From his nearby position, Jim Logan scowled at her in mingled frustration and rage. In his eyes Bryony Hill looked as alluring as ever. The flickering firelight within the dusky cave played softly about her delicate features, revealing the patrician lines of her sculptured cheekbones, the tender curve of her lips, the unextinguishable glow in those bewitching green eyes. He was filled with a savage, single-minded desire that was all the more torturous because it was so impossible to fulfill.

Then, all of a sudden, a dam seemed to burst inside both of them. He pulled her brutally against him, and began to kiss her savagely, releasing the torrent of passion that had been carefully held in check, crushing her limbs in a fierce embrace. It was as if a magnet drew them together, their lips burning beneath the searing flame of kisses that could no longer be controlled . . .

The Wayward Heart
An Adventure in Romance!

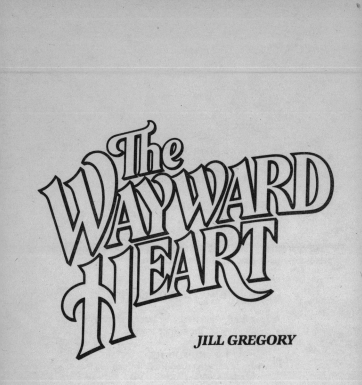

The WAYWARD HEART

JILL GREGORY

A JOVE BOOK

THE WAYWARD HEART

A Jove Book / published by arrangement with
the author

PRINTING HISTORY
Ace trade paperback edition / March 1982
Jove edition / March 1983

ISBN: 0-515-07100-5

Jove books are published by Jove Publications, Inc.,
200 Madison Avenue, New York, N.Y. 10016. The words
"A JOVE BOOK" and the "J" with sunburst are
trademarks belonging to Jove Publications, Inc.

PRINTED IN THE UNITED STATES OF AMERICA

To my beautiful daughter Rachel,
whose smile lights up the world
and brings me joy.

Chapter One

St. Louis, 1874

The clatter of pebbles against her windowpane drew Bryony's attention away from her studies. Pushing the heavy textbook aside, she hurried eagerly to the window to peer down into the moonlit courtyard. Below, Roger Davenport's shadowy form waved and urgently beckoned her to open the window. Laughing with soft amusement, she obeyed, resting her arms along the sill as she leaned out into the brisk March night.

"For heaven's sake, Roger, what is it?" she asked saucily, her jade green eyes brimming with mischief.

"I had to see you," the young man replied in a throbbing whisper. "I couldn't let things rest the way they ended this afternoon! I must speak with you, Bryony!"

"Shall I come down, or will you come up?" she inquired.

Roger made an uncontrollable gesture of impatience. "Don't be absurd! You know I can't come up. Please, Bryony, come down at once. It will be bad enough if I'm discovered here in the courtyard, much less in your room!"

She laughed again. Roger was right, of course. What a scandal there would be if a man were discovered on the premises of Miss Marsh's School for Young Ladies

1

at this unseemly hour. No man was ever permitted in the dormitory wing where the girls resided, and only authorized visitors were admitted to the grounds at all. This afternoon, Roger Davenport had been an authorized visitor. But tonight. . . . There would be quite an uproar if he were discovered lurking in the shrubbery. Pleased and excited that he would take such a risk to see her, she promised to come down to him immediately, and pausing only long enough to lower the window and to dim the oil lamp on the desk before snatching up her shawl, she slipped quickly out of the room and down the long, carpeted hallway to the flight of stairs which led to the side doorway. In very little time she was stealing her way noiselessly through the garden to where Roger waited, just below her window. He was seated on the long, low stone bench, fidgeting nervously at every rustle of the shrubbery. His handsome face wore an expression of restless agitation. When Bryony appeared out of the shadows, he leapt up and hurried to greet her, clasping her hands in his and leading her over to the bench.

She regarded him quizzically. "Roger, what is this all about? I find it very difficult to believe that *you*, of all people, crept in here after dark to see me."

"I had to see you, Bryony! I haven't had a moment's peace since I left you this afternoon. It's terrible, not knowing if you'll consent to marry me or not! Your answer this afternoon was not at all satisfactory, you know. 'I'll think about it, Roger.' What in hell's name does that *mean?*"

Bryony sighed. So they were back to this marriage business, were they? Poor Roger, he really seemed desperate for her answer. But what could she say? She didn't *know* what answer to give him. Her own feelings were clouded and uncertain. She needed time, time to sort things out. When she had tried to explain that to him this afternoon, he had been hurt and a little angry. Now he seemed even more upset. She supposed she ought to be flattered that her answer meant so much to him, but somehow, she had a feeling that Roger was more interested in marriage for marriage's sake than in marriage to her.

"Oh, Roger, why must you press me like this?" she asked uncertainly. "I just don't know what to say."

"Say yes!" His shining brown eyes stared intently into hers. "I'll make you happy, Bryony. You'll see. I'll buy you anything you wish—a new carriage, evening dresses, jewels! We'll travel in the finest circles! I can picture just how it will be—you will charm everybody, my relatives and friends and business associates, and they will all adore you as I do. I swear to you, it will be a wonderful life!"

Bryony tossed her long, silken black hair, impatient with this stream of chatter. Every word Roger uttered reinforced her suspicion that he wanted her only as an ornament, something to show off to his friends and business acquaintants. Well, she wanted something more from life than that!

She was about to speak sharply to him, but she bit her lip instead, remembering the warnings of her friends. They all considered him a most wonderfully eligible suitor: handsome, polished, ambitious. They had told her repeatedly to avoid taking his courtship lightly, for he was a very promising young man. And above all, they had told her, never speak unpleasantly to him, or to any man. That was the quickest way to drive a romantic suitor away for good. So Bryony hesitated. She wasn't ready to drive Roger away for good. After all, he was good-looking: tall and fashionable, with slick dark hair and pleasant eyes, and a most attractive smile. And his future was undoubtedly bright, for Roger was clever and ambitious, and his father was the president of one of St. Louis's largest and most prestigious banks. Mr. Silas Davenport was bringing Roger into the banking business with him, and his son, a quick learner, was obviously destined to become just as successful as he had been. The Davenport family, a rather stuffy, self-consciously dignified group whom she had met on several occasions, knew all of the right people, and were among the city's most prominent citizens. If she married Roger, she would automatically enter their select circle, and her future would be assured. Bryony knew it would be an easy, glamorous life, and she couldn't turn it down flat, not without giving Roger's proposal a great deal of thought. She liked him very much. But did she love him? How did one know when one was in love?

"Bryony, say something!" Roger said urgently, shaking her slightly.

Hesitantly, she raised her eyes to his face. "I'm very fond of you, Roger," she began truthfully, "and very flattered by your proposal. But I'm not entirely certain that I . . . that I love you—or that you love me."

"Not certain? How can you say that after I've gone to all this trouble to sneak in here tonight—just to beg you to marry me! Of course I love you! You're so beautiful, Bryony, and sweet, and you'll be a perfect, charming wife. And if you'll only agree to marry me, you'll make me the happiest man in the world. Please, say yes!"

She studied him silently. For some reason, Roger's pleading tone irritated her. If he loved her, truly loved her, why didn't he sweep her into his arms and show her—passionately. Why didn't he kiss her until she swooned, or carry her off without giving her a chance to refuse? Why didn't he *do* something, instead of begging her like this? Hiding her annoyance, she stood up, saying firmly, "I can't answer you tonight, Roger. Perhaps tomorrow. Yes, tomorrow afternoon. Come see me, and I promise to give you a definite answer."

He grabbed her arm and pulled her back onto the bench, anger and desperation giving his voice a shrill quality. "You're a fool to hesitate, Bryony!" he cried. "You're eighteen now, and in a few months you'll be finished with your schooling. You can't stay on at this boarding school forever! If you don't marry me, what will you do? Where will you go?"

"Please, lower your voice, Roger," she said, breaking free of his hold and regarding him with mounting anger. She kept her tone level, though, as she replied, "I've told you before that I hope to visit my father on his ranch this summer. You know I haven't seen him for several years now, and I've been begging him to let me come west. I intend to set out as soon as this term is finished."

"West? You can't be serious! It's a rough, uncivilized frontier out there, crawling with Indians and the most dangerous, unsavory types of white men. You wouldn't like it at all, believe me." He laughed suddenly, gazing at her with indulgence and continuing in a milder tone. "I understand your passion for horseback riding, Bryony, and I assure you, I'll be happy to provide you with a half-dozen purebreds after we're married, if that will please you, so you needn't think of journeying all that distance merely to satisfy your equestrian desires. Come now, you don't really want to travel all the way to . . . Arizona Territory, isn't it? I'm sure your father would never permit you to do so. He hasn't allowed you to visit before, has he?"

"No." She spoke in a low voice, and quickly turned her head away so that he couldn't see the hurt in her eyes. For it was true. She hadn't seen her father for three years, and on that occasion he had visited her here at the school. She couldn't deny that they had never been particularly close, and that it had been her mother, the lovely Helena, who had raised Bryony with love and great gentleness until her death ten years ago. Ever since that time, Wesley Hill had placed his daughter in the best boarding schools and in the homes of relatives, writing occasionally, always seeing that she was well cared for, and showered with lavish presents on her birthday; in general, denying her nothing—nothing, that is, but his company, and his own precious time.

Wesley Hill was a vital, ambitious man, and he had made it quite clear that he didn't have time for a young daughter to be roaming about underfoot. He had become involved in the mining business, and through several well-placed investments, owned sizable shares in two profitable Colorado gold mines. He had gone on to become one of the first men to begin ranching in the Arizona Territory, setting up his spread on ten thousand acres of rich grazing land near the southeastern frontier town of Winchester, and stocking his range with fifteen thousand head of Texas and Mexican longhorn cattle. In the past five years, since he had begun this project, his herd had multiplied rapidly, despite the persistent raids by Apache Indians, and now more than thirty thousand head of cattle grazed on Circle H land.

Bryony had heard of this success through occasional letters from her father, but though she had for some time longed to go west for a visit, he had never permitted it. She had been greatly disappointed by his refusals, not only because she wished to see him, but also because she had a strong, burning desire to see the great, fabled west of which she had heard so much. She possessed an adventurous spirit that had never been given free rein, confined as she had always been to boarding schools and the very proper homes of her genteel relations. But lately, this adventurous urge had been growing on her, and she was not ready to give up hope. She had a feeling that somehow, someday, she would know more of life than she had previously been allowed to glimpse, and she had a strong suspicion that this would not be achieved by marriage to Roger Davenport.

"Roger, I must go back now," she said, rising once more. "We'll talk again tomorrow."

"No, wait!" he cried, as she moved resolutely away from the bench. In his excitement, his voice rose more loudly than he had intended, and with a little cry of alarm, Bryony peered upward, fearful that one of her classmates would come to a window to investigate the noise. But it was her own window that caught and held her attention, as she saw the oil lamp in her room glow with increasing brightness. Someone was in her room, turning up the lamp.

"Roger, go!" she whispered desperately, suddenly aware of how close they stood to discovery.

"I . . . I'm sorry, Bryony, I didn't mean to shout. . ." he began guiltily.

She pushed him away impatiently. "Please, you'd best leave at once. Don't you see? Someone is in my room, looking for me! They mustn't find us togeth . . . oh!"

She broke off as a dark form filled the window where only a short time before she had laughed down at Roger. But the woman in the window was not laughing. A dark scowl was fixed upon her stern, homely features as she caught sight of the two young people in the courtyard.

Roger stiffened, frozen with horror. "She sees us!" he cried hoarsely.

"Yes, thanks to your stupidity!" Bryony snapped, abandoning the advice of her friends concerning the eternally pleasant tone to be used when addressing a suitor. "Now, Roger, will you please leave before she comes down here? Look, she's left the window; she's on her way already."

"I can't leave you here to face her alone," he said miserably, white with dread over the upcoming trouble, but determined to be a man about it. "It is my duty to. . ."

"No, no, forget your duty! I can handle Miss Grayson," she assured him hastily, though she felt far from confident. Her heart was pounding uncomfortably; she knew the trouble she was in, and dreaded the scene awaiting her. But she preferred to face the scandal alone, without having to worry about defending Roger. "Please, there's no reason why you need be scolded, too. She won't have recognized you, and I promise you that I won't tell her your name. I beg of you to leave—this will be much easier for me if I'm alone.''

He glanced at her uncertainly, and then, as heavy footsteps sounded on the graveled path, he kissed Bryony hurriedly on the lips, promised to call on the morrow, and darted frantically into the shrubbery to escape.

Bryony turned just as Miss Letitia Grayson emerged from the garden path, her puffy, red face lit with triumph.

''Well, Miss Hill,'' the woman said in her loud, grating voice, folding her plump arms across her massive chest in a formidable pose. ''What, may I ask, is the meaning of this outrageous behavior?''

Chapter Two

"Good . . . good evening, Miss Grayson," Bryony stammered. She felt herself flushing under the woman's withering stare, but faced her with head held high, her black hair streaming in the gusty March breeze. She became suddenly aware that it was cold in the courtyard, but how much of this was due to the chilly evening, and how much to the frostiness emanating from Miss Grayson, it was difficult to say. Shivering, Bryony pulled her shawl more closely about her shoulders while the older woman looked her up and down.

"It is *not* a good evening, Miss Hill—not for you, at any rate," the assistant headmistress sneered contemptuously. "And you haven't answered my question! What is the meaning of this despicable conduct?"

Bryony saw faces pressed against the glass of several windows above, and silently wished Miss Grayson would not speak quite so loudly. The commotion she was creating was only worsening an already dreadful situation. But she knew it would be useless to ask the woman to lower her voice. There was a malicious sparkle in the assistant's beady dark eyes that showed she was only too happy to have caught Bryony Hill in a compromising situation. Bryony sighed as she heard one of the upstairs windows slide open, no doubt to permit the observer to hear the entire conversation. Resignedly, she accepted the fact that the scandal would be all over the school by morning.

"I . . . just came down for a walk in the garden," she said quietly, shrugging as if nothing unusual had occurred. "It was such a mild, lovely night . . . I thought. . ."

"Poppycock!" Miss Grayson practically shrieked the word, and Bryony winced as several more curious, white faces appeared at their windows, like sudden stars popping into the evening sky.

"There was a young man here with you!" her tormentor announced triumphantly. "I saw him myself! Who was he?"

Bryony eyed her silently, struggling for composure, although violent anger was surging through her at this public ordeal. She suspected that Miss Grayson was enjoying herself immensely, and resentment flooded through the dark-haired girl. When she made no reply to the assistant headmistress's query, Miss Grayson took a step closer and grasped her arm in a pinching, painful grip. "Are you going to answer me?" she demanded, giving Bryony's arm a vicious shake.

"No!" Bryony cried defiantly, wrenching away. She was trembling now, not from the cold, but from fury that she could no longer control. A savage rush of satisfaction swept over her as Miss Grayson's thin-lipped mouth drooped ludicrously open in shock at her reply. Good! Bryony thought rebelliously. How dare this old sour-face treat me so! As if she thinks she'll intimidate me into betraying Roger! Bryony was determined not to expose him. Her green eyes sparkled with fury as she stared at the square, bullish, gray-haired woman before her. She knew that Miss Grayson had never liked her, though she didn't know why, and she was convinced that the horrid woman was delighting in her predicament. Well, she was sadly mistaken if she expected her victim to burst into tears and plead for leniency! Bryony drew herself up proudly and regarded the assistant headmistress with icy dislike.

"I don't wish to discuss this any further, Miss Grayson," she said coldly. "At least, not out here in the open. But perhaps you'll tell me why you were in my room looking for me? Was there something you wanted?"

The woman reddened with wrath and shook a stubby finger in Bryony's face. "Why, you impudent young hussy!" she gasped. "How *dare* you speak to me in this brazen, insolent manner! You shall be punished severely for your conduct this evening, indeed you shall! And as for why I came to your room. . ." She broke off abruptly, and a stricken look flashed across her homely features.

"I . . . I'd forgotten," she muttered, in sudden confusion. A strange expression came into her beady eyes as she gazed at Bryony standing defiantly before her. It was true, she had never liked the girl. She had never liked any of the girls in her charge, but particularly not this one. Bryony Hill's striking beauty, and her love of laughter and life, made her an automatic enemy of this bitter woman, who hated everything that was pure and unspoiled in the world. Miss Grayson had been born with a sour disposition, and it had not been improved upon when she had realized, as a young woman, that she possessed features that could only be described as plain. Though many such women were able to achieve a pleasing attractiveness despite their flaws, due to an inner beauty and sweetness that reflected itself in their outer countenance, Miss Grayson was not one of their number. Her low-spirited, negative nature took even more secure hold of her personality, and she brooded many hours upon the ill turn served her by nature and by the world at large. Thus, she grew into a woman whose ugliness of appearance matched the ugliness of her soul, a woman whose only pleasure in life lay in spoiling the happiness of others. She had been consumed with spiteful glee at discovering Bryony Hill's

wrongdoing, but now the girl's enquiry as to why the
assistant headmistress had been in her room recalled her
to her duty.

"You're wanted immediately in Miss Marsh's office,
young woman. This other matter will have to wait. You
must come with me at once."

Bryony stared in bewilderment as Miss Grayson
promptly turned on her heel and marched back across
the garden path toward the side doorway. She followed
quickly, conscious of the many gaping eyes upon her
retreating back. She was already regretting her burst of
temper, knowing that she had only created more trouble
for herself. Miss Grayson would undoubtedly report her
to Miss Marsh, the school's headmistress, and she
would certainly be punished, as much for her insolence
as for her rendezvous with Roger. But as she quietly
followed Miss Grayson into the school building, her
mind pondered something else. Why had Miss Marsh
sent Miss Grayson to find her? Why would the headmistress possibly want to see her at this late hour?

She still had no answer to this perplexing question
when she reached the door to Miss Marsh's private office. Knocking softly, she waited for an invitation to
enter, casting a bewildered, searching look at Miss
Grayson, who stood beside her, as silent and forbidding
as a prison guard. Miss Marsh's soft "Please come in"
sounded almost immediately, and Bryony opened the
paneled door. Letitia Grayson hesitated, seemingly anxious to enter the room, but the elegant, small-boned
woman behind the dainty marble desk quietly informed
her that she need not stay.

"But, ma'am, there are certain things you ought to
know," Miss Grayson began indignantly from the doorway, watching Bryony seat herself in a deep pink-and-
white velvet chair opposite the marble desk. "Indeed,
the reprehensible behavior of this young person tonight
should be made known to you most plainly, and in no

uncertain terms! Why, ma'am, I have never in my life—''

"Surely, this report can wait for a later time?" Katharine Marsh suggested in her soft, pleasing voice. She glanced meaningfully at Miss Grayson, who scowled, muttered something, and banged the door shut loudly behind her.

Miss Marsh was a pretty, petite, middle-aged woman, with soft brown hair faintly streaked with gray, and calm, intelligent brown eyes. She had been born and bred in Boston, of excellent family, and this accounted for her impeccably prim, ladylike manner. She expected exemplary conduct from her pupils at all times, and contributed toward this goal by setting a perfect example of good breeding and gentility.

She was loved and respected by all the students, unlike the homely, malicious Miss Grayson, who was privately known among the girls as "Miss Sourface." Miss Marsh was a romantic figure to them, subject to much rumor and speculation. It was known that she had opened her school for young ladies in St. Louis after the tragic ending of a love affair. Her beloved fiancé, an aristocratic young Boston gentleman, had been killed in a stable fire while trying to rescue his prized horse, only weeks before the marriage ceremony, and according to rumor, Miss Marsh had never recovered from his death. She had refused to see any other suitors in the months and years that followed, and had retired almost completely from Boston social life. Finally, after deciding never to marry, she had left her home to start a new life in St. Louis, opening a boarding school for young ladies of good families, and running it with great, dedicated skill.

Miss Marsh was much whispered about by her pupils, who thought of her as a heroine, and who rapturously regarded her life history as the saddest, most beautiful story they had ever heard. In turn, Katharine Marsh took equal interest in the lives and happiness of her students. In addition to personally instructing them in music appreciation (for she was a most accomplished pianist), she took pains to become acquainted with each girl in her care. Now, as she faced Bryony Hill in her tastefully feminine pink-and-white office—lightly scented, as always, with lavender—there was a curious sadness in her fine dark eyes. She liked the girl sitting before her, and deeply regretted the news it was her duty to convey.

"Good evening, Bryony," she said gently.

"Good evening, Miss Marsh." Bryony waited tensely, unable to imagine any reason for this evening summons. As Miss Marsh seemed to hesitate momentarily, that strange sadness shadowing her eyes, Bryony's uneasiness increased.

"Pray, what is it, ma'am?" she inquired, leaning slightly forward in her chair. "Why do you wish to see me? Have I . . . have I done something awful?"

"No, my dear, nothing of the sort. Although apparently Miss Grayson seems to think so. However, that can wait for another time. At the moment, I'm afraid I have some grievous news for you."

"Dear heavens! What is it?"

"I have just received a telegram from a Judge Hamilton of Winchester, in the Arizona Territory." Miss Marsh sighed, meeting Bryony's wide-eyed gaze sympathetically. "My dear," she said gently, "I'm so sorry, but I must tell you that your father has been killed."

"Killed!" Bryony froze, numb with disbelief. Her throat felt as dry as if it were filled with sand. "No! It . . . it isn't possible!" she cried, staring at Miss Marsh in blank confusion. "It can't be true!"

"I understand how you feel, my dear. Indeed, it's a terrible shock. But, unfortunately, it is all too true. You may read Judge Hamilton's message, if you wish."

A cold, numb sensation crept over Bryony. Her

father—dead! She felt slightly sick, and leaned dazedly back in her chair, passing her hands shakily across her eyes. "I can't believe it," she mumbled. Slowly, she raised her eyes to Miss Marsh's face. "You said he was . . . killed? What do you mean? How did he. . ." She swallowed. "How did he die?"

"He was shot—by a gunfighter."

This statement added a new dimension of horror, and Bryony felt her skin grow clammy. She gripped the arms of her chair. "Murdered?" she whispered.

"No, not quite." Miss Marsh couldn't bear to look upon that pale, agonized face, from which all sign of animation had vanished. Averting her gaze, she shook her head slightly, her thin, delicately veined hands twisting nervously atop the desk. "He was killed during a gunfight—a fair fight, as Judge Hamilton calls it in his telegram—with several witnesses present. I'm afraid that this terrible man who shot him, this Jim Logan, cannot be held accountable for murder. Apparently gunfights of this sort are a way of life in the west." She shuddered. "That Arizona Territory must be a dreadful, wild place. This entire episode sounds quite barbaric!"

"But I don't understand! Why would a gunfighter kill my father? There must have been a quarrel, but I can't see why my father should have had any reason to quarrel with this . . . this. . ."

"Jim Logan," Miss Marsh supplied. She shrugged helplessly. "I'm sorry, Bryony, but Judge Hamilton doesn't give any explanation for what happened. I don't understand any more than you do."

Bryony listened in numb silence as Miss Marsh again offered her sincere sympathies, and told her not to worry about any arrangements. She would send for Wesley Hill's lawyer in the morning, and no doubt he would see Bryony within a few days to settle things. She handed Bryony the Judge's telegram, and offered to accompany her back to her room, but Bryony shook her head and declined. In a daze, she returned to her own quarters and closed the door against the outside world. Hot silent tears slid down her cheeks as she rested her head against the door. Her father was dead. It didn't seem possible. But it was true. And now she was alone.

It was strange, she thought dully, that she should feel so bereft. She had not known her father very well; they had been almost strangers for the past ten years. But he was her father, and she loved him, and now he was gone. She felt stunned, and more alone than ever before in her life. Her sense of loss weighed heavily upon her, and when she finally sank into her bed, her burden pressed her into a turbulent sleep, fraught with jumbled, horrible, nightmarish fragments. When she awoke in the morning, she felt drained and dreary, and wondered how she would ever manage to face the day. In addition to everything else, it was gray and raining outside. The rain drummed against her windowpane, whipped by a screeching wind, and the drooping trees in the courtyard looked every bit as miserable as Bryony felt. Gloom had descended upon her world, wiping away all the happiness she had known only a day ago.

Bryony didn't attend classes that day, but many of her friends and teachers came by to express their sympathies, and in the afternoon she met with her father's lawyer, Mr. Parker. On her way to this meeting, which took place in Miss Marsh's office, she encountered Miss Letitia Grayson in the corridor. That grim-faced woman gave her a disdainful nod in greeting, and then strode away with an unmistakable air of contempt. Bryony didn't care, however; her conflict with Miss Grayson didn't seem to matter anymore. Even her rendezvous with Roger seemed distant and unreal.

"Good afternoon, Miss Hill." Mr. Parker came forward solicitously as she entered the headmistress's office. "Please accept my sincere condolences. I'm aware that this has been a terrible shock for you."

"Thank you, Mr. Parker." Bryony smiled wanly at

this short, kindly, fair-haired man. She had known him
since she was a child, and he had always treated her
pleasantly. She trusted him completely, and knew that
he would settle her father's affairs properly. At least
that was one matter she need not be concerned about.

Miss Marsh excused herself to allow them privacy
during their discussion. Bryony and Mr. Parker seated
themselves in pink-and-white chairs, separated by a
small, marble-edged table. A small, cheerful fire burned
in the fireplace, and over the marble mantelpiece, a
handsome, lacquered clock ticked soothingly. The pink
silk draperies were drawn against the dreariness of the
day, making the room seem a haven of beauty and
grace. Under normal circumstances Bryony would have
delighted in glancing around at the attractive china
figurines and crystal vases; today she derived no comfort from the attractiveness of her surroundings. Her
heart was heavy with a sorrow she tried hard not to
show.

"Now, Miss Hill," the lawyer began, "it seems, at
least, that you shall not be burdened by many details. I,
too, received a telegram from Judge Hamilton of Winchester yesterday. As you know, I am responsible for all
of your father's business and legal affairs in the east.
Judge Hamilton has been assisting your father in the
Arizona Territory. He informed me in his telegram that
your father is being buried in a small, respectable
cemetery outside of the town. So there are no arrangements for you or me to make in that respect."

For the first time, Bryony realized that it would not
even be possible for her to attend her father's funeral.

Mr. Parker went on briskly, producing some papers
from his leather case and spreading them on the table.
"As far as financial matters are concerned, you may
rest easy. Your tuition and board here at the school are
paid in full until the end of the term. Not that you
couldn't afford it otherwise, however, for you are now a
very wealthy young woman, Miss Hill."

"Am I?" Bryony asked almost disinterestedly.

"Yes, indeed. Your father had set up a trust for you of twenty-five thousand dollars, which became available to you upon your eighteenth birthday, some few months ago, I believe. And he died with the sum of thirty thousand dollars deposited in his permanent bank account here in St. Louis, in addition to whatever cash he may have kept in Arizona, be it in a bank or personal safe or whatever. Naturally, the entire sum belongs to you. His shares in those Colorado gold mines, which are not inconsiderable, will also be transferred to your name."

Bryony stared at him in astonishment. "I can't believe it! I hadn't realized that my father had accumulated such vast amounts."

"That is not all. According to his will, which I have right here, you are the sole inheritor of his entire estate, which includes the Circle H ranch itself, and all of the property and cattle. There are more than ten thousand acres of fine grazing land, which, I assure you, will fetch a considerable price."

"Price? What do you mean?" At mention of the ranch, Bryony became suddenly interested, regarding Mr. Parker with thoughtful green eyes.

"Why, when you sell it, of course. As a matter of fact, Miss Hill, in addition to Judge Hamilton's telegram, I received a most interesting one this morning from a Mr. Matthew Richards. Apparently Mr. Richards and your father were excellent friends. He very kindly expressed his sympathy for you, and informed me that he would be willing to take the ranch off your hands for a handsome price. It seems that he and your father had the two largest spreads in the region, and now that your father is gone, Mr. Richards wants to buy you out and consolidate his place with the Circle H. He's made a most generous offer."

"Do you mean that I should sell the ranch? Why, I've never even seen it!"

Mr. Parker smiled. "That's hardly necessary. I can assure you that the price Mr. Richards has offered is most fair." As he quoted the figure, Bryony's eyes widened. She stood up abruptly and began to pace about the room.

"It sounds like a fortune, but. . ." she found herself hesitating, searching for words. "I've always had rather a fancy to visit the ranch myself. I'm not sure that I wish to sell it."

Mr. Parker laughed, his mild blue eyes disappearing into a sea of creases. "You can't be serious, Miss Hill," he said. "Of course you must sell the ranch. Whatever would you do with it otherwise?"

"I could live on it," she said slowly, turning to face him. "I could run it myself, just as my father did."

"That's ridiculous." Mr. Parker still seemed inclined to laugh, but something in Bryony's expression caused him to hastily choke back his amusement, and instead, he studied her with faint concern. "Miss Hill, perhaps we should talk about this 'fancy' of yours. You can't be thinking clearly if you're really considering a life in the west. Why, it's a wild, dangerous place—not at all the environment for a delicately bred young woman like yourself. Believe me, I'm sure you have some silly romantic notion of it, but you'd not find it at all pleasant in reality. The west, and in particular the Arizona Territory, is no place for you."

"Perhaps you're right," Bryony said abstractedly. "Perhaps not."

She had a dreamy expression in her eyes as she gazed into space, and Mr. Parker, who had known her for years, couldn't help marveling at what a lovely creature she had become. True, she had always been a charming little girl, but now—well, now she was a woman. Slender and exquisite, with that beautiful mass of rich, coal-black hair, snow-white skin, and those glimmering emerald green eyes. Her features were delicate and lovely, with high, sculptured cheekbones, and a small, straight, patrician nose. And, even attired as she was in a sober mourning-gown of black taffeta, with ruffles up to her swan-like throat, it was obvious that her soft, curvaceous figure was fully blossomed into womanhood, and would surely distract a saint from his prayers. She was enchanting, he concluded admiringly, and in addition to her other charms, she possessed an engaging air of innocence that made her seem terribly vulnerable and appealing. Mr. Parker sighed. This dainty, captivating creature alone in the uncivilized west? It would never, never do.

"Please, Miss Hill, perhaps this is not the best time to make decisions of this importance," he said earnestly, rising to approach her and taking her slender white hands in his. "I'm certain that after you've given the matter some consideration, you'll agree that selling the property is your wisest course."

Touched by the genuine concern she read in his kindly eyes, Bryony smiled at him with real warmth. "You needn't worry about me, Mr. Parker," she assured him. "I promise to think about it most carefully. I do realize that it's a very important decision."

During the following week, Bryony kept her word to Mr. Parker, for she did give the matter a great deal of scrutiny. In fact, it was never far from her thoughts. As she adjusted to her father's death, her natural good spirits gradually returned, and with them, the familiar yearning for adventure. The Circle H ranch provided the ideal means of satisfying her urge to travel west. Despite Roger Davenport's casual assumption that her love for horseback riding lay behind this desire, Bryony knew differently. Oh, it was true enough that horses were a passion with her; she rode in the park at every opportunity, and those who knew her well and observed her with her mounts claimed that she had a magical way with the animals. But it was more than the desire to ride which made her think constantly of the western frontier.

Something about the vast, untamed wilderness held a

powerful attraction for her, a lure that seemed to draw her irresistibly. Sometimes, she felt unbearably stifled by the forces that governed her life. And it seemed to her that the western frontier held out a promise of freedom, of a release from the multitude of restrictions under which she lived. Deep down, her heart yearned for this. Yet, dare she follow her instincts? Common sense advised against such a bold course.

Her eastern life was comfortable, pleasant, and safe. When she had finished her term at Miss Marsh's School, she could marry Roger Davenport, and live the rest of her life in luxury. Or she could go to the home of one of her relations, several of whom had already written to beg her to come to them. She would be pampered and spoiled, and treated to every kindness in their power. Both of these choices promised comfort and security. Why give them up for a life that would be filled with uncertainty? Surely, she would be foolish to do so. At times, she was convinced of this. And at other times, she would think of the open frontier, and her pulse would race. . . .

She was in a quandary, unable to decide what to do.

As if she did not have enough upon her mind, Bryony soon found herself in disgrace at the school. Miss Letitia Grayson had reported her improper conduct to Miss Marsh, and one week following the news of her father's death, Bryony was reproachfully informed that she must be punished for her impropriety. All of her social privileges were revoked for a period of one month, which meant that she must retire to her quarters immediately after dinner each night, and must turn out her light by seven-thirty. She would not be permitted any social visitors during the entire period, but must confine her activities to classes, studying, and meals.

Upon being informed of this penalty by a regretful but severely displeased Miss Marsh, Bryony choked back bitter tears. She listened miserably to Miss Marsh's lecture on the importance of propriety and decorum, unable to control a quirk of resentment at having her life so controlled. She had lived eighteen years under the thumb of society's tyranny and once, just once, she would love to snap her fingers at its dictates and do as she pleased. Instead, she answered Miss Marsh quietly and politely, turning away to seek the sanctuary of her room. At that moment there was a knock upon the office door.

"Yes?" Miss Marsh inquired in her soft, pretty voice.

The door opened, and Bryony started as Roger Davenport entered, looking fit and handsome, his brown derby hat in his hand. He looked surprised to see her and flushed just a bit as he glanced quickly away to address the headmistress.

"Good day, ma'am," he began nervously, fidgeting with his hat. "I . . . I didn't mean to interrupt . . . that is, I can wait outside if this is an inconvenient time, but I . . . I would like your permission, ma'am, for a visit with Miss Hill."

Miss Marsh regarded him suspiciously. Bryony had never revealed the identity of the young man who had visited her in the moonlit courtyard, but Roger Davenport was her most attentive beau, and seemed the likely culprit. Yet, he was such a well-mannered, *proper* young man. Not at all the type to engage in scandalous conduct. Miss Marsh could not be sure that he was the secret visitor. She decided to say nothing of the matter, since she had no specific reason to reproach him. But should she permit the private visit after just informing Bryony Hill of her social restrictions? The headmistress glanced from one to the other of them. Bryony was pale, her eyes wide and anxious. Roger Davenport had reddened in his agitation for her reply. She felt rather sorry for both of them. Despite her primness, Miss Marsh well remembered the urgency of young lovers.

"Very well," she finally assented, rising from her desk. "You may have ten minutes alone in this room.

And then, Bryony, the penalty period shall begin. Do you understand?''

"Yes, Miss Marsh. Thank you."

Bryony could barely contain herself until Miss Marsh departed before whirling to confront Roger.

"Why haven't you come sooner?" she demanded, searching his face. "I sent you a note as soon as I heard the news about my father, begging you to come to me, and I never received even a word in response. Where have you been?"

"I know, Bryony, and I'm sorry. I'll explain everything. But first, tell me what that woman meant about a penalty period. Are you in some kind of trouble because of my visit?"

"Yes," she acknowledged bitterly, sinking into a chair. "All social privileges have been withdrawn for the next month, commencing immediately after you leave today!"

"Forgive me! I never meant you to suffer on my account!" He knelt by her chair, grasping her hands in his own, and gazed at her with sorrowful brown eyes.

Bryony studied him earnestly. After her father's death she had longed to see Roger, to pour out her unhappiness and loneliness to him, to share with him her sense of loss. She had needed him then, and she had sent for him. But he had not come.

"Why didn't you answer my letter, Roger?" she asked softly. "Why didn't you come to me, as I begged you to do?"

His hands tightened on hers. "I wanted to come, Bryony, believe me! But I was afraid, afraid that they would suspect me. If it became known that I met with you so improperly, it could be most damaging to my career. A scandal like that . . ." He broke off at the infuriated expression upon her face.

"Not that I didn't think of you constantly, and yearn to be with you," he added hastily. "Believe me, Bryony,

my darling, you have my every sympathy and con-
dolence regarding your father. I know it must have been
a dreadful ordeal for you, and I'd have done anything in
my power to ease your grief."

"Except come to me when I needed you!" she cried
disgustedly, pulling her hands away and jumping up to
pace agitatedly about the room.

"Please, try to understand," he pleaded. "It was too
great a risk—I could not consider it safe to visit you, or
even write to you, until some time had passed. It does
not mean that I don't love you—I do! But preserving a
respectable reputation is of paramount importance to a
man in my position."

"That's enough!" Bryony trembled with fury, staring
at him out of dangerously sparkling green eyes. Her
voice dripped contempt. "Do not ever again speak to
me of love, Roger Davenport! It sickens me! I do not
consider the love of a man so intimidated by society to
be worthy of my consideration! As far as I'm concerned, you may leave this room immediately, and never
show your face to me again!"

Roger flushed a deep scarlet as her words flayed at
him. "Now, see here," he warned angrily, in a shaking
voice, "you have no right to speak to me that way. If I
were you, Bryony, I'd watch my tongue. This isn't the
first time you've shown what can only be described as
an unladylike temper. It isn't at all becoming, I assure
you."

"Why, you! How dare you sit in judgment upon
me!"

"Who has a better right?" he retorted. "After all, a
husband has a right to demand proper conduct from his
wife. And I can see that I will have my work cut out for
me. I must tell you, Bryony, that there are times when
the liveliness of your spirits causes you to behave with a
shade too much license to suit my tastes. When you
become my wife—"

"When I become your wife?" She stared at him incredulously. "Roger, didn't you hear what I said? Don't you understand? I have no intention of seeing you again, let alone marrying you!"

"Oh, really?" An ugly note crept into Roger's voice; he crossed his arms and stared at her with an expression of smug, cruel satisfaction. "And if I don't marry you, what will you do? You're in disgrace here at the school, your father is dead, and you have nowhere to go, other than the home of some damned relative who probably doesn't want you anyway! You're a woman alone! You need me, Miss High-and-Mighty Bryony Hill! Whether you like it or not, you need me!"

There was a moment of burning silence while Bryony clenched her fists, trying to bring her raging temper under control. For an instant, she wanted to scream at Roger, to throw something at him, but that instant passed. Her sense of dignity took over and instead of attacking Roger, she laughed out loud at him. When he glared at her in amazement, she was able to reply in a clear, cool tone.

"You're wrong, Roger. I don't need you, you or anyone else. I'm perfectly able to take care of myself."

"And what will you do after I walk out that door?" he demanded contemptuously.

She smiled. "I will go west—to the Arizona Territory," she replied calmly.

Chapter Three

The stage depot was located in the front lobby of the
Parkside Hotel, a respectable, three-story, rose brick
building surrounded by a gleaming black wrought-iron
fence. Inside, wooden benches lined the walls of the
small, square lobby, providing seats for the passengers
who were waiting for their coaches. At the early hour of
seven in the morning, the room was already crowded,
and bustling with excitement.

Bryony entered the depot on the arm of Mr. Parker,
glancing eagerly about at the milling people, wondering
which of those in the room would be fellow passengers
on her journey. She had little time for these musings,
however, for Mr. Parker led her immediately to the
ticket window, where he purchased a one-way ticket for
her on the eight o'clock stage bound for San Francisco,
via El Paso and Tucson. There was a worried crease in
his balding forehead as he handed her the ticket. Mr.
Parker didn't approve of this venture in the least, and
he had not hesitated to tell Bryony so often. Both he and
Miss Marsh had pleaded with her to abandon this wild
notion, but to no avail. Even Miss Marsh's desperate offer to repeal the punishment had no effect on her plans.

Bryony looked enchantingly lovely this morning in a
gown of soft, dove-gray velveteen, trimmed at the
throat and wrists with delicate white lace. Her long,

black curls flowed gently about her shoulders beneath a smart little hat of the same dove-gray velveteen as her gown, which tied beneath her chin with ribbons of black satin. Perhaps it was the excitement of the morning, or else the dusky lighting in the lobby, but her green eyes had unusual brilliance as she gazed about her, like flames of green in an ivory face. Her lips were parted, her cheeks flushed, and Mr. Parker felt himself grow almost breathless at the sight of her beauty. His kindly heart was heavy with fear as he contemplated the fate of this ravishing innocent alone in the untamed west.

"Is everything set then?" Bryony asked suddenly, raising her eyes to smile hopefully at him.

"Yes, all is in order," he replied, with a sigh. "Miss Hill, are you quite sure. . .?"

"Quite!" She answered with a laugh. "Now do stop worrying, Mr. Parker! I intend to prove to you and everyone else that I can manage perfectly well on my own!"

Five days had passed since her final encounter with Roger Davenport, and during that time she had set her plans into motion with incredible determination and speed. Each passing day had increased her conviction that she had made the right decision. This was her journey to freedom, to a new life, and she welcomed it with eager anticipation, hardly able to contain her impatience to be on her way, speeding along unfamiliar roads, along plains and prairies, through desert and mountains.

There was a crackling undercurrent of excitement in the depot of which she was thrillingly aware; she felt totally caught up in the mood of adventure that always accompanies travelers. Perhaps later, she reflected, she would miss her friends at Miss Marsh's School, and look back on her eastern life with pleasant nostalgia. But at the moment her mind was filled with the bright new world ahead of her, and she could scarcely concentrate on anything else. She had to force herself to pay attention as Mr. Parker secured seats for them at the far end of one of the wooden benches, and began nervously to review her travel plans yet another time.

The town of Winchester was situated fifty miles east of Tucson, near the banks of the San Pedro River. Fifteen days of night and day travel would be required to reach it, with regular stops at relay stations along the way to change horses and drivers. Winchester itself served as a relay station on the route west to Tucson and San Francisco. It was not by any means a large town, but it was strategically located along the stagecoach road. However, the lawyer warned her, before reaching this far-off destination she would be required to endure a journey that would be long and uncomfortable, and dangerous as well. The latter part of it would be through Apache Territory.

"Yes, Mr. Parker," she acknowledged with a little smile. "You have told me so before, at great length."

"Hmph. Not that it did much good," he frowned.

"Please, go on," Bryony teased, her eyes dancing. "I believe you were going to remind me that you've telegraphed Judge Hamilton, asking him to meet my stage. You've only reviewed *that* part of my itinerary a scant half-dozen times. Surely I need be reminded again!"

Despite his concern, Mr. Parker couldn't help grinning sheepishly. He conceded that she must be quite tired of hearing his instructions, but his conscience would not let him cease until he felt certain she was completely prepared for this journey. So he continued determinedly.

"Yes, that is quite correct. The Judge is to meet your stage and then drive you out to the Circle H ranch house, which is, I understand, only ten or twelve miles outside of town."

At that moment there was a commotion in the doorway, and two women made their entrance into the lobby: one, a tall, buxom matron in a bustled gown of turquoise silk; the other, apparently her daughter, a pale, haughty-looking blonde girl elegantly attired in apricot satin so stiff that it rustled loudly when she walked. Both women wore high, fancy plumed hats to match their gowns, and carried embroidered reticules and parasols. They were followed into the lobby by two servants struggling with an assortment of heavy trunks and bandboxes, but the two women, aside from imperiously directing the servants to be careful of how they handled the baggage in their charge, seemed oblivious of anything or anyone else in the room.

They swept past Bryony and Mr. Parker, as well as the other fascinated occupants of the room, to confront the clerk, loudly demanding two seats on the next stagecoach bound for San Francisco.

"It looks as if those two ladies will be traveling with you," Mr. Parker remarked drily. "Unfortunately, they don't appear to be the most sociable of creatures. I had hoped there would be someone on the stage who could provide you with some friendly female companionship."

"They do appear very fine and haughty, don't they?" she whispered back amusedly, watching the elegant pair oblige several gentlemen to surrender their seats, and then settle down majestically. "One would think they owned the entire hotel and stagecoach line combined, the way they took command of this lobby. I believe it shall be a very interesting journey!"

Bryony was not easily daunted by the airs put on by others. She knew herself to be well-dressed and well-mannered, and felt herself the equal of any company. So, when the pale blonde girl and her imposing mother happened to glance her way, she smiled at them in a friendly manner, quite willing to promote a sociable relationship with two of her fellow passengers. To her amazement, both mother and daughter returned her smile with cold, disapproving stares before letting their gazes travel disinterestedly down the row of travelers.

She felt a blush burn her cheeks at their open disdain, and she looked quickly away in confusion. Snubbed! By those pompous, arrogant peacocks! Her hands clenched angrily into tight little fists in her lap, but after a moment or two she managed to recover her composure. As the indignation drained away, it was replaced by a firm decision. Though she couldn't help wishing that those two unpleasant women were not going to be her traveling companions for the next fifteen days, she was determined that they shouldn't ruin her enjoyment of the trip, and she resolved to ignore them. From all indications, they intended to keep very much to themselves, and from what Bryony had observed of their manners, that would suit her just fine.

As she glanced about the crowded lobby, she became aware for the first time that she was the subject of much bold interest. A young man in a dark suit was studying her admiringly from an opposite bench, and several men lounging about the ticket counter were staring quite brazenly at her. She was glad, suddenly, of the presence of Mr. Parker. For a brief moment, she felt a twinge of uncertainty. Once she boarded the stagecoach, she would no longer be under the lawyer's protection; she would be alone. She would have to handle any such problems herself.

Presently, there was a loud jingle of harnesses outside, and the rhythmic drum of horses' hooves rapidly approaching. Mr. Parker glanced at his pocket watch.

"That's it," he said resignedly. "The eight o'clock stage. I suppose we'd best go outside and transfer your baggage from my carriage. If you're still determined to leave, that is. You know, Miss Hill, it's not too late to change your mind."

Bryony leaned over impulsively to kiss his cheek. "I'm not going to change my mind, Mr. Parker. But thank you for your concern, and for all your help. You've been wonderful. And when I write you from the Arizona Territory telling you how wildly happy I am, you'll realize that you had no cause to worry. Just wait and see!''

The stagecoach was a handsome, egg-shaped vehicle slung between sturdy axles by two thick, strong, leather thorough braces. It appeared to have been freshly painted, and the portraits of two beautiful women adorned the gleaming, finely carved door panels. Four spirited grays pranced before the carriage, obviously restless to be off. As Bryony surveyed them and the coach, a thrill of anticipation ran through her. She, too, was impatient to start.

The stage driver, a thin, wiry fellow, began loading the passengers' baggage in the boot at the rear of the coach. Mr. Parker brought over Bryony's trunk and two bandboxes, and panting ever so slightly from the exertion, exchanged introductions with the driver before indicating the girl at his side.

"Mr. Wilkins, this is my client, Miss Bryony Hill. She'll be traveling as far as Winchester, in the Arizona Territory. I'd appreciate it if you'd keep an eye on her. This is her first journey alone.''

Wilkins ran his shrewd dark eyes over Bryony's willowy form. "Shore seems young to be headin' west all by herself,'' he concluded, between chews on his tobacco. "But if that's what she's doin', I'll be glad to keep an eye on her, leastways as far as I go, until the next driver takes over.'' He winked at Mr. Parker. "Mebbe two eyes, since she's such a looker. Purty girls can get into a lot of trouble, if you know what I mean. And if you'll pardon me for sayin' so, ma'am, you're by far the purtiest thing I've laid eyes on in many a year, east or west.''

"Thank you, Mr. Wilkins, you're very kind. But I assure you, I don't have the slightest intention of getting into any trouble. I'm well able to take care of myself.''

The stage driver gave a loud guffaw. "Good for you, little lady! That'll make things easy for both of us, and that's fine with me.'' With an amiable nod at Mr.

Parker, he resumed his task of heaving baggage into the boot.

Bryony, though a little surprised by the stagecoach driver's frank way of speaking, liked him. He seemed an easygoing, good-tempered sort of man. She only hoped he was as competent with the reins as he was at casual banter. Then her journey, the first stage of it at any rate, would indeed be speedy.

Amid a bustle of last-minute activity and frenzied good-byes, Bryony boarded the stage, sinking into a cushioned seat at the front of the coach. Before she had time to do more than arrange the folds of her skirt about her legs, there was a shout from the driver, the crack of a whip, and then the horses broke into a brisk trot. Hurriedly, she leaned out the window, waving a white silk handkerchief at the short, fair-haired lawyer, who waved back, trying to smile encouragingly at her.

"Good-bye, Mr. Parker!" she called. "And thank you!"

"Take care of yourself!" he shouted hoarsely, and then he, along with the crowd of other well-wishers outside the depot, was lost in a cloud of dust as the horses gathered speed and the coach bowled rapidly along the wide, paved street.

Bryony settled back, suddenly aware of how crowded it was inside the stage. There were seven other people squeezed together within its small, rounded confines, all of them struggling to find a comfortable position for their knees, elbows, and feet. Beside her sat a portly, distinguished-looking man with a long, gray mustache. He wore a dark, well-pressed suit and carried a shiny black cane, which seemed to be very much in the way. After trying unsuccessfully to prop it beside him, he finally laid it down beneath the seat, then straightened up, smiling at Bryony as he caught her friendly, interested glance.

"How do you do? I should have known that cane would be in the way, but I'm in the habit of never being without it. Silly, wouldn't you say? Allow me to introduce myself. I'm Dr. Brady. Dr. Charles Brady."

"I'm happy to meet you, Doctor. My name is Bryony Hill. Are you traveling far?"

"All the way to San Francisco. I'm considering opening a new medical practice there." He chuckled. "My friends all say I'm too old to begin anew in a strange environment, but I've had this urge to try something different ever since my wife passed away last year." He blinked rapidly. "I need the change, you see. My memories of Lucy are too strong here in Missouri." He continued, brightening as he spoke. "I hear that California is a wonderful place, so I'm going to see for myself. If I like it, I just may pack up and move out there for good. Wouldn't that surprise all of my acquaintances in St. Louis!"

She smiled at him. Here was someone else who felt the urge for change, for adventure. Somehow, at the start of her journey, it was comforting to know that she was not alone in her yearning for a new life. "Good luck to you!" she exclaimed warmly. "I hope you find the west to your liking."

"And you, Miss Hill? For where are you bound?"

She explained about her ranch in the Arizona Territory. "So you see, Dr. Brady, I believe we have something in common. Both of us seek a new life in the west, though neither of us knows quite what to expect."

Before too long, the other passengers in the coach began introducing themselves. Across from Bryony and Dr. Brady, in the middle seat, were Tom and Martha Scott, and their small, towheaded daughter, Hannah. Their seven-year-old son, Billy, sat on the far side of Dr. Brady, making faces at his younger sister. The Scotts were a farming family, returning to California from a visit in Missouri. They had moved west five years before to begin homesteading, and this had been their first trip to visit their eastern relations since the move.

After the Scotts had introduced themselves, there was

a brief, awkward pause while everyone looked expectantly at the tall matron and her daughter, ensconced on the seat at the rear of the coach. They, in turn, eyed the other passengers with frigid hauteur.

"Excuse me," Dr. Brady said hesitatingly, breaking the silence. "I'm Dr. Charles Brady, and this is Miss Hill, and Mr. and Mrs. Scott. How do you do? I don't believe we've had the privilege of learning your names, ladies."

"Indeed." The matron sniffed, regarding him with raised eyebrows. "I am Mrs. Oliver—Mrs. Douglas Oliver—and this is my daughter, Diana."

The younger woman nodded coldly to the other occupants of the coach. Her pale blue eyes flitted from one to the other of them, resting briefly on Bryony, at which point they seemed to grow even icier. Diana Oliver was not beautiful by any means, but she possessed an aloof, aristocratic prettiness that was quite attractive in its own way. However, the frosty expression in her pale eyes, and the fact that her thin pink lips were set in a permanent straight line, did nothing to enhance her charm. Her thin, pinched nose and haughtily arched brows added to her appearance of unpleasant superiority. With one hand patting her elaborate blonde coiffure beneath its apricot plumed hat, she spoke in a high, disdainful voice.

"I do hope, Mrs. Scott, that you will be able to control your children during the length of this journey. My mother's nerves will not be able to endure any screeching or crying, and I must say that if we had known children would be present on the trip, we no doubt would have waited for another stage, despite the fact that my dear papa is anxiously awaiting our arrival in San Francisco."

Bryony gasped at the rudeness of this speech, and even Dr. Brady caught his breath in shock.

"Well, now, we'll sure do our best to keep the young 'uns quiet," Tom said in a strained voice. "But you know how children are. I can't make no promises, ma'am."

Mrs. Oliver sighed. "Surely you should be able to control your own children, sir. I assume you don't allow them to behave in an unruly fashion at home—or perhaps you do?"

Bryony glanced at little Hannah and Billy. They were sitting perfectly still, staring unhappily at Mrs. Oliver and her daughter. Hannah, her eyes wide, had snuggled closer to her mother, obviously realizing that she and her brother were the cause of discord amongst the occupants of the stagecoach. Looking at those two little forlorn faces, Bryony felt a sudden burst of anger toward the Olivers, who were causing trouble so needlessly. She had a strong suspicion that they were deliberately trying to intimidate the Scotts, to impress them with their self-importance. And they seemed to be succeeding. Martha had flushed crimson at Mrs. Scott's words, and was glancing uncertainly at Tom, who seemed equally discomfited. The children were looking more miserable every second.

"Tell me, Miss Oliver," Bryony said coolly, "are you and your mother in the habit of anticipating difficulties before they arise? The children seem to me perfectly well-behaved, and I can't see any reason at all why you should be so concerned. Can you?"

Two spots of color appeared on Diana Oliver's thin cheeks, and she stared at Bryony in obvious rage. "I am merely trying to protect my mother from any possible disturbance," she snapped. "As I mentioned before, her nerves are in no condition to tolerate rowdy children. And I really can't see, Miss Hill, why this matter is of any concern to you."

"Yes," Mrs. Oliver remarked disapprovingly. "It is quite impudent of you to interfere, young woman. This discussion involved only ourselves and the Scotts. It is certainly none of *your* business."

"I'm sorry, ma'am, but you are mistaken," Bryony

flashed, her jade-green eyes meeting the matriarch's squarely, then holding the daughter's gaze for one brief, purposeful moment. "If you and your daughter persist in anticipating problems needlessly, you're both going to irritate *my* nerves. And that is very much my business!"

Now it was Mrs. Oliver's turn to gasp. She and Diana exchanged indignant glances, and flounced back in their seats, turning their heads away from the other passengers in a huff to abruptly end the debate.

Dr. Brady gave a stifled chortle of laughter, and squeezed Bryony's arm. "Brave, my girl," he whispered in her ear. "I do admire your spirit!"

The Scotts threw her a grateful smile, and turned their attention to soothing the unhappy children, while Bryony leaned back in her upholstered seat and gazed out the window unseeingly, pondering her exchange with the Olivers. *Those hideous women*, she concluded furiously. *I'm glad I gave them a setdown, for if ever two people deserved one, they certainly did!* Her only regret, upon reflection, was that she may have added to the strain amongst the passengers, and this would make for further unpleasantness during the journey.

Her worries faded, however, as normal conversation resumed between Dr. Brady and the Scott family, and she realized that no one intended to pay the slightest attention to the unpleasant Oliver women. The sound of the children's laughter did much to ease her anxiety.

It was nearly April, and the barren Missouri countryside, showing small signs of the approaching spring, rolled steadily by. Here and there, Bryony caught a glimpse of green buds on the solemn black trees, and flocks of birds frequently swept across the sky from the south, bringing with them the promise of spring. Red-and-white farmhouses and open pastures still blanketed with snow dotted the landscape, giving her a sense of comfort with their peaceful familiarity. She began memorizing every detail of the Missouri scenery, aware that soon she would be viewing landscapes vastly different. The thought was both intriguing and unsettling, and for a moment she longed to cling to the solid farmland she knew. But presently, her sense of adventure rose up to claim her again and she began watching with fresh eagerness for the slightest change in the tranquil scenery.

At first, the cushioned seat in the stagecoach was comfortable, but after the first few hours of continuous travel, Bryony felt every jolt in the road, and her body began to ache. She wondered how she would ever be able to sleep sitting up, and soon learned the answer: she wouldn't—at least, not very well. Throughout that first night, she kept being shaken awake by the pitching, rocking motion of the stagecoach as it lurched along the dark, uneven roads, and by morning, she was so stiff and sore that any movement was torturous for her.

The other passengers were enduring the same agony; they had all chosen to follow the common practice of traveling both day and night in order to reach their destination more quickly, and they were all regretting their decision by the time dawn's first, faint pinkish light tinged the horizon. It was a bone-weary group that climbed down from the stage for breakfast at the relay station, partaking of a paltry meal of unbuttered short-cake, dried beef, and bitter, unsweetened coffee. After an all too brief respite, they were summoned back to resume the journey, feeling none too certain of their ability to withstand such torment for many more days. But eventually, they adapted to the discomforts of their mode of travel, and were even able to snatch a few hours of sleep during the night.

The days passed one by one, and when not involved in a friendly game of whist, or perhaps euchre, with her fellow passengers, Bryony spent many absorbing hours drinking in the scenery. The landscape changed daily, as they crossed the steep stony Ozark Mountain range and entered Indian Territory, progressing gradually across the wide desert expanses of Texas, and the vast, rather frightening wilderness of New Mexico. Gone were the peaceful farmhouses of Missouri; the country through which she now traveled was desolate and forbidding, but breathtakingly beautiful because of its wild, natural splendor. As the stagecoach wound its way precariously around narrow mountain passes, walled in on either side by towering red boulders that stretched skyward like rocky giants, Bryony felt a strange thrill run through her body, and a prickly sensation brushed ghostlike down her spine. How tiny and insignificant she and the other passengers and the stagecoach seemed, dwarfed by the awesome magnitude of their surroundings. This feeling persisted even when they had crossed the mountains and were hurtling across the barren desert floor, with the sun beating down from a vivid blue sky. Here, in the west, nature seemed so strong, so terrifyingly powerful. She hoped grimly that she would have the strength to survive in this harsh, formidable land.

As the journey progressed, a friendly camaraderie sprang up among the passengers, except for the two Oliver women, who maintained a disdainful distance from the rest of the company. But Bryony soon grew fond of Dr. Brady and the Scotts, and she was always eager and happy to help Martha with the children, keeping them entertained with lively, amusing stories that she invented herself, soothing them when they bumped their heads after a particularly jarring jolt in the road, and enfolding them comfortably in her arms when they attempted to sleep. Both she and Dr. Brady were fascinated by the stories Tom and Martha had to tell about life in the west, wanting to glean as much information as possible.

One afternoon, shortly after they had passed through El Paso, Dr. Brady began questioning Tom about the lawlessness that was rumored to be rampant in this part of the country.

"Is it really as bad as they say," he inquired, "or is

all this talk about bandits and desperados an attempt to scare away city folks like myself?"

Tom shook his head. "I'm sorry to say, Doc, that most of the stories are true. In California, the mining boom attracted lots of thievin', low-down fellers seeking a quick way to get rich. And a lot of 'em didn't care if they did it honest or not. Texas, New Mexico, Arizona—they're the same way. Big, wide-open spaces attract a certain breed of men—not that they're all like that, mind you, but many of 'em are just rough, wild characters who figure they can get away with anything. Sheriffs aren't none too plentiful around these parts, and a lawman who's willin' to go after a real dangerous desperado, well, he's more scarce than water in the desert."

Dr. Brady looked solemn at these words, and Bryony bit her lip. "Tom, tell me about Arizona Territory. Is it as bad as Texas and New Mexico?" she asked, leaning forward slightly in her seat.

"Shore is. Why, Tucson is one of the worst towns of the lot, filled with rustlers, thieves, gamblers." Seeing her alarmed expression, he tried to smile reassuringly. "Well, now, Bryony, I wouldn't get too scared just yet. After all, you won't be in Tucson. You're going to Winchester, which is some fifty miles east of there. And besides, there'll be a whole mess of wranglers at that ranch of yours, all bustin' to protect you from any kind of trouble." He grinned, running a large hand through his thick, sandy hair. "I reckon one of those wranglers will pack you off and marry you before the summer's end, and then you won't have to worry about anythin' anymore."

Everybody laughed, except Bryony, who blushed rosily at his forthright words.

"Hush, Tom," Martha scolded, though she was unable to keep from chuckling herself. She turned to Bryony with an apologetic smile. "You'll have to pardon him," she said kindly. "He doesn't mean to be embarrassin' you, but with you bein' so pretty and all, there ain't no doubt but that he's most likely right.''

"Thank you," Bryony replied, "but I'm not in the least anxious to marry! And as for worrying about these terrible men, well, all I can say is that they'd best start worrying about me! I intend to purchase a gun of my own as soon as I arrive in Arizona, and I'm going to learn how to use it. No one is going to intimidate me!''

The men exchanged amused glances at this determined speech coming from such a fragile-looking beauty, but Dr. Brady replied, "Yes, my dear, that is probably a good idea. It doesn't hurt to be armed, and able to protect yourself. In all seriousness, Tom, don't you agree?''

"Shore. But I wouldn't want to see her goin' up against a real gunfighter, like Wes Hardin or Jim Logan.''

"Jim . . . Logan?" Bryony caught her breath as her heart gave a sudden, painful jolt.

"Why, Bryony, what is it?" Dr. Brady exclaimed in concern, reaching quickly for her pulse. "You're as white as parchment, my dear! Whatever is wrong?''

"N—nothing." She shook her head, taking slow, deep breaths. Fighting for composure, she attempted to smile at her worried companions. "I'm perfectly all right, really I am. It was only that name. . .'' Her voice trailed off. That horrible man—that killer! An icy shiver traveled down her spine. How she hated him! And yet, somehow, she felt a kind of morbid curiosity to learn more about the man who had killed her father.

"What do you know about this man?" she asked Tom in an unsteady voice.

"Not much, really. They say he hails from Texas, like Wes Hardin, and is considered one of the most dangerous hombres in these parts. He's like lightning with a gun, so I hear. He's only twenty-eight or twenty-nine years old, but he's killed more'n a dozen men already, and I reckon there'll be a lot more. Bryony, what is it? Why are you so interested in Texas Jim Logan, and why are you lookin' at me so funny?''

"I'm sorry," Bryony murmured, glancing down at her hands. "You must all think me quite odd."

"No, my dear, we don't think you odd at all," Dr. Brady said reassuringly. "But won't you tell us what is troubling you?"

She met his gaze with eyes suddenly brimming with tears. "Jim Logan killed my father," she whispered.

There was a brief, shocked silence. Even Mrs. Oliver and Diana stared at her in amazement. Martha Scott was the first to speak.

"How horrible for you, Bryony," she said awkwardly. "We're awfully sorry. We won't talk about it any more. You just try not to think about it, for I'm sure those thoughts bring you a lot of hurting."

"Yes, I do want to forget about it. I just hope this Jim Logan has left the territory. I think that if ever I encountered him, I'd be tempted to try to kill him myself!"

"Don't even think about that," Dr. Brady said soothingly.

"He'll probably be long gone from Arizona by the time you get there," Tom put in. "You'll never have to lay eyes on him, and we shore won't talk about him any more."

Bryony was relieved when they changed the subject, but as their quiet conversation flowed gently about her, she couldn't help thinking about the man who had shot her father. This Texas Jim Logan, as Tom Scott had called him, sounded like a terrible man, representing everything she loathed: violence, brutality, lawlessness. Yet there was one thing she could not understand. Why had he shot her father? What possible quarrel could Wesley Hill have had with a professional gunman? She fretted over this for some little time, but eventually gave it up. There was no use speculating about it; after all, she knew nothing of her father's affairs in Arizona.

Perhaps Judge Hamilton would be able to enlighten her when she arrived in Winchester. She knew there had to be an explanation.

When the stagecoach at last crossed the border from New Mexico into Arizona, Bryony stared with fascinated interest at the terrain of her new home. She had expected to find Arizona a stark, barren desert, void of color or life, but instead, she was amazed to discover that it was a land of spectacular beauty and contrasts. Spring had already waved its magic wand, and the result was a breathtaking panorama. Silhouetted against a brilliant sapphire sky were towering mountains veiled in a pale lilac mist, their jagged peaks topped with snow. In the distance were immense pine forests, high above rolling green foothills and sweeping, sand-swept plains. There were deep purple canyons and rocky mesas, and the fresh, clear scent of spring in the air, laced with the sweet, delicious aroma of pine trees and orange blossoms. There were desert flowers bursting with color, and cactus blossoms of infinite variety. Paloverde, ironwood, and saguaro cactus were everywhere, decorating the desert. And this magnificent landscape teemed with life. The passengers frequently caught sight of galloping antelope herds, of white-tailed deer, and foxes, and badgers, and once, Bryony insisted, a herd of elk upon a rocky bluff. She no longer missed the tranquil Missouri countryside, for this glorious wilderness was far more exciting.

As the stagecoach advanced further and further into the territory, the much-discussed threat of Indian attacks became frighteningly real. They were in Apacheria, the domain of Cochise, the Apaches' most fearsome and menacing of chiefs. At every relay station where the stage halted to change horses, reports of Indian unrest were rampant, causing the passengers to glance uneasily at each other as they heard the driver summon them back to the coach. Everyone wished nervously that this stage of the journey was over, but they kept most of their fears to themselves, except for Mrs. Oliver and her daughter, who screamed in alarm at every bump in the road or noise in the night.

When at last the day of Bryony's anticipated arrival in Winchester arrived, she heaved an inward sigh of relief. For her, the danger would be over once she disembarked from the stagecoach into the waiting company of Judge Hamilton. And though the other passengers were all continuing on to San Francisco, their danger would also be left behind very soon, for the roughest portion of the journey was almost completed. So it was with a lifting of spirits that everyone boarded the dusty stagecoach after breakfast that morning, eager to pass through the remaining dangerous terrain as quickly as possible.

Bryony had taken special pains with her appearance that day, wanting to make a favorable impression on Judge Hamilton and the other citizens of Winchester. She had found a tiny clear brook near the relay station where they had breakfasted, and stealing away for a few moments, she had rinsed some of the dust and grime of the journey from her face and arms and throat, delighting in the cool, sparkling water. Swiftly, she had returned to the station, and changed her dress in a small dingy back room, her fingers flying to fasten the tiny pearl buttons on her frock. Then, looking fresh and pretty in a soft lavender gown, with its dainty pearl buttons and flattering, rounded neckline, she had carefully lifted her heavy mass of black hair off of her neck and arranged it becomingly atop her head, securing it with pearl hairpins. For a final touch, she had tied a lavender ribbon about her slender white throat, and fixed in its center the lovely cameo brooch that had belonged to her mother. It was very old and very valuable, and Bryony only wore it upon special occasions. This day seemed special. It was the beginning of a new life for her, and she wanted everything to be perfect. With the brooch in place, her spirits soared, and she joined the other passengers to finish the last stage of her journey.

"We shall miss you, my dear," Dr. Brady told her, shortly after noon. "It won't be the same, traveling on without you."

"And I shall miss you—all of you!" she smiled, patting the doctor's hand. "Especially the children."

Hannah and Billy beamed at this compliment, but Martha said almost ruefully, tucking a strand of brown hair behind her ear, "I don't know how I'll manage them without you, Bryony. You're a wonder with the little ones."

"Hmph!" Mrs. Oliver snorted from her seat at the rear of the coach. "I hope you *can* manage without her," she told Martha unpleasantly. "This journey has been tiring enough, without having to put up with any additional disturbances!"

"Now, now, let's not start this again," Dr. Brady interrupted hastily.

"The young 'uns have been behaving better than some of the grown-up passengers, it seems to me," Tom remarked meaningfully, his blue eyes glinting. He was no longer intimidated by the Oliver women; constant contact during the past fifteen days had eliminated all inhibitions, and he seemed to derive great pleasure from standing up to them. When Mrs. Oliver grasped the intent of his comment, she afforded him considerable gratification by clamping her lips tightly together and flouncing indignantly back in her seat.

"Don't be upset, Mama," Diana cried, flashing Tom a contemptuous look. "We won't have to endure such rude company much longer. Soon we will be in San Francisco with Papa, and we can forget the indignities suffered on this wretched journey."

"Yes, if we ever arrive safely, without being murdered by savages!" her mother said plaintively.

She had no sooner finished speaking than a frenzied commotion sounded from without. The previously peaceful afternoon exploded with the thunder of horses' hooves, and wild yelling, and a series of deafening shots that rang out in rapid succession. Its horses screaming in terror, the stagecoach lurched to a rocking standstill, throwing the passengers from their seats. Bryony lifted herself from the dusty floor of the coach to peer through the window, and what she saw made her catch her breath in fright.

"Indians!" Mrs. Oliver shrieked, clutching her head like a madwoman. "Indians! Indians! We shall all be killed!"

Diana, too, began to scream hysterically.

"Oh, hush!" Bryony whispered urgently. "There are no Indians! We're being held up by highwaymen!"

Dr. Brady stared past her. "I'm afraid you're right," he said grimly, as four masked riders converged upon the halted stagecoach.

Bryony's hands grew cold and clammy. She wiped them nervously upon her skirt. Danger had struck only a few short hours from Winchester and safety! Her mind was racing, wondering what the highwaymen would do with them. Suddenly, a thought occurred to her. She frantically snatched the cameo brooch from the ribbon at her throat. Those men must not see it, or they would undoubtedly steal it away from her! She buried it deep inside her reticule, desperately hoping she would not be searched. A frightened sob rose in her throat, but she choked it back, making a valiant effort to remain calm. She must not have hysterics like those odious Oliver women. She must try to be strong.

"Everybody out!" A man's thick, coarse voice suddenly bellowed from outside. "And hurry it up! We got no time for playin' games, and we'll shoot anyone who makes a false move!"

Chapter Four

One by one the passengers filed out. They huddled in a small group beside the driver, who had dismounted angrily and was now spitting disgustedly into the road.

"You fellers are barkin' up the wrong tree!" he exclaimed, shaking his shaggy head. "We don't got no strongbox on this trip, jest passengers. You kin look fer yourselves."

"Shut up!" the leader of the highwaymen barked, waving his large, evil-looking revolver in a threatening way at the driver. "We'll take what we can get! These here passengers look mighty well off to me, and I'm sure they won't mind sharing some of their valuables with us poor banditos."

The other three men with the leader snickered loudly at this remark, though the sound was muffled by the thick scarves they wore across their faces, hiding all but their eyes. Bryony shivered as she looked at them, but it was the leader who really made her flesh crawl. He was a burly, barrel-chested man with a shock of gold hair showing beneath his black sombrero, and his eyes, as they ran swiftly over the group of passengers, were a bright, wicked blue. They rested on her suddenly, and a light sparked in them, a quick gleam of interest as he looked her up and down in a bold, leering way.

"We've got a real little beauty here!" he declared to

his companions, and dismounted heavily from his horse.

Bryony shrank against Dr. Brady, who stood next to her, and he placed a trembling arm about her shoulders. "It's all right. They . . . just want our money," he whispered in a voice that was meant to be reassuring, but which revealed the extent of his own uncertainty and fear. His hand on her shoulder tightened protectively as a tremor shook her body.

"No more talkin' unless you're talked to!" a bandit wearing a red scarf shouted angrily.

The leader approached Tom and Martha, who were standing very close together, with little Hannah and Billy clinging tearfully to their mother's skirt. Tom's face was pale, but he showed no other signs of fear as the highwayman poked the gun into his ribs.

"Say, now, farmer, where you headin' with your missus and those two kids?"

"California."

"California? You don't say. Well, now, that's real nice. But I don't suppose you've got much cash on hand, do you? You don't look to me like a wealthy man."

"No. I don't have much."

"How much?" the leader demanded harshly, his hard, bright eyes narrowing dangerously.

"I've got about forty-five dollars with me," Tom replied in a quiet voice, as beside him Martha began to sob.

"Forty-five dollars! Forty-five dollars! You hear that, boys? We'll be living high off the hog on forty-five dollars, won't we?"

He gave a great, bellowing laugh, and waved the gun carelessly at Tom. "You keep your damn forty-five dollars, amigo. You need it more than we do!" He stepped past the Scotts to Dr. Brady. "Now, this fellow here seems more our type. I bet you have a few pesos on you, pardner, don't you?"

Dr. Brady, without a word, removed his wallet and handed it over to the burly highwayman, who rifled through it and then gave a low whistle. "Well, this is more like it! And I reckon you've got a nice gold watch inside that fancy vest you're wearing. Hand it over, on the double!"

The doctor complied quickly, breathing a sigh of relief as the highwayman sauntered past both him and Bryony to confront the Olivers, who cowered in abject terror against the stagecoach.

His shrewd gaze raked Mrs. Oliver and her daughter for a long, thoughtful moment. "You ladies sure look like you've got a bundle of loot," he remarked. The gun jerked violently in his big, hairy hand. "Pass it over!"

Sobbing, they surrendered to him what appeared to be a considerable sum of cash. But this didn't satisfy the highwayman, who immediately demanded their jewels.

"Oh, please, won't you let us keep *something?*" Mrs. Oliver pleaded, pressing her diamond-studded necklace to her throat. "Please, don't take our jewelry as well as our money."

"Shut up!" he roared, and with a sudden, lunging motion, tore the necklace from her throat. "And give me those rings you're wearing! I've got a real hankering for pretty baubles!" He turned to Diana and gripped her arm ruthlessly. "What about you, blondie? Those pearls you've got around that skinny neck of yours are mighty pretty, but I don't reckon they're worth your life, so you'd best give them to me without any back talk or I might get mad. And I'm awful mean when I get mad."

As Diana thrust the pearl necklace into his waiting hands, a furious cry rose from her throat. "What about *her?*" she demanded in a shriek, pointing a shaking finger at Bryony, who stood rock-still beside Dr. Brady. "She's got a cameo brooch worth more than any of these pieces, and it's hidden inside her reticule! Why don't you take that and leave us alone?"

Bryony gasped at Diana's words, and her entire body froze as the burly, gold-haired outlaw strode over to her and stared harshly down into her pale face.

"Is it true about that brooch she mentioned?"

Bryony couldn't speak. Her body had turned to ice, and she could only tremble uncontrollably as the highwayman's bright eyes hardened.

"What's your name, little filly?" he asked in that same, strangely excited whisper. When she still said nothing, his hand shot out to grip her wrist in a brutal hold. "Answer me!" he barked.

Dr. Brady sought to push the man away from Bryony, but the outlaw rounded on him furiously and delivered a crashing blow to the doctor's chin. Down he went with a grunt of pain, and Bryony immediately knelt beside him.

"Dr. Brady, are you all right?" she cried in horror, as the doctor's eyes rolled dazedly in his head.

"One more move like that and he'll be dead," the highwayman sneered, looming over them with leveled gun. He yanked Bryony roughly to her feet. "I asked you your name, girl, and I want an answer!"

"My name is Bryony Hill—if it's any of your business!" she spat, fury overcoming her previous fear, and making her long to claw at her tormentor, to rake his leering face with her nails. "And don't you dare to touch this man again!"

She drew herself up very straight as she met his evil stare with her own burning green one, but the highwayman only laughed cruelly at her enraged expression. "You're a real fighter, aren't you, little filly?" he boomed. "Well, I'll tell you what. As a reward for bein' so pretty and so brave, we're goin' to take you along with us! How do you like that?"

Terror surged through her. Her knees grew weak and she swayed slightly on her feet. "You can't mean that!" she quavered.

"Sure I do. Don't I, boys?"

There was a chorus of laughing agreement from the other masked men, who had never dismounted from their mustangs, but who were still pointing their weapons at the captured passengers and driver.

The leader again grasped Bryony's wrist.

"Come along now, like a good girl."

"No! Please!" she begged frantically, struggling against his grip. "Please don't take me with you! You can have the cameo!"

"We'll have you and the cameo!" he growled, and began dragging her relentlessly toward his mount, while the other bandits trained their guns on the horrified passengers.

"Here now, let her alone!" Tom Scott implored desperately, while Martha sank, weeping, to her knees.

"Please, don't hurt her!" she pleaded. "Let her stay with us!"

Dr. Brady, struggling painfully to a sitting position, added his gasping voice to their pleas, but the highwaymen paid no attention. The big, barrel-chested leader shoved Bryony over to his horse, but when he attempted to hoist her into the saddle, she whirled and fought with him, clawing, kicking, and biting like a tigress. The other masked riders chortled gleefully as their leader struggled with the wisp of a girl who was putting up such a fight. Finally, he wrapped his arms about her slender body so that she was helplessly pinioned, and dumped her onto the saddle. Then he kicked his horse into a gallop, and the others followed quickly, brandishing their weapons in the air as they left the shocked stagecoach passengers beside their dusty vehicle. They rode swiftly over the rough terrain, in a hurry now to reach the safety of shelter where they could divide up their spoils. And they were in a hurry for something else, too. The girl. She was part of the reward for this day's work. Each of them meant to enjoy her before the long night was over.

Bryony clung desperately to the saddle horn as the

horse scrambled wildly up twisted mountain paths strewn with boulders and thick mesquite shrubs. Tears streamed down her cheeks as she and the band of highwaymen headed deeper and deeper into the rugged mountain wilderness. She was a prisoner, a prisoner of this ruthless outlaw band! It had all happened so quickly that she could barely believe it was really true, but the heavy pressure of the bandit leader's hulking body against hers, and his hot breath down her neck, was proof enough. Where were they taking her? What were they going to do?

The hours dragged interminably past, and still they rode, on and on beneath the hot, relentless yellow sun, the ruddy mountain walls rising up to engulf them, the sky a blue-mirrored glare overhead, stretching into eternity. Bryony's dark hair had tumbled loose from its pretty chignon to hang limply in her face, which was caked with sweat and dust, and her throat felt so parched she found it difficult to swallow. When at last the band halted by a thin stream that wound its way along a sloping, rocky path studded with thorny cactus plants and scrub brush, she felt a kind of numb relief. The horses drank thirstily from the stream, while the highwaymen gulped at their canteens. But when the leader of the band, with a bawdy wink and a grin at his companions, wiped his mouth after drinking lustily, and offered his canteen to Bryony, she shoved it away disgustedly and instead sank down beside the stream to cup her hands and sip the icy droplets from them. The highwaymen all roared with laughter.

"So, you won't drink from my canteen, eh, little filly? Never mind! Soon enough you'll be drinking in my kisses, like it or not! Might as well get used to the idea!"

From her kneeling position by the stream, Bryony raised her head to stare at him in hatred. Her jade green eyes were narrowed and sparkling with fury as she studied the outlaw leader. Once removed from the stagecoach trail, the men had taken off their masks, and now she saw her captors plainly. The leader had thick, heavy features beneath those wicked blue eyes; his nose was bulbous, his lips full and sneering. With his shock of gold hair and those vivid eyes, some might have thought him attractive, in a bold, vulgar way, but to Bryony, the sight of him was repulsive.

"I'd rather die than have you touch me!" she hissed, crouching in the dust. "You're no better than an animal —you and your thieving friends!"

The leader's eyes gleamed evilly at her. "It don't matter what you think, little filly, because we're going to have you one way or 'nother! And as for dying, we'll see about that later. But we won't let you die until we're good and ready, and I've a hunch that won't be for a spell. Right, boys?"

At these ominous words, Bryony's terror overcame her. She leaped up and began to run wildly down the slope. Even as she fled, she knew it was useless, but desperation drove her blindly to attempt this mad escape, and for a few brief seconds she clattered over rocks and shrubs, scraping her hands and elbows as she stumbled past rough-edged boulders in frantic haste. She heard a yell behind her, and panic made her flee even faster, but within seconds there was a triumphant "Whooeee!" close behind, and the next thing she knew, she went down hard in the gritty sand, tackled by a hurtling, unseen figure. She screamed, and tried to twist away, but her captor turned her roughly onto her back on the trail and held her there securely, his weight pressing her into the hard ground, his small, dark eyes alive with glee as he gazed triumphantly down into her flushed, grimy face.

Bryony recognized him as the highwayman who had worn the red bandana, the one who had ordered her and Dr. Brady to be silent. He was short and pug-nosed, with a stubby dark growth of beard on his swarthy face.

"Please," she whispered as she struggled to throw him off. "Please, let me go!"

"Go! You're crazy, lady! You'd jest die of thirst in this desert before you ever caught sight of another living creature, unless it was a band of Apaches, in which case you'd be better off dying from thirst! And Zeke already told you that we're not going to let you die until we're good and ready, now didn't he?" His eyes, bright as pennies, slid over her body, raptly studying her breasts as they rose and fell heavily with the effort of her struggle.

"Don't fight it, lady. You'll only make it worse on yerself. There's no way me or any of my pardners is going to let you off. It's not every day we get our hands on such a fine-looking filly, and we mean to enjoy you."

To Bryony's horror, his hand groped at her breast and began to squeeze it eagerly. "No!" she screamed frantically. "No! Please!"

At that moment, the outlaw leader's voice rang out angrily from somewhere above. "What the hell are you doin', Ned? I told you to fetch her back! We don't have all day to wait around for you!"

"Aw, Zeke! I'm jest having a little fun! She's sure a beaut, all right."

"Damn it, we don't have time for that now!" the leader shouted impatiently from above. "Get off of her and bring her back pronto! Another hour's hard ridin' and we'll be at Gilly's. Then you can have all the fun you want."

"Jest give me ten minutes with her right now," Ned begged urgently. "Jest ten minutes!"

"Later! You've got ten seconds to get her back to the horses, or we're leavin' you here without your mount. Savvy?"

With a reluctant grimace, Ned got to his feet and stared down at Bryony, who lay weeping in the dust.

"Let's go, lady," he muttered. "You and me'll have to wait 'til later to git acquainted."

He seized her arm and pulled her to her feet, hustling her up the sloping trail alongside of him. Bryony had no more will to resist. She felt weak and drained from the effort of her foolish escape attempt, and barely had the strength to stumble up the stony path. Her hands and elbows were cut and bleeding, her ankle ached painfully where it had twisted when Ned threw her to the ground. She was exhausted, almost beyond caring. Silently, she allowed Zeke to hoist her onto the saddle. Deep inside, a cold, horrible dread was piercing her heart. She knew all too well what lay ahead of her, and she knew there was no hope of escape.

For almost another hour they rode up and down zigzagging, tortuous mountain paths, until at last they overlooked a deep, purple canyon below. At Zeke's command, the outlaws began their descent, the tired horses picking their way carefully along the steep ravine. Despite the fact that new terrors awaited her when they reached their destination, Bryony longed for the end of the journey.

At last they reached the bottom of the canyon. The band headed through a narrow, rock-walled passage that had been invisible from the top. It was like a secret hole in the heart of the canyon walls, and Bryony stared in wonder as they rode single file through the small, hidden opening. When they finally emerged from its narrow, suffocating confinement, they were on a wide, cactus-covered bluff, having ridden completely through the canyon walls. It appeared that the hidden passageway was the only entrance to the secluded bluff, for on all other sides rose a sheer rock wall that would be impossible to scale or descend. Zeke noticed her staring at those steep, towering walls, and chuckled softly in her ear.

"There's no way anyone can climb those rocks from either side, little filly. The only way in or out of this place is through that passage we just rode through, and even that is hidden from above. Pretty smart, huh? This way, we only get *invited* guests at Gilly's. Know what I mean?''

With a sinking heart, she turned her face away from his triumphant, sneering countenance. Yes, she knew all too well what he meant. There was not a chance in the world that anyone would find her here, or that she could get away. Tears stung her eyes. Through their blur, she saw a ramshackle wooden building ahead, set well back from the edge of the bluff. There were horses tethered outside, and as they approached, raucous sounds of merriment drifted outside from within.

Zeke jerked her down from the saddle, snickering as Bryony landed upon weak, unsteady legs and almost collapsed. Half carrying her, he dragged her up a dirt path to the rickety wooden door, shoving it open without hesitation. The other highwaymen followed noisily.

''Look here, boys,'' Zeke announced, pushing Bryony roughly ahead of him into the noisy, smoke-filled room. ''We've brought back this here pretty little city girl, and she's real anxious and eager to meet you all!''

Chapter Five

The men in Gilly's grew strangely quiet as they stared at the trembling young girl thrust suddenly before them. Their eyes widened with admiration as they greedily gazed upon her dusty, disheveled form. Despite the fact that her hair had loosened from its chignon and was trailing haphazardly about her face and shoulders in dark, wispy curls, despite the fact that her creamy white skin was caked with dust and sand, that her gown was torn at the knees and covered with grit, and that her small white hands were scratched and bloodied, there was not a single doubt that before them stood a superbly beautiful woman. Her lavender gown was so damp with perspiration that it clung tightly to every curve in her slender body, revealing firm, rounded breasts, a tiny waist, and temptingly curved hips. Her large green eyes seemed brilliant against the pallor of her skin, and her ripe, red mouth, soft and sensuous with youth, and tumbling midnight hair even further heightened her bewitching loveliness. The men stared, fascinated, at the luscious creature before them. Every one of them yearned for the opportunity to bed her, and there wasn't one among them who wouldn't kill to have his way.

Bryony stood as if transfixed, her frightened gaze taking in the dusky room crowded with men. Near the far wall, there was a long bar where several cowboys stood drinking. There were several tables where men sat, cards and chips spread before them. There was no activity now, no sound; every man's eyes were on her—she felt naked beneath the eager intensity of their looks. Behind her, Zeke gave a great roar of laughter, and shoved her across the bare wooden floor.

"I reckon you'all like what you see!" he declared, striding over to a corner table. "Well, she's available to any or all of you—for the right price, that is."

A hearty cheer went up in the smoke-filled room, followed by much laughter. As the other highwaymen joined Zeke at a round wooden table covered with scratches and sticky with spilled whisky, Zeke called to Gilly, the stout, sleazy-looking bartender, for drinks. Bryony leaned weakly against the knotted-pine wall in the corner, feeling like a caged animal.

There were perhaps a dozen men present, some clad in bright, dandyish cowboy garb, others in dark, grimy, worn-looking clothing that appeared not to have been washed for weeks. Despite their varied dress, however, to Bryony they all seemed to have something in common: they were all desperate men. She could see that in their hard, swarthy faces, in the way their cruel eyes darted quickly, calculatingly about the dingy room, like snakes in a darkened pit. It was borne in upon her with sudden dismay that this secluded wooden building in the wilderness must be a meeting place for outlaws, gamblers, and thieves. And here she was, trapped amongst them, a prisoner, a helpless captive.

Her heart was pounding so thunderously she thought they must all be able to hear it, and she rammed her dirtied fist against her mouth to keep from screaming her despair. If only there was some way to escape—but it was hopeless. And tonight, these men intended to have her—and nothing was going to stop them. Nothing!

She slumped wearily to the floor in the corner, wondering dully whether she would be able to survive the degradation in store for her. At the thought of all of these hideous men touching her, probing her most intimate parts, brutally using her body to satisfy their animal lusts, something inside of her died. Sobs shook her as she huddled in the corner, but she tried valiantly to choke them back, to keep as quiet as possible, hoping that the outlaws would forget about her. At the moment they were engrossed in counting their loot. If only they would remain that way!

"It sure was a nice haul," Zeke remarked, fingering Mrs. Oliver's diamond necklace with satisfaction. "All in all, boys, a good day's work."

"Hey, what about this?" Ned snatched up Bryony's reticule and dumped the contents onto the table. "Maybe the city girl's got some cash in here."

The cameo brooch spilled out with a clatter, along with the money Bryony had brought with her, a silk handkerchief, and a small hand-mirror.

"Whoopee, look at this!" Ned exclaimed, whistling in admiration as he held up the brooch for inspection. "This one's a dandy! What do you suppose it's worth, Zeke?"

At his words, Bryony forgot her intention to remain quiet and unobtrusive. She rushed over and snatched the brooch from Ned's hands before she realized what she was doing. When he turned incredulous eyes upon her, she recoiled, clutching the brooch desperately.

"P—please," she began brokenly, glancing beseechingly at the grinning circle of bandits at the table. "Please let me keep the cameo. Please let me go! If it's money you want, I can get it for you! I have money! It's in the bank, I can send for it! I promise, I'll pay you anything you like if you'll just let me go."

Deafening laughter greeted her words and her heart sank. Zeke Murdock looked as though he were about to burst with laughter, and Ned was grinning from ear to ear. *How did I become the victim of such monsters*, she wondered wildly, her entire body beginning to tremble as she backed futilely away from them. They were heartless, totally without mercy. She spoke dazedly, in a whisper, the words quivering with fear. "You're . . . no better than animals. You're wicked, inhuman, despicable. . ."

Ned stalked her until her back was against the wall. A malicious grin was spread across his weasel-like face. "That's enough out of you," he snapped. "Now you jest give me this purty little trinket, and I might forget about your rude talk."

He tried to grab the brooch from her hands, but Bryony, engulfed by helpless rage, shrieked a protest, and before she could stop herself, she slapped him as hard as she could, a stinging blow to the cheek. As soon as she did it, she knew she had made a terrible mistake, for she saw the insane fury light in his eyes and immediately, he raised his fist and struck her a stunning blow that knocked her back against the wall. Tears stung her eyes as pain exploded in her face. Gasping and sobbing, she still resisted as the pug-nosed outlaw tried again to wrench the brooch from her clenched hand, and he struck her once more, even harder than before. Bryony sank to her knees as the room swam above her and a horrible aching agony pierced her cheek. The cameo brooch rolled from her limp fingers. Ned grabbed it up, and then yanked her roughly to her feet, sneering down into her tear-filled eyes.

"I guess that shut you up, didn't it?" he crowed. His eyes fell upon her pearl hairpins, and with a triumphant chortle, he began tearing them eagerly from her hair, ruthlessly pulling several long, black strands in his haste to collect the jewels.

"Hey, Zeke, look at these! This little lady is sure full of surprises!" he called gleefully, tossing the hairpins onto the table, while Bryony's thick mane of long, dark hair cascaded freely about her shaking shoulders. Ned turned back to her, grinning. "Now, lady, I've got a few surprises in store for you," he chuckled.

"Hell, why should Casper get her first?" one of the others protested to Zeke as Ned closed in upon Bryony, who had shrunk back against the wall. "Why shouldn't we have our chance?"

"And what about the rest of us?" A chorus of voices chimed in from around the smoky room. There was an angry buzz as the men argued amongst themselves.

"I'm willing to pay a good price for the first round with her," a tall, sly-looking cowboy announced from the bar.

"So am I!" retorted another. "And I can better afford it!"

Zeke pushed back his chair and stood up. "All right, boys, simmer down," he ordered. He glanced briefly at Ned, who had stopped in his tracks. "Set yourself down, Casper, and try to control yourself. It appears we're goin' to have a little bargaining session concernin' this filly. You'll have to put in your bid like everyone else and wait your turn."

"That ain't fair!" Ned snarled, turning upon the outlaw leader with a suddenly vicious expression. "You tole me back on the mountain that when we got to Gilly's—"

"Shut up! You'll have your turn with her, just like I said. Every man here will. But the hombre who gets her first, the one who gets this virgin territory for his own—well, he'll have to pay a steeper price. And it seems like plenty of these boys are willin' to pay it. Especially since she happens to be such a beauty." At that, Zeke grabbed Bryony's arm and jerked her forward, his fingers biting cruelly into her tender flesh. "Now, what do you boys want to offer for this pretty little filly?"

"How about a free sample of what's in store?" the sly-looking cowboy suggested. "Let me have a kiss from those sweet red lips and then I'll tell you how much I'll pay."

Zeke threw back his head and laughed. "Fair enough! I'll tell you what, boys. One kiss apiece, and then we'll start the bidding. I've got a feeling you fellows are gonna like your little taste, and want to go for the whole damn meal!"

Then, to Bryony's horror, Zeke shoved her into Ned's

lap, and proceeded to roar with laughter while the highwayman eagerly fastened his small, wet lips on hers and
kissed her. Nauseated and terrified, she struggled to
break free, but Ned held her securely, his mouth sucking
greedily at her trembling, revolted lips, his tongue darting in and out in quick exploration of her mouth.

"That's long enough!" Zeke declared.

"Pass her on to Hendrickson. Every man gets his
turn."

And so it went. Bryony, who in her sheltered eighteen
years had never before been kissed with anything but
polite respect by the genteel young men of her acquaintance, found herself passed roughly about the room like
a limp, helpless rag doll, while each man in Gilly's
tasted her lips and mouth, held her close and hard in a
crushing embrace, and eagerly fondled her breasts and
buttocks before Zeke commanded them to let the next
man have his chance. Breathless, bruised, and sickened,
she was tossed about until her knees buckled beneath
her, and her lips were bleeding and sore. At last, dizzy
and sobbing, she was returned to Zeke, who held her
sagging body upright, smiling down into her tear-
streaked face with unbridled pleasure.

"Now it's my turn, little lady," he muttered softly,
and his brawny arms swept her into a stifling embrace,
while his full, sensuous lips pressed hungrily against
hers. Slowly, desperately, with her last ounce of
strength, she raised her small foot and kicked at his
shin, but though he grunted in pain, his lips never left
hers; instead they sucked all the more viciously at the
soft recesses of her mouth. Finally, when Bryony had no
more breath left in her slender body, he released her,
chuckling as she collapsed in his arms. With one arm
snaked tightly about her throat and the other clamping
her body against his, he held her facing the throng of
men who watched eagerly, their eyes shining with
awakened desire.

"Now, how much will you pay?" Zeke boomed, his
wicked blue gaze sweeping the crowd. "How much will

you pay to bed this here little city girl and show her a bit of western hospitality?''

The bidding began. Fifty dollars. Sixty dollars. Eighty dollars. At first, Bryony struggled weakly against Zeke's grasp, but she soon realized how futile it was, since her own strength was nearly spent, and even if she wasn't exhausted and bone-weary, she would have been no match for the burly outlaw leader. Her head reeled with numbers as the men shouted their bids. The atmosphere in the room was merry, but beneath it she sensed an undertone of charged excitement and tension. Each of the men wanted her, and meant to have her. Their basest passions had been kindled by that one tempting kiss, and now they were anxious to satisfy their animal craving, to beat out their fellow men for the coveted prize. Despair closed in upon her. Soon it would all be over; the bidding would be closed. And she would be handed over to one of those brutal, disgusting men who stank of whisky and sweat and tobacco, who whispered vulgar obscenities in her ear as he kissed and fondled her. She wished fervently for death.

"Well, it seems we've got a little problem here," Zeke was saying, in a slow, thoughtful tone. "Sam, you've bid two hundred and ten dollars, and Ned here has bid two hundred and fifteen. Now, I'd hate for one of you boys to lose out by a mere five bills. Sam, why don't you offer a clean two hundred and fifty? That would settle it for sure.''

"Hey!" Ned scrambled to his feet in protest, flushing furiously. "That ain't fair!"

"Oh, hell, I don't know," the sly-looking cowboy called Sam replied uncertainly. He regarded Bryony with obvious longing in his squinted eyes. "Two hundred and fifty—that's a lot of loot."

"Don't you think she's worth it?" Zeke queried shrewdly. Suddenly, his arm left Bryony's throat to tear savagely at her lavender gown, ripping open the bodice and the chemise beneath to reveal the full, creamy-white mounds of her breasts. She screamed and renewed her

desperate struggles, to no avail. He continued to hold
her ruthlessly as the outlaws whooped and leaned forward excitedly in their chairs.

"Now, don't you think she's worth it?" Zeke
wheedled, eyeing Sam's fascinated face with satisfaction. "Two hundred and fifty dollars and she's yours!"

"Done!" Sam shouted, leaping away from the bar
hastily to approach the helpless, dark-haired girl before
him. His squinting eyes glowed with delight as he gazed
at his prize.

Bryony, held fast in Zeke's clutches, gave a low, tortured moan that rose from her throat like the anguished
cry of a captured animal.

At that moment, the door to the hideout swung open
and a man entered, pausing in the doorway to survey
the scene before him, as all eyes swerved instinctively
in his direction. He seemed to fill the narrow doorway
as he lounged there, coolly studying the occupants of
the room. He was tall—well over six feet—lean, and
bronzed, with a dark sombrero worn low over his eyes,
almost concealing his dark brown hair, and shadowing
the cold, light blue of his eyes. A pale blue linen shirt,
open at the throat, where a white silk neckerchief had
been expertly tied, covered his brawny chest and fit
snugly over wide, powerful shoulders. Dark blue
trousers encased his muscular thighs, and gleaming
black leather boots shone at his feet, which were planted
apart in a relaxed but ready stance. But the thing one
noticed first and foremost about the stranger was his
gunbelt. It was worn low over his hip, and contained a
long-barreled Colt .45 Frontier. Somehow, the weapon
seemed an integral part of the man in the doorway. One
couldn't imagine him without it.

Upon the stranger's entrance, the place grew
strangely quiet. Bryony, staring at him out of wide,
terrified eyes, felt a new fear descend upon her. As his
cold blue eyes raked her, taking in her cloud of mid-
night-black hair, her parted red lips and frightened
green eyes, her exposed breasts, she felt a sudden chill

sweep over her. Something about this stranger had a tremendous effect upon her, as it seemed to have upon everyone else in the room. She waited in growing dread as he advanced leisurely into the dimly-lit hideout, moving with a slow, purposeful stride to stand before her and Zeke.

"H—howdy, Texas." Zeke spoke in a voice that made an effort to be casual, but for the first time since she had met him, Bryony heard a note of nervousness in the outlaw leader's tone.

"Howdy, Murdock," the stranger drawled, with a slight, arrogant smile that just barely curled his lips, but never even approached those cold, light blue eyes. "Mind if I ask what's going on?"

Zeke laughed uneasily. " 'Course not. This here is just a little city girl me and the boys fetched off the west-bound stage. Quite a beauty, ain't she? We've been havin' a little fun, decidin' who gets the first go at her."

The stranger's gaze flicked from the burly outlaw leader to the girl locked in his grasp. No change of expression was perceptible in his icy eyes. He appeared relaxed, casual, totally at ease as he studied her. No one suspected that beneath his cool, nonchalant exterior, he was thinking hard and fast.

Damn! the stranger thought, as he met the girl's terrified gaze with his own outwardly indifferent one. She *is* beautiful. She looks like a butterfly caught in a hornet's nest—and every one of these hornets wants to put his sting in her. Not that he could blame them. Never before had he beheld a lovelier creature. He wondered, with an inward spark of excitement, what it would be like to touch those long, ebony tendrils cascading about her shoulders, to feel the fullness of her ripe, creamy breasts in his hands, to kiss those soft, tempting lips. Her jade green eyes, huge and brilliant in her terror, seemed to hold him spellbound for a moment. Perhaps it was her delicate features, or the milkiness of her skin, or the way her slender body seemed dwarfed by Zeke's hefty bulk, but she seemed so fragile, like an innocent young angel. With an effort, he withdrew his gaze from that captivating face to meet Zeke's nervous stare.

"Sounds like good, harmless fun," he commented lazily, hooking his strong, well-shaped hands in his gunbelt. "What was the outcome? Who's the lucky man?"

"Sam Taylor here won out," Zeke answered, jerking his head toward the cowboy who had backed off a few paces when the stranger named Texas had entered. "And I reckon Ned there will get her after he's done, seein' as he placed the second highest bid." The outlaw leader seemed suddenly struck with an idea. "Say, Texas," he said eagerly, wetting his dry lips with his tongue, "would you like a turn with her?"

The stranger nodded. "Yes, Murdock, I reckon I would. But you see, I don't like waiting for any man. I want her first."

There was a sharp intake of breath by all the men in the room at this remark. Little beads of perspiration broke out on Zeke's swarthy brow. "Well, now Texas, that's between you and Sam," he said hurriedly, his voice thick with nervousness. "I don't want any part of it."

"I don't blame you, Murdock," the tall, lean stranger replied with a mocking smile, and turning slightly, faced the cowboy who a few moments earlier had been gloating over Bryony. "Well, Taylor?" he remarked easily. "Did you hear what I said? I have a hankering for this city girl. And I don't feel like waiting until you've finished with her. Any objections?"

Bryony's heart, which had been beating rapidly before, now seemed to stop completely for one horrified moment. There was something about this arrogant stranger that frightened her far more than had any of the other outlaws. Beside him, they seemed merely common ruffians. She sensed instinctively that the stranger was of a different ilk. He was dangerous, like a coiled rattlesnake. Well-dressed, calm, with that deep, drawling voice, and those eyes—so cold, so ruthless. And that unmistakable air of arrogance! From the first moment she had laid eyes on him, she had known that he was far more deadly than the others.

"Well, Texas," Sam Taylor was saying, in a strangely choked voice. "I've . . . already . . . agreed to pay two hundred and fifty dollars for her."

The stranger regarded him coolly. "I don't give a damn what you've done, Taylor," he drawled. "I'm prepared to offer Murdock the same amount, and I'm sure he'll be happy to accept my money instead of yours. Right, Murdock?"

"Sure, Texas, whatever you say," Zeke agreed hastily. He still held Bryony, and she was aware that his hands had turned cold and clammy since the stranger's entrance. Obviously, he was just as intimidated by the man called Texas as everyone else appeared to be. As the stranger continued to fix his steely gaze upon Sam Taylor, the other men drifted to either side of the room, out of the line of fire. Sam faced the tall stranger alone. The room grew deathly still and silent.

"Well, Taylor, what's it going to be?" Texas asked. "If you have any objections, we can settle them here and now."

Sam Taylor swallowed, a look of helpless fury upon his face. His fingers twitched in a convulsive movement as if itching to draw his gun, but a powerful fear kept him from acting. He had paled considerably under the stranger's cold scrutiny; perspiration beaded on his brow. He hesitated, glancing longingly at Bryony, then back to the hard-eyed stranger.

"I . . . I don't want no trouble," he spurted in a hoarse voice. "But I bid for her—and I won. It jest ain't fair!" he cried out bitterly.

The stranger smiled slightly, a mere curling of his thin, sardonic lips. "You have my sympathies," he drawled, his eyes never leaving the sweating face of the man before him. "But I'm certain you've made the right choice. No woman—however beautiful—is worth dying for. Do you savvy what I mean?"

Taylor nodded, fists clenched tightly at his sides.

With an abrupt, frustrated movement, he turned on his heel and stalked over to the bar, gruffly ordering a drink.

The stranger turned back to Bryony and Zeke. "I'll take the lady now," he said politely.

"Sure, Texas, she's all yours." Zeke cleared his throat uneasily. "Uh, what about the money? The two hundred and fifty dollars?"

"I'll pay you after I'm finished with her. Providing she's worth it," the man replied insolently, his gaze sweeping Bryony's slender body with critical appraisal. He chuckled softly. "Something tells me she will be," he remarked.

Throughout the entire scene between Sam Taylor and the tall stranger, Bryony had become increasingly consumed with rage. Being bartered about, back and forth, like a slab of beef! It was insufferable! Now, with the stranger's arrogant, insulting words, her fury mounted to new heights, and she began struggling anew in Zeke's grasp.

"I promise you," she vowed wrathfully, in a low, hissing tone, her green eyes burning into the stranger's icy blue ones with unconcealed hatred, "I'll fight you or any man who touches me with every last ounce of my strength! I'll never give in, not as long as I have a breath left in my body!"

Her eyes locked with those of the stranger; to her fury, his were gleaming with amusement. Zeke threw back his head and roared with laughter. "Is that so, little lady?" he chortled gaily. "Well, in these here parts we know how to deal with back-talking women!" And he whirled her suddenly in his arms, his fist raised to deliver a punishing blow. But with blinding speed the stranger's strong arm shot out to intercept his fist.

"Hold it, Murdock," he ordered, his eyes hardening dangerously. "Don't damage my property. I know how to handle stubborn women as well as any man."

With these words, he pried away the outlaw leader's husky arm and seized Bryony, tossing her slim body over his shoulder with careless ease. This act was met by raucous merriment and approval from everyone in the place except Sam Taylor, who nursed his drink sulkily, and Ned Casper, who had regarded all the proceedings with a dark eye. The stranger, ignoring them all, strode purposefully toward the narrow passageway behind the bar, where he knew several small bedchambers were located, while Bryony kicked and struggled helplessly on his broad shoulder.

"The first one on the left is empty," Gilly said as Texas stomped past, followed by the cheers and whistles of the assembled crowd.

The stranger nodded curtly, disappearing into the dim hallway. He halted beside the first door on the left and opened it, entering the room swiftly. With unruffled ease, he lowered Bryony from his shoulder, setting her abruptly upon the bare wooden floor of the tiny bedroom. As she steadied herself, he turned and bolted the heavy door.

Bryony glanced with loathing at the narrow cot haphazardly covered with a faded green quilt, and at the soiled, torn curtains screening the room's only window. For the rest, the room was empty of furniture, except for a rough, three-drawered pine chest in the far corner. The only light was provided by the weak glimmers of the almost setting sun, which filtered faintly through the worn, faded curtains. In the dimness, the stranger's tall, muscular physique seemed to fill the room. When he turned back to face her after bolting the door, Bryony darted instinctively across the floor to the far side of the narrow cot.

"D—don't you t—touch me!" she began desperately, holding her hands across her exposed breasts as pathetically flimsy protection. "I'm warning you!"

"Shut up!" he ordered roughly, advancing purposefully toward her. "Keep quiet and do exactly as I say!"

"I won't!" she shrieked in renewed terror, striking out at him with her small fists as he closed in upon her.

"I won't give in to you—no matter what you do or say!"

"You stupid fool!" He grabbed her flailing wrists in his strong hands and shook her violently. "Shut up and listen to me!"

"I won't, I won't! Stop it!" she sobbed. He continued to shake her until her head was spinning. At last she grew silent, except for the racking sobs, and he ceased shaking her, though his powerful grip on her wrists never slackened.

"Tell me your name," he demanded.

"Wh—why?" She raised wet, blurred eyes to gaze at him in frightened confusion.

"Don't ask questions!" he said impatiently, giving her another shake. "Tell me your name!"

"Bryony . . . Hill," she managed in a weak, unsteady voice. She twisted futilely in his grip, but though he had grown suddenly preoccupied and thoughtful, he still held her securely.

"I knew it," he muttered, almost to himself. "Damn, isn't this a pretty situation?" He seemed to recollect her suddenly and, looking down, was about to speak when Bryony stopped him.

"Please," she pleaded, her beautiful, tear-filled eyes appealing to him more powerfully than any words she might have used. "Please don't hurt me. Please let me go."

"I'm not going to hurt you, you stupid little fool!" he told her, his blue eyes flashing. "I'm planning to get you out of here—but if you don't stop sniveling and start obeying me, I might just give up and let those coyotes out there have their fun with you!" His fingers tightened warningly on her wrists; his eyes glinted with anger. "Now, for the last time—*will you shut up and do as I say?*"

Chapter Six

For a moment there was dead silence. Outside, the shrill cry of a mockingbird split the dry air. Inside, Bryony stared in blank astonishment at the face of the man whose fingers enclosed her wrists like steel bands. She swallowed painfully, barely able to believe what he had just told her.

"You're going to help me?" she whispered.

"That's right." His steely blue eyes stared down into her upturned face, unconsciously noting how clear and deep were the depths of her emerald eyes. "If you'll allow me . . . ma'am," he added sarcastically.

"I'm sorry, just tell me what to do!" she exclaimed breathlessly, scarcely able to believe her ears.

He pulled her over to the window and drew the faded curtains aside. "My horse is tethered around the corner. Follow me as quietly as you can. They'll hear us once we're riding off, but by then there won't be much they can do." He laughed softly. "I very much doubt that anyone will come after us. They'll be mad as hell, of course, but there's not a man in the place who will want to trade shots with me." He threw one powerfully muscled leg over the sill of the opened window, then glanced back at her small, white face. "Stay right with me now," he warned, "and don't make a sound."

Bryony nodded mutely, unconsciously rubbing the

bruises his fingers had caused on her wrists. As she followed him carefully out of the low window, his hands reached up to help her, holding her by her slender waist as she landed in the pebbly dust. Then he moved off, with long, catlike strides, and she hurried with him, taking small, quick steps to keep up with him. As she ran, Bryony wondered at his incredible calmness—her own heart was beating frantically.

They edged up to the corner of the building and peered cautiously around the bend. She saw the same group of horses that had been tied in front when she'd arrived, only now there was an addition: a tall, handsome bay stallion with distinctive white markings on its feet and forelocks, tethered to a hitching post less than twenty-five feet from where she stood. Pausing only long enough to make sure that no one was about, the stranger pulled her away from the security of the building's shadow and they sprinted along the open ground toward the stallion. She froze, aghast, as the horse whinnied in greeting to his master, but the stranger never hesitated. Untying the animal with practiced speed, he hoisted Bryony up as easily as if she were a doll, then got on behind her. An instant later, he turned the bay stallion with one smooth movement and they were off, hurtling across the bluff at a stunning pace, leaving behind a thick cloud of dust.

As they entered the narrow, hidden passageway, Bryony glanced back. Men were running from Gilly's, their dark, swarthy faces contorted with fury and amazement as they realized, too late, what had happened. She choked back an almost hysterical desire to laugh, facing forward again as the rocky walls of the passageway closed in upon her. The warm desert wind whipped at her hair and face as they sped through the narrow opening in the walls of the canyon. Her palms, clinging desperately to the leather saddle horn, were sweaty. Every moment she expected to hear the thunderous pounding of hooves behind them, and the prospect of being caught by Zeke and the other outlaws made her want to scream in panic. She couldn't refrain from constantly peeking over her shoulder, until finally, upon emerging from the hidden passageway, the stranger spoke drily in her ear.

"You can stop worrying now, ma'am. They're not going to come after us. And even if they did, I reckon Pecos can outrun any of their mustangs without even breathing hard."

"Are you quite sure?" she asked uncertainly, twisting about to peer anxiously into his face.

His steely blue eyes glinted with amusement as he grinned down at her. "Quite sure," he drawled. "Now why don't you just sit back and enjoy the ride? We've quite a ways to go to Winchester."

"How did you know that I wanted to go to Winchester?" she inquired in astonishment.

The amusement in his eyes deepened. "Let's just say I've heard things in town—about your expected arrival, that is."

"Oh." Bryony digested this in silence as he expertly guided the horse toward the steep, winding path that led up and out of the canyon. But though her tongue was silent, her mind was crowded with whirling questions.

Who was this cold, ruggedly handsome man behind her? Why had he helped her? And why had every man in the dilapidated hideout been completely intimidated by him?

She had no answers, but as they reached the crest of the canyon and started along a straighter, more open trail flanked by mesquite shrubs and golden poppies, she realized that he knew his way in and out of the outlaws' secret meeting place as well as Zeke had. With a sudden chill came the knowledge that he too must be an outlaw, else how would he know about Gilly's, or be accepted so readily inside it? Yet, she felt certain that he was not like Zeke and Ned and the others. There was a deep intelligence in those hard blue eyes, and a deadly quietness in his manner that set him apart from the common desperados in Gilly's. She didn't think he was a bandit. Perhaps, she reflected, he was a gambler. At any rate, one thing was certain. The man riding behind her was a man accustomed to getting his own way. And she could only be grateful that he had chosen to help rather than harm her.

As they rode through the mountain paths, descending at length to the rugged foothills, sunset painted the azure sky with streaks of rose and orange and gold, casting deep purple and soft lavender hues upon the distant mountain peaks. A stillness came over the rainbowed desert, broken only by the melancholy cries of occasional golden eagles who wheeled and circled overhead before swooping away. With the disappearance of the flaming red sun behind a gilt-edged mountaintop in the western sky, the air cooled refreshingly, fanning Bryony's face as they galloped across the sandy plains. They whipped past barrel cactus and yucca trees and lovely green paloverdes with their bright yellow blossoms fluttering gently in the breeze. It was a relief to be crossing level ground again, and Bryony found herself relaxing against the strong, solid body of the man riding behind her, unconsciously leaning against him for support as weariness crept over her sore, aching body. She watched in fascination as the twilight deepened, and stars bloomed in the purple sky. If only she could sleep . . . if only she could forget about this nightmarish day, about the long ride ahead, about the explanations when she arrived in Winchester; if only she could forget about everything. . . .

She was jerked awake by the abrupt halt of all movement as Pecos slid to an obedient stop beneath a towering, fifty-foot saguaro cactus, whose long, spiny branches stretched out like witch's claws to rake the night. Bryony blinked, staring about her in startled confusion as the stranger lightly dismounted and reached up to pull her from the saddle.

"Why are we stopping?" she asked half-fearfully as his strong arms lifted her easily and set her upon the ground. He stared down at her from his tall height, his black sombrero almost completely hiding his eyes. In the shadowy starlight, his powerful form was even more intimidating than usual and she found herself shrinking from him. She made an attempt to cover herself with her torn gown as best she could. A grim smile touched his lips as he noticed her nervous movement, then he reached casually beneath his saddle to pull forth a drab brown woolen blanket, which he handed to her, his eyes glinting.

"Don't panic, little tenderfoot," he remarked calmly, as she hurriedly wrapped the heavy blanket about her shoulders, clutching it tightly closed across her breasts. "We're just resting a spell. It's a couple of hours yet to Winchester, and I figured you might want some refreshment. I reckon you haven't eaten anything in some time."

With a little shock, Bryony realized that she hadn't had a morsel since breakfast early that morning. She was famished. "Have you some food?" she asked eagerly.

"Not much, but you're welcome to whatever is here."

He removed a thick packet from his saddlebag. Wrapped inside were a half-dozen hard little biscuits and a chunk of beef jerky. None of it looked especially appetizing, but to Bryony's half-starved eyes it was a feast. The stranger removed another blanket from his pack and spread it on the ground beneath the giant saguaro. Wearily, Bryony sank down upon the rough woolen blanket. The stranger, kneeling beside her, offered her his canteen. Bryony drank from it with deep gulps. An instant later her eyes widened in shock, tears springing to them as the strong burning liquid scorched her throat. Choking and gasping, she dropped the canteen, pressing her fingers to her throat.

"Ugh! What is that?"

The stranger laughed, picking up the canteen and drinking from it. "Whisky. I thought it might help revive your spirits. You look pretty worn out."

"It's horrible! Haven't you any water?"

Grinning sardonically, he handed her a second canteen, which she raised cautiously to her lips, sending him a wary, distrustful look. This time there was water, and she drank her fill before handing it back to him without a word. Then she turned her attention to the meager food spread before her, eating ravenously. Texas also lounged on the blanket, chewing on the biscuits and beef, and occasionally taking a drink from the whisky canteen. Bryony stole a glance at him between bites of food. He looked thoughtful, relaxed, as at home out here on this bizarre desert picnic beneath the stars as most people were in their own front parlors.

His cold, handsome face held a strange fascination for her. She had never met a man like him before—he was so cool and assured about everything, so obviously accustomed to being in command. She knew that she owed him a great deal for rescuing her, and she wanted to thank him, but for some reason she didn't know how.

He made her feel like a little girl, all shy and tongue-tied. And that was unusual for her, she reflected in surprise, for at Miss Marsh's school, she had a reputation for vivacity and high-spiritedness. She was accustomed to flirting and chatting charmingly with every man of her acquaintance. But then, the sheltered life she had led in St. Louis had not permitted her to meet an extensive number of gentlemen, and certainly none at all to compare with this handsome, steely-eyed stranger.

Suddenly, his light blue eyes lifted, meeting hers with a keen, glinting stare, and to her embarrassment she felt a slow blush stain her cheeks, and her pulse quickened automatically.

"Yes, Miss Hill?" he drawled politely, the faintest note of mockery in his deep voice.

"I've been meaning to ask you something," she began. She met his intent gaze steadily, though she was conscious that her heart was thumping rapidly in her breast. Being alone in the dark, ghostly desert with him was having a strange effect on her, an effect she didn't understand at all, but which was oddly exciting. With an effort, she dragged her straying thoughts back to the matter at hand.

"Why weren't you surprised back at Gilly's when I told you my name? You said that you knew it all along."

"Did I say that?" he inquired coolly.

"You know that you did!" Bryony replied tartly. She had decided to gather her courage together and face him squarely, for she wanted to know precisely what was going on. Concealing her inner trepidation, she schooled her features into an expression of assurance that she hoped matched his own nonchalance, and lifted her chin proudly.

"You must understand that I appreciate everything you've done for me," she told him with dignity. "But I am also very curious. I'd like to know who you are, how you knew my identity, and also," she paused, regarding him thoughtfully, "why you helped me."

"Why I helped you? Well, ma'am, it just so happens that I'm not in the habit of raping every silly little schoolgirl who happens to cross my path. You see, I like my women wild and willing, and I don't have any interest in naive little virgins who don't know anything about pleasing a man. Does that answer your question?"

"How dare you!" she began furiously, forgetting to be afraid of him as indignation swelled within her.

"Hold it, Miss Hill," he ordered, quelling her with the steely expression in his eyes. "I'm not in the least interested in your opinion of my manners or morals, which I reckon is what you intend to lecture me on." He continued smoothly, ignoring her incensed expression.

"If you don't like my answers, maybe you'd better forget about asking the questions. It's time for us to be going anyway."

"Wait a moment!" she cried, as he began gathering up the remnants of their meal. "Please—just tell me how you knew my name! I must know!"

His voice was curt. "As I told you before, I'd heard in Winchester about your expected arrival. When I saw you at Gilly's, and heard you'd been grabbed off the westbound stage, I just put two and two together. Your identity was an obvious conclusion. And your predicament—well, let's just say I wasn't very surprised."

She felt more confused than ever at this last statement. "Not surprised? I don't understand."

"Don't you?" He looked grim. "Never mind. I've answered enough questions for one evening. We'd best be going, unless you wish to spend the remainder of the night bedding down on this very spot. It's possible, you know. We could always ride on to town in the morning if you're unwilling to go on."

"Stay here tonight? With you? Alone?" she exclaimed uneasily. "You must be joking!"

He shrugged. "Well, if you're tired."

"No, I'm not tired! At least, not that tired!" she retorted, tossing her head. She had no intention of sleeping under the stars with this cold, mysterious stranger, that was certain! She was amazed that he had the boldness to suggest anything so improper! "I think we'd better go on at once," she informed him frigidly, letting him know by her tone and manner that she was a lady of propriety, duly shocked by his suggestion. But to her irritation, the stranger only laughed, and began competently repacking his saddle bag with the canteens and blanket.

"That suits me just fine. There's a pretty little woman in town who's expecting me to show her a good time tonight. I'd hate to disappoint her." He grinned arrogantly.

"Oh. Yes. Of course. Then we certainly must go on," Bryony returned stiffly. But when he turned to help her mount the bay stallion, she stopped him with one hand upon his chest, raising her soft green eyes to him appealingly.

"Please, just tell me one more thing," she said quietly, searching his face with an earnest expression.

"What is it?" the stranger asked, all too aware of the gentle pressure of her small hand upon his chest. He stared down at the raven-haired girl before him, wondering if she had any idea how utterly beautiful she was. Despite his contemptuous words a few moments ago, calculated to insult her, he knew full well that the girl before him was no tame, sniveling schoolgirl to be lightly dismissed. She was a lovely, tantalizing creature, with the refreshing, innocent charm of an angel and the striking beauty of a born temptress, a combination guaranteed to drive every man in the territory wild with desire. And, he reflected admiringly, she has the temper of a she-devil to boot. He well remembered the fiery wrath with which she had vowed to resist him or any man only a short while ago, and the way her huge, emerald eyes had burned vividly into his, flaming with passionate hatred. She was as spirited as she was beautiful, and he guessed, taking in the small, determined chin and the smooth, patrician lines of her profile, she was probably stubborn besides. A reluctant smile touched his lips as he studied her. She was enchanting, no doubt about it.

"Who are you?" The words came out as a whisper, echoing strangely in the silent desert night, with only the stars as witness to the two people standing so close together beneath the velvet sky.

Something flickered behind the stranger's eyes. For a moment he said nothing, merely staring at her inscrutably, though from the way his thin, cynical mouth was set, Bryony sensed that he was angry.

"Who are you?" she repeated softly.

"Folks in these parts call me Texas."

"I want to know your real name," she insisted. "Surely Texas is just a nickname."

Suddenly, he reached out and grasped her arms. "That's enough questions, Miss Hill. If you're going to live long in this part of the country, you'll have to learn that asking a lot of questions about a man's name or his past can be dangerous. Mighty dangerous. Do you understand?"

"No, I don't!" Resentfully, Bryony struggled to free herself from his viselike grip, but she was no match for his overpowering strength. The blanket slipped from her shoulders to crumple in a heap on the ground, leaving her breasts exposed to his view; still he held her. Her green eyes glared up at him in fury. "Let me go!" she cried. "I only asked you because I wanted to thank you and to give you a reward for saving me, but now you can forget about *that!* I wouldn't give a penny to a brutal, uncivilized beast like you!" She winced as his grip tightened painfully on her tender flesh. "Let . . . me . . . go!"

"So you were going to offer me a reward, eh?" he muttered, staring down at her upturned face. Both anger and desire coarsed through his lean body, and before he knew what he was doing, he pulled her close, twisting his hand in her tumbling black hair as he crushed her slender, trembling body against his. A grim smile curled his lips, and his blue eyes flashed like daggers. "I'll take my reward here and now!" he vowed huskily.

And before Bryony had time to do more than gasp in terror, his mouth closed upon hers in a kiss she was helpless to prevent. She fought feebly in his iron arms as the force of the kiss bent her head back, but he held her with effortless strength. He kissed her ruthlessly, demandingly, with the power and passion of a man experienced at lovemaking, and suddenly, Bryony found that something incredible was happening. She was no longer resisting. Her rigid body was melting against his, her lips yielding of their own accord to his tremendous, conquering will. Her knees buckled beneath her, and it was fortunate he held her so tightly or she would surely have collapsed. Then, her arms instinctively encircled his neck, drawing him close. As his lips moved hungrily on hers she felt herself responding with wild passion, her own mouth parting to welcome him eagerly as he plunged his tongue into the honeyed recesses of her mouth. A thrill shot through her entire body, a new sensation that licked through her veins like wildfire, igniting her with feverish desire. At that moment she wanted nothing other than to remain in his arms, with their lips locked together in this blissful ecstasy. It seemed like forever that he held her, his mouth crushing hers, as excitement and delight flamed within her. Then, he lifted his head, his lips leaving hers reluctantly. He stared down into her flushed face, with her rapturously closed eyes and eager, parted mouth. Her eyes fluttered open to meet his compelling gaze.

Triumph glowed in his cold blue eyes. "Thanks for the reward, ma'am," he drawled softly. "It sure was my pleasure."

Reality flooded back, sending a horrified shudder through her as she realized where she was and what had happened. Something inside of her shattered as she beheld his mocking face, realizing that he was trying to embarrass and humiliate her, to enjoy her submission. The wonderful delight of a moment before vanished, leaving behind shame and fury at her own weakness. How could she have been so idiotic? She had let him make a fool of her! She gave a stifled groan, hate filling her green eyes.

"I'll kill you!" she screamed, flailing at him with her hands.

He pushed her away contemptuously, sending her flying downward into the dust at his feet. "I doubt that,

little tenderfoot. Better men and women than you have
tried and failed!"

"Go away! Go away and leave me alone! I never want
to see you again!"

He laughed at her outraged expression as she leaped
to her feet, clutching the retrieved blanket to her body.
She stood shaking before him, her lovely face flushed
with a fury that went beyond words. He gestured to
Pecos, waiting restlessly beside them.

"But, ma'am, I'm afraid you must be subjected to
my company for a short while longer. We must ride
back to town together, in case you've forgotten."

"Never! I won't ride anywhere with you!"

He shrugged and turned away indifferently to mount
the bay stallion. Sitting astride the saddle, he gazed
down at her, laughter glinting in his eyes. "Suit yourself, little tenderfoot. I don't have time to put up with
your temper tantrums. As I told you before, there's a
fine-looking woman waiting for me in Winchester, and I
always hate to keep a lady waiting." With these words,
he kicked the horse into motion, and rode off at a fast
trot.

Bryony stood frozen, her mind a blank. Suddenly, it
registered that he was leaving, riding off and leaving!
She would be alone out here in this wilderness for the
rest of the night!

"Wait!" she screamed, beginning to run frantically
after the now galloping stallion. "Wait! Please!"

At first there was no noticeable slowing of the horse,
and her heart leaped to her throat as the distance between them widened. Then she saw that the stallion was
halting, and the rider turning slightly in the saddle, as if
waiting expectantly for her to approach. She took off at
a run, stumbling wearily across the darkened desert to
where he waited, a cold expression on his hard features.

"Yes?"

"Take me with you!" she managed through clenched

teeth, breathing hard from the exertion of running. Her legs felt as if they were about to give way.

"I offered and you refused, Miss Hill," he returned coolly. "Remember? But I reckon that if you were to ask me nicely, I'd give you another chance."

Her face was livid with loathing. "Take me with you—please!" she grated, tears of misery at having to beg him brimming from her eyes.

"That's better," he complimented her with an arrogant grin, and, reaching down, pulled her into the saddle before him. Once again the bay stallion darted off, his powerful hooves thundering swiftly over the level ground.

Choking back a sob of helpless outrage, Bryony forced her tired body to sit very stiff and straight in the saddle, refusing to relax against the man behind her in the slightest way. She couldn't help the fact that his arms were tight against her body as he held the reins, and that his lean, muscled form pressed intimately against the curve of her back and buttocks, but she was determined to avoid any contact with him that wasn't absolutely necessary. She had never met such an arrogant, heartless, detestable man in her life!

She hated him, hated him with all her heart! The burning memory of his kiss, and her wanton response to it, caused her to blush scarlet with shame. She was supposed to be a lady of good breeding and gentle refinement, and ladies didn't react that way when forcibly kissed by dangerous strangers. She should have fought him with the last ounce of her strength, she should have kicked and screeched and clawed until he gave up and released her. That was what she should have done. But she hadn't. She had been swept up in an ecstasy she had never known before, and had nearly swooned as waves of delight had washed over her. She trembled, remembering. No one had ever kissed her like that before, leaving her breathless and weak and bursting with rapture. And she had never responded to any man with the fer-vent ardor she had shown to this hard, indifferent stranger, this man called Texas. When she thought of the way his eyes had glittered triumphantly at her, she almost screamed with mortification. The kiss had not meant anything to him! It had only been a means of humiliating and subduing her, of exercising his superior power. She itched to have revenge; her mind spun a dozen murderous fantasies. She was more determined than ever to purchase a gun as soon as possible, and then, if this odious stranger ever crossed her path again, ever dared to molest her in the slightest way. . . . .

A smile of grim satisfaction played across her lips as she contemplated the vengeful scene, but it didn't last long as the uncomfortable realities of her situation brought her back to the present with a jolt. The night air had cooled considerably, whistling about her body as Pecos's long legs swallowed up mile after mile of desolate land, and she pulled the blanket snugly across her shoulders. Her body ached dreadfully in places she hadn't even known existed, and weariness crept over her like heavy, bruising hands, dragging relentlessly at her drooping form. *Would they ever reach Winchester?* she wondered dismally, as tears of pure exhaustion stung her eyes, though her pride kept the racking sobs locked inside her, forbidding her to reveal the extent of her misery to the man riding behind her. *Not that it would make any difference if she* did *complain*, she thought bitterly, blinking back the tears. He would hardly care if she was to drop dead before his very eyes. She bit her lip in silent anguish, and resolutely stiffened her throbbing back, feeling that the traumatic nightmare of this day would never come to an end.

Behind her, the man called Texas rode with harshly set features, his body tense and rigid in the saddle. Contrary to Bryony's beliefs, he was intensely aware of the slender, black-haired girl pressed close against him. Despite his outward indifference to her after their kiss, he had been deeply affected, more affected than he cared to think about. And he didn't understand why. He'd kissed many women in his day, most of them dance-hall girls or saloon women who were experts at pleasing a man in a variety of sexual activities, but none of them had ever aroused in him the fierce, unexplainable emotions stirred by this beautiful, raven-haired innocent, with her honeyed lips and soft, melting body. Damn her! Even as they rode, her soft, dark hair tickled his chin, making him want to caress it. Her slim, lovely body was trembling with the cold, and he longed to stop right there in the midst of the starlit desert, to spread his saddle blanket on the ground and throw her down upon it, to warm her with the heat of his own desire. He felt a strange urge to comfort her, for he knew she must be exhausted and miserable, and furious with him as well. Poor kid, he thought, she doesn't know what she's getting into here. That kidnapping was only the beginning.

Then the grimness returned to his momentarily softened expression. He remembered angrily who she was and who he was, and he knew that this was the way it must be. His lips twisted in a hard, unpleasant smile that contained neither mirth nor joy, but only a kind of bitter cynicism. So, she wanted to know his name, did she? Well, he thought coldly, hardening his heart, that is something she will find out soon enough.

Chapter Seven

It was quiet in the hotel, except for the tinny sounds of the piano drifting in from the Silver Spur saloon down the street, accompanied by the faint rumble of voices raised in uproarious merriment. The two men in the deserted hotel dining room stared at their half-filled coffee cups, the coffee long gone cold. Their expressions were troubled and thoughtful as they sat at the little round table, each immersed in his own private contemplations. They couldn't help glancing every now and then at the fancy brass trunk with its ornate, expensive gold trim, which sat in the corner of the lobby beside the two elegant bandboxes. One of the men, a paunchy, balding, weathered-looking fellow in his late fifties, at last raised his head to gaze at his companion. He sighed.

"Well, Matt," he said tiredly. "Maybe we'd best try to get some sleep. We can start hunting for her again first thing in the morning, provided you're willing to give up some of your men to search the mountains."

Matthew Richards nodded, regarding the Judge through shrewd black eyes. He ran a hand through his shock of black hair in a gesture of despair. "Sure, Judge, I'll let you have a dozen men, if you think that'll help, but from what those other stagecoach passengers said, those outlaws could be anyone, and they could be hiding anywhere. I don't know if we'll ever find where they've taken the girl."

Judge Hamilton banged his fist on the table, frustration making the tired wrinkles on his face even more noticeable. "Damn those low-down, chicken-hearted scoundrels!" he cursed, his faded brown eyes sparking with rage. "When I think what they must be doing to that poor, helpless child."

"I know, Judge, I know. Hanging is too good for whoever's responsible for this," Richards put in. He was a tall, powerfully built man, with thickset shoulders and hips, and suave, handsome features. Above his dark, hooded eyes, heavy black eyebrows gave him a somber appearance, which was further emphasized by his black, curling mustache. There was an aura of power and assurance about him, for although Matt Richards was only thirty years old, he had built his Twin Bars ranch into one of the territory's most prosperous spreads, rivaled only by the ranch of the now deceased Wesley Hill.

Richards' wealth was clearly evidenced by his fine, well-cut clothes: gray silk shirt, dark breeches, and red embroidered vest. His tall boots were of finest kid leather, and his expensive Stetson was only one of a collection that would make any cowboy envious. But then it was only appropriate that Winchester's most influential citizen should take pains with his appearance.

As the clock struck nine o'clock in the little hotel dining room, Richards stretched out one long leg, examining the shine on his boot. When he spoke, his voice was quiet, almost hesitant, as he glanced soberly at the despondent Judge.

"You know, I hate to say this, Judge, but there's a chance we might never find the girl. I mean, there's a lot of territory out there, and we don't even know where to begin. What's going to happen to the Circle H if we don't? The hands won't stay on forever without an employer to pay them and give them orders. And since

Wes's death, I've had my doubts about Rusty Jessup's loyalty as foreman. According to rumor, he's been stirring up some kind of trouble.''

"True enough," Judge Hamilton sighed. "But I suppose we'll work something out if it comes to that. If we don't find Miss Hill within a week or two, I reckon I'll have to contact that fancy eastern lawyer about making some arrangements.''

"Well, you know I'd be happy to buy the place and add it on to my acreage and stock," Richards remarked. "I wanted to do that in the first place, right after Wes was killed. It seemed to me that I'd be doing his daughter a favor by taking it off her hands." He shook his head ruefully. "If only she had agreed to sell then, none of this would have happened. She'd still be safe and happy back east with all her city friends, instead of. . . .''

"Please, don't say any more, Matt," Judge Hamilton interrupted him wearily. "I can't bear to think about it.''

"I feel the same way, Judge," Richards agreed. "But I can't help hoping that by some miracle she'll turn up. I'd like to own the Circle H, naturally, but I'd hate like hell to think that I was profiting by the poor young girl's misfortune." He started to sip absently at his half-filled coffee cup, then pushed it away in disgust as the cold, bitter liquid touched his lips. "Damn, I feel so helpless, Judge! Wesley Hill was my closest friend, one of the finest men I knew! It's frustrating as hell to know that his daughter is out there somewhere," he waved his arm vaguely, "in trouble, and that there's nothing I can do to help her. Poor kid. She's only a schoolgirl, scarcely used to the kind of treatment she's sure to get from those desperadoes. And Judge, from the photograph I've seen in Wes's study, she's beautiful, too. So soft and delicate-looking. . .''

His voice trailed off as the Judge groaned miserably, and both men lapsed into silence, thinking of the lovely young girl they'd seen so often in the photograph, the girl they would in all likelihood never have the opportunity to meet in the flesh.

"Can . . . can someone help me . . . please?"

A breathless female voice moaned suddenly from the hotel doorway, and glancing up, the two men were shocked into frozen silence by the apparition they saw there. A young woman leaned against the door frame, her long dark hair a tumbling, tangled mass hanging about her face, a drab woolen blanket clutched tightly around her shoulders, below which could be seen the tattered remnants of a soiled, dust-caked lavender dress. Her face was pale and dirty, her green eyes swollen with recently shed tears.

"Please, can you help me?" she said again in a voice that was barely audible. "I . . . I need a room for the night."

By this time, the two men had sprung into motion, scraping their chairs back hastily as they rushed to her aid.

"Miss Hill?" Judge Hamilton demanded incredulously, as his arm encircled her waist.

"Yes, oh, yes," she nodded tearfully, leaning weakly against him. The Judge exchanged an astonished look with Richards, whose expression was one of total disbelief. For a moment, Matthew Richards seemed completely stunned, as though a ghost had entered the hotel, but then he recovered his composure, and hurried to assist the Judge in helping the girl to a table.

"You're all right now," the older man was telling her reassuringly as he lowered her into a hard wooden chair, his eyes studying her white, dazed face. "I'm Judge Hamilton, Miss Hill, and this is Matthew Richards, your father's very good friend. So you see, you're in good hands now. There is nothing more to be frightened of."

"Thank you," Bryony whispered, closing her eyes in a gesture of utter exhaustion. She opened them a moment later to gratefully accept the glass of water Matt Richards brought her. The cool liquid tasted delicious as it soothed her parched throat. Placing the empty glass on the table, she gave a small shaky smile to the two men hovering worriedly over her. "I'll be fine now," she told them. "I only need to rest."

"Can you tell us what happened to you, child?" Judge Hamilton questioned, sitting down beside her and taking her limp hand in his. "The other passengers on your stagecoach told us they'd been robbed, and that you'd been abducted by the bandits. They were mighty distraught, and that's the truth. One of them, Doc Brady, offered a hefty reward to any man who found you. We were out searching for you until dark, but to no avail. Where did they take you? How did you escape?"

Bryony shuddered uncontrollably as the horrible memories came flooding back. "I was taken to a . . . a vile place called Gilly's," she murmured, staring up at the Judge with slightly dazed, bleary eyes. "Have you heard of it?"

"Heard of it? Why, girl, it has a notorious reputation—it's a known hangout for all the rustlers, thieves, and gunmen between here and Tucson!"

She nodded. "I can well believe it."

"How did you ever get out of there alive?" Matt Richards spoke for the first time. Bryony pushed her hair out of her eyes, gazing up at his thickset, bearlike form.

"I was rescued. A man helped me escape and brought me back to town. He left me in front of the saloon." Her eyes darkened in anger as she recalled the way the insufferable stranger had refused to take her as far as the hotel, insisting that she go on alone once they reached town. He had claimed that she had made him late enough for his intended date that evening, and he wasn't going to delay his pleasure one moment longer just to escort her along a perfectly safe street to the perfectly safe premises of the hotel. Her fists clenched furiously as she remembered his insolent smile as he watched her stagger off down the street, but she was interrupted from dwelling on these rage-provoking memories by another question from Matt Richards. His voice cut urgently into her thoughts.

"Who was the man who rescued you, Miss Hill?" he asked, his black eyes staring hard into hers.

"I . . . I don't know. He wouldn't tell me his name."

Judge Hamilton put a hand on Richards's shoulder. "I think she's had enough questions for one night, Matt. Let's wake up Frank and his missus and have them settle her in a room. We'll find out more about this business tomorrow."

Richards nodded curtly and strode off to awaken the hotel owner and his wife, who had already retired to their modest room across from the hotel kitchen. He returned shortly, followed by the disgruntled couple who were hurriedly pulling on dressing robes over their nightwear.

"What in tarnation is this all about, Judge?" Frank Billings demanded irritably, until he saw the dark-haired girl sitting at the dining table. A low whistle sounded from between his lips. "Is that her? The kidnapped woman?" he cried in amazement.

"It sure is. This is Miss Bryony Hill, in the flesh." Judge Hamilton looked as pleased as though he personally had rescued the lady from her recent peril. "She needs a room, Frank. As you can see, she's pretty worn out."

"Land sakes, 'course she is." Edna Billings pushed past her startled husband to bustle solicitously over Bryony. "You jest come with me, honey. We'll fix you up in a real nice soft featherbed and you'll be as good as new come mornin'." She surveyed her charge's bedraggled appearance severely. "Hmmm. Looks like a nice hot bath is a good idea first off. It'll help ease those aching bones, I promise you that. Come on, honey, I'll help you upstairs. Frank, for heaven's sake, don't jest stand there like a ninny—bring her baggage along and fetch some water for her bath. Hurry it up now, or I'll give you a tongue-lashing you won't soon forget!"

With these words, the peppery little gray-haired woman took charge of the situation, sending her hapless husband scampering into action, while Judge Hamilton and Matt Richards watched in silence. When Bryony had disappeared around the second floor landing, supported by Mrs. Billings's solid arm, Judge Hamilton turned away to pick up his old black hat, settling it upon his head with an air of relief. But Matt Richards continued staring at the now empty stairway. He started when Judge Hamilton spoke suddenly beside him, breaking his reverie.

"Shall we go, Matt?" The Judge inquired, looking at him curiously.

"Oh, yes, of course." Richards's sober, handsome face immediately broke into a smile. "Well, Judge, it appears that all our worrying was for nothing. Bryony Hill turned out to be one lucky young woman."

The Judge readily assented, and the two men left the hotel, each headed for his separate lodgings.

Upstairs, Bryony sank dazedly into the bath that had been so hurriedly prepared for her. Mr. Billings had vanished, but his wife still scurried about the small, tidy room. Bryony's torn clothing and the woolen saddle blanket had been tossed into a careless pile on the floor beside the tub as their owner hurried to wash away the grime of her day's adventures. She groaned as her sore muscles protested each little movement, but the hot, sudsy water felt wonderfully relaxing to her tortured body. While she was washing the sand and grit from her hair, Mrs. Billings bade her good night and departed, shutting the door behind her to leave Bryony alone in the small, spotless hotel bedroom with its pretty print wallpaper and drawn muslin curtains. By the time she finished rinsing herself clean and patting her aching

body with the thick towel the woman had left, Bryony
was too tired to look through her trunk for a nightgown, so she climbed into bed completely nude. The
sheets felt cool and refreshing, the bed exquisitely soft.
Her eyes fluttered shut as she basked in the sublime
comfort of the moment. But tired as she was, sleep did
not come to her immediately. Her mind whirled with a
jumble of disturbed thoughts. The awful events of the
day haunted her, as did unnerving doubts about the
future.

Maybe she wasn't cut out for life in the west, she told
herself bleakly. Maybe Roger and Mr. Parker and Miss
Marsh were right when they said that the frontier was no
place for a girl who was alone in the world and completely dependent upon herself. Maybe she should have
listened to them, and sold the Circle H to Matthew
Richards when he first offered to buy it, and married
Roger, despite his faults. After all, he had wanted her,
and he would have taken care of her, however super-
ficial his reasons. She moved restlessly on the bed. *It
wasn't too late*, she thought miserably. She could still go
back. She could catch the next stage bound for St. Louis
and return to the life she had been bred to lead, a life
vastly different from the barbarism and hardships she
had already encountered in this wild land. The prospect
was dismal, for she hated the idea of having to admit
failure, but she couldn't dismiss it from her mind, not
after the harrowing experiences of this day. Finally,
besieged by doubts, her spirits sagging with defeat, she
drifted off to sleep, granting her a brief reprieve until
the morning.

Chapter Eight

Sunshine streaked into the room, unhindered by the thin blue-and-white-print muslin curtains that rustled softly in the April morning breeze. The glow of light and warmth spreading over the clean, bare wooden floor, touching the bed, and the girl sleeping deeply in it, grew increasingly brighter and more intense as the hours of the morning wore on and noon approached. It was this shimmering glow that finally awakened Bryony, as the warm brightness at last penetrated the heavy oblivion of her slumber.

She stretched, yawned, and opened her eyes, staring blankly at the unfamiliar surroundings. At first, nothing registered; her sleep-fogged mind sluggishly struggled to recall where she was, but then her memory returned with a sudden jolt that coincided with a knock on the hotel-room door. She hurriedly snatched the cool bedsheet and wrapped it about her before padding quickly to the door.

"Who's there?" she called, leaning cautiously against the paneled wood.

"Edna Billings. I've brought you a bite of breakfast," the hotel keeper's wife answered promptly. "Open up this here door, honey. This tray is getting mighty heavy."

"Here you go, honey," Edna said, setting the tray

down on the night stand. "Some coffee and my fresh
home-baked bread. When you come downstairs I'll
whip you up a batch of eggs and some buttered short-
cake, but this'll tide you over 'til then. I figgered you'd
be 'bout half-starved."

"I am!"

She began to eat ravenously, and Mrs. Billings, with a
satisfied smile, left to begin preparing the rest of her
breakfast. Bryony devoured every crumb of the home-
made bread, heartily convinced that she had never
tasted anything so delicious, especially after she
smothered it with butter and honey. The coffee was the
first she'd drank with the benefit of sugar and cream
since she'd departed St. Louis, and it was wonderfully
strong and flavorful. The entire meal was a delight,
rapidly bolstering her spirits, which, with the dawning
of a sunny new day, were already reviving.

It was spring, and she was young, and a whole exciting new world stretched before her. Gone were the
doubts and fears of the previous night; yesterday had
been a horrible nightmare, but all that was over now
and this was a new day, a chance for a fresh start. All
thoughts of returning to St. Louis disappeared as she
experienced a new determination to make a success of
her life in the west, to prove that she could survive in the
toughest of conditions.

With surging confidence she finished her meal and
went through her trunk for some clothes. She selected
one of her prettiest gowns, with the eager intention of
making a smashing impression upon everyone she
should meet. After last night's unpropitious beginning
she knew she must do everything in her power to show
the people of Winchester that she was not weak, or
helpless, or given to defeat; and that she was, instead, a
competent, independent woman, strong enough to
conquer life on the frontier.

She washed and completed her toilette quickly, and
stood before the tall chipped mirror that hung from the

wall opposite the window, studying her reflection in its shining surface. Completely without vanity, she knew she looked splendid. Her gown of white muslin was charmingly pretty, with a low décolletage that was just daring enough without being boldly immodest. Her dark hair contrasted dramatically with the white gown. She had dressed it in a cluster of ebony ringlets that dangled prettily about her small, oval-shaped face, enhancing the sculptured look of her high cheekbones, and calling attention to her vivid jade green eyes. Surveying herself, she frowned. Something was missing. But what? With a sudden inspiration she began rummaging once more through her trunk. Her jewel box was inside and contained just what she needed to complete her toilette: a dainty gold heart-shaped locket on a solid gold chain. She found it quickly, but paused for a moment to stare at the assortment of jewels in her possession as a startling thought struck her. How strange that the highwaymen yesterday had not ordered her or any of the other passengers to open their baggage. The outlaws must have known their victims possessed other valuables in addition to the ones they were wearing, yet they hadn't insisted on searching for them. Why not? It was very odd. Almost as if they'd been in a hurry to collect what was readily available, without caring to bother about the rest. But if robbery was their motive for stopping the stagecoach, why didn't they take the time to do a thorough job of it? Why hadn't they stripped the passengers of every single valuable item they owned? Perhaps, she thought, they'd been in a terrible hurry, fearful of being apprehended. But the road had been lonely, deserted, and the highwaymen had not seemed uneasy in the least. They *had* been in a hurry, though. In a hurry to hustle her away with them. She bit her lip uneasily. Something about this situation disturbed her, but she wasn't sure exactly why, or what.

At last she shrugged and closed the lid of her trunk

with a snap. Instead of questioning the outlaws' behavior she ought to be grateful they hadn't bothered to search for her other jewels. Wasn't it bad enough that they had stolen her mother's cameo brooch? She sighed sadly, and decided to try to forget all about the robbery, and about everything else that had happened yesterday. She turned back to the mirror to fasten the gold locket about her throat.

Despite her resolve, her fingers trembled as she secured the locket's clasp. She couldn't help wishing that this was the cameo brooch instead. But she would never see the brooch again—that she knew. Her eyes clouded with sadness at the thought, for that brooch had been one of the few keepsakes she had left of her mother, and she had treasured it for years. Most of her jewelry had been gifts from her father, as was this locket, but they didn't have the same meaning for her as those items her mother had worn. For years, ever since her mother's death, her father had bought her gifts that were used as a substitute for his own attention and affection. They were beautiful, it was true, and lavishly expensive, but they had never been able to compensate for love.

Thinking of this, a lump rose in her throat. During most of her life she had borne a very private pain: the pain of terrible loneliness and rejection by her nearest living kin. Her father's indifference had hurt her deeply, wounding her more cruelly than harsh words or beatings would have done. But she had never let on to anyone how unhappy she was; she had never complained. Now, standing before the mirror in the Winchester hotel room, fingering the locket he had bought her last winter in Paris, she was gripped by a sudden pang, more searing than any she had known previously. She realized with a forlorn wrenching of the heart that now it was too late to ever remedy the coldness in her relationship with her father. She would never have the chance to bridge the gap between them, to show him that she loved him and wanted his love and affection more than any gifts he could purchase for her. Death had provided a final gulf, a permanent, insurmountable distance that she must learn to accept. All that was left now was to try to build a life for herself on the ranch he had bequeathed to her; try to know him by learning about the ranch he had loved and nurtured in a way he had never loved and nurtured her. Today she would drive out to the Circle H and begin to make it her home. Today would mark a turning point in her life, a time for a fresh new beginning.

She descended the stairs and entered the hotel dining room, glancing about for Mrs. Billings. The dining area was a moderately sized room opposite the main desk and stairway. Faded green-and-yellow patterned wallpaper decorated the walls; the tables were small, scrubbed, and polished, and the wooden-shuttered windows were open, allowing the bright spring sunlight to pour into the room in a pool of dazzling warmth. There were half a dozen other people in the dining area at various tables, and they all turned to stare as she appeared. Bryony took a seat at a table in the corner, uncomfortably aware of all the attention she was receiving.

In a town like Winchester, strangers were instantly conspicuous, especially if the unfamiliar face was both young and beautiful. Self-consciously, Bryony smoothed the skirt of her gown. She wished everyone would stop staring so openly. She felt as though she was a prize steer being inspected before a cattle show. As Mrs. Billings bustled out of the kitchen and made her way quickly to Bryony's table, relief washed over her at the sight of a familiar and friendly face.

"Well, now, honey, don't you look nice!" Edna declared, placing her hands, which were slightly coated with flour, on her broad hips. She smiled with genuine friendliness and Bryony returned the smile, glad that she seemed to have at least one friend in Winchester already.

"I must thank you again, Mrs. Billings," Bryony replied. "You've been much, much more than kind."

"It wasn't nothin' at all, honey." The woman dismissed the praise offhandedly, though her pale blue eyes glowed with pleasure. "And listen, you just call me Edna, like everyone else in town. I don't go for puttin' on airs, and Mrs. Billings reminds me of my Frank's mother, which is something I don't like to think of!"

They laughed together, and then the older woman turned briskly away. "I'll be back in a jiffy with the rest of your breakfast, so don't you be going anywhere!" she ordered, and hastened off to the kitchen.

After this show of friendliness from the hotel-keeper's wife, the other people in the dining room ceased staring quite so fixedly at Bryony, and she was able to consume her breakfast in relative peace, though she was still aware that every now and then someone cast her a curious glance. When she had finished her meal, and Edna had cleared away the dishes, Bryony began to rise, intending to seek out Judge Hamilton, but before she had done more than get to her feet, he walked in, his kind features lighting up as he caught sight of her. Beside him strode Matthew Richards.

"Good morning, my girl! You look prettier than a poppy in the desert!" the Judge enthused, grasping her hand in his. "I'm sure glad to see you're none the worse for your experience of yesterday. Doesn't she look fine, Matt?"

"Yes, indeed." Matt Richards gave her a warm, admiring smile, his black eyes taking in her fresh, innocent loveliness, the enticing swell of her breasts beneath the thin muslin gown, the fine delicate features and clear, expressive green eyes fringed by dark, sooty, incredibly long eyelashes. She was a beautiful woman, and he was a man who appreciated beauty. His eyes lingered on her face, and Bryony, gazing up at him, blushed slightly under his scrutiny.

She was surprised that Matt Richards was such a

young man, certainly not more than thirty years old; she had expected her father's friend to be considerably older. He was undeniably handsome, with dark features and a smooth, polished air that was very attractive.

"I hope you're feeling well enough this morning to discuss what happened yesterday," Judge Hamilton ventured questioningly, his faded brown eyes searching Bryony's face for some sign of distress at his suggestion.

"Yes, I'm feeling much better today, Judge. And I want to tell you everything so that you can apprehend the men who abducted me." She sat down again, and the two men joined her.

"Well, that might not be easy," Judge Hamilton began, clearing his throat. "You see, Miss Hill. . ."

"Oh, it shouldn't be difficult at all! I know the name of the outlaw leader—it's Murdock, Zeke Murdock. And one of the men with him was called Ned, and I can describe him and the others perfectly, and surely if you go to Gilly's—" She broke off at the regretful expression on his face and stared at him in confusion. "I don't understand. What is the problem? Why can't you apprehend those men and see that they're punished?"

"Listen to me, Miss Hill," the Judge said heavily. "Those men *could* be apprehended—if there was a lawman in town to do it. But there isn't. And I'm afraid it'll be quite a spell before such a man arrives."

She stared at him blankly and he continued in a tired voice. "You see, I'm not a lawman. Neither is Matt here. I'm just a judge, a justice of the peace, able to pronounce sentences, marry folks, and help out with legal documents. Matt's a rancher, a powerful one to be sure, but not a sheriff or a marshal, which is what it takes to go out and arrest desperadoes like these men who kidnapped you. Now, I've heard of Zeke Murdock, and he's one bad hombre. He's a suspected rustler who usually hangs out in Tucson with a pretty wild bunch of boys. But no one has ever been able to prove anything against him, or catch him in the act, which is the reason he's alive today. Rustlers who get caught red-handed are usually hanged on the spot."

Bryony's eyes widened at this brutal pronouncement, and she shivered slightly. Seeing her shocked reaction, Matt Richards smiled ruefully. "You see, Miss Hill, this is a rough, almost barbaric civilization you've entered. A man who steals another man's cattle or horse is considered as bad as a murderer in these parts. If we didn't take tough measures, stealing would be even more widespread than it is already. Brutality is sometimes necessary in a wild frontier territory like Arizona. In order to preserve what little there is of law and order, we must sometimes take the law into our own hands and act decisively against these outlaws."

"Well," Bryony replied quickly, "it still sounds rather horrible—hanging a man without trial just for stealing some animals! But if that's the policy out here, I understand even less why you can't capture and punish the men who stole *me*! After all, what they did was far worse than rustling." Her voice shook with pent-up rage as she remembered what had almost happened to her yesterday. "Fortunately, I was rescued before they could do me any real harm, but if I hadn't been. . ." She broke off as her emotions threatened to overwhelm her, and it took a moment to calm herself. Her green eyes were bright with tears of anger.

Judge Hamilton tried to calm her. "Now, try to settle down, Miss Hill," he urged, glancing at Richards for help as the incensed girl bore into him with her flaming green eyes. "I'll explain it to you if you'll just simmer down and listen to me for a moment." As she unclenched her fists and settled back in her chair expectantly, he went on in a firmer voice. "Catching someone rustling cattle red-handed is one thing. Usually a group of wranglers catch the thief and punish him on the spot. But to go after a whole band of outlaws hiding out in the wilderness, well, that's something else. It's a job for a lawman, and they're pretty scarce in this territory.

Every so often a marshal passes through town, but those visits are few and far between, and in the meantime we have to fend for ourselves. And even if there was a lawman in town, it would be pretty hard to track down those hombres who grabbed you off the stage. There's a hell of a lot of wilderness out there in the desert."

"But I *told* you that they took me to Gilly's hideout. You've even heard of it! Surely it wouldn't be difficult to ride out there and—"

The Judge shook his head. "I'm sorry, Miss Hill, but that would be impossible. Sure I've heard of Gilly's— who hasn't? But the fact of the matter is, no one knows exactly where it's located. No one, that is, but the outlaws and gunmen who hang out there. I'm afraid its location is a secret to all law-abiding men. Oh, one or two have tried to find it, without any success. It's my opinion that looking for that outlaws' den in the wilderness would be like searching for sunken treasure in the ocean—without a map. A worthy cause, but doomed to failure just as sure as I'm sitting here."

Bryony sat silent with frustration. She hated to admit it, but the Judge's words made sense. How could she expect him and Matthew Richards to volunteer to risk their lives going after a dangerous band of criminals? It wasn't their job or their duty, and they had no legal authority. Apparently, no one in Winchester had such authority. She had to keep in mind the fact that she was no longer in St. Louis, but in a wild, primitive frontier territory where lawlessness reigned. Tom Scott had warned her on the stagecoach that good lawmen willing to track down hardened desperadoes were scarce. Apparently, he had spoken the stark, bitter truth, and she had better learn to accept it. Besides, she reflected with a defeated sigh, what Judge Hamilton had said about Gilly's was all too true. She clearly remembered the secret passageway in the heart of the canyon walls, the passageway that was impossible to detect from above, and that led to the hidden, secluded bluff where

Gilly's was located. Even if she was able to describe the setting to the Judge and Matt Richards, she would never be able to pinpoint precisely where it was, or to differentiate the canyon from any one of hundreds of other canyons that looked identical to an inexperienced eye. No, there was no way they could find the hideout. As the Judge had said, only outlaws and gunmen knew its location. Suddenly, she gave a gasp and leaned forward excitedly in her chair, gaining the full attention of both men.

"Texas knows how to find the place!" she exclaimed triumphantly, her eyes flashing. "He could lead a lawman there!"

"*Who?*" Judge Hamilton and Matthew Richards boomed the word together, their eyes riveted incredulously on Bryony's face.

She glanced uncertainly from one to the other of them. "Texas," she said falteringly, confused by their sudden, intense silence. "The man who rescued me."

The men exchanged shocked glances. Matt Richards was about to speak when he was interrupted by a bustle of excitement. A tall, bow-kneed cowboy burst into the hotel doorway and announced excitedly to the patrons inside, "Hey, folks, there's goin' to be another gunfight! They're comin' out of the saloon now!"

The few other people in the room put down their coffee cups hurriedly and hastened to crowd out the doorway into the street. Bryony and her two companions stared after them.

"A gunfight?" Bryony cried in alarm, forgetting the strange turn their previous conversation had taken in light of this startling new development. She felt sickened by the thought that at any moment another man would die in the streets of Winchester, just as her father had done. . . .

"I'm afraid so." Matt rose to his feet, his thickset, powerful form looming over her as he glanced down at her pale face. "These gunfights are all too common. In

Winchester, a man is killed nearly every day."

"How awful." Bryony shuddered. She gazed upward as Judge Hamilton also rose and the two men prepared to leave her. In the street outside there were sounds of commotion as people hurried to get out of the way. There was a queer note of frenzied excitement in the air, an excitement that was as contagious as it was unnerving. She swallowed painfully, feeling an iciness down her spine.

"We'll be back, Miss Hill," Judge Hamilton informed her as he and Matt moved to join the onlookers in the street.

Bryony nodded, watching their retreating forms. She felt shaken and cold and more than a little sick. Something was acting upon her, a force she didn't recognize or understand. She only knew that she wanted nothing more than to sit here with her hands over her eyes and ears, and to block out all sound and sight of the violence that was about to take place, to banish its ugly brutality from her mind. Yet something was telling her to get up, to move. Something was drawing her outside, to the street where the tragic scene was taking place. She closed her eyes for a moment, fighting for control, struggling to regain logic and thought and reason. And then she rose as if drawn by an unseen, magnetic force, and moved slowly, irresistibly toward the hotel door.

Chapter Nine

Texas buckled on his gun belt, fitting it tightly about his slim hips, letting the gun ride low and hard against his body. Poised in front of the tall, gaudy, imitation-gilt framed mirror, he studied his reflection impassively in its dusty surface, totally oblivious of the narrow, tawdry bedroom over the Silver Spur Saloon in which he found himself, and of the girl in the red negligee who was carelessly asleep in the rumpled bed only a few feet behind him. His eyes met those of the tall, lean man in the mirror and narrowed appraisingly. The man who stared back at him looked formidable, his blue eyes cold and hard beneath the black sombrero that almost hid his curly, dark brown hair from view. His black bandana was tied about his neck with just the right touch of care-less skill, his red shirt fit well over his wide shoulders and broad chest, and the snug-fitting black vest with small pearl buttons added a dark, dangerous tone to his appearance. His black trousers and dark leather boots emphasized the fine strong shape of his powerful legs and thighs. And then there was the gunbelt, ever present, ever needed, with the gleaming black Colt fitted snugly into the holster.

For a moment he regarded the weapon coldly, and then, as he did every morning of his life, he slowly dropped his hands to his side and let them hang for an instant. Suddenly, with blinding speed, his right hand flashed to his gun with one swift fluid movement, yanking it from the holster into shooting position. The entire action took less than two seconds, far too rapid for the eye to accurately measure. He replaced the gun silently in the holster and went through the process again. And again. And again. Time after time his hand flashed to his hip and produced the gun in a lightning stroke, his fingers sure and tight around the weapon, his eyes relentless and unblinking in the mirror. The ritual was the same day after day, a period of practice imperative to his survival. At last, satisfied, he turned away from the mirror. He was ready to begin another day.

As he moved with the smooth, quiet grace of a panther toward the bedroom door, he could hear the sounds of men's voices in the saloon below. The girl on the bed shifted restlessly, her almond-shaped eyes slowly opening, enabling her to see the man advancing quietly toward the door. Sleepily, she propped herself up on one elbow, surveying him, her coppery hair tumbling over her smooth bare shoulders as the red negligee dipped forward, impudently revealing her enormous breasts. "Texas, where are you going?" she demanded poutingly, her eyes fixed accusingly on his tall, powerful form.

At her words he paused and turned to face her, a slight sardonic smile twisting his lips. "Well, well, awake at last. I thought you were going to sleep all day, Ginger," he replied mockingly. "I reckon our activities last night tired you out. Too bad. A girl in your position ought to have more endurance."

His mocking words seemed to have no effect on the girl curled catlike on the bed. Her tawny eyes smiled seductively up at him.

"Why didn't you wake me if you wanted me this morning?" she inquired softly. "You know, Texas honey, I'm always ready and willing whenever you want me."

"I know," he agreed, sounding somewhat bored, and once again turning away.

"Wait!" Ginger leapt from the bed and ran to him, coyly pressing her abundantly curvaceous body against his and entwining her long arms firmly about his neck. "Don't go, honey," she whispered huskily, her full, pink lips warm against his solid jaw. "Stay with me just a little longer. We'll have a wonderful time, sugar, I promise you."

Without a word, the tall, lean cowboy lowered his head and kissed her roughly, his lips devouring her mouth with careless brutality. She moaned ecstatically, her hands groping downward for the male hardness she loved to touch. But he pushed her away with a laugh, watching as she tumbled backwards upon the bed, the negligee falling open to reveal her nude magnificence. "I don't have time to play games with you this mornin'," Ginger," he chuckled, moving toward the door. "But, maybe, if you play your cards right, I'll stop by and see you again tonight."

She shoved her coppery hair out of her eyes with an impatient hand. She was angry that he was leaving her so abruptly, depriving her of the pleasure she had looked forward to throughout the night. They had made love until very late, and she had finally drifted off to sleep, possessively expecting more entertainment in the morning. Instead, this indifferent bastard was leaving her without satisfying the craving he had aroused in her by his mere presence. She scowled at him. Where was he going that was so damned important? Did he think she had forgotten that he had arrived hours late last night, all because of that stupid little bitch from the east who had gotten herself into well-deserved trouble?

"Well, sugar, don't bother to show up if you're going to be late again!" she flung at him sulkily. "Next time you can just turn to your little Miss Bryony Hill for company!"

At this, he spun around to face her amusedly, his eyes glinting beneath the dark rim of his sombrero. His voice was cool. "What does Miss Hill have to do with this?"

Ginger sat up on the bed, giving her head a petulant

toss and reaching smugly for the hairbrush she kept on the night stand beside the bed. She began brushing her long curls with languid, self-consciously sensual strokes as she talked. "Well, Texas, honey, you told me last night that the reason you got here so late was because that prissy little eastern bitch got herself kidnapped off the stage. And you had to volunteer to bring her back to town! Now, really, Texas! I don't see why you didn't leave well enough alone. Who wants her here in Winchester? If you ask my opinion, she deserved whatever she got. And I'd think *you'd* feel the same. Why you should go out of your way to help her is beyond me, let me tell you! Have you forgotten about Daisy? Have you? Now, honey, don't narrow your eyes at me that way. I know you haven't. But if that's how you feel about it, why bother to help Wesley Hill's spoiled little brat? She's probably no better than her old man, and I *know* how you felt about him!"

Texas smiled coldly. "Even you, Ginger, can't hold the girl responsible for her father's sins. That's going a bit far, don't you think?"

"No, I don't! Like father, like daughter, that's what I think!" she snapped, throwing the hairbrush down on the night stand with a clatter. She lay back in the bed, stretching seductively on the pink satin sheets, allowing her long, lithe body to wriggle invitingly as Texas watched her with his cold, hard blue eyes. "Tell me something, Texas, honey," she urged sweetly, slowly inching the red negligee upward across her shapely thigh. "Is she pretty, this Bryony Hill? Is she prettier than me?"

The man opposite her laughed shortly, a harsh, merciless sound full of mockery and contempt. He ignored her deliberately sensual movements as she bared her body for his scrutiny, instead watching her narrow, pretty face with its wild, tawny eyes and full pink lips that seemed permanently set in a pout. "Don't tell me you're jealous, Ginger. Do you have so little confidence in your own charms?"

"No, honey," she replied sweetly, though her eyes had hardened viciously. "I know there's not another woman in town who can please you the way I do, and you know it, too. I'm not worried—just curious, that's all. Daisy once saw a picture of Wesley Hill's daughter and she said she was a real looker. I just wondered if it was true."

"You'll have to see for yourself," he replied carelessly. But he advanced slowly across the room and grinned wickedly at Ginger, who had removed the filmy red negligee and was now lying nude before him, her eyes shining with desire as she gazed at him. He reached out and yanked her up against him, crushing her soft flesh against his, his hands expertly caressing her breasts and hips and buttocks while he kissed her with rough, bruising passion. She responded delightedly, wriggling against his lean, muscled form like a snake.

After a moment, Texas lifted his head and stared down into her flushed face. He took her head between his hands, holding it firmly in his grip while his eyes pierced her. "I want you tonight, Ginger. Eight o'clock. We'll spend the whole night up here," he ordered.

Ginger's lips parted in protest. "But, sugar, I have to work in the Silver Spur tonight. Meg won't let me off. Why not come back to bed now? Please?" She began squirming in his grasp, trying to pull him down with her onto the bed, but he held her strongly, his arms now wrapped about her heated body as his lips took hers once again. "I don't have time now, but tonight, Ginger, I want to spend the whole night up here alone with you—savvy?"

"But I can't! Last night I was off work at eight, but you weren't here, and tonight, Meg expects me to work until two in the morning! Don't you understand?"

"Square it with Meg!" he ordered roughly, his lips silencing any further protests. Then, abruptly, he slapped her resoundingly on the buttocks and once more pushed her away, back down onto the bed. He turned and strode toward the door, pausing as he reached it to glance back at her frustrated expression. "Tonight, Ginger. See that you're free. Or else you'll answer to me and I promise you that my anger is worse than anything you'll get from Meg Donahue!" With these words, he left the room, shutting the door behind him, while Ginger screeched her frustration and banged her fist wrathfully into the pillow.

Texas chuckled softly to himself and proceeded down the creaking, uncarpeted stairs leading to the saloon. He was looking forward to the evening, when he would have Ginger all to himself. She was wickedly pretty, and deliciously wanton in bed; she knew more ways to please a man with her lips and tongue than any other whore he'd ever met. He didn't mind the fact that despite her youthful twenty-four years, her eyes and mouth had the harshness of a much older woman, and her voluptuous body had been used by a multitude of other men. He understood the rigors of her position. She worked as a dance-hall girl and waitress in the Silver Spur, and prostituted herself on the side, giving a cut to Meg Donahue, the saloon's proprietor, in exchange for the use of the tawdry little bedroom upstairs. Ginger was alone in the world, like most of the other girls who worked in the Silver Spur, and she made her living the only way she knew how. He thought no less of her because she was a prostitute; in fact, he admired the way she had made a success of herself. Ginger was the most sought-after girl in the saloon, probably because her reputation of expertise at lovemaking was widely known. From his own considerable experience with women of her ilk, he knew that she was one of the best, and that was why he chose to spend the night with her whenever possible. The only thing that annoyed him was her possessiveness, which had been getting progressively worse. The way she had behaved this morning was a perfect example—clinging to him, trying to seduce him every moment, wanting him to stay with her for longer and longer periods. It was getting to be a bore. She was so predictable and dependent in her constant

yearning for his attentions that there wasn't the same
excitement he had once felt in bedding her. And her
jealousy was equally irritating. She had actually
sounded jealous of Bryony Hill, a naive little schoolgirl
from the east! Even worse, she'd been very upset lately
whenever he spoke with one of the other dance-hall girls
in the saloon. Like that Lila, the attractive brunette with
the long, slinky legs, who always wore black-netted
stockings. Ginger had thrown a fit the other night when
he had merely slipped his arm around the woman's
waist after she brought him his drink.

Texas sighed as he approached the main room of the
Silver Spur. Ginger had better watch out. Possessiveness
was one quality he would not tolerate. He wasn't about
to be owned by any woman, and she had better face up
to that fast. He liked the life he had chosen for himself.
He had grown accustomed to facing danger whenever it
arose, to seizing pleasure whenever he felt so inclined, to
doing precisely what he liked without having to answer
to any man—or any woman. And he had no intention of
changing his ways. It had been a long time since he'd
lived any other kind of life, and it was too late now to
pick up the old ties, or begin new ones. He thought of
the letter he'd received last week and had thrown in the
pocket of his saddlebag, along with a half-dozen others
he'd received from Danny in the past months. Sometimes, when he was alone in the mountains or the desert,
he'd stare into his campfire and imagine what it would
be like to go back. But he knew he never would. He had
too much guilt, too much pride, too much stubbornness. Besides, he told himself, he was much better off
like this, free to live—or die, as he chose. He resolved to
teach Ginger not to interfere in his personal life, for he
intended to sleep with that long-legged Lila before his
stay in Winchester ended and he rode on to another
town. She was the only one of the girls in the Silver Spur
he hadn't taken to bed—except of course, for Daisy. . . .

At the memory of that small, frightened face framed
by yellow curls and dominated by huge, cornflower blue

eyes and a tiny pink bow of a mouth, he jerked his thoughts harshly back to the present and to the business at hand. He had a job to finish here, and he wasn't going anywhere until it was done. Enough thinking about Ginger LaRue and her problems. It was time to attend to important matters.

Upon entering the main room of the saloon, he instinctively noted its other occupants. The room was relatively empty, with only a handful of men lounging at one of the card tables, smoking and talking aimlessly between gulps of whisky. It was barely noon; the saloon wouldn't fill up until later in the day. Now, in the glowing April sunshine that streamed through the windows, it looked vastly different than it would tonight, when the room would be crowded with boisterous cowboys and shrilly laughing dance-hall girls, when the smells of whisky and tobacco and cheap perfume would mingle freely, and the piano player would bang out his bawdy tunes while the girls danced on tables and sang atop the piano, hiking their colorful skirts up tantalizingly to boldly reveal colorful fishnet stockings and spiked high heels. The enormous crystal chandeliers would sway dangerously, casting bright, reeling light off the vivid red-and-gold wallpaper that adorned the walls and the high, arched ceiling. But that would be tonight, when the Silver Spur would be rowdy and festive, alive with noisy merriment and drunken gambling. At the moment it was only a quiet room with a dozen small, round gambling tables, a handful of customers, and the long, curving bar with its assortment of glasses and bottles. Texas seated himself on one of the black leather bar stools. He ordered black coffee from Luke, the broad-shouldered, dark-bearded bartender, who grunted a greeting and turned away to pour him a cup of the steaming liquid.

Texas half-turned in his stool so that he could have a view of the swinging double doors leading into the saloon from the street, and of the group of men at the card table. He knew them; they were local range hands who were probably in town to buy supplies, but despite their apparent harmlessness, he thought it wise not to turn his back to them. He had learned that the only man he could trust was himself, and he made an automatic practice of taking every precaution in every situation. He had no intention of becoming a victim. So he lounged on his seat, drinking his coffee, hat pulled low over his eyes, to all appearances relaxed and careless, while inwardly his reflexes were needle-sharp, his mind alert and keen for any hint of trouble.

A woman entered from a back room and approached him, her flaming red hair artfully arranged in an elaborate coiffure upon her head, crowned by a huge aqua blue hat containing bunches of tall blue feathers and trimmed in blue sequins. Her long satin gown matched her hat, the sequins glittering gaudily as the blue satin flowed over her tall, statuesque form, scantily covering her bosom and clinging tightly to every curve in her queenly body. Meg Donahue was a big, handsome woman, with large blue eyes that sparkled like the sequins on her dress. Enormous rhinestone earrings decorated her ears, flashing brightly with each movement of her head. About her clung the strong, heady scent of jasmine and lilac, an almost overpowering fragrance that seemed to fill the saloon. She sat down on the stool next to Texas and gave him a saucy, sidelong smile.

"Well now, Texas, honey, don't you look fine and ready for trouble this morning! Just like always!" she laughed heartily.

He returned her smile coolly, pushing his dark sombrero further back on his head to give her a long, raking stare that held both approval and a hint of amusement.

"Mornin', Meg," he replied nonchalantly.

"Where's Ginger?" the woman inquired, downing the gin the bartender brought her in one gulp. "Is she still in bed at this hour? I swear to you, Texas, I don't know what you do to tire that girl out so! She's never this late coming down after being with any of these

other hombres in town!" There was a hint of exasperation mingled with playfulness in the saloon owner's
tone, and Texas raised one eyebrow at her in mock innocence, but made no reply. Meg Donahue studied his
calm expression a moment, then burst into raucous
laughter, her dangling rhinestone earrings flashing
gaudily as she shook her head.

"You're sure a cool one, Texas, aren't you?" she
declared admiringly. "Well, any time you get tired of
Ginger, you can always come back to my bed. We sure
had some good times when you first came to town,
didn't we?"

Texas grinned at her, a wave of affection washing
over him. Meg Donahue was as good-natured as she was
handsome. She had lived in Winchester for the past fifteen years, coming with her husband as a twenty-year
old bride to the town that was barely more than a
cluster of wood-shingled buildings and horse manure.
She worked side by side with him in the Silver Spur
saloon, serving the rough, violent men who frequented
this wild part of the country. Six years ago, her husband
had been shot accidentally by a stray bullet during a
saloon brawl, and she had worn widow's black for a full
six months before returning to the bright, gaudy, glittering world she loved.

In the five and a half years since she'd come out of
mourning, she had made up for her previous faithful-
ness to her husband by choosing many lovers, content-
ing herself with the use of their strong, tough bodies,
but never giving them a second thought outside of the
bedroom. Her heart had been sealed off when her husband's coffin had been lowered into the grave, but her
flesh was still very much alive and sought satisfaction
from any man with a strong body and handsome face.
In Texas she had found both, and for the first few weeks
after he'd ridden into Winchester, they had both enjoyed themselves immensely. But she had seemed to
understand from the start that Texas was a roving man,
not to be satisfied by any one woman, and when he had

moved on to the other girls in the saloon for his night-time pleasures, she had shrugged, slapped him on the back, and wished him well. Meg was aware that he'd been enjoying Ginger's abundant charms almost exclusively of late, and couldn't help wondering when he would tire of the copper-haired girl and move on to new quarry, perhaps Lila, who had made her interest in him quite obvious, and who felt rather slighted that she was the only girl in the saloon he had not bedded. Except for Daisy, Meg reflected. He had never once slept with Daisy. . . .

"I'd appreciate you doing me a favor, Meg," Texas was now saying, arms folded relaxedly across his chest.

"And what might that be, cowboy?"

"Give Ginger the night off." He smiled wickedly at her. "I want her all to myself tonight—all night. I told her to square it with you."

"The hell you did! Damn, what do you think this is, mister, a brothel? This is a saloon! Now if those girls want to make a little extra loot on the side, I don't want to stop 'em. But first things first, and that means I expect them to put in a full work week, serving drinks and dancing with the customers and sitting on the piano swinging their legs." She glared at him. "There's no way on this earth Ginger can have tonight off! I don't have no one else to replace her. It's just her and Stella working, and I'm expecting a big crowd. So forget it, Texas. I just won't allow it!"

Meg fumed on in this fashion for several moments, her blue eyes flashing like sapphires, her face flushed angrily beneath her flaming red hair and that outrageous blue-plumed hat. Texas watched her impassively, until she at last fell silent, her chest heaving with indignation.

"Are you finished?" he inquired lazily.

"You're damn right I am! And the answer is no! No, no, no!" She banged her fist on the bar for emphasis. Texas took her fist and unbent the long fingers gently. Into her opened palm he placed a considerable wad of green bills. Meg's eyes widened as she saw them, and she quickly raised her eyes to his face which, as usual, was set in a careless, inscrutable expression.

"You're willing to pay all this—for Ginger?" she asked suspiciously.

"That's right. Take it or leave it," he returned mockingly.

Meg hesitated only an instant before a wide smile brightened her heavily rouged face. She stuffed the wad of money inside the bodice of her dress, winking broadly at Texas. "I'll take it, honey, damned if I don't," she chuckled. "I'll tell Lila or Gracie that one of them will have to take over tonight for Ginger. No problem." She happily patted the spot between her breasts where the wad of money rested. "Anything to make you happy, Texas!"

He nodded and turned back to the bar to order more coffee, having already lost interest in her; but her next words won his attention back in spades.

"I hear there's going to be some trouble, honey," Meg confided in a suddenly lowered voice, one eye on the three range cowboys still at the card table. They had taken out a deck of cards and begun a round of stud poker, seemingly oblivious of her and her conversation with Texas. Encouraged by this, and by the suddenly interested look on the tall cowboy's face, Meg leaned closer to him and gave him a sultry, secretive smile. "I heard that Zeke Murdock is after your scalp," she whispered. "And he's not the only one. A whole pack of hombres are riled with you for some reason. What'd you do to stir 'em up so?"

Texas merely shrugged. "It beats me, Meg," he said. "You know me—just a peace-loving cowboy who'll cross the street to avoid a fight. I can't imagine why those boys are gunning for me."

"Ha!" she chortled so loudly that the range hands glanced up from their game. But before she could say anything further, the swinging doors leading into the saloon burst open and a man stormed into the room. He was short and wiry, with bright, wild eyes and greasy dark hair that looked as if it hadn't been washed or combed in a week. His flat pug nose flared in anger and his animal's eyes glistened with satisfied excitement as his gaze fell upon the man he had come to town to kill. The cardplayers stared, open-mouthed, as he stalked swiftly over to Texas.

"I've been huntin' fer you!" Ned Casper rasped, his dark, leering face stubby with unshaved beard, his eyes like dirty pebbles fastened on Texas's impassive face.

"So what?" Texas drawled insultingly, as calm and untroubled as though he were passing the time of day with a kindly old lady instead of facing an obviously enraged outlaw whose reputation was known in every corner of the west. Ned Casper was wanted for bank robbery and murder in California, and like many desperadoes on the run was hiding out in the vast untamed wilderness of the Arizona territory. He was known to be as quick with his gun as he was with his temper, a man who made a potently dangerous enemy. But as Texas coolly studied the other man, he didn't seem in the least affected by his knowledge of the outlaw's fierce reputation. He appeared merely bored and slightly disdainful.

"You . . . you cheated us!" Casper grated, his fists clenched convulsively at his sides, his breath coming hard. "You stole that city girl right out from under our noses and if you think you kin git away with it, you're dead wrong. You hear me?" His eyes narrowed into vicious slits. "Why did you do it?" he growled. "You had first go at her—why in hell didn't you use it and pay up? 'Stead of runnin' out with her and leavin' the rest of us high and dry, without the girl and without the two hundred and fifty bucks you owed us?"

Texas was amazed by the man's audacity, to come brazenly into town to discuss his crime of the previous day. He concluded shrewdly that Ned Casper, for all his threatening reputation, was a stupid swine of a man without the brains necessary to make him a truly perilous foe. Now Zeke Murdock, he was the one who had lost most by yesterday's events, for he had lost not only the money, but the girl, and whoever had hired him would not like that one damn bit, but Murdock was too smart to come openly into town to face him. He would try something, sometime, but it would be a sly, stealthy attack, perhaps a shot in the back or a knife thrown suddenly out of the darkness. . . .

Texas brought his attention back to the matter at hand. Casper would have to be dealt with, that was obvious. However, maybe he could be of some use before he was finished off. With slightly raised brows, he gave the furious outlaw his most mocking smile. "If you're really interested, Casper, I'll tell you why I grabbed the girl from under your filthy nose. I thought it was a good joke on all you two-bit coyotes, and I couldn't resist the opportunity to glance back and watch your weaselly faces as I rode off with your prize catch of the day." He chuckled coldly, satisfaction in his glinting blue eyes as Ned's face exploded into scarlet-colored rage. "I laughed the whole way back to town. And you know what? I reckon I'll enjoy telling that joke for many years to come."

"The hell you will!" Contorted with fury, Casper could barely choke out his words. "I'll kill you first, you low-down son of a bitch, and if I don't, someone else will! Either Murdock or. . ." He caught himself abruptly, and finished in a rush, "or one of the others."

"You meant to say the name of the man who hired you in the first place, didn't you?" Texas asked softly, his keen eyes riveted to Casper's face. "Who is it? Who hired you to kidnap the girl?"

Casper's mouth opened and closed in consternation, but he recovered quickly, and snarled, "What are you talkin' about? No one hired us! We saw her and we wanted her! That's all!" He glanced nervously about the room, for the first time aware of the other men. "No one hired us, you hear?"

Texas laughed derisively. He'd hoped to anger him

into making a slip, but the outlaw had recovered his wits in time. Well, it didn't really matter. He already had a damn good suspicion who had arranged the stagecoach robbery as a coverup for the girl's kidnapping, and he knew the reason behind it. The man who had hired the gang of outlaws had wanted Bryony Hill out of the way—permanently. Texas had no doubt that eventually she would have been killed—after all the men in Gilly's had had their way with her, that is. But things hadn't worked out that way. The girl had been rescued, leaving the man who had masterminded the plot in a very dangerous and vulnerable position. Texas wondered what his next move would be. Whatever it was, Miss Bryony Hill would be the target. She was in imminent peril of her life because her unknown enemy was a desperate man. He was fighting for his very survival against the danger she unwittingly presented to him. He wouldn't rest until he was assured of either her total harmlessness or her death. Texas knew he didn't have much time.

"Supposing you tell me what you want, Casper," Texas suggested lazily. "I don't have all morning to waste with a no-good rattlesnake like you."

"I want you—dead!" Ned snarled, his anger banishing all caution as he issued his challenge for everyone to hear.

The cowboys at the card table gaped in astonishment at his words, and Meg Donahue gave a clearly audible gasp, but the man called Texas just smiled, his lips twisting unpleasantly at the prospect of a fight.

"Now look here," Meg put in swiftly. She placed her hand on Casper's arm. "Mister, I don't know what kind of trouble you're after, but do you know who this man is?"

"I know!" Ned rasped, shaking her off roughly. "And I ain't scared of him or any other man! And this is none of yer business, lady, so keep out of it!"

"Suit yourself, mister," Meg returned archly, leaning back to rest her elbows on the bar behind her, her expression frosty and disdainful. "But when they bury you tomorrow mornin', don't say I didn't warn you."

"Are you goin' to fight me or not?" Casper roared, his infuriated gaze boring into Texas's lean, calm face. "Or are you too chicken to face a man with a price on his head?"

"You're shore the braggart, aren't you, Casper?" Texas drawled coolly. "Don't you ever worry that a lawman might overhear your boasts and decide to earn himself a nice fat reward?"

"Lawman! Haw! There's not one damn lawman for miles around and you know it. Unless you've taken on the job and not seen fit to tell no one? After all, rescuin' that girl was the kind of thing I'd expect from a man with a badge. Sure you're not hidin' one under that purty black vest?"

"No, I'm not a lawman," the other responded softly, his eyes gleaming. "But I'm man enough to help rid the world of pack rats like you—which is what I intend to do, pronto." His voice became suddenly, frighteningly steely. "Outside, Casper! I wouldn't dirty Meg's floor with your filthy hide!"

Casper's face darkened with his vicious rage, but he whirled on his heel and without another word stalked quickly to the saloon door. Texas followed, his smooth, graceful walk indicative of his supreme coolness and confidence. His purposeful step left little doubt in anyone's mind what the outcome of the fight would be.

The street itself was deserted but the wooden boardwalk lining the street was crammed with excited onlookers. For Bryony, this was her first glimpse of Winchester in daylight. Flanked by Matt Richards and Judge Hamilton, she had time to notice little more than that it was a dusty, colorless little town, with long, dreary rows of unpainted frame buildings on either side of the narrow main street, and groups of sweating horses tethered to a broken line of hitching posts along the road. And people—an assortment of people—clustered together like cattle beneath the imperturbable cerulean sky to witness a killing.

"And I am one of them," she thought dazedly, dismayed by her own behavior. Yet she couldn't help herself. She had to see what was going on. To her chagrin, a tall woman wearing a high, stiffly starched yellow bonnet blocked her view of the two combatants already standing in the street, but just as she ducked her head in a vain attempt to peer past the woman, her attention was caught by a noisy crowd of people emerging from the saloon. A large, red-haired woman in a glittering blue satin gown shoved her way through the swinging doors and onto the wooden platform of the boardwalk, followed closely by a handful of eager, grinning cowboys whose boots scraped loudly, breaking the hushed silence that preceded their arrival on the scene. Then a door flew open suddenly on the upper floor of the saloon and a girl scrambled out onto the narrow balcony over the Silver Spur, a sheer, red silk robe trimmed with red maribou draped over her body, her coppery hair spilling wildly about her shoulders as she rushed to the guard rail surrounding the balcony and stared intensely down into the street. Bryony could read the fearful anxiety in the girl's face, and wondered which of the two men about to engage in the duel was the recipient of this anxious concern. Bryony, raised strictly in proper eastern society, had never seen anyone like the copper-haired girl before in her life. She had never known anyone who would dare emerge into public view in a dressing robe, especially a robe as daring and revealing as this vivid red silk one.

A moment later her attention was reclaimed by the event taking place in the street. The crowd shifted suddenly, and the woman in the yellow bonnet no longer blocked her view. Bryony squinted her eyes against the hot white brilliance of the noonday sun, straining to see the two men facing each other alone in the deserted road.

All at once, her eyes widened, and a startled gasp

escaped her lips. She felt a tiny shock vibrate throughout her body as she recognized the two men. Ned Casper
stood nearer to her, turned so that she could only see his
profile, but she knew him at a glance; the sight of his
short, wiry body, unshaven face, and pug nose was all
too familiar. Then her eyes traveled to the other man.
He faced her fully, his hat pulled low on his brow to
protect his eyes from the sun's glare, his lean, muscular
form poised for action as his hands waited at his sides
for the moment he would draw his deadly black gun. It
was the man called Texas. Her heart began to beat
violently, and she pushed her way desperately through
the crowd to its very edge.

Movement suddenly exploded in the narrow street.
Ned Casper lunged for his gun, jerking it rapidly from
his holster to fire at the tall stranger. But the shot never
came. Texas drew first, whipping the big black Colt
from its well-oiled holster, squeezing the trigger just
once, with deadly accuracy. With his gun still raised in
midair, Ned Casper crumpled brokenly to the ground,
bloodying the gray dust as he sprawled like a misshapen
puppet in the dirt, a terrible scream tearing from his lips
to echo agonizingly in the stunned silence. His body
twitched convulsively for what seemed like an eternal
moment, and then lay completely still and silent beneath
the bright, impassive blue of the Arizona sky. Slowly,
slowly, the crowd came to life, buzzing with excitement
as they surged forward toward the fallen form. The man
called Texas returned his gun to his holster and began to
turn away.

Then his gaze fell upon Bryony, who was leaning
against a supporting post as if she could not stand
alone, her emerald eyes huge and vivid upon him.
Beside her stood the paunchy, white-haired figure of
Judge Hamilton, and the dark, powerful form of Matt
Richards. The stranger smiled slightly, and lifted his hat
in a brief, insolent salute to the beautiful girl in the soft,
white dress. Then he turned arrogantly away and continued in a leisurely, unconcerned fashion toward the

saloon, where Meg Donahue waited with a beaming smile on her rouged face. Overhead, the copper-haired girl leaned over the balcony railing and called out her congratulations. Her filmy red dressing robe blew enticingly in the breeze.

Bryony Hill watched mutely as Texas disappeared into the saloon. A terrible feeling of dread stole through her and she began to shake. Her voice emerged as a dry, breathless whisper in the thin, desert air.

"Who . . . who is that man?" she said, her eyes still fixed on the spot where he had disappeared into the saloon. She gripped the wooden post for support as a horrifying premonition swept over her.

Beside her, the Judge and Matt exchanged grim glances, hesitating. "You'd best tell her," the Judge finally muttered in a low voice.

Richards nodded, glancing down with his intense dark eyes into Bryony's pale face. "That man is a gunfighter, Miss Hill," he began slowly, and to his surprise, she nodded, closing her eyes weakly in anticipation of his next words.

"His name is Texas Jim Logan," Matt continued, his tone hardening. "He is the man who killed your father."

Chapter Ten

The gun was small and compactly made, with a shiny pearl handle and gleaming black barrel, exquisitely tooled. It was a Remington .22 derringer, guaranteed by the merchant who had sold it to her to be deadly at a range of twenty feet. Bryony found that its unfamiliar weight inside her reticule was unexpectedly comforting, and she had to deliberately control herself against continually opening her bag to glance at the weapon. Instead, she focused her gaze purposefully on the trail ahead as the buggy in which she rode rolled forward at an easy pace under Judge Hamilton's guidance. Matt Richards rode alongside, mounted on a fine-looking gray gelding that seemed impatient of the sedate pace the Judge was setting.

Bryony felt impatient herself. After the events of the morning she was more anxious than ever to reach the sanctuary of the Circle H, to settle herself in and temporarily shut the world out. Judge Hamilton seemed unmindful of her inward tension, and unconcernedly passed the time while they drove to the ranch by recounting to her some of the details of Arizona's history. Bryony tried to concentrate on the conversation, but her mind churned with confused thoughts and emotions as she sought to recover from the shock she'd experienced only a short while before.

She'd gathered her belongings and checked out of the

hotel, and then insisted on being taken to the gunsmith to purchase a weapon before leaving town. Matt and the Judge had tried to discourage her, but she had been adamant. Finally, they had escorted her to the gunsmith and helped her to select the derringer. Both men were uncertain about her intentions for its use, and Bryony had given it little thought herself, only knowing that she had wanted it. She firmly intended to learn how to shoot it with expertise. But that would come later. Now she only wanted to calm the tumult whirling madly in her mind, to think about her discovery that the stranger called Texas who had rescued her from the highwaymen and then brazenly kissed her beneath the desert stars was the feared gunfighter who had killed her father.

Strangely enough, she had known this even before Matt Richards had put it into words. Something had clicked inside her head when she had seen the tall, lean stranger in the street. A distant memory of a conversation on the stagecoach, when Tom Scott had talked of "Texas Jim Logan" and his dangerous reputation, had begun to return, and she had realized the awful truth an instant before Matt Richards actually voiced it. The agony of that moment! Realizing that she had been boldly and passionately kissed by her father's murderer, and worse, she had shamefully enjoyed it! Her only consolation, however slim, lay in the fact that at the time she had been unaware of the stranger's identity. Surely if she had known the truth, she never would have responded with such wild ardor to his advances. She would not have felt such rapturous delight in being held so close against his iron body, while his lips crushed and caressed hers so masterfully. She cringed with shame at the accursed memory, and silently vowed vengeance on the loathsome stranger who had used her in this way, knowing full well who she was and what he had done to her father. She gripped her reticule tightly, thinking of the little black gun inside. She would learn how to use it. Oh yes, indeed, she would learn.

With an effort, she returned her thoughts to the present. It would not be long now before they reached the ranch. The countryside was magnificent as they trotted along a winding trail where wild geraniums, violets, and poppies grew in colorful profusion beside the road, and green shrubs and flowering cacti added their own special charm to the scene. Above, the brilliant blue sky was dotted with small, fleecy clouds like tufts of lamb's wool, and the sun bathed the entire landscape in dazzling golden light. It was hot, and very still. In the distance, mesas and jagged bluffs rose up from lavender-misted foothills and sloping valleys. And then, as always, there were the mountains, their rainbow-hued colors ever changing with the light and angle of vision. Just now, their towering, carved formations loomed against the sky in breath-taking shades of blue and purple and lavender. Somehow, their solid, imposing presence was reassuring.

She felt a strange bond to this rough, colorful, untamed land, a sense of kinship that deeply pierced her innermost soul. But how could she explain her feelings to Judge Hamilton and Matthew Richards? She barely understood them herself. She only knew that all of her life she had yearned for adventure, for excitement, for something beyond the ordinary. She wanted to draw from the strength of those towering mountains, to discover life's secrets and treasures, its richness and joy. She had a feeling that here in Arizona she would have the opportunity to taste Life, to embrace it as one embraces a cool wind on a sultry summer's day, to know the happiness of real freedom. She was overwhelmingly glad that she had come.

The Circle H ranch was an incredibly impressive hacienda nestled in the foothills of the Dragoon Mountains. It overlooked a sprawling green and yellow valley carpeted with golden poppies and purple owl's clover, and studded with mesquite shrubs, paloverde trees, and cacti of all shapes and sizes. Groves of cottonwoods flanked the ranch-house grounds, and Bryony spotted orange groves ringing the rear of the house. The range, dotted with peacefully grazing cattle, spread lavishly over a vast amount of land. In the distance, the thin blue ribbon of water that was the San Pedro River wound its way northward through the plunging valley. Looking down upon this gorgeous scene from an over-hanging bluff, Bryony caught her breath in rapt admiration. She had never seen such splendor in her life!

The ranch house itself was a handsome, two-story red adobe building with numerous wooden-shuttered windows. Around the outside of the house ran a wide, roofed porch supported by wooden posts, giving the structure an open, airy appearance. Judge Hamilton explained that porches of this type were common in the southwest, for they helped protect the inside of the house from the intense heat inflicted by the desert sun. A wide road led up to the front of the building, where a white-painted wrought-iron fence guarded the path leading to the shaded entrance within the porch. Bryony gazed upward at the ranch in delight as Richards, dismounting quickly from the gelding, helped her to alight from the buggy, while Judge Hamilton got down heavily and fastened the horses to a hitching post. Before following the men up the steps and into the ranch house, she glanced swiftly about, noting the long, low bunk house where the range hands undoubtedly slept, the gable-roofed barn and stables, the storehouses and corrals.

A group of cowboys in the nearest corral had been watching a young wrangler breaking in a fiercely bucking black stallion, but upon Bryony's arrival they'd swung their attention over to her. Their eyes seemed to bore into her as she paused on the ranch house steps. The wrangler, thrown to the ground by the horse, rolled free of his plunging hooves, narrowly escaping death, but he seemed oblivious of his danger as he calmly climbed the corral fence and joined the rest of his companions in staring openly at the elegant young woman who was now mistress of the Circle H cattle ranch.

Slightly disconcerted by the bold, appraising way the wranglers were regarding her, Bryony crossed the wide shaded porch swiftly and entered the open doorway of the adobe ranch house. Inside, to her surprise, it was remarkably cool, and the decor of the house, in striking contrast to the rugged simplicity of the exterior architecture, was lavish with tasteful, expensive luxury.

Her father had obviously spared no expense in furnishing the ranch house. The hallway in which she stood boasted as fine a parquet floor as one could wish to see, its gleaming wood polished to a high bronze, the rich color reflecting off the finely paneled walls, which extended, she could see, into the other rooms. A large parlor branched off to the right of the hallway, and Bryony caught a glimpse of handsome, carved oak furniture, and a beautiful Indian-woven rug of intricate geometric design in colors of brown and tan and beige, which hung from the far wall, while another, even larger and in sunset colors, graced the expensive parquet floor. Brass lamps and colorful Indian pottery brightened the handsome room, which looked as if it had just been freshly cleaned and polished. Everything glowed with a rich, elegant beauty that bespoke a man's solid good taste and an abundance of wealth.

Straight ahead through the hallway rose a plushly carpeted staircase leading to the second floor bedrooms, as Judge Hamilton informed Bryony. And behind the stairway was the kitchen and the room in which Rosita, her father's Mexican housekeeper, slept. Beyond the parlor there was a large, formal dining room furnished with a long oak table and finely carved chairs, a massive china cabinet, and an oak sideboard. The sideboard and china cabinet displayed lovely dishes and trays of pewter, French crystal goblets, and several bowls and candlesticks of fine sterling silver. A highly polished silver coffee service sat in the center of the long oak dining table, glittering proudly. It was a splendid room, and Bryony felt a rush of pleasure as she surveyed it. French windows along one entire wall opened onto the porch and the rear courtyard, where orange groves clustered prettily against a distant background of the Dragoon Mountains.

After a brief tour of these downstairs rooms, Judge Hamilton took Bryony's arm and ushered her into her father's study, which branched off to the left of the front hallway. Here she stopped short in complete amazement. It wasn't that the room wasn't as carefully appointed as the others in the ranch house—it was; her attention was solely claimed by the gaping hole in the wall above the dark walnut mantelpiece, a large, jagged black cavity where perhaps a painting should have been, and wasn't. She stared in astonishment until Matt Richards came up behind her and spoke ruefully over her shoulder.

"Not a very pretty sight, is it? I'm afraid Judge Hamilton and I didn't really know what to do with it— I mean, whether you'd want us to have another safe installed for you, or to just repair the wall and cover it with a painting, or what. . ."

"What happened here?" Bryony demanded, whirling to face him. "I'm afraid I don't understand what you're talking about."

"It seems, ma'am, that someone broke into the house shortly after your father's death. The whole place was ransacked, and the wall safe your father had installed in this room was blown open—dynamited. Whatever money he had in there was stolen. We're really not sure how much was there."

"The ranch was robbed? How awful! Was anything else of value stolen?" Then she caught herself up short. "No, of course not. The silver coffee service and all those beautiful things are still in the dining room where they belong, aren't they?"

"That's the odd thing about it," the Judge answered. "The place was turned upside down, but only the contents of the safe were missing."

"But how was all this allowed to happen, Judge? Didn't anyone hear the commotion and come to investigate? There are dozens of range hands on this property—why didn't they do something to stop the thieves?"

"It happened on the wranglers' night off. All the men were in town, whooping it up at the Silver Spur. Rosita was here alone, asleep. When she heard the explosion, she got up to see what was happening, but was knocked unconscious from behind before she could see anyone." He shrugged. "I'm right sorry, Miss Hill. I've no idea who those hombres were who ransacked the place. And believe me, they really tore it apart. It took Rosita nearly a week to clean everything up."

"Si, es true. A whole week it took—*mucho trabajo!*"

The heavily accented Mexican voice spoke softly from the doorway, and Bryony turned curiously to view Rosita, her father's housekeeper. The Mexican woman was short and plump, with a fat, pretty brown face, dark hair braided severely atop her head, and a hint of a mustache along her upper lip. She wore a loose-fitting white blouse that hung limply over her sagging breasts, and a long, colorful print skirt that almost touched the floor. Her thick brown arms were crossed in front of her, and this, added to the unfriendly expression on her broad face, gave an impression of sullenness.

"Howdy, Rosita. This is Miss Bryony Hill, your new mistress." Judge Hamilton grinned at Bryony. "Rosita Lopez, Miss Hill, is the best housekeeper in the territory. Mrs. Banks, my landlady at the boardinghouse, has been trying to steal her away for the longest time, and so has Edna Billings at the hotel, but I guess they can't match the money your pa paid out. Rosita's worth it, though, every cent of it. Right, Matt?"

The rancher nodded, while Bryony smiled politely, wondering if Rosita's housekeeping talents were worth the price of having her sour face continually present in the house. She decided to wait and see; perhaps she could eventually melt down some of the woman's aloofness. In the meantime, she said with a sincere effort at friendliness, "How do you do, Rosita? I'm happy to meet you. And I can see that the Judge isn't exaggerating; the house absolutely sparkles. I do hope you'll stay on with me."

The woman shrugged stoically. "Buenas dias, señorita. Si, I will stay." Then she lapsed into sullen silence, as if waiting for further orders.

"That's fine, Rosita, just fine." The Judge filled the uncomfortable silence with his hearty voice. "Now why don't you start rustling up some supper for Miss Hill? This desert air stirs up an appetite, and I don't think she's had a bite of chow since breakfast."

Mutely, the woman turned and lumbered away, her sandaled feet moving with remarkable quietness for so large a woman.

Bryony glanced hesitantly at Judge Hamilton. "I don't think she likes me very much," she ventured.

"Oh, Rosita's not the talkative type. And besides, she'll like you just fine after she's been paid. I reckon that seeing the pesos she has coming to her will bring a smile to that sour old face."

Bryony started. "What do you mean?"

The Judge sighed. "Well, ma'am, the woman hasn't been paid since a week before your pa died. Neither have any of the hands. Matter of fact, they're all about ready to up and quit. No one was here to take care of the payroll—you see, the money was locked in the safe." He nodded toward the wall with the gaping hole.

"Do you mean that the payroll money was stolen from there?" Bryony cried, her green eyes widening in dismay. "That's terrible! How am I to pay Rosita and all the others?" This new problem was worse than all the rest. It was bad enough that the ranch had been broken into, but a missing payroll and disgruntled employees were even more unsettling. What was she going to do?

"I'm sorry, Miss Hill, but it looks like this is your most pressing problem," Matt Richards spoke from the window, where he was gazing out toward the corrals. "A whole pack of wranglers are on their way over here right now, with Rusty Jessup, your father's foreman, in the lead. And they look madder than a band of Apache braves on the warpath.'' He turned from the window, frowning. ''I'm afraid they're going to want their pay before the day is out.''

''But that's ridiculous. I don't have that kind of money with me!'' Bryony gasped, rushing to the window to see for herself. Sure enough, about a dozen men were stalking purposefully toward the ranch house, their chaps flapping against their denim jeans and high, pointed boots. Beneath their wide sombreros, their dark-tanned faces were set in hard, determined expressions, and Bryony's heart jumped at the prospect of a confrontation with such fierce-looking men. She spun about to stare wildly at Judge Hamilton.

''What am I going to do, Judge? I don't have the money with which to pay them!''

''I reckon you're going to have to stall them off a bit,'' he replied thoughtfully. ''There's probably plenty of cash to cover the payroll in the bank in Tucson, where your pa had an account. Once you're settled in here, I'll drive you over to Tucson and you can withdraw it.''

''But is that going to satisfy their demands today?'' she asked nervously.

Judge Hamilton gave her a long, measuring look, taking in her slender, lovely figure, the long, ebony curls flowing softly about her shoulders, the small white hands twisting nervously together. He spoke in a quiet, serious voice to the beautiful young girl waiting anxiously before him.

''Miss Hill, if you're going to run this ranch, you're going to have to face all the problems that go along with the job. Those men out there worked for your father, and now they work for you. *You* have to handle this. No one else.''

She met his gaze silently. He was right, of course. Unconsciously, she had been hoping that he or Matt Richards would step in and pacify the angry cowboys for her. Now she saw that that would never do.

She took a deep breath as she heard a pounding on the ranch house door. Then without a word she turned, her white skirts swishing behind her as she walked gracefully into the hallway and to the front door. Despite her calm exterior, her heart thudded nervously. She knew that this confrontation would be a real test of her ability to survive here in Arizona, where rough, brutal men and smoking guns ruled the day. It was vital that she succeed with the angry wranglers or else she may as well give up her dream of running this ranch, of making Arizona her home. So much depended on the next few minutes!

The man facing her on the opposite side of the doorway was tall and slim, in his middle twenties, with a thick crop of curly red hair beneath his pushed-back brown hat. He was dressed in typical cowboy garb: denim Levis, chaps, pointed boots with intricate, fancy stitching, and a plaid shirt with a brown neckerchief tied about his throat. The expression on his narrow face was not encouraging, as Bryony studied him swiftly; he had sharp, cruel blue eyes beneath bushy red brows, a prominent nose, and thin lips that were set in a contemptuous sneer. As she took his measure, he did the same with her, his sharp eyes lingering on the generous swell of her breasts, traveling downward along her body as though she were not wearing any clothes at all. When he returned his gaze to her face, there was a jeering expression in his eyes, not unmixed, she noted, with a look of desire.

"Yes, what is it?" Bryony asked coolly, trying not to expose her inner anxiety. She must retain control of this situation and make the wranglers respect her. If they thought she was weak and easily frightened, the battle would be lost before she even spoke a word.

"So you're Miss Hill—the new owner of the Circle H," the red-haired cowboy remarked derisively.

"Yes, I am. What do you want?"

He leisurely drew himself up to his full height to

tower over her intimidatingly. "Well, ma'am," he drawled, "I'm Rusty Jessup—your father's foreman, and these are some of the boys who worked for your pa." He jerked his thumb to indicate the restless group of cowboys waiting in the dust at the foot of the porch steps. "We've come for our pay, ma'am," Rusty continued, his deceptively easygoing tone toughening. "We stayed on after your pa died out of respect, but now that you're here, we expect you to make it up to us. Pronto." He leaned closer, so close that she could smell the strong, nauseating aroma of his hair tonic. "In case you don't know, city lady, pronto means *now*!"

Bryony flushed at his rude tone, wishing she could slap that sly, self-satisfied expression off his face. For some reason she couldn't fathom, Rusty Jessup had made up his mind that he was going to dislike his new employer without even giving her a chance, and Bryony sensed that it would be futile to try to reason with him. Moreover, she returned his dislike, wondering why her father had ever hired such a contemptible, unpleasant man as his foreman. But she had no time to ponder that question now.

She stepped coldly past Rusty Jessup without another word, pausing in the center of the porch to sweep her gaze over the group of discontented range hands. She heard Judge Hamilton and Matt Richards emerge from the house to stand silently behind her, while from the corner of her eye she saw still another wrangler making his way toward the group on the porch. She recognized him as the man who had been riding the wild mustang when she arrived, but she had no time to think further about him, for even as he loped up to join the group at the foot of the steps, Bryony became aware that everyone was waiting for her to speak. Rusty Jessup breathed heavily beside her and the range hands watched her with evident hostility. She drew a deep breath, casting frantically in her mind for the right words with which to address them. Having lived all her life in the homes of her kindly relations and in boarding schools where others made the decisions, Bryony was unaccustomed to being in command. Desperately, she wondered what Miss Marsh would say in this situation. That slender, soft-spoken woman, for all her delicate appearance, was universally respected by all those who came into contact with her; she seemed capable of handling any situation with grace and firm efficiency. She swallowed once, and then began to speak as she imagined Miss Marsh would if faced with this problem.

"I'm glad you have come here to see me this afternoon," she began steadily, her gaze traveling calmly over each listening man as she spoke. "I want to thank you all for remaining here on the Circle H during the period following my father's death. I greatly appreciate it." She paused, wondering if she should smile at them, then deciding against it. She had once overheard Miss Marsh warning a new teacher at the school that she should not bestow even one smile on her students for the entire first month of the term—the students would have to learn to respect her; later there would be time for them to like her. Bryony sensed that the same principle applied now. "As you all know, the payroll money that was kept in the safe in my father's study was stolen shortly after his death. Consequently, I do not at this moment have the money that is due you." A chorus of angry muttering and oaths sounded at these words, but Bryony held up a hand for silence and continued speaking, her heart pounding. "I regret this delay deeply, believe me I do, and I intend to make it up to you."

"Oh yeah? How?" Rusty Jessup demanded, glaring down into her face. "The only way you can make anything up to us is by giving us our pay here and now! We've waited long enough already!"

"That's right. We want what's owed us!" another cowboy shouted from the crowd, and others agreed rowdily, discontent spreading through them as rapidly as a wildfire. Only the tall blond wrangler who had ridden the bucking mustang remained silent, studying first Bryony and then Rusty Jessup. As the foreman continued to argue, deliberately inciting the other men, and preventing Bryony from speaking, the young range hand shouldered his way to the front of the crowd.

"Maybe if you shut up a minute, Jessup, the lady might have a chance to speak her mind," he boomed, and instantly the other men fell silent, glancing in surprise at the angered cowboy.

"What's with you, Monroe—don't you want your money?" Jessup sneered, his cruel blue eyes knifing into the younger man. "Or are you more interested in making a good impression on this fine-looking little filly?"

A second later the young blond wrangler was on the porch, one large fist slamming into the foreman's narrow face. Jessup went down in a sprawl on the porch, clutching his jaw in pain and confusion. As he realized what had happened, he surged upward toward the lanky wrangler looming over him, but Judge Hamilton and Matt Richards intervened, pulling the two men apart. Bryony watched the exchange in horror, shocked by how quickly the situation had exploded. The range hands seemed to have forgotten all about her. They were buzzing excitely among themselves, commenting on the fight. She began to feel angry. The situation had gone beyond her control; somehow, she must regain mastery of it.

"All right, that's enough!" she suddenly shouted, placing her hands on her hips in a posture of authority. The men quieted, staring at her in surprise.

Her eyes burned like fiery emeralds as she scorched each man with her gaze. Her lovely face was set coldly; the dainty features might have been carved from white marble. Her voice rang sharply in the air. "I will not tolerate another instant of this conduct," she warned. "The next man who speaks before I have finished is fired—effective immediately. Is that understood?" She paused, waiting until each man had nodded, amazement registering on their faces as the exquisite young girl before them took on a startling new dimension. The wranglers were not ready to throw in their jobs without hearing what she had to say. It was Jessup who had stirred up their ire these past few days, kindling their resentment into fury with the new owner of the ranch. But now that they had seen her, the men were intrigued. No one made a sound as Bryony Hill once more began to speak.

"Within the next few days I'll ride to Tucson and withdraw sufficient sums from the bank there to cover the payroll for every man and woman on this ranch. I am also prepared to pay an extra week's salary to every person who remains in my employ without another word of complaint. But there are two things I expect from those who work for me—loyalty and respect. Mr. Jessup has shown neither, and as of now he is dismissed from his duties here. And anyone else who feels as he does is free to leave, because I don't want people on this ranch who will not be loyal to me. Those of you who choose to leave will be paid as soon as I return from Tucson with the money. Those who stay will have bonuses in addition to their regular pay, and they will also have my appreciation. But stay or leave, I will not tolerate grumbling and complaints. Those who do so will quickly follow in Mr. Jessup's footsteps—straight off this ranch. Is that clear?"

For a moment there was a shocked, tense silence. Rusty Jessup began swearing furiously, but Judge Hamilton still held him firmly in his grasp. The young blond wrangler was grinning from ear to ear. Suddenly, he gave an earsplitting yell.

"Whoopee!" he crowed, drawing reluctant smiles from the other wranglers. They eyed Bryony with new respect as she waited on the porch for their reaction to her speech. She'd exhibited a toughness today that they hadn't expected from such a young, lovely-looking girl, and they began to think that perhaps she really could make a go of running this ranch after all. She'd have a lot to learn, but she seemed plenty game enough to tackle the job. And the men working for the Circle H were well paid. They weren't eager to look elsewhere for work, not if there was a chance the new owner would keep the ranch prosperous. One by one they began doffing their Stetsons to her, informing her that they would stay on and wait for their money—and the accompanying bonuses. Bryony responded coolly, thanking them, and sending them back to work. As the group broke up she turned to the wrangler as he leaped jubilantly from the porch.

"Just a minute!" she called quickly, and he turned back to her, his warm brown eyes sparkling.

"Yes, ma'am?"

"What's your name, cowboy?"

He swept his dusty Stetson off his head in a comic salute. "Buck Monroe, ma'am, at your service."

"Thank you. I appreciate your efforts to help me a few moments ago, Buck," Bryony smiled, disarmed by the cowboy's earnest friendliness. He was staring at her as if he had never seen a woman before, his eyes glowing with admiration. Unlike Rusty Jessup's lewd appraisal, Buck Monroe's attitude was sweet, and very flattering. She went on swiftly, "I'm going to need a new foreman for the Circle H, and I wonder if you have any suggestions."

"Well, now, ma'am, it just so happens that I'd be perfect for the job," he informed her brashly, swaggering toward her. "And you shore won't find a more loyal man—I was tickled silly when you told off those ungrateful varmints!"

Bryony couldn't suppress a laugh at his infectious smile and comical way of speaking. Buck Monroe had temporarily made her forget the heavy cares of this afternoon. Before she could reply to his offer, though, he went on in a more serious tone.

"Actually, ma'am, if you really want my advice, I wouldn't hire no one for Circle H foreman but one man: Shorty Buchanan. He's got a few years on me, y'know, and he's got the kind of experience the other boys will respect. Shorty's a wily old cowpoke—born and raised in California, rode herd for years up the

Chisholm Trail. He's worked for your pa about three years now, and he's as fine a man as you'll ever see.'' He regarded her solemnly. ''Shorty is shore the best man for the job.''

''Was he here this afternoon?''

''Shorty? Naw, he's out on the south range checking up on a calf that took sick yesterday mornin'. Shorty doesn't have time to sit around and get riled up by the likes of Rusty Jessup!''

At these inflammatory words, the incensed foreman, who still stood on the porch between the Judge and Matthew Richards, began swearing and struggling anew in an attempt to reach Monroe.

''I'd like to meet this Shorty Buchanan,'' Bryony stated. ''Will you ask him to come see me early tomorrow morning?''

''I shore will, ma'am. Glad to help.'' He grinned roguishly. ''And if you change your mind about Shorty, I'm right here in line for the job. Never let it be said that Buck Monroe wouldn't be ready and willing to aid a lady in need!''

Bryony laughed. ''I'll remember that. Thank you.''

Buck carelessly plopped his Stetson on his sandy head, grinned at her, and sauntered cockily off in the direction of the corral, where the black mustang still fretted. She sensed instinctively that Buck was honest and reliable, and would be a valuable friend. She was smiling as she turned away from him, but the smile quickly faded from her lips as Rusty Jessup's cruel, narrow face glared back at her from the porch. The Judge and Matt Richards released him, the Judge advising him to pack his gear and get out, but instead, the ex-foreman advanced threateningly toward Bryony.

She froze, watching his livid face in alarm. Her voice was calm with an effort.

''I have nothing more to say to you, Mr. Jessup. You may leave my property at once.''

''Your property!'' he sneered, his eyes ugly with hatred. ''We'll see how long this ranch remains your property! Unless I miss my guess, lady, you won't last a month. You won't live that long!''

Bryony gasped, and Judge Hamilton quickly grabbed the red-haired cowboy's arm, jerking him about.

"Now see here, Jessup, is that a threat?" the Judge growled.

Jessup glanced from the Judge to Matt Richards's frowning face and back again. He shrugged. "Take it any way you want to," he replied, and wrenched away from Judge Hamilton's grip. He stalked across the porch and down the steps, then turned back for a moment, his thin lips twisted into a malicious smile. His cruel blue eyes held Bryony in a hypnotic gaze as he pointed one lean finger at her in warning.

"All I have to say is that we'll meet again, fancy lady," he promised. "And when we do, I reckon you'll be mighty sorry!" With these words he spun about and marched across the dust toward the bunk house. Bryony and the others waited uneasily until a few moments later, when they saw him emerge from the building and strap his bedroll to his pinto horse. He swung into the saddle and rode off at a hard gallop.

Bryony turned wearily back to the ranch house, her face pale and drawn from the strain of the afternoon. She was followed into her father's study by the Judge and Matt Richards, but to her relief, the Judge soon took his leave, promising to call the next day to drive her into Tucson. She thanked him, and watched him depart, wanting desperately to be alone with her thoughts, but Matt Richards remained, his dark, handsome face watching her concernedly as she dropped tiredly into a brown leather easy chair. Bryony felt too drained to speak. All she could think about was the venom she had seen in Rusty Jessup's eyes. She had made an enemy in the man, a dangerous enemy, and it was not at all a pleasant thought. She was shaken, and exhausted. But she managed a small, wan smile for the man who had been her father's friend.

"Are you all right, Bryony?" Matthew Richards

asked, coming over to stand beside her chair. "I hope you haven't let that coyote upset you too much. Men like Jessup are full of idle threats. But I wouldn't worry about it; he'll probably drink himself out of his rage and forget all about it."

"Do you really think so, Mr. Richards?" Bryony gazed up at him hopefully, comforted by his reassuring words and his strong, solid presence. Matthew Richards, with his powerful, thickset physique and dark good looks, seemed like a man who could take care of himself. She trusted his judgment automatically, and if he thought Jessup was only talking, then almost certainly it must be true.

"I'm sure everything will work out fine," he smiled, and pulled up a chair beside her. "And won't you call me Matt? I sort of hoped we could be good friends, and I hate to stand on ceremony with my friends."

"Of course," Bryony agreed warmly, her heart gladdened. If there was one thing she needed in Winchester, it was friends, and Matt Richards would be a welcome one. The wealthy rancher was kind, handsome, and a powerful figure in the town. She had seen that when he had accompanied her to the gunsmith earlier that morning. Everyone they'd encountered on the street had greeted him with deference, and the gunsmith had treated him with the utmost respect, even more so than he had Judge Hamilton. She was pleased that he had chosen to befriend her, especially since she had refused to sell him the Circle H in the first place, instead coming to claim it for her own. She had been afraid he might be angry about this, but when she mentioned it hesitatingly, he laughed.

"Angry? With you? That's nonsense! Sure I wanted the ranch—it's a valuable property, and would make a fine addition to my own land. And I hardly expected you to want it—I thought you'd be happy to be rid of it and have the cash instead. But I'm sure not mad because you wanted to keep it!" He smiled frankly. "I'll tell you, Bryony, I never expected you to come here like this, to make the Circle H your home. It's the damndest thing I ever saw, but I admire you for it!"

She blushed. "Thank you. I'm glad you understand how much this ranch means to me."

He nodded thoughtfully. "I do. You know, the way you handled those wranglers this afternoon reminded me of your father. He had the same kind of determination you showed today. Building this ranch into one of the largest spreads in Arizona meant more to him than almost anything. Maybe that's why he and I got along so well. You see, I feel the same way about my Twin Bars ranch." His voice trailed off and he seemed lost in contemplation. When he continued, he seemed to be talking almost to himself. "The Twin Bars had only three, maybe four thousand head of cattle when I started it years ago. But I worked hard—damned hard —and now I've got thirty-five thousand head of the finest cattle you've ever laid eyes on. I built that spread into one of the best ranches in the territory, and I'm not finished yet. The Twin Bars will grow even more; it will make me the wealthiest cattleman in the whole west before I'm finished. . ." He stopped abruptly, as if awakened from a dream, and smiled apologetically at her. "I'm sorry. You must be tired and hungry, and here I am going on and on about my own affairs."

"Oh, no, it's fascinating! I'm sure you'll succeed with all your ambitions, though from what I've heard, you've already accomplished more than most men do in a lifetime. The Twin Bars must be a magnificent ranch."

"It is." Matt beamed at her in a pleased way. "I hope you'll come visit me sometime and let me show you around the place."

"I'd love to."

They stood up together as he prepared to leave, but before turning toward the door, Matt paused a moment and stared earnestly into her jade green eyes. He took her small hand in his large, calloused one, holding it tightly. "I must ask you one thing, Bryony," he said soberly. "Don't ride out alone if you can help it. Arizona is not the safest place in the world for a man, let alone a woman. There is not only danger from Indians, but from all kinds of natural hazards— mountain lions, rattlesnakes, Gila monsters. And there are plenty of lowdown hombres who wouldn't hesitate to attack a woman alone—men like those who brought you to Gilly's. So please be careful. And feel free to call on me if you need anything, or if you want me to accompany you anywhere. I'll be happy to oblige any-time."

Touched by his concern, and by the generosity of his offer, Bryony thanked him warmly, and watched almost fondly as he strode out the ranch house door and down the porch steps, vaulting easily into the saddle of the gray gelding. He waved back at her once as he rode off, and she felt a little surge of regret at being left alone. She liked Matt Richards, and she felt safer when he was around. But she realized almost immediately that she must not come to depend on him too much—or on anyone else, for that matter. Now she was in Arizona, and she must learn to depend upon herself.

It was much later that evening when Bryony knelt by the window of her bedroom, staring out at the darkened valley. A chill breeze from the distant, shadowy mountains ruffled the blue silk curtains, and caused her to shiver involuntarily as she pulled her ice-blue dressing robe closer about her body. But she stayed by the window, heedless of the comfortable brass bed waiting to receive her weary form, and of the pleasant prettiness of her room, which she had scarcely noticed. She was troubled by thoughts and feelings for which she had no explanation, and her mood grew ever more lonely and depressed as she gazed out at the dark, threatening wilderness beyond her window.

Hours earlier, she had devoured a dinner of thick, juicy steak and chili beans, served by a silent Rosita, and then she had wandered aimlessly about the ranch house, exploring the rooms, trying to gain some impression of her father by examining her surroundings. She hadn't succeeded in learning much, other than that he had excellent, expensive taste in furnishings. There were three bedrooms upstairs: his own, a massive chamber decorated in dark woods, with a handsome mahogany bedframe, a thick tan carpet, and bronze lamps, and two other bedrooms that were apparently available for guests. The one Bryony had chosen to make into her own quarters was a spacious room with a gleaming parquet floor adorned by an Aubusson carpet, a blue silk quilt upon the plump bed with its brass frame, and pretty fruitwood furniture, including a wide chest of drawers, a night stand beside the bed, a dressing table, and the hand-carved rocking chair in the corner by the window. In the opposite corner was an attractive Oriental screen behind which was a porcelain hip bath. It was a very comfortable room, and a very lovely house, but Bryony was less interested in the physical trappings of her surroundings than in the gloomy mood that had descended upon her as the sun had disappeared in a bloody red fire over the western mountains. She had no explanation for this sense of desolate foreboding; she only knew that it was as thick as a heavy mist, and just as intangible.

Outside her window, dark, scudding clouds rolled ponderously through the inky, moonless sky, seeming to weave a murky pattern of their own mysterious design. They obscured the stars that had brightened the desert the previous night, and only the dim, jagged shapes of the distant mountains were discernible in the resultant blackness, like eerie shadows on the horizon. She shivered again as the wind whipped sadistically at her loose cloud of coal-black hair, sweeping it away from her small, lovely face. Her eyes searched the darkened wilderness for some clue as to the source of her newfound sense of foreboding, but found none.

Her thoughts shifted gradually to the people she had encountered that day, and the events that had taken place. She pictured Judge Hamilton, with his weathered, friendly face and reliable good sense, and then thought of Matt Richards: suave, handsome, kindhearted. The memory of lanky Buck Monroe made her smile, but when Rusty Jessup's cruel, narrow face swam into her mind's eye, a cold finger of fear brushed her spine. She didn't understand why he had tried to lead the wranglers in a revolt against her, or why he had behaved so rudely, forcing her to fire him as foreman, and she understood even less why he had threatened her, warning that she might not live out another month. It seemed to her that ever since she had arrived in Arizona, events had taken place that seemed designed to frighten her, to force her to abandon her intention of settling in the region. First her abduction by Zeke Murdock and the highwaymen; then the problems at the ranch, with the house having been ransacked, the study safe blown open and robbed, the payroll money missing. And finally, Rusty Jessup trying to turn the range hands against her. It almost seemed as if there was a conspiracy to frighten her away, to make her throw up her hands and turn her back on her inheritance, to send her flying back to St. Louis and Miss Marsh's School for Young Ladies. But that idea was preposterous. Why should anyone want to drive her away?

Suddenly, the melancholy cry of a faraway coyote shattered the ominous silence of the night, and she remembered Texas Jim Logan. Bryony knew that she would always think of him when she heard that sound, that she would always remember the way he had held her in his arms and kissed her beneath the desert stars. . . .

Abruptly, with a curse that would have shocked Miss Marsh, she drove this unwanted memory from her mind. Her emerald eyes narrowed in the darkness, and her heart swelled with hatred. That murderous gunslinger! He was a cold, vicious, despicable man! She hated him with all her heart!

It was then that she realized that she had forgotten to

ısk Judge Hamilton why her father had quarreled with the legendary Texas Jim Logan, and she determined that on the morrow she would learn the answer. And she would have Rosita burn that disgusting saddle blanket he had given her.

As she hurried across the cold wooden floor to her bed, discarding the dressing robe and snuggling between the sheets in nothing but her pale blue satin nightgown, her black mass of hair spread upon the pillow, she couldn't help but envision the tall gunfighter's lean, bronzed face, with those cold light blue eyes and his thin, cynical mouth. He loomed before her mockingly, his lips twisting into an arrogant smile, his eyes light and steely as they pierced her consciousness. She shut her own eyes tightly to block out this disturbing vision, aware that her heart was racing strangely. She chewed her lip, staring tensely at the ceiling, ignoring the gloomy sense of desolation that had troubled her all evening, and which still hung over the silent ranch-house. Fervently, she wished that she would never have to lay her eyes on Texas Jim Logan again. Never!

Little did she know how quickly her wish would be denied.

Chapter Eleven

Bryony's interview with Shorty Buchanan the next morning was both brief and productive. She took an immediate liking to the blunt, grizzled little man whose legs were permanently bow-kneed from so many years in the saddle, and whose small beady eyes took her measure unwaveringly. Shorty Buchanan was gravel-voiced, wiry, and cantankerous, and at first he had been openly skeptical of his new boss's ability to run the ranch, but after a few moments alone with Bryony in the study, he became convinced that she was no ordinary city girl, and that she meant what she said when she told him that she was going to devote herself to maintaining the Circle H as one of the finest ranches in the territory. In a very short time she had won him over completely. They parted in mutual satisfaction; the wrangler pleased with his new mistress's firm determination, and Bryony relieved that she had an experienced foreman to guide her. She was also glad that Shorty had agreed to teach her to shoot, and they scheduled her first lesson for the next afternoon.

Later that same day, she drove to Tucson with Judge Hamilton, withdrawing the payroll funds from the bank without incident, and staying in Tucson—a wild, noisy town filled with drunken cowboys and stern-faced gamblers—only long enough to purchase several bolts of cloth from the general store so that she might sew some of the pretty Mexican skirts and blouses that had taken her fancy. That particular style of clothing seemed lightweight and ideal for the hot, dry climate, and she was eager to feel more a part of this Spanish-influenced region. With her errands accomplished and the noon sun glaring mercilessly overhead, Judge Hamilton turned his buggy back toward Winchester, while Bryony straightened the skirt of her peach-colored muslin gown and tucked a few stray ebony curls inside her ribbon-trimmed bonnet, wincing every time the buggy hit a particularly deep rut in the road and sent her bouncing up in her seat.

It was just outside of Winchester that she asked Judge Hamilton the question that had disturbed her for so long, but his answer, instead of relieving her mind, only puzzled her more. He seemed very evasive about the reason Jim Logan had shot her father, and when Bryony pressed him for an explanation, the Judge pursed his lips together and looked uncomfortable.

"Don't fret yourself about the past, Miss Hill," he admonished her at last, his eyes fixed rigidly on the sweating team of horses. "What's done is done. Unfortunately, nothing can bring your father back to this earth. So why don't you just forget about what happened and concentrate on the future."

"Call me, Bryony, Judge—please," she replied quickly, her eyes scanning his craggy face. "And please tell me the truth. I want to know why Jim Logan quarreled with my father."

"I don't rightly know!" the Judge answered, rather too loudly. "I wasn't there when it happened, and all I heard was a lot of gossip—I reckon you know how unreliable gossip is!"

"Tell me anyway," Bryony persisted. "What did people say?"

The Judge hesitated. When he spoke again, he seemed to be picking his words very carefully. "Well, supposedly, there was a woman involved. There were plenty of rumors—none of them proved, mind you—about a girl named Daisy being the cause of the fight.''

"A woman! Well, where is she? Perhaps if I spoke with this Daisy myself, she might explain to me—"

"She can't explain anything, Bryony. Daisy Winston is dead.''

Bryony absorbed the shock of this news, and felt more confused than ever. "When did she die?" she queried, shaken. "H—how?"

"She was murdered. Beaten to death. The night before your father shot it out with Logan. Now that's all I know, Bryony, and that's all I'm going to say. If you follow my advice, girl, you'll forget all about this business of digging up the past and put it completely out of your mind.''

Bryony never had a chance to respond. The peaceful silence of the sloping trail was broken abruptly by the rumbling of horses' hooves as a wagon rolled suddenly into view from around a bend. The Judge pulled his team quickly aside to avoid a collision. Both vehicles drew up, and Judge Hamilton doffed his hat to the man and young girl sitting in the wagon.

"Afternoon, Sam. Miss Annie. Let me introduce you to Bryony Hill—Wes's daughter.''

Still digesting the information she had just learned, Bryony smiled automatically as the Judge presented Sam Blake and his daughter Ann, the owners of a small cattle ranch just east of Circle H land. To her astonishment, the pair in the wagon returned her polite greeting with blatantly hostile expressions. Samuel Blake, tall and gaunt, with graying hair and mustache, and worn, old work clothing on his spare frame, stared right through her with frosty gray eyes, while his daughter, a girl of about seventeen, seemed openly antagonistic, her features set in an angry, contemptuous expression. Annie Blake might have been a very pretty girl, Bryony

observed, with her thick chestnut hair and large hazel
eyes, but her appearance was rough and untidy, her hair
knotted carelessly at the nape of her neck, with long
tangled strands escaping haphazardly to swirl about her
face, her eyes almost hidden by the floppy old sombrero
on her head. Whatever feminine figure she might have
possessed was disguised by the loose, tomboyish jeans
and flannel shirt she wore, giving her body a bulky,
shapeless appearance. But Bryony felt certain that an
attractive young woman lurked somewhere inside the
angry tomboy opposite her. She couldn't understand
why the Blakes treated her so coldly, responding in an
almost surly tone when she spoke to them, and ignoring her the rest of the time as they immersed themselves
in conversation with the Judge. Puzzled, she made a
further attempt at cordiality as the two groups prepared
to part.

"Please, Mr. Blake," she said, giving him her nicest
smile, "I'd be very pleased if you and Annie would
come to call on me sometime soon. We're neighbors,
after all. Can I look forward to it?"

He received this invitation with stony silence, but
Annie Blake shot her a withering look. "Hah!" the girl
snorted. "Don't hold your breath none!"

"Well, now, we'd best be getting on our way," Judge
Hamilton put in quickly, gathering up the horses' reins.
"Nice seeing you folks. Adios."

Bryony turned to Judge Hamilton in complete
bewilderment as the buggy rolled on toward home.

"What's the matter with *them*?" she cried. "They
behaved as if I was their worst enemy! And I've never
even met them!"

"Don't judge the Blakes too harshly, Bryony," he
answered, speeding the horses to a fast trot as the trail
suddenly opened onto smooth, level ground. Miles of
golden poppies fluttered in the afternoon breeze as they
thundered along the open prairie. Overhead, the orange

sun was slowly shifting into the western sky. "They're decent enough folk, when you get to know them. Sam's a widower, like me, and he's raising his daughter as best he can. He lost his son not long ago. They've been having a pretty rough time of it lately. Rustlers have been stealing their cattle, and they don't look too kindly on strangers. Also," he added, glancing at her hesitatingly, "they're one of the few people in these parts who weren't on the best of terms with your pa, so you can't expect them to welcome you with open arms."

"Oh. I see," Bryony said, but in truth, she did not. Her father's life in Arizona was becoming more of an enigma to her every day. She had no idea who Daisy Winston was, or how she was involved in her father's gunfight with Jim Logan, nor did she understand why Sam and Annie Blake had disliked her father. She sighed in exasperation. Instead of answers, she kept coming up with more and more questions, but she sensed that she had put Judge Hamilton in an awkward position, and decided to refrain from questioning him further. Perhaps Matt Richards could enlighten her. She would ask him about these matters when the right moment arose.

The days began to pass quickly. Bryony became immersed in payroll and bookkeeping activities, in supply lists and household chores. She had her first shooting lesson with Shorty Buchanan, who instructed her in the mechanics of loading and firing her derringer, advising her to keep it on her person at all times. By the evening of her third day on the ranch, Bryony felt exhausted. Never had she been so busy, so pressed for time in which to complete her responsibilities. She hadn't even had an opportunity to write to any of her friends yet, informing them that she was safely installed as mistress of the Circle H. She decided that the very next day she would take care of all her correspondence.

It was midafternoon of her fourth day in Winchester

when she finally finished her letter-writing, having written to Dr. Brady and the Scotts, and Mr. Parker and Miss Marsh, assuring them all that she was well and happy. She considered writing to Roger Davenport, then decided against it. She had severed all ties with Roger when she had refused to marry him, and it seemed best not to renew their relationship in any way. Besides, she reflected wryly, no doubt Roger had already found himself another fiancée, one more suitable to his oh-so-proper taste. The thought did not trouble her in the least; life in Arizona was too rich to waste time regretting lost opportunities. She knew that if she had it all to do again, she would reject Roger's proposal just as firmly as she had the first time.

Having completed her letters, she rose and peered out the study window, wondering if Buck Monroe was nearby. She knew that he was planning to ride into town for supplies later that day, and she wanted to give him her letters for the mail. But Buck was nowhere in sight. In fact, the ranch was rather deserted, with Shorty and most of the other wranglers having ridden out to the northern range to check on the herd, while Rosita was busy in the kitchen, baking a tortilla pie. The day was peaceful, still and clear, with the scent of pine in the air, and Bryony decided to look for Buck in the stable, where he'd been spending a lot of time on that wild mustang he'd been trying to break. Holding the skirt of her pale yellow cotton gown in her hand to keep it from dragging in the dust, she left the house and crossed the ranch-house grounds toward the barn and stable. She heard the dull pounding of a horse's hooves and, staring into the distance, she saw a rider approaching swiftly.

She paused, one hand shading her eyes as she watched the rider approach, wondering who this visitor could be. She waited curiously as he drew nearer, but had little time to discern his identity, for the horse made no effort to slow down as he drew closer and closer, and alarm showed in Bryony's lovely features as steed and rider swept almost upon her in a thunderous roar. She screamed in panic as the beast bore down upon her, but suddenly, only inches from the terrified girl in his path, the rider pulled the horse to a screeching halt. As the dust settled around them, the lean, bronzed man in the saddle calmly regarded the black-haired girl before him.

"Y—you!" She gasped disbelievingly as Texas Jim Logan swept off his sombrero in a mocking salute. She stared wide-eyed at his tall, powerful frame outlined against the diamond-blue sky, hardly able to believe the man's audacity in coming here. Her breath came in short, ragged gasps as fury mounted inside her. "What are you doing here?" she demanded. "And just what are you trying to do—run me into the ground? Wasn't it enough that you killed my father, *Mister* Logan, without adding me to your list of victims?"

A cold smile touched Logan's lips. "Now don't be melodramatic, ma'am. I knew damn well Pecos wouldn't stampede you. I wouldn't let him. There was nothing for you to be concerned about."

"Get off my land!" Bryony ordered through clenched teeth, the blood rushing furiously to her face as the gunfighter baited her. "I want you off of my property this instant—and don't you ever dare show your face here again, you . . . you murderer!"

His only response to her command was to swing unconcernedly from the saddle. He led Pecos to a corral post and tethered him there. Bryony watched wildly, infuriated almost to speechlessness by his cool contempt of her demands. She glanced quickly about for some sign of Buck or one of the other range hands who could bodily remove Texas Jim Logan from her land, but there was no one about. They were alone except for some horses whinnying in the corral.

Suddenly, she remembered the derringer in the pocket of her cotton dress, and she hurriedly reached for the weapon. But even as she raised it, a hand clamped brutally over her wrist, and Logan's steel-blue eyes glinted into her frightened green ones. He wrenched the weapon from her with a violence that hurt her wrist, but though he held the weapon securely in one hand, his other did not leave her arm. Instead, it tightened cruelly about her tender flesh, holding her with an iron strength.

"I want to talk to you, Miss Hill. And there's no way you're going to stop me."

She paled. The ruthless expression on his handsome, tanned face was terrifying. He was hurting her arm dreadfully, and she had to fight back tears. Before she could protest or resist, he began dragging her firmly toward the barn, his hand on her arm propelling her along helplessly. He thrust her roughly into the dusky interior of the hay-filled building, bolting the barn door behind them so that no one could enter from outside. The only light filtered in from a high window against the far wall, and the atmosphere was close and dark, pungently scented with hay.

"What . . . what do you want with me?" she gasped, the terror building inside her. "Let me out of here before I scream and bring a dozen range hands running to my aid. They'll probably shoot you down without asking any questions!" But her voice quivered, belying the confidence of her words.

Logan laughed mockingly. "Scream away, ma'am. I doubt if any of your wranglers will hear you down on the north range."

"How . . . how did you know. . ."

He shrugged coolly. "I checked, of course. You see, I've been waiting for the right moment to talk to you—alone."

Bryony tried desperately to still her pounding heart. "What do you want?" she cried.

Contemptuously, Logan tossed her little derringer into the hayloft above. He hooked his thumbs in his gunbelt, lazily studying her. "Well, ma'am, I reckon the first thing I want is my saddle blanket," he drawled slowly. "I lent it to you a few nights back so you could cover up your nakedness, if you remember, but now I've come to claim it. Where is it?"

Bryony swallowed. Her emotions had been changing rapidly from fury to fear, and being alone in the locked barn with this tall, steel-eyed gunfighter was quickly increasing her alarm. She had no protection against the anger she feared would come when she told him what had become of his saddle blanket, yet she had no choice. It was impossible to run away and escape him, escape his wrath. And he was waiting for her reply.

"I burned it," she said at last, wiping her clammy hands nervously upon her yellow cotton skirt. There was a trace of defiance in her tone. "Or rather, I ordered Rosita to do it. It's gone."

The gunfighter smiled unpleasantly. "That was my property you destroyed, Miss Hill. And I don't take kindly to having my property stolen or destroyed." There was a cold gleam in his eyes that she didn't like at all. "You'll have to settle with me, little tenderfoot. I figure you owe me something to compensate for the loss."

He moved menacingly toward her, but Bryony reacted swiftly, spurred by her terror. She whirled to run away from him across the darkened barn. A sob rose in her throat as she heard his quick pursuit, and snatching up her skirts, she clambered onto the rickety ladder leading up to the loft. Logan was right behind her, but her fear gave her unexpected speed and she reached the top alone, breathing hard and sobbing frantically. Where was the gun? It was her only hope against her attacker. She hunted desperately for the derringer in the soft mounds of hay, but just as she spotted it, she was grabbed from behind and pushed roughly down into the hay, her struggles to free herself useless as Texas Jim Logan straddled her, pinning her writhing body to the ground. Bryony screamed, fighting him with all of her strength, her head tossing desperately from side to side, sending her long black curls flying about her tear-streaked face. All her efforts were futile, though, for the gunfighter held her helpless beneath him, his iron-muscled body pressing her relentlessly into the hay as his strong hands gripped her wrists in an unbreakable hold.

"Shut up and lie still!" he ordered, his eyes cold and angry. But it was several moments before Bryony finally gave up in total exhaustion, her chest heaving, her hair clinging damply to her face. She raised her jade green eyes to stare fearfully at the lean, bronzed man who held her prisoner with his body. There was an expression of ruthlessness in his eyes that made her moan in helpless terror. Then he leaned closer, his face directly above hers, his cold blue eyes shining into her fevered face with a desire that demanded quenching. Even as Bryony groaned a protest his lips found hers and crushed them, brutally exploring the softness of her mouth. He kissed her with such ferocity that Bryony whimpered with pain, yet at the same time a tide of pleasure washed over her, drowning her resistance. His hands released her wrists, moving hungrily to her breasts, the strong fingers caressing the soft white mounds beneath the thinness of her cotton gown. Her nipples hardened and grew erect beneath his expertly massaging hands, and Bryony gave herself up to the sensations of sweet, ago-nizing ecstasy that overwhelmed her. The pressure of his body against hers was almost painfully exciting, and his rough, devouring kisses left her breathless, robbed of all power to think or speak, capable only of reacting with the same animal passion that drove him. She entwined her arms about him, pulling him closer, closer, her lips parting to welcome his mouth as she ardently returned his kiss, lost in a magical world of torment and pleasure, aching with a desire she had never experienced before and didn't understand, consumed by a delight she had never dreamed possible. She moaned softly as he nib-bled at her earlobe, his lips scorching her flesh as they traveled down her slender white throat to the throbbing pulse that jumped when he touched it with his mouth.

"Bryony, Bryony, you're so damn beautiful," he whispered huskily, his fingers tearing at her gown and chemise, baring her breasts to his caressing hands and lips. Then, driven by a need that had been building torturously inside him, he began pulling at her skirt, hiking it up above her hips. His hands reached up toward her thighs, but at the first touch of this virgin spot, Bryony gasped in instinctive terror, the spell that had bound her breaking abruptly as she realized what was about to happen.

"No!" she cried wildly, cringing from his probing hands. "You mustn't . . . we mustn't . . . oh, no . . . let me go!"

But Logan continued to kiss her fiercely, his hands deliberately exploring the secret part that no man had ever touched. He began unfastening his trousers, easing his body over hers so that the pressure of his powerful male hardness pushed against the warm, moist flesh of her virgin body.

Terror superseded all her desire. Bryony screamed, hysterical in her desperation. "No! Stop! What kind of a man are you? How can you do this to me?" Her fists beat futilely against his broad, muscular chest. Her voice rose to a panic-stricken, agonized wail that at last seemed to penetrate the gunfighter's urgent determination. He froze, flushed with desire, a muscle throbbing in his jaw and his eyes alive with a glowing passion that urged him to go on, to ignore her protests and teach her what a man and woman were made for. But he did not. He pushed her away violently and stood up, fastening his trousers with shaking fingers, while Bryony lay back on the hay and sobbed, shame and misery rising up to engulf her as she realized in horror what she had allowed to happen—what had almost happened. She was no better than a harlot to melt in the arms of the man who had killed her father, this vile, wicked, murderous stranger who cared no more for her than for a flower he would uncaringly crush beneath his boot! Her hysteria mounted as she recalled the shameless way she had responded to him, the mad craving she had allowed to run wild.

Texas Jim Logan watched her in silence, breathing heavily. His lean face struggled to find the mask of careless composure he always wore, while his heart gradually slowed to a normal pace after his heady encounter with this intoxicating, raven-haired beauty.

He wanted her, wanted her with a fierceness that bordered on madness, but he was still sane enough to realize that taking her by force was something he could never do. She was so young, so fragile, so innocent. She should not be initiated into womanhood with a scream of terror in her throat. No, he wanted her warm and willing, and wild with the same driving need he felt for her. But he knew damn well how unlikely *that* was, for she hated him with a loathing that could never be overborne, and for which, he reflected bitterly, he could not really blame her. After what he had done, he knew well enough that there was little chance this lovely, spirited girl would ever turn to him with anything but hatred in her heart.

"Go away!" Bryony cried, her slender body racking with sobs. "Leave me in peace . . . alone."

"With pleasure, ma'am," Logan said harshly, his frustration and bitterness hidden now, his face once again controlled and impassive, except for the glint of anger in those steely eyes. "But first I'm going to talk to you, for that's what I came to do."

She raised her head, her green eyes swollen with tears, but still flashing fire. "What can you possibly have to say to me that I would want to hear? Don't you know that I despise the very sight of you?"

"It didn't seem so a few moments ago, ma'am."

"Oh! How dare you!" she raged, her fists clenching as she stared up at his tall, broad-shouldered form. He looked huge and intimidating, standing over her like that, his booted feet planted apart, the muscles in his arms bulging powerfully. He was frowning, and his eyes were hard.

"Just go away!" she begged.

"That's odd. Those are the very words I came here to say," he drawled. "Go away. That's what you'll do, Bryony, if you have an ounce of sense in that beautiful head."

Shocked into speechlessness, she merely stared at him for a long moment. "Why should I?" she demanded at last, anger sparking once again in her breast.

"Because you won't live long if you don't."

Almost the very words Rusty Jessup had spoken to her! A cold shiver of fear brushed the hair at the nape of her neck. "Is . . . is that a threat, Mr. Logan?" she asked, sitting up and pushing her tangled hair out of her face. "Are you planning to murder me as you did my father?"

"Don't tempt me!" he grated, his eyes narrowing. "Though for your information, I didn't murder your father—he died in a fair gunfight, and if I had it all to do again, I'd shoot him still, only this time I'd riddle his body with bullets, instead of only drilling him with one."

She gasped, stunned by his cruel, arrogant words, sickened as if he had struck her a blow to the stomach with one of those powerful fists. A sudden fury swept through her, crazing her, and she leaped, screeching, to her feet, falling upon him with raking fingernails, kicking and biting viciously as he attempted to hold her off. She bit his hand as it closed over her arm, and her nails dug a scratch across his cheek, but then he gained control of her, holding her struggling, slender body tightly against his muscle-hardened one.

"Stop fighting me and listen, you idiotic little bitch!" he commanded, shaking her as he had that first day in Gilly's. "I didn't come here to threaten you. I came to warn you. Your life isn't worth a wooden peso if you stay in Arizona. Now don't look at me that way—I'm not the one who's going to harm you, though believe me, I'd like to wring your pretty neck." He laughed mirthlessly. "Someone else is planning your demise, little tenderfoot, and I reckon I know why. But that's none of your concern at the moment. All you have to do is get the hell out!"

"You're mad!" she spat, her green eyes narrowed furiously. "You come here with a lot of vague warnings and predictions, refusing to tell me the basis for your suspicions, and expecting me to trust and believe you—*you*, of all the people on this earth! You must think me a complete fool, and I promise you, Mr. Logan, that I am not!"

"Prove it," he ordered coolly. "Leave Arizona today—before it's too late."

"Never!" Bryony's voice quivered with anger.

He shoved her roughly away, down into the soft mound of hay. "Damn you!" he muttered savagely. "And damn Wesley Hill!"

With those words, he grabbed up his fallen hat and spun about to descend from the loft, stepping down the ladder with the lithe, graceful movements of a cat. Bryony had landed face down in the pile of hay, and as she struggled to sit upright, her hand came across something hard and cold only inches from her head. The gun. The derringer she had searched so hard to find only a short while ago. She watched Texas Jim Logan stalk swiftly across the barn toward the bolted door. She scrambled quickly to her feet, her breath coming hard, a terrible thudding in her heart. Her temples ached with a cruel, blinding pressure. Without stopping to think, she raised the gun, her finger on the trigger.

Chapter Twelve

It must have been some sixth sense of danger that made Jim Logan glance back at the girl in the loft. He saw her raise the gun and aim it at him; he had only an instant to react. Leaping into a half-crouch, his hand flew to his hip and drew out the Colt. He fired in the same instant. His face had turned a ghastly white.

The bullet struck Bryony's derringer with a shattering impact, sending the reverberations through her hand and wrist in shock waves of pain. Her lips parted, but no sound emerged as she dropped her weapon and sank dazedly to her knees, her face contorted with pain, her hand dangling limply before her.

In three huge strides, Logan had crossed the barn and swung himself up into the loft to kneel beside her, a string of epithets streaming from his lips. If Bryony had been in a fit state to observe him, she would have seen the fear in his eyes as he bent over her, a fear which no man had ever been able to kindle, but which threatened to overwhelm him as he realized that for the first time in his life he had shot at a woman, that he could have killed her if his aim had not been faultless.

"You damn little fool!" he cried hoarsely, examining her hand. "I might have killed you! A fate you deserve as sure as hell, but I'll be damned if I'm the one who's going to be responsible for it!"

160

Bryony barely heard his furious chastisements, or noticed his distraught concern. Her hand had gone numb, but there was a dreadful ache in her wrist and she felt waves of blackness rushing over her intermittently, blotting out sight and sound. Seeing her stunned, half-fainting state, and observing with relief that there was no real physical damage to her hand, only the aftermath of pain and shock, he carried her to the edge of the rickety ladder and helped her descend it, supporting her swaying body. When they finally reached the bottom rung, he swept her into his arms and bore her quickly out of the darkened barn and to the ranch house, glad that none of the wranglers had returned yet to impede him. He kicked open the ranch house door, carrying Bryony through the hallway, and there halted momentarily as the stolid brown form of Rosita blocked his path. The Mexican woman's dark eyes widened at the sight of her mistress's limp form in the arms of the tall gunfighter she recognized immediately. Her usually stoic expression changed to one of astonishment, but Logan was not in the mood to explain.

"Where is your mistress's room?" he demanded brusquely, in a tone that invited no questions.

"*Arriba.*" She pointed up the staircase and then followed hurriedly as Logan climbed the stairs swiftly. Rosita showed him where Bryony's room was located and he brought her there, lowering her with unexpected gentleness onto the brass bed. As quickly as he could, he explained how Bryony had been hurt. If Rosita was shocked by the tale, she showed no evidence of it; after that first moment of amazement her usual complacence had returned, and she merely listened silently until Logan had finished.

"*Un momento*," she murmured then, and left the room.

He paced anxiously about the bedchamber, glancing worriedly at Bryony, who had closed her eyes and was moaning softly. Her small, lovely face was very white,

framed by the dark mass of long black hair that fell
about it in soft, thick curls. She looked unbelievably
beautiful and fragile as she lay unmoving upon the bed,
and Logan's features darkened into a bitter scowl as he
observed her. A moment later Rosita returned with cold
cloths with which she bathed Bryony's face and the
injured hand, swathing her wrist in the cool wrappings
and placing it on pillows. Bryony seemed to be relieved
by these ministrations, and her eyelashes fluttered open.

"Oh, Rosita," she whispered gratefully, but then her
gaze fell on Texas Jim Logan, who was standing over
her bed. Fear darted into her green eyes. "You!" she
cried in alarm.

"At your service, ma'am," he drawled grimly, his
face set like a granite mask.

"You tried to kill me!" she whispered as the full
memory of what had happened came rushing back to
her.

"On the contrary, Miss Hill. If I had been trying to
kill you, you'd be dead this very moment. I only wanted
to deflect your shot, for you see, *you* were trying to kill
me."

"Go away!" she muttered tiredly, suddenly too
exhausted to continue the argument. Her weariness
overcame her and she no longer had the strength to deal
with this tall, powerful man who seemed to delight in
tormenting her. "Go away," she repeated in a weak
whisper that was barely audible.

"I'm going," he promised coldly, "but remember
one thing. The next time you take up a gun against me,
be prepared to die on the instant, for woman or no
woman, I won't spare you a second time."

With these words, he turned on his heel and strode
from the room, his boots thumping as he went down the
stairs and out of the ranch house. Seconds later, the two
women heard a horse's hooves thundering away from
the ranch.

"Are you all right, Señorita Hill?"

Bryony glanced wearily at the plump, pretty Mexican woman. She had been surprised that Rosita had been the one to care for her injury. But then who else was there? A wan smile curved her lips.

"Yes, Rosita, I'm fine now. My wrist aches a bit but it's much better than it was. *Gracias, muchas gracias.*"

The housekeeper shrugged. "*De nada.*" But some of the aloofness she had shown toward Bryony in previous days was gone, and she seemed to be looking at the girl with quiet compassion.

"Rosita," Bryony began, encouraged by the woman's softened attitude, "I must ask you a favor. *Por favor.*" She paused, blushing scarlet as she realized that her gown was torn away, as well as her chemise; Rosita must have guessed something of what had gone on in the locked barn. Mercifully, the housekeeper wasn't the type of person to ask questions, but Bryony had no desire to have the whole ranch talking of her encounter with Jim Logan.

"Please," she pleaded, meeting Rosita's solemn gaze. "Please don't tell anyone what happened this afternoon. About my injury or . . . or anything. I'd like to forget the whole episode, and I don't think I could bear a lot of questions or gossip." Her eyes clouded with unshed tears. "Will you do this for me, Rosita? Will you not mention it to a soul?"

"Si, Señorita, I will keep silence," the woman answered simply. "Do not worry yourself about this. Try to rest." For the first time since Bryony had met her, Rosita smiled. It transformed her face. "I will go to the kitchen now and cook for you *una deliciosa cena*. It will make you strong." She departed noiselessly, her heavy bulk disappearing through the doorway.

Bryony lay back against the fluff of pillows, thoroughly shaken by the tumultuous events of the afternoon. She tried to think only of the supper Rosita was preparing for her, but her mind kept returning to her violent encounter with Jim Logan, and to the question that was dominating her thoughts. Would she have pulled the trigger on the derringer? If he had not prevented her, would she have killed Texas Jim Logan?

She covered her face with her hands, knowing the answer. If any man deserved death, she firmly believed that he did. After all, had he not killed her father? Had he not molested her in the locked barn? Surely he deserved to die!

Yet she would not have killed him, could not have. It was the plain, simple truth and it set upon her heart like a cold gravestone. She felt sick and clammy and dreadfully frightened.

It wasn't fear for her life, however. It was a fear of Texas Jim Logan himself, a fear that went beyond his size and his strength, and his prowess with a gun. It was a fear of his power over her, for she could not deny that when he touched her or kissed her or stroked her, she melted like candle wax, losing all her resolve and her common sense, and becoming soft and pliable in his strong hands. This terrified her more than any threat or warnings, for no man had ever wielded such power over her before in her young life and she did not understand its source or its meaning. She only knew that she ought to hate him more than anyone in the entire world, and instead, she felt. . . .

She didn't know what she felt. Filled with shame, panic-stricken by her own confused, tempestuous feelings, Bryony buried her face in the softness of her pillow. As the April afternoon waned, the wranglers returned to the ranch, their rowdy voices filling the warm desert air outside her bedroom window. But Bryony didn't even hear them. She was caught up in her own world of confusion and doubt.

And she could not ignore the warning Jim Logan had issued—the warning that her life was in danger if she remained in Arizona. Was he speaking the truth? Even so, how could he expect her to believe him? Yet, his warning somehow coincided with her own instinct that someone was trying to frighten her away. She didn't want to panic, to run away like a frightened child. She wanted to stay and make her home on the land that was rightfully hers. For the time being, she decided to wait and see. She would be alert; she would be careful. If anything happened to give credence to Logan's suspicions, then she would decide what to do.

A sense of uneasiness settled over her, and would not go away. Even when Rosita brought her supper on a tray, and turned up the oil lamp as the dusk deepened outside her window, the uneasy feeling persisted. And when late that night the coyotes called to each other from the hilltops, their melancholy wails piercing the night, she felt a chill deep in her heart, and her sleep that evening was filled with nightmares.

Chapter Thirteen

The following day Bryony wanted to ride to town with Buck Monroe. She came out of the ranch house with her letters in hand, dressed for riding. She was determined to shake off the misery of yesterday, and the way in which she meant to do this was by occupying herself with pleasant diversions. First, she intended to select a horse for her personal use. She hadn't had an opportunity to ride since she'd arrived at the ranch, but she intended to change that at once, and she had already decided which mount to make her own.

It was a beautiful spring day, with a cool breeze sweeping down from the mountains. The sky, the sun, the mountains, the valley—everything was radiant with color, bright, majestic, wild. She spotted Buck and some other hands in the far corral and started toward them. To her surprise, they stared at her in wide-mouthed amazement as she approached. She flushed, made acutely uncomfortable by their scrutiny.

"Wal, I'll be a dog-eared Gila monster!" Buck exclaimed, his jaw dropping.

"What are you talking about? What's the matter?" Bryony demanded, gazing from one to the other of the men's astonished faces. "For heaven's sake, haven't you ever seen a riding habit before?"

Grinning, Buck shook his head, studying the slim,

elegant figure she presented in her dark blue velvet outfit, with her glistening black kid boots up to her knees, and her riding crop in gloved hand. Atop her head, contrasting markedly with the cowboys' wide-brimmed Stetsons, she wore a smart little derby cap of blue velvet to match her habit. To Buck and the others, she looked as foreign as a dainty English tea cake set amidst their steak and beans, and they couldn't help gaping at her. But Bryony felt dismay surging through her, along with a trace of resentment.

"Well?" she asked Buck, fire kindling in her eyes. "What is it? I'll have you know, Buck Monroe, that this is my very nicest habit. I always wore it when riding in the park on Sundays, and if it was good enough for St. Louis society, I believe it's good enough for you!"

Buck burst into a loud guffaw, then fought to control his amusement as he saw the hurt look in her vivid jade green eyes.

"I'm sorry, Bryony. Uh, Miss Hill. You look fine—mighty fine. I swear it. It's not that at all."

"Then what?"

"Well, ma'am," his brown eyes gazed at her earnestly, "that's a real pretty outfit and all—real pretty. But it doesn't seem too practical for Arizona. For one thing, it's too heavy for desert heat; you'll be hotter'n Rosita's chili in no time. And for another, well, hell, ma'am, it just looks so danged dandyish. Citified, if you know what I mean."

"Oh. Yes, I believe I do. How stupid of me," Bryony replied slowly, her expression crestfallen. Of course. Riding in Arizona was not at all like riding in the park in St. Louis. Even she should have realized that immediately. Her English riding habit must look ridiculously out of place in this rugged, untamed region. If she wanted to fit in here, she must make more of an effort to become westernized. She remembered the baggy, shapeless clothes Annie Blake had been wearing that day in the wagon, and shuddered inwardly. Well, she

would not have to dress quite like that. She would have
to find a style of dress that would not make her look like
a lumpy sack of potatoes. Though Bryony was not vain,
she took pride in her appearance, and derived pleasure
and confidence from being well-groomed. She would
have to change her wardrobe accordingly as soon as
possible, but decided that for today, her velvet riding
habit would have to do. She refused to give up her pro-
posed ride to town merely because she didn't yet have
proper attire.

"Until I get some other riding clothes, this will just
have to do," she told Buck firmly. "With your permission of course, Mr. Monroe."

This jibe drew a burst of laughter from the other
wranglers, and made Buck blush. He grinned good-
naturedly, a light sparking in his warm brown eyes.

"You're the boss, ma'am," he acknowledged ami-
ably. "I was just trying to give you some friendly
advice." There was no mistaking the admiration in his
eyes when he smiled down at her. Buck seemed to
delight in these playful conversations, and she had
already observed the way his face lit up whenever she
appeared. Now there was a certain wistfulness in his
expression as he gazed at the stunning picture she
presented, her raven-black hair pinned atop her head
beneath the derby, her ivory skin glowing in the sunshine. When her emerald eyes met his, his color
deepened. Bryony sensed that he was developing a crush
on her. She recognized the symptoms readily, having
observed them in any number of young men in St.
Louis. She felt flattered, naturally, but she didn't return
Buck's feelings, and she hoped the situation wouldn't
become painful or embarrassing for either of them. She
liked Buck and wanted him as a friend. Only as a friend.
She had no desire at the moment to fall in love with
anyone. She wanted only to devote herself to the ranch.

She pretended not to notice the rapt way he was
staring at her. "I heard you didn't go to Winchester

yesterday, as you'd planned," she went on smoothly. "Are you going today instead?"

"Yep. I have to pick up some supplies Shorty ordered last week, and I'm also aiming to buy me a new pair of boots with the bonus money you gave us."

"Good." She smiled. "I'll ride in with you. Are you ready to leave now?"

"Shore. Which horse should I saddle up for you?" He grinned rather mischievously. "As the boss, you get your pick of the lot."

"Saddle up the black stallion you've been breaking in. I fell in love with him the first time I saw him."

If she thought Buck had been astounded before, the expression in his eyes now mirrored absolute incredulity. The other wranglers, who had been listening, matched his reaction.

"Miss Hill," he said quickly, "I can't do that. That black horse will kill you. He's still half wild!"

Bryony met his gaze evenly. "You've been breaking him, haven't you?"

"Shore, and he's coming along, but that's one stubborn horse, and it'll be a long time before he's fit for riding by anyone but an experienced wrangler."

"I'm a good rider, Buck," she assured him. "I can handle the stallion, and I've made up my mind that he is going to be mine. Beginning today."

His concern for her made the lanky, sandy-haired wrangler speak with sudden anger. "He's a strong, half-wild animal, ma'am, not the kind of pony you're accustomed to riding in the park on Sundays! He'll kill you!"

The other wranglers shuffled their feet nervously. They thought it utter madness that their new mistress wanted to ride the mustang. After the way she had spoken to them on her arrival at the ranch, they had hoped she possessed good sense, but this wild notion to ride the spirited mustang undermined their confidence in her. She must be just another ignorant tenderfoot, underestimating the hazards of western life. If she had been a man, they would have shrugged their shoulders and willingly let her learn her lesson the hard way, but she was a woman, a young, lovely woman, and they didn't want to see her hurt or killed because of a stupid, reckless fancy.

"Buck is right, Señorita," a plaid-shirted vaquero named Tomas interjected with a frown. "Forget that black horse. He is not for you, that one."

"They're right, ma'am. That mustang's too dangerous for anyone but a seasoned cowpoke," another wrangler added. "Now there's a real pretty little mare who'd suit you much better—she's gentle and sweet-tempered, just perfect for a lady."

Bryony controlled her rising temper with an effort. She knew they were just trying to protect her, but she'd heard enough. Men! They thought they knew everything; they thought they could tell every woman under the sun what to do. She had already made up her mind to ride the black mustang, and she wasn't about to be put off by anyone, especially her own employees. She tossed her head, and her green eyes glittered with determination.

"Saddle up the black stallion immediately!" Her tone was imperious. "I'm not going to waste another moment arguing about it—I'm in a hurry to get to town." She glared at Buck. "Do as I say, damn it!" She felt surprised at her own words. Miss Marsh would have been horribly shocked to hear one of her girls use such language, but Bryony already felt herself growing away from her St. Louis restrictions and she was in a hurry to prove that she could survive in this rough land, and on equal terms with the cowboys who inhabited it. At any rate, her strong words spurred Buck to reluctant activity. Without another word he stamped off to the stable and returned shortly with the saddled mustang. His expression was furious, yet fearful. Inwardly he was cursing this ravishing girl who was as stubborn as a mule, and equally as stupid. He was certain she would manage to get herself killed—or at least horribly maimed by the wild mustang's mighty hooves.

Bryony smiled slightly as Buck brought the stallion before her. What a magnificent creature this black horse was, as proud and majestic as the mountains that he had so freely roamed. His long, powerful legs pawed restlessly at the ground, and there was fire in the bright, intelligent eyes that watched the humans so warily. Bryony felt a kinship with this wild, free creature, for she herself had a spirit which others had always wanted to tame. She understood how he felt, no longer able to roam the desert and mountains at will. She was sorry for that, but sensed instinctively that there would be a bond between them. She approached him slowly, her voice soft and gentle as her hand lightly stroked the shining black mane.

"There, boy," she whispered, "don't be afraid. I won't hurt you. We're going to be friends, great friends. Easy now. Take it easy."

She spoke to him for a few moments, while Buck, Tomas, and the others watched doubtfully. All of Bryony's anger had evaporated. She concentrated only on the stallion. In St. Louis she had loved to ride, and everyone had agreed that she had a special way with horses, like a gypsy or a witch. But that had only been with tame city horses, and this situation was completely different. She had to focus all her energies on winning his confidence. She hoped the magic she had always possessed would be potent enough to reach this fiercely spirited creature, for she knew that no other horse would satisfy her. This black stallion was probably the only horse in the territory magnificent enough to rival Texas Jim Logan's Pecos. They were of the same height, and carried their beautiful heads in the same proud, fearless manner.

At last, she placed a foot in the stirrup and sprang lightly into the saddle. She wasn't seated more than an instant before the mustang reared straight up, clawing the air before him, sending Bryony flying backwards with a mighty heave from his sleek black form. She hit the dust hard, sprawling well away from the horse's fatal hooves, and Buck sprinted to help her up, while Tomas grabbed the stallion's reins.

"Miss Hill! Are you all right?" Buck's skin had paled beneath his tan. "You danged fool! I *told* you what would happen! You're just lucky he—"

"Shut up!" Bryony gritted her teeth, and shook off his hands. She dusted off her velvet habit impatiently. "Hold his reins, Tomas," she ordered curtly.

"You're loco!" Buck shouted, grabbing her arm as she started to place her foot in the mustang's stirrup.

She shook him off and turned her attention back to the horse. This time she wouldn't expect too much. She'd be prepared. She swung deftly into the saddle.

The mustang reared again, but Bryony now knew what to expect. She clung with her hands, her knees, her whole body moving with the animal's contortions. The stallion wasn't really trying to throw her; he was rearing and dancing and side-stepping, but Bryony guessed he was trying to test her more than to actually rid himself of her. She hung on.

"Wal, I'll be a . . ."

"Dog-eared Gila monster?" Bryony supplied the words for Buck, a gurgle of laughter escaping her throat as the mustang's movements resolved into prancing. "Be careful, Buck, or you might really turn into such a creature!"

She felt wonderfully exhilarated. Gloominess vanished as she exulted in the sense of freedom she experienced upon the back of this beautiful, strong creature. She turned the horse toward Buck and the wranglers, who looked appropriately shocked by her success.

"Well, Mr. Monroe, are you riding to town with me or not? I don't have all day to wait for you!"

He shook his sandy head incredulously, mounting his dappled palomino. There was open admiration in the eyes of the other wranglers as Bryony and her wild mustang raced off toward town, while Buck, with a yell to his horse, gave chase, galloping down the valley trail. Once again their new mistress had surprised them, and their respect for her grew. They grinned to themselves, anxious to relate to the other cowhands what they'd witnessed this morning.

Bryony's heart filled with joy as the stallion's hooves flew across the desert. He was swift and sure-footed; his gait beautifully even. This was the kind of riding she had always yearned for during those sedate afternoons in the park. This was freedom, delightful freedom. Her cares and doubts fell away as the cool mountain breeze fanned her flushed face, and boulders and cacti flashed past. She cast about in her mind for a name for this fleet-footed horse, and decided upon Shadow. It suited him admirably. Eventually, she slowed his pace to allow Buck and his palomino to catch up.

In town, she accomplished her errands efficiently, posting her letters for the mail, and making a few purchases in the general store. She was warmed by the reception given her as soon as the townfolk she met learned her name. A beaming Clyde Webster at the general store pumped her hand up and down.

"It's a real pleasure to make your acquaintance, Miss Hill, a real pleasure," he declared. "Your pa was the finest man in the territory, and anyone in Winchester'll tell you the same. Always had a smile for folks, ready to help a body out if they was in trouble. Yep, a fine man, a fine man. He's sorely missed, ma'am, I can tell you that for a fact."

"Thank you." Bryony felt a rush of pleasure at these words. How wonderful to know that her father had been so respected, so well-liked by his neighbors. It somehow made her feel closer to him. When she stopped to visit Edna Billings at the hotel, the peppery little woman introduced her to several women who had stopped by to gossip, and each woman told her most sincerely how well her father had been thought of. Bryony enjoyed her visit with them, and was sorry when it was time for her to meet Buck. She left the hotel expressing a wish that they call on her at the Circle H.

As Bryony made her way along the dusty boardwalk lining the street, her elegant riding habit drew many stares, but quite a few of these glances were inspired more by her beauty than by her unorthodox attire. No man touched her as she passed by them, head held high, but their eyes molested her without compunction. And from the doorway of the saloon, unbeknownst to Bryony, Rusty Jessup licked his lips, a cruel smile twisting his narrow mouth. Only when she neared the saloon did he duck back inside, his eyes sly as he returned to his whisky and cards.

When Bryony passed the Silver Spur moments later she felt an almost irresistible desire to peek inside. From within came the harsh sound of men's voices and the occasional shrill laugh of a woman. She knew it would be wrong to peer over the swinging double doors into the saloon; such places were wicked. However, it was this very fact that attracted her interest. The forbidden and unknown were always more intriguing than the acceptable. Her natural curiosity drew her to the doorway and she paused an instant, standing on tiptoe to peek inside. The room was half-filled with cowboys who sprawled at card tables or leaned against the curving black bar. A tall, red-haired woman in a sequined dress threw back her head and roared with laughter at something one of the cowboys said, and a long-legged brunette in a shamelessly tight-fitting crimson dress and high-heeled red shoes was serving a tray of drinks to the loudly swearing players at the foremost card table. Bryony's gaze fell accidentally upon one of the men at that table, and she gave a startled gasp, drawing hastily away from the doorway. She had no desire to let Rusty

Jessup see her. She was just moving swiftly away when a mocking voice from the street brought her up short in her tracks.

"Well, as I live and breathe, if it ain't Wesley Hill's little daughter—in the flesh."

She whirled in surprise to face the voluptuous, copper-haired girl she remembered from the gunfight, the girl in the sheer red dressing-robe who had leaned daringly over the second floor railing to view the fight. Today she was clad in a dress of gaudy hot pink trimmed in black lace, which left no doubt as to the magnificence of her figure, emphasizing her large breasts and wide, rounded hips. The long, coppery hair flowed freely over her bare shoulders, beneath a little pink hat adorned with long black plumes. Her tawny eyes held a sly, contemptuous expression as she cocked her head to one side and looked Bryony up and down. Bryony had no idea how this girl, who obviously worked at the saloon, knew her identity, nor why she had spoken to her. She stared in amazement until the copper-haired girl spoke again.

"You're pretty all right, just like I heard," she remarked, her eyes hard as stones. "But you can't be too smart, sugar, or you wouldn't be hanging around the Silver Spur."

"I beg your pardon?" Bryony began stiffly, but the girl cut her off with a derisive laugh.

"Don't go putting on your fancy city airs with me, Miss Bryony Hill! I don't care a hot damn for them!"

Bryony clenched her fists tightly, longing to deliver a resounding slap to this odious girl, but she controlled the impulse and instead drew herself up with all the dignity she possessed. "I've no idea who you are or what you're talking about," she stated airily, "but I have no desire to further our acquaintance, nor to hear any more of your vulgar conversation. So, if you'll excuse me, I'll be on my way." After this crushing speech, delivered in her best boarding-school style, Bryony started to sweep on down the boardwalk, but the copper-haired girl sprang quickly into her path, a red stain of anger seeping across her cheeks.

"Well, that's just fine with me, Miss Fancy Boots, because I don't want to further *your* acquaintance none either! But just remember to stay away from the Silver Spur, and away from me, because Daisy Winston was a friend of mine, and I remember my friends. Get it? Just stay out of my way!"

Then, she shoved Bryony aside and stomped into the Silver Spur, her high heels clattering on the wooden planks. Bryony recovered her balance and straightened her derby cap, staring in bewilderment at the swinging door of the saloon. What was that disgusting girl talking about? Why had she mentioned Daisy Winston? And why was she so angry with her when they'd never even met?

As Bryony continued along the boardwalk, turning the incident over and over in her mind, she collided with Annie Blake coming out of the general store. The girl was dressed in the same unkempt, unattractive manner she had been the first time Bryony met her, and her expression hadn't changed either. She scowled darkly when she saw who had bumped into her, causing her to drop a hefty bag of sugar and spill some potatoes from a sack. When Bryony stooped to retrieve the fallen items, apologizing, Annie's expression remained unsoftened. She muttered something unintelligible, and reached for the items Bryony held, but the black-haired girl shook her head and smiled.

"No, let me help you. Your arms are quite full. Where shall I bring these things?"

Surprise flickered in the Blake girl's hazel eyes at this unexpected offer, and for a moment it seemed she was about to refuse, but then she shrugged and jerked her head. "My wagon's down there," she muttered.

"Good. My horse is tethered nearby. I'll walk with

you to the wagon and give you a hand with these purchases.''

"Suit yourself.''

There was silence as they walked along. Bryony glanced appraisingly at her companion, and hostility was the only word to describe Annie Blake's demeanor. Her angular face was set harshly and her lips clamped tightly together. To Bryony, she looked about as friendly as the rocky face of a mountain. Bryony sighed. She was tired of this. She didn't understand the enmity she was encountering in the most unexpected of people, and though in the case of the saloon girl she had no desire to pursue the matter, Annie Blake was a different story. Bryony wanted to know why the girl—and her father—seemed determined to dislike her, without even giving her a chance! She handed Annie her things, then touched the girl's arm as she began to climb into the wagon.

"Wait a minute, please. I'd like to talk to you, Annie. If I may call you that?''

"Call me whatever you want,'' the girl returned. "I don't have to answer to it.''

"Now that's exactly what I want to talk about,'' Bryony snapped, exasperated. "What have I ever done to make you dislike me? We only met the other day, and I can't possibly have done anything to offend you in such a short time. You and your father both behaved as if I had the plague from the first moment we were introduced.'' Bryony's eyes flashed fire. "And I want to know why.''

"Need you ask?'' Annie retorted, her breast heaving, her voice shaking with emotion. "After everything that's happened, need you ask why we hate you—why the sight of you sickens us?''

Taken aback by the vehemence of this reply, Bryony could only stare in wonder.

"My brother,'' Annie continued tremulously, "is

lying in a grave not far from that of your father. My brother was only fifteen. And you ask why we hate you? You ask what you've done? My brother is dead, we're about to lose our ranch, my father has aged long before his time, and you have the gall to ask why we despise you! Well, lady, if you had the brains you were born with, you'd know the answer to that question without having to ask!" Hatred and grief shone from her eyes as she glared down at Bryony from her seat in the wagon. She looked as if she'd like to run the dark-haired girl down, and never look back to see the damage.

"I . . . I don't understand . . ." Bryony's voice trailed away. Her eyes, wide and dark, mirrored her confusion.

Annie Blake stared at her a long moment. "You don't know, do you?" she finally said, her voice filled with incredulity. "You really don't know."

Bryony began to speak, but at that moment, Buck Monroe's hearty voice sounded at her elbow and she jumped.

"Howdy, Miss Hill. I'm all set to ride for home. Hope you haven't been waitin' too long. Afternoon, Annie."

"H—hello, Buck."

Bryony immediately noted the change that came over Annie Blake in Buck's presence. A flush entered her cheeks, and her work-roughened hands trembled as she held the reins to her horses. She couldn't draw her eyes away from the husky young wrangler's handsome face. Buck, though, had eyes only for Bryony. He was beaming down at her, barely sparing a glance for the ranch girl in the dilapidated wagon.

Why, she's in love with him, Bryony realized instantly, recognizing the despair in Annie's eyes. *And Buck doesn't even know she's alive. All he does is stare at* me. Sympathy stirred in her. Annie, too, had noticed Buck's absorption in his employer, and her lips quivered as she spoke in a dull voice.

"Pa's waitin' on his supper—I've got to go. Buck?"

The wrangler tore his gaze from Bryony to grin at Annie good-naturedly. "Yeah, Annie, what's on your mind?"

Whatever she'd been about to say, Annie abruptly changed her mind. She just shook her head, and without another word to either of them, she struck her horses into motion. Bryony watched in dismay.

"Oh, Buck," she sighed, and was on the verge of inquiring how he could be so blind when she realized that it was not her place to betray Annie's secret. Even if Buck knew, it would not make him return her affection.

"What is it, ma'am?"

Bryony turned toward the horses. "Never mind. Let's go," she said. "I've had enough of this town for one day."

While they rode back, she remembered what Annie had been saying before Buck's appearance. Though she didn't feel free to discuss the girl's feelings for him, Bryony could see no reason why she shouldn't discover if Buck could shed some light on the other situation. She repeated the words Annie had told her, but Buck merely shook his head, frowning.

"Well, what does it mean?" she demanded, guiding Shadow back toward the valley. "I haven't the faintest idea what she's talking about."

Buck seemed hesitant. "It's not worth discussing. Annie shouldn't have mentioned it. Dang it, don't pay no attention to her; nobody else does. You just forget Annie Blake."

"I can't do that, Buck. I won't. Please, if you have any idea what Annie means by all this, I wish you would tell me."

Buck was staring straight ahead, his voice sober. "Well, ma'am, it's a fact of western life that cattle ranches are always plagued by rustlers. Big spreads and small ranches alike get their share of trouble, but in these parts there's always been some hard feelings between the larges ranches and the small ones. Your pa and Matt Richards, and the other big ranchers in the area were always expanding their herds and their lands, and some of the smaller ranchers, like Sam Blake, complained that they were being pushed out of the picture.'' Buck grimaced, noting her worried expression. ''Now you've got to understand, that's a common complaint in these parts, where men have a habit of taking what they want. But Sam and a few others accused your pa and Mr. Richards and the other big cattlemen of stealing from them to increase their own herds, of trying to drive them off the range.''

''Oh, Buck, no!'' Bryony cried in dismay, and the black mustang, sensing her disquiet, suddenly grew skittish, snorting and fighting for his head.

''Whoa, boy, take it easy,'' Buck ordered, as Bryony worked to bring the horse under control. When she had succeeded in calming the animal, Buck went on in a reassuring tone.

''Now, don't get yourself all upset, Miss Hill. No one ever proved any of these accusations—especially where your pa and Mr. Richards were concerned. If you knew the west better, you'd know that there is always talk like that goin' on, and folks are used to it. Anyway, a feud sprang up here in Winchester between your pa and Mr. Richards, and this group led by Sam Blake. One night, Sam's young son was killed while he was laying in ambush to catch some rustlers, and Sam . . .'' Buck hesitated, then went on staunchly. ''Sam always insisted it was your pa's and Richards' men who did the killing. Well, no one ever believed it; both those men were too well-known and respectable to be guilty of such dirty business, and most folks figured the killing and thieving were done by renegade Apache.'' He shrugged and glanced solemnly at Bryony, whose expression was horrified. ''Don't go on worrying about it, ma'am. These feuds happen all the time, and they're usually triggered by some stupid misunderstanding. I'm shore there's no basis for any of the things Sam or Annie Blake says, or else I wouldn't have stayed on working for your pa, and neither would Shorty, or a lot of other cowpokes I know. So just forget what Annie told you, put it right out of your thoughts.''

This was something she could not do. A terrible, terrible misunderstanding—Buck had to be right about that. Her father couldn't possibly have been involved in anything unscrupulous. The idea was ridiculous.

Still, a heaviness of heart settled over her as she thought of Annie Blake's young brother, dead at so early an age. It was a tragedy. But neither she, nor her father, could be held in any way responsible for it, and she intended to make that clear to Annie the very next time they met.

Chapter Fourteen

The days slipped by. May arrived, and the giant saguaro cactus, so prominent in the region, gave forth its beautiful white blossoms, filled with the long, purplish fruit that the Indians had long used for food. The flat, sandy desert grew more exquisite daily, adorned with its yucca trees, greasewood, jumping cholla cacti, flowering organ-pipe cacti, and barrel cacti, from whose trunk, Bryony learned, candy was made. In the valley, the grass-covered rangeland was dotted with pink-blooming ironwoods. Geraniums, violets, snowberry, and fernbush carpeted the mountains and their foothills, and dazzling, sun-golden poppies spanned the mesas. Each day Bryony was greeted by a brilliant, sapphire-domed sky and hot sunshine, and the air was always scented with pine, mingled with the citric aroma from her own orange groves. As ever, the mountains loomed deep blue and purple in the distance, a pinkish haze tinging their starkly jagged edges.

Bryony reveled in the magnificence of her surroundings. Her days were full as she occupied herself with the running of a large and prosperous cattle ranch, aided in her efforts by Judge Hamilton, who showed her how to manage the books and payroll, and by Shorty Buchanan, who kept the wranglers in line and handled all matters of daily management, reporting to Bryony several times each week. She frequently visited her father's grave in the cemetery outside of Winchester. Though she managed to find time for horseback riding occasionally, most of her hours were spent helping Rosita with the cooking and housework, writing up supply lists, and balancing the books. One thing she never missed, however, was her daily shooting lesson. Her derringer had been chipped by Jim Logan's bullet, but it was otherwise in good working order, and Bryony saw to it that she and Shorty Buchanan rode out into the foothills for a practice session every afternoon. She had grown quite fond of the feisty little cowpoke, though she soon learned that he was anything but a patient teacher. His grizzled face often screwed itself into an expression of exasperation when she didn't follow his instructions exactly, but he knew more about shooting a gun than most men knew about breathing, and under his tutelage, she became surprisingly proficient with the weapon. Her aim was good, her hand steady, and her reactions were quicksilver. Though he never admitted it in words, Shorty was proud of her.

Matthew Richards was a frequent caller at the Circle H, and his attentions to Bryony had become quite marked. At first she thought he was being kind to her because of his friendship with her father, but eventually she came to realize that he was genuinely attracted to her, and she couldn't help but feel flattered and pleased. Matt Richards, with his jet-haired, dark-eyed good looks, his vast cattle holdings and impressive Twin Bars ranch, and his warm, polished personality, was considered the matrimonial catch of the valley. He was a man respected by everyone in Winchester, and here he was, dangling after a girl fresh out of boarding school. It was a compliment indeed. Bryony enjoyed his company, and was always pleased when he rode up in the cool of the evening to share a glass of lemonade or elderberry wine with her on the porch. He often brought gifts, such as a wild turkey he had personally shot for

her Sunday dinner, or the fine-looking white Stetson he
had ordered especially for her in Tucson. There was
something so comforting about his solid, friendly
presence that she found herself looking forward eagerly
to his visits.

One Saturday morning in mid-May, Bryony stood
before her bedroom mirror, carefully twisting her hair
into two long dark braids, which she subsequently
wound about her head in a soft, pretty chignon. She was
dressed in a ruffly white blouse and long, brightly
flowered skirt, with thin sandals on her feet. She turned
this way and that before the mirror, studying her appearance. Today she and Matt were going on a picnic
near the banks of the San Pedro, and she wanted to look
especially nice for him. She had been looking forward to
this outing all week, and now that it was finally here,
her heart fairly sang with pleasure. How much she enjoyed being outdoors in the fresh, clean mountain air,
drinking in the spectacular western scenery. Especially
in the company of a man she was so fond of, and who
always took every care for her enjoyment. She smiled
into the mirror, her lovely face with its fragile, sculptured cheekbones and luminous jade green eyes
radiating her happiness. She dabbed on some of the
French cologne she saved for special occasions, then set
a crisp white sunbonnet over her dark, braided chignon,
tying the silken ribbons jauntily under her chin. She was
ready. It was ten o'clock exactly, and even as she turned
away from her mirror, she heard the crunch of carriage
wheels on the pebbles below. Matt had arrived.

Dancing eagerly down the stairs, Bryony encountered
Rosita in the parlor, vigorously polishing the handsome
brass lamps with beeswax.

"Rosita, how do I look?" she cried gaily, pirouetting
to show off her Mexican-style blouse and skirt.

Rosita's eyes shone with approval. *"Muy bonita,*
Señorita," she assured her mistress with a smile. "Very,
very pretty!"

"*Gracias*," Bryony returned dimpling. She had been making an effort to learn Spanish, but her progress had been necessarily slow since her time was so fully occupied with her duties. She often reflected ruefully on how much time she had spent in school mastering French, and now that she was fluent in that language, she had absolutely no need for it. She was determined that before the summer was out, she would be able to converse respectably in the Spanish language, for there was no doubt that the Spanish and Mexican cultures had a profound influence on many aspects of life in Arizona, such as the local architecture, mode of dress, and diet. She found it fascinating and wanted to assimilate herself into the southwestern culture as much as possible.

A purposeful knock on the ranch house door sent Bryony hurrying to open it. Matt was waiting on the porch, looking tall and extremely handsome in a blue-and-green plaid shirt and navy trousers, with a green bandana knotted at his neck, and handsome leather boots glistening upon his feet. His deep-set, hooded eyes lit up when he saw her, and the smile she had grown so fond of curved his mouth.

"You're a sight for sore eyes, Bryony," he said, grasping her hands. "I can't tell you how much I've been looking forward to this day."

"So have I." She smiled warmly up into his dark eyes. For a moment it seemed that he was going to kiss her, but just as he leaned forward, Bryony suddenly broke away with a laugh. "Good heavens, I'm so excited, I almost forgot the picnic basket! Come in while I get it." She drew him into the hallway and then disappeared like a whirlwind in the direction of the kitchen.

Matt strode to the doorway of the parlor, nodding at the housekeeper, who had straightened from her work and was regarding him with a darkened expression.

"*Buenas dias*, Rosita."

"*Buenas dias*, Señor," she returned in the surly voice she frequently used. In the days following Bryony's injury, her attitude toward the girl had altered considerably and they had been getting along quite well. Few people were impervious to Bryony's impetuous charm and effervescent personality, and Rosita had warmed to the girl as she had grown to know her. But with the appearance of Matt Richards in the doorway, the housekeeper's previous aloofness returned, a fact Bryony noticed immediately upon returning to the hallway, a wicker picnic basket in her arms.

"Ready?" Matt smiled, gently taking the heavy basket from her. "I sure don't want to waste a minute of this fine morning."

"Neither do I! Rosita, Señor Richards and I will be picnicking near the banks of the San Pedro, just south of Cougars' Bluff. If Shorty or one of the men need me, I can be reached there."

The Mexican woman nodded brusquely. Her thick dark brows were drawn together in a frown. Bryony stared at her a moment in half-amused exasperation. For some reason she couldn't fathom, Rosita strongly disliked Matt Richards. She was one of the only people in the valley who did.

A short time later she was seated in Matt's handsomely painted carriage, drawn by a pretty, spirited white mare that trotted down the valley trail, weaving its way toward the banks of the river. It was a scenic drive, affording Bryony an opportunity to view the flowering white saguaro blossoming everywhere. She watched and listened in delight as the cactus wrens and egrets flitted through the clear, cloudless azure sky, turning her head continuously to view the dark, rolling foothills to her right, Cougars' Bluff ahead to the left, and straining to catch a glimpse of the San Pedro, their destination.

They camped on a lovely spot, a wide stretch of grassy land near the water, where they could watch the river wind its way peacefully downhill, gurgling past the jutting rocks and thick mesquite shrubs overhanging the shore. Just now, the river was a thin, pretty ribbon, since the season was hot and dry, but she had heard that during the rainy season, or when a sudden summer thunderstorm hit the region, the banks could swell with a mammoth flood of water, washing away everything in its path. Today, though, all was peace and tranquility. Bryony spotted a yellow-necked mud turtle crawling ponderously along the muddy edge of the river bank, while on the opposite shore, a herd of elk calmly drank from the flowing water.

Matt spread a large blanket upon the grass, and as Bryony knelt upon it she was momentarily reminded of another blanket she had rested upon, one cool spring night under the desert stars. She checked herself, and quickly began unpacking the picnic basket, chasing the unwanted memories of Texas Jim Logan from her mind. In the past weeks, her thoughts had turned all too often to the lean, bronzed gunfighter with the cold, frightening blue eyes, and she had grown increasingly angry with herself for her inability to forget him. Every time her thoughts centered on his tall, broad-shouldered form, remembering the touch of his lips on hers, so warm and demanding, and oddly tender, her heart gave a painful lurch in her breast, sending her blood sizzling through her veins. Oh, how wicked of her to react so to her father's murderer! A man who was despicable in every way! She hated herself for her weakness. And today of all days was not the time to be thinking of the man who deserved only her loathing, for now she was in the company of a gentleman, a kind, decent man who treated women with respect and consideration. She felt no painful jolts of the heart when Matt looked at her, and her blood didn't pound furiously in her temples at his slightest touch. He was a pleasant, enjoyable friend, and she ought to appreciate the comfortable serenity she found in his company, instead of letting her mind wander to that mocking, dangerous gunfighter with his heart of stone.

They munched on chicken enchiladas and corn tortillas for lunch, followed by fresh oranges and delicious *sopaipillas*, fritters rolled in sugar and ground cinnamon. Bryony had prepared everything herself and was proud of her culinary accomplishments. The more accustomed she became to Mexican cooking, the more she enjoyed it. A warm glow of pleasure spread through her when Matt complimented her upon the meal.

"Rosita has taught me a great deal," she told him, pouring plum wine from the flask into the two crystal-stemmed goblets she had carefully packed. "She's a wonderful cook, and has promised to teach me her own special recipe for chili."

"Rosita is a talented woman," he smiled. "It's too bad she doesn't like me. I sure wish I knew what I've done to earn her disapproval."

Bryony felt a blush steal into her cheeks. She was sorry if Rosita's attitude had hurt Matt in any way, and in a rush, began to apologize for her housekeeper, but Matt interrupted her with a wave of his hand.

"It's all right, Bryony. I don't care what the woman thinks of me. It's your opinion I value."

Her blush deepened at this. "You needn't worry about that. My opinion of you is quite high, I promise you."

"I'm glad." He was regarding her so intently that Bryony began to feel a little embarrassed. She started repacking the remnants of their picnic lunch, mentally searching for a more neutral topic of conversation. It was Matt, though, who changed the subject, remarking in a quiet tone, "I hear you go quite often to visit your father's grave. I hope those visits haven't been too upsetting for you."

"No, I've accepted what happened," she replied gently, raising her soft green eyes to meet his penetrating gaze. There was a tiny pause while she tried to think how best to express her feelings in words. "I . . . I can't quite explain why I visit the graveyard so often," she went on earnestly. "Maybe I'm searching for some sense of my father, something to which I can relate. I . . . I didn't know him very well, you see.'' He nodded sympathetically, as if he understood. Bryony realized that she barely understood it herself.

She could picture vividly the way it was each time she visited the graveyard, with its queer silence and sense of eerie peace. Her father's grave was neat and well-tended, adorned by a massive white headstone inscribed with the words: WESLEY HILL—1829–1874. No matter how long she stood there, staring down at the patch of land that would house her father's body for all of eternity, she could not gain any sense of the man that he had been.

Once, she had hunted for the grave where Annie Blake's brother rested, and she had found it some distance from her father's site. She had learned that the boy's name was Johnny, and it was true, he had been only fifteen years old when he died. Without quite knowing why, Bryony had left his grave feeling more shaken and depressed than ever. She remembered the unutterable grief and hatred in Annie Blake's eyes, and her heart went out to the girl. How terrible that she believed that Bryony's father and Matt Richards were responsible for the boy's death. Bryony wanted fervently to make her realize how foolish and misplaced were all her bitter feelings, but she wondered if that would ever be possible.

Matt's voice, quiet and gentle, brought her thoughts back to the present. ''I understand how you must feel,'' he sighed. ''Wes's death was so sudden. It wasn't as if he had a chance to say any farewells.'' His hooded eyes searched hers. ''I don't suppose he left you any sort of letter or anything . . .''

''A letter? Why, no,'' Bryony said, surprised. ''How could he have—he didn't know he was about to die.''

''Of course not,'' Matt assured her hastily, taking her hand. ''I just wondered if he left you any personal papers that might sort of, uh, comfort you now.''

She stared at him. "Do you mean a diary—or something of that nature?"

"Yes, something like that, I reckon."

She shook her head. "No, unfortunately, there's nothing like that to be found. At least, I haven't come across it yet. The only papers I have are his will and the deed to the ranch, and legal documents of that sort." She glanced up at him with the sudden dazzling smile that had fired up so many male hearts in fashionable St. Louis. "Maybe I should start a search!" she exclaimed. "Maybe my father had a secret diary hidden away that he meant only for me to read!" Her eyes danced as she toyed with this fanciful possibility, but Matt looked far from amused.

"Now, Bryony, don't go raising your hopes with farfetched ideas," he advised her quickly, frowning. "Forget I mentioned it to you." He paused, and then said slowly, gently, "I don't want to see you hurt, you know."

He reached over with one of his husky arms and pulled her closer to him, smiling warmly down into her small, ivory face. "I didn't bring you on this picnic to talk about your father," he told her. He leaned closer to her, and was just about to kiss her mouth, when for the second time that day, she broke the spell of the moment and pulled excitedly away from him.

"Matt, listen to me!" she exclaimed rather breathlessly, intensely aware of his arms holding her close to him. "There's something I've been meaning to ask you. It's important. I meant to discuss it with you sooner, but then I became so busy with the ranch and all. It's something I dearly need to know."

He released his grasp on her. "What is it?" he asked warily.

Her vivid green eyes burned deeply into his. "Why did Jim Logan kill my father?"

There was a long silence. "I wish to hell I knew, Bryony," he finally replied.

"Judge Hamilton told me that according to local gossip, a girl named Daisy Winston was involved."

Matt looked grim. "Yes, but just how she fits into this, I'm not sure."

"Who was she?"

He leaned back, propping an elbow on the blanket, studying her. "Well, Bryony honey, you might as well know since you seem hell-bent on asking a lot of questions. Daisy Winston was a saloon girl who worked at the Silver Spur." He was watching her carefully as he spoke the next words. "She was also your father's lover."

Bryony gasped. "I don't believe it!"

"It's true. Pretty little thing she was, barely nineteen years old. Yellow-haired, big blue eyes, as wild as the flower she was named after." He regarded her intently. "Now, Bryony, don't be shocked. There's no reason to be. Your ma's been dead many years now, and you can't have expected your father to lead a monk's life out here in the wilderness. Right?"

She nodded, still stunned by this revelation. What he said was perfectly true. There was no reason why her father should not have become involved with a woman. But—a saloon girl? Nineteen years old? It was a shock.

"Are you sure about this?" she asked. "Did you know this girl well?"

"Pretty well. She was nice enough, though ignorant, and of a poor background. I think your father felt sorry for her, Bryony. He met her at the saloon and sort of took her under his wing. She didn't have any family or anything, I gather. They were seeing each other for nearly a year before she died. Before she was killed, I mean. She was beaten to death the night before your father and Logan shot it out." He paused, considering. "I reckon that Daisy's death might have had something to do with their gunfight, but," he shrugged, "no one can say for sure."

A sick, cold feeling swept over Bryony. The pieces of

the puzzle were beginning to fit together at last, only the picture that was emerging was altogether terrifying. It was clear to her now why her father had fought with Texas Jim Logan. All too clear. Her father had been in love with Daisy. Daisy had been murdered. The next day, he had fought a gun duel with Jim Logan. Why? Because Logan had killed Daisy Winston! And in grief and fury, Wesley Hill had gone hunting for the gunfighter, seeking vengeance. It was the obvious answer, the only answer. Why else would her father have quarreled with a professional gunman, a cold-blooded killer? There could be no other reason than revenge for the death of his lover.

Bryony covered her face with her shaking hands. She found herself remembering all too vividly her violent encounter with Jim Logan: the cold fury in his eyes; the brutal strength in that hard, muscled body! He could have killed her at any moment, and it was a miracle that he hadn't. The man must be mad to have beaten to death that poor, defenseless girl. He was a monster, she realized chillingly, and she had allowed him to kiss her, to touch her, to hold her. It was unbearable.

As sobs shook her, she felt herself enveloped in warm, strong arms. Matthew Richards gently pulled her hands away from her face, and forced her chin up so that she had to meet his eyes. There was concern in them, and tenderness. His arms tightened around her.

"Don't cry, Bryony, honey," he said softly. "I'm sorry I told you all this. I didn't mean to upset you."

She spoke in a ragged voice. "You know, don't you, Matt? Jim Logan must have killed Daisy. That's right, isn't it?"

His dark, hooded eyes were sad. "I reckon so, honey. That son of a bitch killed the girl, and your father went after him. That's my guess, and I'd give a lot to know for sure."

"Oh, it's true, it's true, I'm sure it's true," she cried,

and shuddered in his arms. "I just can't believe that same awful man saved me from those men in Gilly's! Why? It doesn't make any sense!"

"Damned if I know, honey. Men like Logan are a strange breed. He's not good, that's for sure, but maybe he had his own reasons for getting you away from those hombres." Matt stroked her cheek. "Don't cry, Bryony," he said tenderly. "Try not to think about any of this. There's no need now for you to be unhappy or scared. It's true that this is a wild, brutal region, where terrible things can happen, especially to a young woman alone. But, honey, you've got no reason to be frightened. You're not alone. I'm going to take care of you. I'll see to it that no harm comes to you. Believe me, I will."

Before she could speak, he pulled her gently down to lie upon the blanket. He leaned over her, his lips fastening warmly upon her mouth. He kissed her, a long, tender kiss, filled with reassurance. Her bonnet had slid down at a haphazard angle upon her head, and laughingly, he removed it and began to stroke her silken black hair. Some of the long, dark strands came loose from the braided chignon and wisped delicately about her face. He moved closer, and kissed her again, his hands lovingly caressing the length of her body.

Bryony closed her eyes and tried to relax. Matt's kisses were pleasant, and his strong arms holding her tightly were comfortably reassuring, but she felt no surge of passion at his touch; his kisses failed to ignite her. Much as she wanted to respond to his lovemaking, her heart and body remained calm and unexcited, like the waters of a small, clear, rippleless pond. As she parted her lips to receive Matt's kiss, willing her body to respond, she couldn't help but remember another man, another kiss—one that had swept her into a swirling torrent of passion, like an ocean driven by a storm into a frenzied, raging sea of excitement. As this memory intruded into the placidness of the moment, she felt herself shrink instinctively from Matt's embrace, her body tensing of its own accord.

He stopped kissing her abruptly and stared down into her face, studying the wide, luminous green eyes gazing rather unhappily at him, and taking note of the soft, sensuous curve of her full red lips. A chuckle escaped him as he held her body in his arms.

"Bryony, honey, you're as innocent as a little kitten, aren't you?" he remarked indulgently. He took her chin between his fingers and planted another kiss upon her mouth. His dark eyes shone warmly down into hers. "Don't worry that I'm trying to take advantage of you. My intentions are honorable."

"It's not *that* . . ." Bryony began, struggling to sit up, but this time he held her firmly in place upon the blanket. She stopped squirming and stared helplessly up at him, not knowing how to explain. "It's just that . . . I don't feel . . . that is, I . . ."

Matt threw back his head and laughed. "You're adorable. Now stop stammering and listen to me." He paused and smiled at her. "Ever since you arrived in Winchester, Bryony, I've admired your beauty, your spirit, your determination to carve out a life for yourself here on the frontier. We're alike, you and I. We're both devoted to building our ranches into the biggest, grandest spreads in the territory. Isn't that true?"

"Well, yes," she allowed, wondering uneasily where all this was leading. She wished Matt would let her go so that she could sit up and stare him frankly in the face, but he seemed determined to keep her lying upon the blanket, her head tilted rather awkwardly up at him. "I do want to run the ranch successfully, to achieve my father's goals for the Circle H, but—"

"But that's exactly my point, Bryony! We both want the same thing—and together, we can achieve our goals!"

"Together?" she echoed faintly.

He nodded, his black eyes glowing down at her, his breath warm and rapid on her upturned face. She felt the pent-up excitement charging through his thickset, powerful body.

"Yes, together," Matt repeated, and kissed her again, letting his mouth linger on hers. "I want you to marry me, Bryony," he said. "The frontier is no place for an ttected woman, but if you marry me, honey, you'll know complete safety and security. We'll join our ranches into the largest spread this territory has ever seen—and you'll live with me up at the Twin Bars, never wanting for comfort or safety." His grip on her tightened almost painfully with his excitement. "Marry me and I'll make you happier than you ever dreamed possible!"

Bryony's heart sank. With dismay she realized that her fondness and admiration for Matt Richards had encouraged him to expect more from her than she was prepared to give. She wanted his friendship, not his name in marriage. "Oh, Matt," she began miserably, tears of regret stinging her eyes. "I'm flattered—very flattered—that you want me to be your wife. But I can't accept. I'm truly, truly sorry, but a marriage between us isn't possible."

He stared at her with disbelief. It was obvious that the possibility of rejection had never occurred to him. "Come on, Bryony. You don't mean this!" he rasped finally, his voice hoarse. He cleared his throat and went on quickly, "Do you realize what you're saying? You're giving up the chance for a cattle empire! For wealth, security, comfort—everything a young woman could possibly want!"

"No." This time, when Bryony struggled to sit upright, he released his hold upon her. "No, there is something more that I want some day from life—from the man that I marry. Love! I'm sorry, Matt, but there is no love between us, and without it . . ." She spread her hands helplessly, leaving the sentence unfinished.

Matt's confused expression underwent an abrupt change. One moment he was glaring at her, the next, sunshine spread across his dark features. He grinned, reaching out for her. "Apparently I've given you the wrong impression, Bryony," he remarked ruefully. "With all my talk about cattle empires and security, I've overlooked the most important reason for our marriage." Again his arms encircled her, but this time, instead of returning his embrace, she kept her arms limply at her sides. "I do love you, honey," he told her firmly. "If I didn't make that clear before, I'm sorry. I want to marry you as much for love as for any of those other reasons. You've got to believe that."

She stared intently into his eyes, searching for confirmation of his words. His eyes were glowing with strong emotion, and there was great tenderness in his face. She'd never suspected his feelings for her ran so deeply. They'd been friends, they'd flirted in a light way, they'd been comfortable together—but love? She was surprised, and sorry for him. "Matt," she returned softly, wishing she could spare him this pain. "I don't love you. I'm sorry. I'm fond of you. I admire you and respect you greatly, but I don't love you."

He drew in his breath sharply, but after a moment he laughed, and there was a derisiveness in the sound that did not escape Bryony's ear. "Love! What does a young girl like you know of love?" he retorted. "You're a child! I'll teach you all you need to know about love, honey. I promise you, all that will come in time. But right now, isn't it enough that we care for each other, that there is affection and respect between us? I reckon you've read more than your share of those silly romantic novels, and you probably have some downright foolish ideas about the subject of marriage. But this is reality, Bryony, honey, and you've got to face it. If you stay on at the Circle H without a husband to protect you, you're letting yourself in for all kinds of trouble. The frontier is more savage than anything your pretty little head can imagine. All kinds of things could happen—things that would make your blood curdle." To Bryony's shock, she thought she detected a threatening note in Matt's tone, as if he was deliberately trying to frighten her.

"If you marry me, Bryony, and come to live up at the Twin Bars," he went on, "I'll see you're cared for like a little china doll. You'll never have to fear man or beast again. I promise you that." His lips moved lovingly over her hair. "I'll make you happy, Bryony, and you'll grow to love me in time as I love you."

Then he began to kiss her again, but this time Bryony drew violently away. "No!" she cried, tearing her lips from his, and writhing in his suffocating embrace. Once before, when Roger Davenport had begged her to marry him, she had wondered if she was truly in love, and how she would know it if that were so. But today she had no need to wonder. Marriage for the sake of security or comfort held no appeal for Bryony. If ever she married, she knew that it would be purely for reasons of the heart, influenced neither by monetary concerns nor those of safety, but only by a driving, insatiable love that would bind her joyfully to one man. Maybe these were schoolgirlish dreams, as Matt seemed to think, but even so, she would stand by them, and fall by them, if need be. To her chagrin, Matt Richards appeared unwilling to accept her decision, and as she struggled in a rather undignified fashion to free herself from him, he only held her more closely, soothing words of love streaming from his lips as he sought to subdue her protests.

"Matt, no, you must let me go," she gasped as he began to fondle her breasts, his legs wrapping themselves around hers as they rolled upon the blanket. "I said *no*!" she practically screamed, as he continued to nuzzle her, heedless of her growing anger. "I won't marry you, and I never will, and you had better accept that as fact!"

These words at last penetrated his ardor, for he stopped nipping at her neck, and removed his hand from her breast, staring at her. His expression slowly darkened.

"You won't . . . marry me?" he repeated grimly.

She shook her head, breathing hard. "No. I tried to explain it to you, but if you don't understand, there's nothing more I can say. I . . . I'm sorry." She was aware that her own voice sounded stiff and awkward, but she couldn't help it. She *was* sorry to have hurt him, but she also felt angry at the way he'd been mauling her, refusing to listen to her protests, refusing to respect her wishes.

"Matt, please take me home now."

"All right, Bryony. I reckon I don't have any choice but to take you at your word." He released her abruptly and began rolling up the picnic blanket, then tossed it into the carriage. Bryony tied the silken ribbons of her bonnet beneath her chin with trembling fingers. In silence, she handed him the wicker basket, and allowed him to help her onto the carriage seat. The picnic was over, ending on a note far different from the way it had begun. As the white mare drew the vehicle over the valley trail, neither occupant of the carriage seemed much concerned with the glorious summer scenery, or the heat, or the heavy stillness in the air. The silence between the couple was intense, the strain tremendous. When at last Matt set her down before her own front door, Bryony had lost almost all her anger, and remained feeling merely sad and empty, as if she had lost something that meant a great deal to her. But there were other emotions in Matt Richards's breast as he drove swiftly off toward the Twin Bars, and if Bryony had been able to read his mind, she would have been more than a little surprised.

Chapter Fifteen

A letter from Roger Davenport arrived on Monday afternoon, two days after the picnic. Bryony tore it open curiously, dropping into the upholstered easy chair in her father's study to read the elegant, even lines Roger had written across the expensive, monogrammed stationery. She had been depressed ever since the unfortunate conclusion of Saturday's picnic, but this diversion immediately claimed her interest, making her wonder with a surge of excitement why Roger had written. As she scanned the letter, her eyes began to sparkle with amusement.

Roger had sprinkled his letter with protestations of love, assuring her most fervently that he had not met anyone who could replace her in his affections, and insisting that he still wished to marry her as eagerly as ever. He expressed certainty that she had by now tired of her rough new life, and that she was more than ready to return to civilization, and the fashionable society she had so impulsively abandoned. And, Roger blithely informed her, he was prepared to give her a second chance to reclaim her place in proper circles. It was necessary that he travel by stagecoach to El Paso and San Francisco on banking business for his father in June, and he was going to make a special stop in Winchester solely to see her. Though he did not say so explicitly, Roger hinted in a most unsubtle way that he meant to propose marriage once again, this time with the certainty of acceptance.

Bryony laughed aloud. How conceited he was! She wondered how she had tolerated it for so long. Nevertheless, she felt strangely glad that Roger would be passing through town. It would be good to show him just how well she was doing on her own, to let him know that she didn't need him to look after her.

An idea then popped into her head so suddenly that she sat bolt upright in her chair. At that same moment, Judge Hamilton entered the room, having been admitted to the house by Rosita.

"Well, my girl, what do you have on your mind?" he asked heartily, noting her rapt expression.

"Oh, Judge Hamilton, I've just had the most marvelous idea!" she exclaimed, jumping up in her excitement. "What do you think of my throwing a party—a real party, with dancing and refreshments and music? A fiesta!"

"Sounds fine to me. What's the occasion?"

"An old friend of mine from St. Louis will be passing through town in June and I'd like to show him that life in Arizona is not as uncivilized as he seems to think! And it would brighten things up around here a bit—you know, life *can* be a little dull without social amusements."

The Judge grinned appreciatively at her. "Wanting to kick up your heels, are you? Can't say that I blame you, my girl. When are you planning to have this party, Bryony?" he asked.

Bryony did not answer immediately. Although she didn't say so, she inwardly thought that this would be an ideal way to smooth things over with Matt. She would invite him to the party within the next few days, and then he would see that there were no hard feelings on her part about his behavior on Saturday. They could become friends again, without strain or tension between them. More than anything else, she wanted to return to their old, comfortable relationship. She began planning her list of guests in growing excitement. She would ask the Judge, of course, and Matt, and Frank and Edna Billings, and Buck Monroe, along with the other range hands, and some of the neighboring ranching families, as well as a few of the cavalry officers and their wives from Fort Lowell. And Samuel and Annie Blake. This would be her opportunity to make peace with them, as well as with the handful of other small ranchers who had feuded with her father, and who remained unfriendly and distrustful toward her. The more she thought about it, the more the party sounded like a lovely way to improve relations in the valley. She could hardly wait to issue her invitations.

"Bryony, my dear, when were you set on throwing this shindig?" the Judge repeated.

"Roger is arriving by stage on June 18, or thereabouts, depending on the conditions of the roads and the absence of Indian problems," she told the Judge speculatively. "So I'll plan the fiesta for the twentieth, since he plans to stay in Winchester a few days at least. Does that sound right to you?"

"Sure, Bryony," Judge Hamilton agreed. "But don't you reckon you'd better let Rosita in on all these plans? After all, she's the one who'll have to do all the cooking for these hordes of guests you'll have flocking to your door."

"Heavens, yes! Wait a minute, Judge, I'll be right back!" She flew off to inform Rosita of her plans and returned a short time later, flushed and excited and happy, to find Judge Hamilton staring absorbedly out of the study window.

"Rosita suggested we hire some women she knows to help out with the cooking and serving," she began, but broke off when the Judge turned around and she saw the worried expression on his face.

"What is it?" she inquired, coming swiftly into the room.

"I don't like the looks of that sky," he replied grimly, scanning the horizon with a narrowed eye. The study window was open, but no mountain breeze fanned the room. There was a hazy stillness outside; the sky hung bright and blue overhead, like a heavy canopy. No cloud disturbed its vast blue expanse, except over the southernmost mountains where a black, foglike shroud lurked above stark red cliffs.

"It looks to me like we're in for a dust storm," the Judge continued. "Maybe a rainstorm to boot. I've seen it happen this way many times. This strange, silent peacefulness is the only warning of what's to come. Yep, it's calm, all right. Too calm. Something's going to bust."

"Is that all?" Bryony laughed, relieved. "From your expression, I thought something terrible was about to happen. It seems to me we could use a little rain. It's scarce enough in these parts."

Judge Hamilton turned sharply from the window, his weatherbeaten face looking grave as he regarded her. "Bryony, you don't understand. These storms are killers. The dust can blind you and flail your flesh like a million tiny whips. The rain can wash half a mountain away, wiping out everything else in its path right along with it." He shook his head. "If you take my advice, you'll send the men out pronto to round up the strays and try to get the herd under some sort of cover, away from the steep trails. As for you, my girl, stay in this house and keep it bolted tight. There's going to be trouble before the day is up, or I'm a lovesick coyote!"

Bryony stepped over to the window and peered upward at the sky, wanting to see for herself what kind of danger threatened. She could see nothing but the calm, placid sky, and those shreds of dark mist over the mountaintops. There didn't seem anything unusually ominous in this, but she knew that Judge Hamilton was wiser than she in such matters. "Well," she said doubtfully, "perhaps Shorty and I will have a *brief* lesson today."

The Judge continued to look concerned. He insisted on following her out to the corral where Shorty waited with their mounts. As they drew up, Bryony saw that Shadow was even more restless than usual today, pawing the ground and stamping his powerful hooves, his handsome head held high, sniffing the heavy, windless air uneasily.

After a brief conference with Shorty, in which he agreed with the Judge's prediction, and assured Bryony that he had already dispatched men to secure the herd, the wiry little foreman scratched at his grizzled beard, thoughtfully studying the girl before him.

"Wal, Miss Hill, if you're set on havin' yer shootin' lesson today, I reckon I ain't aboot to disappoint you," he remarked in his low, gravelly voice.

"Do you think that's a good idea. Shorty?" Judge Hamilton interjected. "That storm could rush down from the mountains like a herd of loco cattle. And before suppertime, too, by my reckoning."

The foreman squinted into the distance, his mouth moving rhythmically as he chewed his tobacco. "Shore, that storm's a'comin', Judge, but I'd be mighty surprised if it hits sooner'n two, mebbe three hours from now. We've got time for a little ridin' and shootin', if that's what the boss lady wants."

"Oh, yes, Shorty, I do," Bryony chimed in quickly. She flashed a warm smile at the Judge. "Please don't worry. We'll ride back long before the storm breaks. Everything will be just fine."

Judge Hamilton saw them off, and with a frowning glance at the sky, mounted his own horse and headed home to his lodgings in town. Bryony, meanwhile, rode beside her foreman in silence as they galloped west of the ranch, toward the foot of the massive, stone-faced mountain that was their customary site for her lessons.

When they reached the foot of the mountain, Bryony and Shorty dismounted and tethered their horses to a nearby paloverde. They were on a rolling plain dotted with cacti and ironwood, with the mountain at their backs. Golden eagles glided overhead with huge, outspread wings, their cries filling the still, leaden air as they hunted for prey. It was a desolate spot, this lonely plain, ringed by small, parched hills, a forsaken place where Bryony could practice her shooting undisturbed by the appraising eyes of her range hands. She liked its privacy, the fact that no one but Shorty could witness her blunders—although when she managed to hit five out of six of the tin cans Shorty arranged on nearby boulders, she did wish that someone else could see her skill. But today, concentrating on improving her speed, she was glad that no one else was present. One day she would demonstrate her skill for others to see, and then they would be impressed by her expertise, but in the meantime, she must simply practice patiently and do her best to follow Shorty's instructions.

It was a good session. Shorty gave her some tips on how to draw her derringer in one smooth, fluid motion, from the holster she wore about her hips, saving what could amount to precious instants in a dangerous situation. She practiced with a Colt revolver also, noting its heavier weight, and taking advantage of its six-shooter capacity to fire at the tin-can targets in rapid succession, hitting three out of five that Shorty had set up. *Not bad*, she thought, rather pleased with herself. Roger would indeed be surprised.

She became so intent upon her shooting that she forgot all about the approaching storm until Shorty began gathering up the tin cans, announcing in his gruff way that it was time they were heading back.

"I reckon we've tested this here storm long enough, ma'am," the foreman drawled, stretching out a thick-knuckled hand for his six-shooter, which she still held.

"We'd best ride on back to the Circle H before she breaks wide open. Matter of fact, the wind 'pears to be pickin' up a bit already. The dust'll be flyin' soon."

Bryony glanced upward, alarmed to see that the previously hidden shreds of clouds now had grown larger and more ominous. The same heavy stillness hung in the air as it had before, only now the wind seemed to have awakened as if from a deep sleep, and it stirred restlessly, sending the dust and sand of the plains into little dancing whirlwinds. Shorty had already mounted his horse and was waiting for her, his sharp eyes studying the clouded horizon. He spat out his much-chewed tobacco and smacked his lips. "She's movin' in faster than I thought, Miss Hill. We'll have to make tracks if we want to git back 'fore the big dust starts blowin'."

Shadow snorted nervously in the rising wind. Bryony was just about to place her foot in the stirrup when the shot rang out of the growing darkness.

Startled, she glanced back in time to see Shorty Buchanan slide from his saddle to crumple in the dust beside his skittering mount. For one horrifying moment, Bryony couldn't move. She could only stare in gaping shock at the foreman's limp figure sprawled face down in the dirt. A scream rose in her throat, and echoed across the plain, and then, as if it had broken the spell that held her frozen, she bolted toward Shorty and pulled frantically at his unmoving form. As he flopped onto his back, his head rolled loosely backward at a grotesque angle, and blood spouted from his chest, staining her hands and clothes. She screamed again, recoiling from the horror before her. Somewhere in the back of her mind she heard the pounding of hooves and wild yells. Another shot rang out, zooming directly over her head, and she leaped up from her knees to stare in stunned terror at the approaching riders.

Two Indian braves, their feathers and warpaint and buckskin garments clearly apparent even from this distance, were descending upon her at a furious pace. Their warlike shrieks tore through the air, striking awesome terror into the depths of her heart. All of the terrible stories she had heard about Apache atrocities flashed through her mind in one agonizing instant, and then, driven by sheer, blood-curdling panic, she began to run. Shadow neighed with fright, sensing danger, as Bryony sprang wildly into the saddle, spurring him into motion. Another shot rang past her, so close that her skin prickled, but she didn't look back. The Indians were closing in. There was nowhere to go—nowhere but straight ahead, toward the mountain. Leaning low over Shadow's mane, she sobbed desperate pleas to the galloping stallion, begging him to be swift enough to save her. Her hands that clung to the reins were sticky with Shorty's blood, and nausea threatened to engulf her. Shadow tore across the remaining open land like a flash of lightning, but even as they reached the base of the stone-faced mountain, Bryony heard sounds of swift pursuit from behind, and the war whoops struck dread into her heart. Gasping and sobbing in hysterical desperation, she urged Shadow on, on up the steep, winding, treacherous path of the mountain, even as the wind began to roar and a great whirling cloud of dust rose up from the earth.

Chapter Sixteen

Though it was only late afternoon, the Silver Spur
had begun to fill up for the evening. Cowboys,
ranchers, and townsmen sought shelter from the
approaching storm, preparing to spend the whole of
what promised to be a wild evening within the big,
gaudy confines of the brightly lit saloon. The piano
player was pounding the keys as the saloon girls
swarmed between the gambling tables and the bar
attired in their most provocative, gaily colored gowns.
Meg Donahue, with diamonds swinging from her ears,
and a skintight dress of russet taffeta hugging her
buxom form, was helping Luke at the bar, while Lila
Garrett, the tall, long-legged brunette in gold satin, was
dancing atop one of the card tables, swishing her skirts
teasingly about her black-stockinged knees to the
uproarious approval of the leering cowboys. Ginger
LaRue, busy refilling the glasses of five already-drunk
miners passing through town, kept glancing impatiently
at the swinging doors to the saloon, and swearing
exasperatedly every time a man strode through them.
She swore because none of them was the man she was
waiting for—Texas Jim Logan.

Where the hell was he? she wondered angrily, hastily
arranging the miners' glasses on a tray. Texas had
promised to buy her dinner tonight at the hotel, and she

had gone to a damned lot of trouble getting permission
from Meg to leave the saloon for an hour. She had also
spent the whole afternoon fixing herself up for him.
Why, her arm positively ached from brushing her cop-
per hair until it gleamed like newly minted pennies, and
she had tried on four of her best dresses before deciding
on the slinky purple silk gown that dipped brazenly
across her breasts. Jet earrings dangled from her ears,
and an assortment of sparkling bracelets and rings
adorned her hands and wrists, while a glittering rhinestone necklace flashed at her throat. Her lips and cheeks
were painted bright red, and her tawny eyes shone with
anticipation. Ginger's evenings with Texas had been less
frequent lately; he hadn't been around much and apparently had been staying at night in his hotel room. Or so
he had implied. Ginger suspected he was involved with
someone else. As she worked in the saloon, her shrewd
glance darted from Lila to Gracie to Ellie Sue, wondering furiously which of them he was taking to bed these
days. For even when she and Texas were together,
Ginger plainly saw his lack of interest. Texas no longer
kissed her with the fierce pleasure she had come to
expect; his caresses were absent-minded, dutiful, while
his thoughts . . . his thoughts were elsewhere. It enraged
her, but she was helpless to do anything about it.
Except—except try to reclaim his straying interest. And
she would do that the only way she knew how—by making herself so seductively irresistible that his passion
would be kindled anew. That was why this dinner
tonight was so important. She was going to give him the
full treatment, and she defied any man to resist her
when she turned on her well-practiced charm.

"Hurry up with that whisky, honey pie," one of the
miners yelled suddenly. With a curse muttered under her
breath, Ginger lifted the tray of drinks she had prepared. As she did so, the swinging doors opposite the
bar parted, and Jim Logan strode into the saloon, paus-

ing briefly to appraise its occupants with a quick, cool
look from under his sombrero, and then proceeding
leisurely to a table in the corner, facing the door.

Relief made Ginger smile quite gaily. She carried the
tray to the drunken miners and deposited it hurriedly,
then scooted over to Logan's table, leaning over to kiss
him gleefully, letting her voluptuous breasts dangle
almost completely free of her daring gown as she bent
over him.

"Texas, honey, I thought you were going to stand me
up," she cooed, her hand caressing his cheek so that the
scent of her strong perfume clearly assailed his nostrils.
"Where have you been, sweetie?"

"That's my business," he stated shortly. "Bring me a
drink."

She slid onto his lap, wrapping her arms around his
neck and allowing her soft fall of coppery hair to brush
his face. "A drink? Aren't we going to have us some
dinner at the hotel? You promised, Texas, honey!"

"And I'm shore not one to break a promise to a
lady," he drawled mockingly, infuriating her with his
cold, sardonic smile. He looked undeniably handsome,
his blue-and-white checked shirt perfectly cut to accen-
tuate his wide, powerful shoulders, tapering to a slim
waist where dark blue pants encased muscular thighs
and legs. His handsome leather boots were dusty, as if
he'd been riding hard. As always, his gun holster
reminded everyone who glanced his way that he was an
uncommonly dangerous man. His dark sombrero
almost completely hid his brown, wavy locks, although
a few curls tumbled carelessly over his brow. His lean
features were bronzed by the sun, bringing out even
more attractively the deep, cold blue of his piercing
eyes. Ginger took all of this in with one narrow, longing
glance, and her arms tightened about his neck.

"So, honey, what about dinner?" she murmured,
rubbing her cheek against his jaw.

To her chagrin, instead of softening toward her, he responded with a hint of impatience. "We'll go to dinner when I'm finished here, Ginger. If you're sure you want to venture outdoors. There's a bad dust storm blowing up, and it looks like a thunderstorm is hot on its heels." Suddenly, he pushed his sombrero back on his head and grinned at her. His arms tightened about her waist as she sat upon his lap. "It shore seems to me like a good night for staying indoors. Know what I mean?"

For answer she kissed him long and hard, oblivious of the crowded saloon and noisy patrons clamoring for service. "I want that, too, Texas honey," she purred, "but you promised me a nice dinner at the hotel, and I'm sick of Meg's beef stew! There's plenty of time for keeping warm and dry later, isn't there, sweetie? And I've been lookin' forward to this all day!"

"All right, Ginger, all right. But first, bring me that drink."

With a final, parting kiss, she obediently jumped off his lap and went to the bar. There, Meg Donahue read her a few blistering words on the evils of neglecting her customers, but Ginger, secure of her position in the Silver Spur, merely tossed her head at Meg and replied in a belligerent way that she'd see to her customers when it damn well suited her. Still, she did agree angrily to serve refills for a rowdy group of cowboys as soon as she'd delivered Texas his drink. Shrilly shouting to the impatient customers to shut up and wait their turn, she stalked over to Logan's table.

"Here you go, honey." She placed the drink carefully before him. "I've got to take care of those hell-raisin' cowpokes, but I'll be back as soon as I can."

He watched her hustle off, unable to suppress an amused smile as Ginger tried to hear the cowboys' shouted orders for drinks over the banging of the piano and the noisy rumble of men's voices in the rapidly filling, smoke-filled saloon. To add to the confusion,

Ellie Sue, a wildly uninhibited saloon girl with frizzy blonde curls and provocatively laughing brown eyes, began dancing atop the cowboys' table, her hips swaying bawdily to the blaring piano music, her high-heeled shoes stomping the table so loudly and heavily that several glasses broke before Ginger could sweep them aside.

Logan chuckled softly to himself. Poor Ginger. She'd been trying so hard to spend time with him, to please and attract him, and here she was being obliged to wipe up the broken glass and spilled whisky, to take drink orders, to fight her way to the overflowing bar. He felt a little sorry for her, but only a little. Ginger could take care of herself. She'd been doing it for a long time now. He knew she wondered why his interest in her had waned, and he also knew that whatever spark there had once been between them was now extinguished. Ginger was nothing to him but a pretty whore who knew her way around the bedroom, and he was more than a little tired of her.

Logan was aware that Ginger suspected he was involved with another saloon girl, probably Lila, who had been flirting outrageously with him lately. Thinking of this, he grimaced, and drained his whisky glass. If only it was true, he thought bitterly. If only it was Lila or one of these other frisky saloon women who haunted his thoughts, tormenting him. But it wasn't. It was someone else, someone completely different. His strong fingers tightened about his empty glass. Harshly, he called for another drink.

Bryony Hill had consumed his thoughts for many weeks now, ever since that afternoon when he had cornered her in the Circle H barn. The memory of her raven-haired beauty and burning green eyes was engraved upon his mind, and when he thought of her soft red lips parting to welcome his kiss, of the way her slender body had melted into his, he went almost wild with frustrated desire. Never before had any woman

had such a profound impact on him. He had always
found the women who interested him more than willing
to share his bed, and he had taken what he wanted from
them and afterward, his needs fulfilled, forgotten them
without a second thought. They had been used for the
moment's pleasure they provided and then discarded,
like an empty bottle of liquor. But Bryony Hill was
unlike any woman he had ever met. Where the others
had been experienced, she was innocent. Where they
had been cheap and pretty and wild, she was exquisitely
beautiful, and spirited, and well-bred. Where they had
quickly lost their charm in their availability, she was all
the more tantalizing because she was unattainable. He
spent every waking hour trying to forget her, and every
night dreaming of her loveliness. It was sheer hell.

Desire for Bryony Hill was driving him loco, and that
was the quickest way for a gunfighter to meet his
demise. He couldn't afford to be distracted by some
fancy little rich girl from St. Louis. To survive, all his
energies had to be focused on his gun, on shooting
faster and straighter than any one else—*everyone* else.
If he didn't watch out, Bryony Hill would kill him yet,
whether or not she was the one to pull the trigger. A
grim smile twisted his lips. He bet she would like that.
That little wildcat would love to know that she was the
cause of another man beating him to the draw.

Logan banged his clenched fist on the table. He'd
be damned if he'd let it come to that. He'd drive that
damned girl from his mind if he had to bed every whore
in the territory to do it. When Lila brought him his second drink, a warmly inviting smile lighting her painted
face, he took it without a word. He set it upon the table,
and pulled her roughly down into his lap.

"Why, Texas," she gasped in pleasure, more than a
little surprised by his sudden interest. She kicked her
long, black-stockinged legs out before her and with a
little whoop gave herself up to his kiss. The next moment she screamed in agony as her long brunette hair

was ripped viciously from its ribboned coiffure by
Ginger LaRue.

"Owww!" Lila screeched, falling out of Texas's lap
to stare balefully at the copper-haired saloon girl standing above her with both hands on her hips.

"Stay away from my man!" Ginger shrilled. Her face
was flushed scarlet with rage; she looked as if she would
scratch the other woman's eyes out. Lila struggled to
her feet, equally ready for a brawl, but Logan spoke
coldly from his seated position at the table.

"That's about enough, ladies," he drawled, his blue
eyes flicking contemptuously between them. "Lila, I appreciate the drink, and the offer of other services, but I
reckon you'd better get back to work before Meg goes
on the warpath. Ginger, come over here and sit down.
I'm in no mood for one of your tantrums."

His steel-edged tone and commanding gaze had the
effect of throwing cold water on the women's burning animosity, and with nothing worse than loathing
glances exchanged, they parted. Lila flounced to the
bar, where Meg Donahue had been watching the episode
with raised eyebrows. As Lila began to loudly air her
grievances, showing the older woman her tumbled hair
and stamping her spike-heeled feet upon the floor,
Ginger sat defiantly on a chair beside Texas, her eyes
livid with rage.

"Why were you kissing that no-good hussy?" she
demanded. Ginger's temper was always short-fused,
and at this point her patience was nearly exhausted. Just
when she thought she was making some progress with
this hard-hearted bastard, he turned his attentions to
that brazen brunette, who knew less than nothing about
pleasing a man! She watched his face for some sign of
apology or excuse, but she was not surprised to find that
he appeared indifferent to her anger, his features set like
granite. It was as if her feelings were of no concern at
all to him. Which, she realized sinkingly, was probably
true. He was bored with her, and disgusted by her

behavior. She was losing him faster than she had realized.

"Stop making a jackass out of yourself, Ginger," Logan said. "If you want me to escort you to the hotel for dinner, I suggest you try to behave a little more like a lady."

"Like a lady?" Her laugh was high-pitched. "Hah! Like a lady, eh? Like that fancy little daughter of Mr. Wesley Hill?" She snorted derisively. "I saw her, honey, one day in town! All decked out in her velvet riding clothes, pretty as you please. Just like a little princess. A little bitch-princess, if you ask me!" Her eyes shone with hatred. "Well, honey, I sure hope you don't plan on getting to know that little bitch any better, cause for one thing she'd probably rather die than have anything to do with the man who shot down her father, and for another . . ." she paused, letting her tongue slide slyly between her full pink lips, "and for another, little Miss Hill is getting married before long, and it hardly seems fittin' for the great Texas Jim Logan to be chasing after another man's lawful wife, now does it, honey?" She laughed spitefully. "You'd look right silly hankering after Mrs. Matthew Richards! Ain't that so, Texas, honey?"

Logan was acutely aware of her shrewd glance upon him, watching for his reaction to these words. It took all of his tremendous will power to refrain from displaying the emotions that assaulted him at that moment. Only his whitened knuckles as his fingers tightened around the whisky glass betrayed his inner turmoil. His eyes, his mouth, his entire demeanor remained calm, indifferent, casual. But his knuckles were very, very white.

"I hadn't heard they were going to be married?" he drawled, and his penetrating blue gaze made Ginger shift somewhat nervously in her chair.

"Well, not yet exactly. But I reckon it's bound to happen soon."

"Why?"

Ginger stood up abruptly. "Look, honey, are you buying me dinner or not? I'm sick and tired of talking about that black-haired little bitch. Let's go get some chow before the dust storm starts. I'm hungry as a grizzly."

Logan's arm shot out and gripped her wrist. His eyes had a deadly glint to them as slowly, slowly, he forced her back down into her seat. "Tell me what you know about this marriage business, Ginger," he said, and though his voice was soft, there was a frightening edge to it. Ginger swallowed nervously.

"Let go of me, Texas," she began uneasily, but the gunfighter's powerful grip became even more viselike.

"Talk, Ginger." There was no pity or mercy in his eyes, and Ginger winced.

"But why . . .?"

"I'm asking the questions," he responded in an iron tone. "You're answering them. I reckon you ought to remember that."

"Matt Richards was in here Saturday night—late. He was in a terrible rage, drank himself right under the table. I've never seen him like that before. Real mean and ornery and gettin' drunker all the time." She couldn't help gasping as Logan's fingers bit into her flesh, and even as she did so, he released her, leaning back in his chair, his cold blue eyes boring into her painted face. She began to rub her wrist, watching him warily from across the table. Despite his apparent calm, she sensed his tension, and silently prayed he wouldn't vent his suppressed violence on her. Unlike many of the men she had known, Texas had never struck or mistreated her, but then she had never seen him so intense about anything as he was about this saloon gossip. She felt a familiar surge of jealousy at his interest in another woman—in this case, Bryony Hill. Her voice was filled with resentment as she continued her reluctant narrative.

"Anyway," she went on sulkily, "Meg tried to talk to

him, but by then he was dead drunk and in a worse temper than ever. Finally, old Judge Hamilton came in and then *he* tried to reason with him, sending Luke away when Matt yelled for another bottle.'' She shrugged. ''I don't know what the Judge said, but soon after they left together—him and Matt. I didn't find out what it was all about 'til afterwards.'' A sudden smirk played across her cheap, pretty face. ''Some of Richards' men were in here the next day and I heard them talkin' all about how the boss was fit to kill—seeing as a certain Miss Bryony Hill turned down his proposal of honorable marriage!'' She shook her head and her eyes were spiteful. ''Imagine that, honey! She turned down the richest rancher in the valley. That little girl's either stupid or loco, or both! But don't you worry none, darlin', I've a hunch that little bitch is just playin' hard to get. You watch— she'll turn around and accept old Matt the next time around.'' She touched his hand possessively, her fear evaporating as she finished her recital.

Beneath his sombrero, Logan's face paled. A terrible feeling of foreboding rushed over him as Ginger's words sank in. Long ago he had developed a sixth sense for danger; it was something all men in his profession needed to stay alive. And now this extra sense was warning him once again.

He had to find Bryony Hill.

''Well, now, Texas, are you riling up my girls!'' Meg Donahue inquired cheerfully at his elbow.

Logan glanced up at her, his face a grim mask. Ginger, glad of the interruption, jumped to her feet. ''It was all that whoring Lila's fault!'' she declared defensively, but Meg only chuckled and patted her coppery head. ''Don't rear up like a wild mustang, Ginger, I'm just teasing you—and Texas.'' She grinned good-naturedly at the gunfighter. ''What do you have to say for yourself, cowboy?''

For answer, he gazed at her long and hard. ''What did Matt Richards say to you that night he was in here drunk?'' he asked curtly. There was an urgency in his tone that Meg noticed immediately. She raised her eyebrows in surprise.

"Answer me, Meg!" There was no arguing with his forceful tone and Meg shrugged.

"Why, he just babbled on and on about that Hill girl, that's all. Seems like she turned him down—marriage-wise and every other way, I reckon." She cocked her head to one side. "Why're you asking, Texas? You're not usually the nosy type when it comes to other folks's business."

Ginger draped herself on her chair once again and sent a long, sidelong smile up at Meg. "Oh, Texas has an uncommon interest in little Miss Fancy-Pants Hill. I figure he's developing a taste for virgins—which cuts out all of us girls around here, doesn't it, Meg?" Her laughter was hard, almost vicious. She was no longer frightened, not with Meg supervising. Texas wouldn't strike her with Meg around, or she'd have him thrown out. Meg took care of the girls who worked for her. So Ginger continued boldly, eager to torment him with more details of Matthew Richards's ardor. "Come on, Meg, what else did Matt say?" she prodded. "I heard you and he were real friendly years ago when he first came to Winchester, so he must have confided in you. What did he say about that black-haired bitch?"

Meg shook her fiery head with a laugh. "Well, I must say, me and Matt did share a few drinks, among other things, back when he first came to town, but that was a long time ago, Ginger." She winked bawdily at Logan, her eyes bright with merriment. "I'll tell you—I wish he *had* told me more about what happened with that city girl. You know, Texas, I like a bit of juicy gossip as well as the next fella. But I've got to own, he didn't talk much sense that night. Just a lot of lover's gibberish. Damned if I could make it out." She settled down in one of the vacant chairs at the table, seemingly ready to chat for hours, but Logan had heard more than enough.

With a nod to Meg, he got to his feet and started toward the double doors. But Ginger grabbed his arm and clung to him, all of her desperation to win him back welling up in her once more.

"Hey, honey, where are you going? I thought we were going to the hotel."

He disengaged himself from her clutching hands. "Sorry, Ginger, this won't wait. Maybe you'd better try to wangle a dinner out of one of those cowpokes over there. And while you're at it, see if one of them wants to warm your bed tonight when the storm hits, because I don't know when I'll be back. And I'd shore hate to think of you lying there all alone."

And with these mocking words, he strode from the brightly lit saloon into the gray calm of the threatening dust storm, leaving Ginger open-mouthed and indignant, her outraged shriek drowned in the din as the music blared on, and the miners and cowboys yelled for more whisky.

Chapter Seventeen

Bryony clung frantically to Shadow's reins as the mustang whipped around a curve in the mountain path, his hooves pounding past boulders and scrub brush, oblivious of the swiftly rising, whistling wind that engulfed them. Her hat had blown off, leaving her head unprotected against the whirling dust, but she paid no heed. Her ears strained for the sounds of pursuit and she thought she caught a horse's neigh from farther down the mountain, and even more alarmingly, the drumming of galloping hooves. It seemed to her that the sounds were not as close as they had been at first, so perhaps she and Shadow had gained some distance from the Indians. Unfortunately, she immediately realized that the fainter sounds might be due to the wind that muffled everything as it tore past, hurling clouds of swirling dust and sand down from the mountain. A little sob rose in her throat. How could she possibly hope to escape? The going was bound to get rougher as she climbed farther up the mountain, and in the end, the Apaches would catch her. What then?

She shuddered in agonizing realization of her probable fate, and a horrible chilling terror turned her body to ice. But she could not give up without trying to save herself, however futile the attempt, and she bent low over Shadow's billowing mane, letting it brush her tear-streaked face as she desperately urged the mustang stallion on. He virtually flew along the mountain path, his mighty hooves remarkably sure-footed on the treacherous terrain. Bryony knew that if she had been riding any other mount, her attackers would have probably caught her already, and she blessed the horse that carried her so swiftly. Even still, she knew that she could not ride forever; it was only a matter of time before the Indians overtook her, and even if she tried to hide somewhere on the mountain, the Apaches were skilled trackers and would find her with ease. Petrified by this knowledge, she buried her face in Shadow's mane. She almost envied Shorty his quick, relatively painless death, for she knew that her own fate would be far more hideous.

Suddenly, an ominous rattling sound pierced the thick air. Before she could react, Shadow reared up, panic-stricken, his forelegs raking the air. With a scream, Bryony slid helplessly from the saddle. Shadow bolted wildly up the slope, crazed by the nearness of his long-time enemy, whose rattle he had instantly recognized. As she lay sprawled on her side, watching him disappear around a narrow bend in the mountain, Bryony, too, saw and recognized the dreaded rattlesnake that had so terrified her black horse.

It was a diamondback, the most dangerous of all rattlers. Her eyes widened with fright as the enormous southwestern killer bared its fangs in preparation to strike, its long, spiny body a full five feet in length as it rose up less than three yards from where she'd fallen. Its thin, forked tongue flicked in and out in frenzied excitement. It was ready to strike.

Bryony had had no time to cry out, even to think. Her hand flew to her hip and yanked out the derringer. She fired, the shot ringing out just as the snake lunged forward. The rattler collapsed in a writhing heap only paces away, its tongue still moving. Its spiny body shud-

dered, and then lay immobile. Unbelievingly, Bryony
stared at the limp form. It took a full minute before she
realized that she had killed it.

She had no time to recover from the shock. Horses'
hooves thundered directly behind her, and she knew
that her pursuers were close. She tried to stumble to her
feet, but gave a soft moan as pain shot through her
ankle. She had twisted it when she fell from her horse,
and when she tried to step upon it, the throbbing pain
was almost unbearable. She could no longer flee, even
by running. She was trapped, helpless, at the mercy of
her attackers. Fresh terror bubbled up within her, and
with it, hopelessness.

Then her gaze fell upon an opening in the rocky wall
of the mountain. It was only a crevice, a small, thin in-
dentation beneath a slight outcropping of rock, but it
was nevertheless a place to hide. She began to crawl
toward it, her heart hammering, her fingers clawing the
gritty, swirling dust, her hands scraped by sharp-edged
stones and pebbles as she dragged herself across the
path to the edge of the mountain wall. The opening was
very slight; she flattened herself on her stomach as she
tried to squeeze beneath the rocky lip into the narrow
crevice. The dust storm would help her, she realized,
with a faint, desperate gleam of hope, for it would make
her trail difficult to follow. Already, as she lay tense and
unmoving beneath the overhanging rock, she saw that
her tracks had been erased by the blowing wind. Unfortunately, however, the dust was whirling into her
hiding place, stinging her face and choking her. With an
effort in that tiny space, she pulled her neckerchief over
her mouth and nose so that it protected part of her face.
Her eyes she would not cover. Whatever happened, she
must try to see what was going on.

She didn't have long to wait. The thunder of hooves
rose over the wind, and then the lower bodies of two
horses came into sight. To her horror, the beasts halted

less than five feet from her, and two large, buckskinned riders dismounted quickly to bend over the lifeless form of the rattlesnake, their feathered headdresses trailing down their broad backs.

Bryony cringed in her hiding place, hardly daring to breathe. Her heart was thudding so loudly she was certain it would betray her. The Indians were not facing her as they examined the dead rattler, but she knew that if they were to turn their heads ever so slightly in her direction. . . .

Then she received a heart-stopping shock.

"Looks fresh killed, don't it?" one of the figures said, in English, in a voice she recognized instantly. "It probably spooked her horse and she shot it. That how you figure it?"

It was all she could do to keep from gasping aloud. She would recognize that thick, harsh voice anywhere! Zeke Murdock! Her fingers dug into the hard ground. Her flesh crawled. Zeke Murdock!

Both men straightened, leaving only their boots in view. Bryony could scarcely believe her ears. All of this time she had believed her pursuers to be Indians, renegade Apaches out for blood, and now she discovered that they were white men. Zeke Murdock and . . . and who else?

She found out soon enough. Rusty Jessup's voice replied disgustedly, "Yep, sounds right to me. She can't have gotten far. Mebbe we can still catch her."

The two mounted their horses once again, and Bryony found it more difficult to hear them. The whistling wind drowned some of their words, but she strained desperately to catch what they were saying. Stunned and frightened as she was, one question drummed in her head. Why? Why? Why did they hate her so much that they would hunt her down like an animal?

"This damn dust is gettin' real bad," Murdock growled. Though Bryony couldn't see his face, she pictured it vividly enough: the shock of gold hair, those brawny, gloating blue eyes, and thick, sneering lips. This brawny, barrel-chested man had kidnapped her off the stagecoach and auctioned her off to the highest bidder in Gilly's. She would rather die than be in his power ever again. She closed her eyes tightly against the blinding dust that stung them, and listened tensely to his muffled words.

"I say we turn back," he went on roughly. "We won't find no tracks with all this dust blowin' around, and I don't aim to get caught up here in a thunderstorm or flash flood—which looks mightly possible. That sky is gettin' darker every damned minute!"

"But we've got orders to kill the girl!" Jessup argued. "She could blow our whole operation sky-high if she—" His next words were swept away by a sudden raging gust of wind. When Bryony heard him again, he was shouting above the increasing roar of the storm. "And besides," he yelled, "she saw us shoot Buchanan. We've got to finish her off!"

"She can't identify us, Jessup!" Murdock exploded. "Come on, let's get out of here before those storm clouds burst wide open. We killed her foreman, and I reckon we've given her a mighty good scare. If this don't chase her out of town, nothin' will. Anyway, the storm'll probably kill her, even if we don't. The boss'll be satisfied, so why in hell should we get ourselves soaked to the skin? Damn it, this here dust is bad enough. I can't see more'n five feet in front of my eyes. Let's go!"

Rusty Jessup's reply was lost in the wind, but he must have assented, for the two horses turned about and disappeared in the direction from which they had come. Bryony lay shaking in her pitiful hiding place for several moments, unable to move. Every muscle in her body trembled, and tears rolled down her face. She still had no idea why Zeke Murdock and Rusty Jessup were trying to kill her, but the knowledge that they were in league, that someone had hired them to see to her death, was chilling. She wanted to stay hidden beneath the rocky ledge forever, away from the terrors of the outside world. But the stinging dust was worsening, making it difficult to breathe, and she knew that she couldn't remain there much longer if she wanted to live. Somehow, she had to find shelter from the ferocity of the storm. She couldn't afford to think about Murdock and Jessup now; she couldn't waste whatever energy she had left wondering who had hired them, and why.

As she crawled wearily from her hiding place, shielding her face with her arms, since the tiny black particles bit right through her neckerchief, she became aware that the sky had indeed grown very black. Thick, immense clouds of dust spun everywhere, driven by a howling wind that whipped at her hair and face, almost knocking her over. A jagged flash of lightning illuminated the inky sky for a bare instant, indicating that the thunderstorm was not far away. She glanced despairingly about, not knowing which way to turn. She vaguely remembered that Shorty had once told her that the mountains were filled with natural caves. If she could find one of them, it might provide some shelter.

Head and body bent almost double from the blistering force of the wind, she began to climb the uneven trail, limping in anguish as she was forced to put weight on her throbbing ankle. Buffeted by powerful gusts, enveloped by a frenzied whirlwind of dust and sand and tumbleweed, her progress was agonizingly slow. When at last she had fought her way around a narrow, twisting bend in the mountain, she frantically scanned the stony side of the mountain. To her dismay, it was solid rock. Sobbing raggedly in frustration, she bowed her head once again and struggled on.

She had no idea how long she labored, fighting the pain in her ankle and the blinding dust, while the wind wailed in her ears, driving her nearly mad with its savagery. She felt her strength slipping away as her fruitless search continued, and once, glancing back, realized that she had not come very far after all. Despair rose in her heart, and a sudden, violent gust sent her to her knees on the rocky trail. She huddled there, weeping, too weak to continue, able to think only that she wished the dreadful pain in her ankle would go away, that this hideous noise would stop hurting her ears, that the dust would not prick her like so many sharpened needles stabbing her flesh. She tried to rise, and failed. The wind rushed even more fiercely about her spent form, and slowly, a great blackness rose up before her eyes to engulf her in a deep, silent void. She lay unconscious on the mountain path, while all around her great dark clouds of dust billowed and swarmed like maddened insects.

Bryony came back to consciousness with a low moan on her lips, slowly aware that hands were touching her, turning her. Her eyes flew open and she perceived, through a swirling haze, that a man was bending over her, shielding her body from the storm. He was wearing a dark blue bandana across his face and a sombrero low over his forehead, but she immediately recognized the broad-shouldered physique and light blue eyes, and a cry of thankfulness sprang instinctively to her throat.

"Please, help me," she managed to gasp, and though her words were muffled by the neckerchief she still wore over her mouth, Jim Logan nodded, his strong hands tightening on her slender form. He lifted her in his arms, and heedless of the powerful wind that had knocked her helplessly to her knees, he settled her not ungently in the saddle of the big chestnut stallion, and then got on in front of her. Neighing unhappily as the forces of nature assailed him, Pecos moved laboriously up the trail. Bryony collapsed exhaustedly against Logan, grateful for the warmth and protection of his body.

She never knew whether it was minutes or hours later

that Pecos picked his way down a steep, half-hidden in-
cline against the northern face of the mountain, coming
to a halt before a yawning gap in the jagged stone wall,
directly beneath an overhanging cliff. Carved out of the
sheer red-rock face of the mountain was a cave, its entrance of mammoth proportions. The interior loomed
black and ominous before them. Just as the horse
halted, Bryony felt the first drops of rain strike her face,
and a boom of thunder split the sky. Logan eased her
from the saddle and carried her into the cave, leading
Pecos right beneath the towering, jagged opening.
Soon, Bryony was lying quite comfortably on a thick,
heavy blanket near a small fire, her head resting on a
saddle bag, with Logan kneeling beside her. Just
beyond, Pecos was tethered to a boulder near the mouth
of the cave, safely out of reach of the wild torrent
of rain streaming down the mountainside. Thunder
cracked, lightning flashed a vivid silver-blue streak
across the leaden sky, and Bryony's wide green gaze
returned to rest on the face of her rescuer.

"Thank you," she whispered, and found her throat
dry and cracked.

"Don't try to talk," he told her roughly. "Drink
this."

He raised his canteen to her lips, but Bryony protested, remembering the last time he had given her
whisky instead of water. He ignored her feeble cry and
firmly held the canteen to her lips, pouring the whisky
down her throat.

"You'll do as you're told for once!" he ordered
angrily. "It's time someone took charge of you. For
your own damn good." His cold blue eyes glinted suddenly with mocking amusement. "Somehow, I don't
think you're in any condition to argue with me. Now if
you'll stay quiet like a good little girl, I'll get you a
damp cloth so you can clean your face, and perhaps I'll
give you something to eat. Then we're going to have a

little talk, you and I. And this time, you'll listen to me.
You'll listen good and hard.''

"I have no interest in anything you have to say!"
Bryony managed, infuriated by his high-handed treatment and attitude. The whisky had soothed her parched
throat and done much to revive her strength. She sat up
weakly, glaring at Logan. Why, oh why, had she been
so glad to see him on the mountain just a short while
ago? The feeling of relief had been monumental, but she
told herself now that at that point she would have been
overjoyed to see anyone who would have helped her
find shelter from the storm. *He* had nothing personally
to do with it. In fact, she would rather be shut up in this
cave with a mountain lion than with this arrogant,
domineering man who persisted in telling her what to
do. Her chest heaved with indignation as she watched
him stride to the cave entrance and soak a clean neckerchief in the streaming rain. He returned to her side and
flung the wet cloth at her, folding his arms across his
chest as he leaned against the wall of the cave. "Here,
little tenderfoot, wipe your face. What would your
friends in St. Louis think if they could see you covered
with grime, your pretty clothes all filthy and caked with
dust? I reckon they'd be shocked out of their fancy
skins.''

"As if I care a fig for that!" she snapped, her eyes
like green daggers. But she took up the cloth and began
to wipe the gritty dust from her face and hands, wishing
she could take off her clothes and jump into a hot bath.
Ignoring Logan, she untied the ribbon that now held
only a few wisps of hair and shook her head, sending
her long, wavy black curls spilling over her shoulders
and down her back. She knew she must look a mess, but
so what? She didn't care how she looked in the presence
of this despicable man whom she loathed more than
words could describe. If he thought her dirty or unattractive, so much the better. Perhaps he would refrain

this time from forcing himself upon her. Yes, she decided grimly, a defiant expression settling on her face as she met his intent gaze, it would be the best thing in the world if he found her totally repulsive. Which, under the present circumstances, was more than likely.

From his nearby position, Jim Logan scowled at her in mingled frustration and rage. In his eyes she looked as alluring as ever. The flickering firelight within the dusky cave played softly about her delicate features, revealing the patrician lines of her sculptured cheek-bones, the tender curve of her lips, the unextinguishable glow in those bewitching green eyes. There was a sensual, earthy quality about her as she sat on the floor of the cave, her coal-black hair tumbling loose about her shoulders, her breasts straining against the tight-fitting plum-colored shirt she wore with her jeans and boots. He was tormented. Damn, how he wanted her. He was filled with a savage, single-minded desire that was all the more torturous because it was so impossible to fulfill.

"I thought you mentioned something about food." Bryony's icy voice broke into his thoughts, and with an effort, he mastered his emotions, regarding her with every appearance of nonchalance. "I shore did, but I reckon I changed my mind. First, we'll talk. Then we can see about the grub." A gleam came into his compelling blue eyes. "All I've got is a hunk of beef jerky and some biscuits, like we had that other night—in the desert. Do you remember that night—Bryony?"

She looked away, flushing. A strange warmth heated her blood, but she managed to say, although a little breathlessly, "Y—yes, I do, but I prefer not to think about it." She straightened her shoulders, assuming a businesslike air. "So let's get on with this, shall we, Mr. Logan? You see, I wish to speak with you, also. I'd like to know how you found me on the mountain." She lowered her gaze to stare at the pale orange flames of the fire. "That's twice now that you've saved my life," she observed in a low voice. "I don't understand how it came about."

He hooked his thumbs in his gun belt, watching her. "I rode out to your ranch to see you, and learned that you weren't there. Your housekeeper told me that you had gone off for a shooting lesson with your foreman." A slight smile twisted his thin lips. "One of your wranglers tried to stop me going after you, so I had to use a little violence, but I reckon it didn't take too long to find out where you and Shorty Buchanan had gone."

"One of my wranglers?" Bryony asked in sudden anxiety. "Who was it?"

He shrugged indifferently. "A tall, light-haired cowpoke who talked mighty big for his breeches. Your housekeeper called him Señor Monroe."

"Buck!" Bryony exclaimed, jumping up to face Logan with clenched fists, a terrible fear rising in her breast. "You didn't kill him, did you?" she cried, panic-stricken. "Oh, you murderer, you vicious killer!"

Logan grabbed her wrists as she began to beat against his chest, and he stared grimly down into her distraught face. "Relax, little tenderfoot. I didn't kill the wrangler. I used my fists, not my gun, and though I reckon his jaw will be a mite sore for a few days, he's not about to throw in his saddle for a coffin." His eyes hardened at the vivid relief that flooded across her features. "So, you're sweet on him, are you?" he remarked harshly. "And I thought it was Matthew Richards who had won your heart."

"What are you talking about?" Bryony demanded, wide-eyed. "What do you know about me and Matt Richards?"

"That he asked you to marry him. That you turned him down. For now, anyway." His eyes nailed into hers. "That was part of the talk I heard in the Silver Spur. The other part, the part that made me ride out to see you, was that he drank himself under the table that night. Gossip has it he was in a black rage—a killing rage. When I heard that, I knew, I just knew that . . ." He broke off suddenly, not quite ready to explain it to her yet. He didn't know if she would believe him, and he had to put the facts before her in the most convincing way he could. He studied her face, wondering what she was thinking. Then he asked her a question that had nothing to do with the matter at hand, but that he suddenly needed to know. "Are you considering marriage to him, Bryony? Is that what you want?" His voice was rough, edged with tension, and Bryony flushed to the roots of her hair.

"That is none of your business!" Eyes blazing, she struggled free of his grasp and flared furiously at his mocking, handsome features. "How dare you question me about Matt or anyone else?" she stormed. "I won't stand for it! There isn't a reason on earth why I should answer to you, a common murderer, a man who kills respectable ranchers and helpless women—like Daisy Winston!"

The words were out before she could stop them, and in horror, she realized what she had said. For a while, she had forgotten that Jim Logan had beaten Daisy Winston to death, but upon uttering these unthinking words in hasty anger, full realization of her own vulnerable position made the color drain from her cheeks. She took an involuntary step backward under the look that came into his eyes, and winced as her ankle again began to throb. She ignored the pain as deadly fear sliced through her heart like a cold steel blade. She was alone in this mountain cave with a cold-blooded murderer, and now that he knew she was aware of his crime, what would he do? She thought fleetingly of the derringer in her holster, then remembered sinkingly that she hadn't had an opportunity to reload after shooting the diamondback. The cartridge was empty. And besides, she reflected, her lower lip quivering in fright, Texas Jim Logan had already warned her that the next time she raised a gun against him, he would kill her. There was no doubt that he could easily beat her to the draw. She glanced at the cave entrance, wondering desperately if she dared brave the howling wind and vicious torrent of rain in an attempt to escape him, but before she could make a move, he had taken three giant steps forward and jerked her into his arms, the pressure of his fingers biting into her flesh.

"Is that what you believe?" he demanded violently, his eyes glittering like blue daggers while he held her in an iron clasp. There was a dangerous expression on his rugged face, an expression that made Bryony gasp in terror. He shook her savagely, his eyes nailing her gaze to his own. "Do you believe that I killed Daisy Winston? Do you? Damn it, Bryony, I want an answer!"

Her eyes locked with his. Her heart pounded. And she knew the truth, knew the answer spoken by her heart, overruling logic and reason. Her lips parted, but they trembled so much that for a moment no words emerged. At last, she managed to whisper in a barely-audible voice, as she found herself drowning in the blue depths of his eyes, "No, no. I don't believe you did. I don't believe you could have killed her. Never, never, in a million years."

Then, all of a sudden, a dam seemed to burst inside both of them. He pulled her brutally against him, and began to kiss her savagely, releasing the torrent of passion that had been carefully held in check, crushing her limbs in a fierce embrace. It was as if a magnet drew them irresistibly together. She kissed him fiercely, starvingly, her arms tight about his broad back, thrilling to the hammering of his heart against her breast, moaning with pleasure as his strong hands urgently caressed her, and his mouth devoured her. Then they found themselves sinking onto the blanket, their writhing bodies pressed desperately together, their lips burning beneath the searing flame of kisses that could no longer be controlled.

Hungrily, they undressed each other, caught up in a whirlwind of seething passion, and Logan's hands cupped her breasts, his strong fingers caressing the hardened nipples and sending waves of delight across her swimming senses. His lips moved tenderly over her breasts and up to her throat, searing her lips and cheeks and eyelids and ears with those sweet, flaming kisses. He explored the warm curves of her slender body as she ran her fingers ecstatically over his muscular back, crying out softly in pleasure at the touch and smell and sight of him, reveling in his overpowering nearness. But when he pressed himself atop her and she felt the warmth and powerful hardness of his manhood between her naked thighs, she gave a stifled moan, half-desire, and half-apprehension. Her luminous eyes flew open to stare at him in sudden fright.

"No, we mustn't . . . it's wrong," she gasped, but he soothed her with the gentlest of kisses, and holding her head between his hands, he spoke to her in a voice she hadn't heard from him before.

"No, Bryony, it's not wrong," he said, his heartbeat quickening at the wide, innocent expression in those beautiful green eyes. He kissed her silken hair as it flowed over her shoulders and moved his tall, strong body purposefully over hers. "It's beautiful, my love, beautiful. I won't hurt you, I promise. Don't be frightened."

She wanted to protest once again, but her heart and her body betrayed her. She opened her mouth to receive his kiss and pulled his body closer against her, rocking with him as a strange, heady excitement raced through her. As he pierced the last of her barricades against him, she screamed softly, but he soothed her with kisses, and as the pain ebbed, she felt a hard, pulsating warmth inside her, thrusting strongly. Gasping, she closed her eyes and her lips locked with his, and she was no longer aware of any pain, but only of a wonderful aching sensation building relentlessly inside her as his movements aroused her to a powerful intensity. Her arms tightened around his neck, her body quivered and writhed to match his movements, and her back arched to receive him more fully, as she became wild, joyful, consumed by an overwhelming desire and urgency, her only thought to fulfill it, yet wishing fervently that this moment could go on and on and on. Then they were one, welded together in wondrous, throbbing unison and it was breathtaking, and almost unbearably wonderful. Sobbing, and holding him tightly against her as though she would never let him go, Bryony was swept up in a rush of frenzied delight, and her pleasure was savage, and sweet, and when at last their passion peaked and they reached the sublime ecstasy of fulfillment, she gave a long, shuddering sigh of happiness, and there were tears on her sweating cheeks. Logan moved carefully to her side and pulled her trembling body against him, warming and caressing her gently. Outside, the storm raged, but their own torrent of passion had been spent, and they lay quietly together for a brief time, wrapped in a fragile cocoon of blissful contentment as night descended on the storm-swept mountain.

Chapter Eighteen

The rain had stopped. Only a drizzle fell from the grimy sky as dawn tried to break through the clouded horizon, sending a pale, watery glimmer of whitish light around the edges of shredding black clouds to indicate that the new day was attempting to arrive. Huddled at the mouth of the cave, Bryony watched in silence as some of night's darkness lifted, leaving a bleak, rain-washed scene of muddied mountain and barren, soaked plains. The wind was now only a low, faint echo of what it had been last night, like the moaning of a weary ghost. Her bones chilled as she listened to it, and looked out over the desolation of the storm-ravaged landscape.

Bryony had been awake for some time, and had taken the liberty of removing Jim Logan's buckskin jacket from his pack to wrap about her nakedness. The pain in her twisted ankle had subsided, but she still felt a few twinges as she turned back into the darkness of the cave. The fire had dwindled to a few glowing embers, giving off little heat or light. In the few flickering sparks that remained, she could make out the ruggedly handsome features of the man sleeping on the saddle blanket. She stepped closer to kneel beside him, staring with wondering eyes at his sleeping face.

In sleep, Jim Logan looked peaceful, and unexpectedly young. Bryony judged his age at about twenty-eight, though he seemed at the moment somehow boyish. His long dark eyelashes curled upon the lean, tanned cheeks, and his mouth had lost its sardonic twist. Her gaze shifted to his bronzed, muscular form, and she remembered the power of those arms as they held her clamped against him, the hard leanness of his tall body as it had locked last night with her own. A thrill went through her at the memory, but even as it did, she was also filled with an aching sadness and remorse. She was ashamed of her behavior last night, ashamed that she had allowed herself to yield to the one man she had sworn to hate, the one man she must not love. She knew it must never happen again.

As if aware of her thoughts, Jim Logan shifted restlessly in his sleep. He awoke with a suddenness that said much about his way of life, for he sat up fully alert, as if ready for any danger. When his eyes fell upon Bryony kneeling beside him, they softened. "Good mornin'," he drawled in his slow, deep voice that never failed to make her heart beat a shade faster.

Bryony blushed, embarrassed at having been caught staring at him. Suddenly, she felt shy. What was there to say to him after what they had experienced together last night? What was he thinking about her—about everything? She met his gaze with an effort, all too aware of the crimson color staining her hot cheeks as his eyes pierced hers, seeming to touch her innermost soul. In confusion, she looked away.

As it happened, there was no need for her to say anything. Logan pulled her down into his arms and kissed her very gently. His hands were vibrantly warm on her silken skin as the buckskin jacket slid away. Bryony felt the now familiar warmth stirring within her, but before it could build to an irresistible intensity, she pulled away from his embrace.

"No, oh no, Jim, we can't—not again!" she cried.

An unexpected smile crossed his features at her words. "Jim?" He laughed quietly. "Do you know how long it's been since anyone has called me by that name?" There was a note of bitterness in his voice. "Lawmen and my enemies call me Logan, and my 'friends,' if you can call them that, call me Texas. It's been nine years since anyone has used that name for me. I reckon I like it coming from you, Bryony."

"You don't seem at all frightening this morning," she said gently.

"You're probably the only person in this part of the country who would say that," he remarked grimly. Once again his eyes were cold and hard. "Don't you know I'm a wicked, cold-blooded monster, Bryony, a man without a heart or a conscience? I'm slightly less than human, despite," he smiled mockingly, "my all too human behavior last night."

Something in his voice suggested that for once, his sarcasm was turned not upon others, but upon himself. Watching him in surprise, Bryony caught a sudden glimpse of pain behind the mockery. It came to her with such blinding clarity that she wondered why she had never seen it before. As the bleak morning light poked its uncertain way into the depths of the cave, she saw clearly what lay beneath the surface of his cool, mocking nonchalance. There were lines around his eyes that revealed deep pain, and a tenseness in his mouth due not to cruelty, but to cynicism about life. Jim Logan, she thought suddenly, wears a mask to the world, a stone-hard mask to disguise the unhappy, bitter man inside. She realized in astonishment that the cool carelessness that seemed so much a part of his personality had been developed to cover up whatever feelings he might nourish deep in his heart. He was hiding, hiding from whatever emotions plagued him beneath that stony surface. Texas Jim Logan, the legendary, feared gunfighter whose reputation was known all over the west, was just a human being after all, a man who had known pain and unhappiness, who struggled through life with a hidden burden he shouldered wordlessly.

She reached out impulsively to touch his hand, wanting to take him in her arms and comfort him. But then the moment of vulnerability was gone, and he was the old Texas Jim Logan again, smiling sardonically at her, the mocking gleam back in his eyes. "Don't feel too sorry for me, ma'am," he told her harshly. "I reckon I'm just as bad as anyone else—no better, no worse."

"Really?" she replied softly. "I'm not so sure. I've just realized that I don't know anything about you."

He shrugged indifferently. "What is there to know?"

"Who you really are, where you came from. Is Jim Logan your real name? Do you have a family?"

At the word "family," a muscle twitched savagely in his jaw, and he surged to his feet. He stalked over to their pile of clothing and began to dress, pulling on his dark blue trousers almost fiercely. "I told you once before, little tenderfoot, you ask too many questions. That's a sure way to get yourself killed in these parts."

"I'm not frightened of you."

His face contorted with sudden anger; he took three quick strides toward her and jerked her to her feet. "You're not, are you?" he rasped. "Don't you know I could kill you in less than an instant? I could shoot you dead in a flash, or better yet, beat and strangle you to death as you think I did to Daisy Winston!"

Despite the furious blazing in his eyes, and the vicious grip in which he held her, Bryony met his burning gaze fearlessly. "I already told you, Jim! I don't think you killed her. And I don't think you'll kill me either. So what are you going to do now?"

She stared at him challengingly, her beautiful eyes soft and smoky green in the cave's dimness. Staring down into her upturned face, something snapped inside Jim Logan. He made a strangled sound and then drew her close against him, wrapping his arms crushingly around her.

"Oh, Bryony, you're so sweet, so damned sweet!" he muttered hoarsely. "I could never hurt you—and I'll be damned if you don't know it!"

A feeling of warmth and tenderness the likes of which she had never known before flooded through her and she raised her luminous eyes to his face. Gently, she kissed him and then touched his cheek with her hand. "There is so much I don't know," she whispered. "Please, won't you tell me? Tell me how this man who has twice saved my life came to be the most dangerous gunman in the west."

Slowly, he turned away from her and began busying himself with building up the dying fire. Pulling the buckskin jacket closely about herself, Bryony sat down upon the saddle blanket and watched him, a lump in her throat. Every word he uttered seemed to engrave itself upon her memory.

"I grew up in Texas," he began in a voice oddly devoid of emotion. "My father owned a ranch there, a mighty big ranch." He paused. "More than seventy-five thousand acres, to be plain about it. He had a cattle empire."

She waited as he stared down at the now crackling fire whose little fingers of blue-and-orange flame licked hungrily outward in long, brilliant sparks, sending strange shadows dancing up the walls of the dusky cave. Jim Logan turned away from the fire and removed a tobacco pouch from his saddle pack. He rolled a cigarette, a slight frown creasing his forehead. Bryony remained silent. When he had finished his task, he began to smoke carelessly, pacing up and down the cave as if trying to collect his thoughts. Eventually, he went on.

"I never got along very well with the old man," he said curtly. "I was a wild kid, I guess, always getting into trouble, always raising some kind of hell." He grinned unexpectedly. "My kid brother, Danny, used to try to cover for me, but my father always found me out somehow—he had a sixth sense for it, I reckon."

"And your mother?" Bryony ventured.

His face was shadowed as he stood tall and thoughtful, bare-chested in the glowing firelight. "My mother used to try to protect me," he said, "but she had enough problems of her own. She was a small, frail woman, and my father was a giant of a man. He was like a Texas longhorn bull; he'd charge over anything in his way to get what he wanted, and my mother had her hands full just trying to live up to what he expected of her, to please him, and keep his temper from exploding. It wasn't any easier for her than it was for me or Danny, though at the time, I didn't always understand that." He turned abruptly to face Bryony, his voice sharp. "It wasn't that my father was a bad man," he told her forcefully. "He was a good man, a hell of an honest man, and not afraid of hard work. But he was strong. Maybe too strong. He had to rule everyone around him, and his word had to be law." Logan threw the stub of his cigarette into the fire. It disappeared in a blaze of golden flames. "I reckon I inherited most of his disposition. Right from the start, I hated being told what to do, how to behave. I fought him every inch of the way, and it was hell for both of us. Even though I was just a kid, I had every ounce of his stubbornness. We were just too alike to get along together."

"I think I understand," Bryony said gently. She could picture him, a young, wild, unruly boy, filled with high spirits and determination, eager to have his own way in life. And the father, an older, stronger version of the son, accustomed to tyrannical power, to obedience from all those around him. Conflict was inevitable.

"Things came to a head when I was fifteen, and the War Between the States was heating up like a red-hot branding iron. It was 1861, and Texas seceded from the Union to join the Confederate States."

"Your family was in favor the secession?" she asked.

"Hell, yes. My father was violent in his opposition to

Lincoln. He didn't make it a practice to own slaves personally, but Texans, you know, are fiercely independent and he opposed any violation of what he felt to be his state's rights in the matter." He grimaced. "Naturally, I disagreed." Suddenly, he gave a short, mirthless bark of laughter. "I guess I was just a natural rebel, Bryony. You see, I rebelled against the rebels—or at least, against one rebel, my father. Though I'd like to think I was aware of some of the larger issues involved, too." He sighed, and looked out over the vast stretch of barren plains. "I reckon I was so hell-bent on being independent and free of my father's influence that I had a natural sympathy for anyone shackled," he reflected slowly. "Slavery rubbed me the wrong way right from the beginning. Soon after Texas seceded, in April of that year, Fort Sumter was attacked by the Confederates and Lincoln issued his call for troops. That's all I needed to hear. I ran right off to join up with the Union forces."

"But you were only a boy—fifteen years old, no more, surely?" Bryony said. "You can't mean that you became a soldier at that age."

The smile he turned upon her was amused. "You're forgetting, little tenderfoot, that we're not talking about St. Louis or New York or Philadelphia. Out west, boys become men at an early age. I learned how to shoot a gun when I was nine, rode my first wild bronco at eleven, and went with the range hands on cattle drives from the time I was twelve. When I was fifteen, it seemed only right and natural to become a soldier. And I was sure that by joining the Union Army I'd prove to my father that I was a man—free and independent."

There was silence as she waited for him to continue, her eyes never leaving his face. When he did speak again, it was brusquely, as if he was in a hurry to conclude his story.

"Naturally, there was a tremendous split between me and my family. There was a violent argument the night

before I left, and my father threatened to disinherit me
if I carried out my plan to leave. He told me I could consider myself dead and buried if I turned against the Con-
federacy.'' His voice hardened. "It was probably the
worst thing he could have said. At that point, wild
horses couldn't have kept me from enlisting. I didn't
write to a single member of my family all during the
war, and they had no way of knowing whether I was
dead or alive. Afterward, when I was a few years older,
and should have known better, pride kept me from con-
tacting them.''

"You mean you haven't seen them since the day you
ran away?''

"I never returned to the ranch,'' he replied quietly.
"But five years ago I wrote to my brother from a town
in New Mexico, and he answered my letter with one of
his own. He told me that my father had died a year after
the war ended. He'd been speared by a longhorn during
the fall roundup—the damn stubborn fool that he was,
he always insisted on hitting the trail with the hands and
he worked harder than any of them.''

By now, the morning's faint light better illuminated
the cavern, and Bryony could more clearly see the bitterness in Jim Logan's eyes. "My mother had died of the
fever six months after he was buried,'' he continued
grimly. "Only Danny was left. In his letter, he begged
me to come home. He said that on his deathbed, my
father had repeatedly asked for me, that he had wanted
my forgiveness, my return to the family. He had even
. . .'' He broke off, his deep voice shaking momentarily
with suppressed emotion. After a moment, he regained
control, and continued in a low tone. "He had even
written me into his will, leaving half of the ranch to me
and the other half to Danny. He wanted us to own it and
run it together.''

There was a brief pause, and Bryony waited for him
to go on. He did so abruptly, turning his head to glare
at her almost angrily. "I wrote back and refused, of

course. I didn't deserve my father's forgiveness, his generosity, not after the years I'd spent hating him and punishing him by staying out of touch. As far as I was concerned, and still am, for that matter, the ranch belongs to Danny—all of it. I could never go back and live there again.''

"But it's what your father wanted in the end, isn't it?'' Bryony implored softly. ''His final wish was for you to return to share the ranch with your brother.''

"I told you, I don't deserve his forgiveness. If it wasn't for my pigheaded pride I would have contacted him when the war was over; we would have made it up then and worked out our differences reasonably, man to man. But once he was dead, it was too late. Can't you see that? *He* may have forgiven me, but *I* can never forgive myself!''

He began to pace about the cave again, while Bryony watched helplessly. He was obviously just as stubborn now as he had been as a boy. Proud, stubborn, angry— and filled with pain. All of these years, he'd been living with this burden. ''What did you do—when the war was over?'' she asked at last.

He shrugged indifferently, his anger now coming under a rigidly disciplined control. The cool, careless mask was back in place; the vulnerability and sorrow might have been only a mirage. Except that Bryony remembered it only too well, for it had stirred her heart in a deep, powerful way, never to be forgotten.

"I traveled around the country with a chip on my shoulder and a gun in my holster, looking for trouble,'' Logan said. ''I was only nineteen, but I'd seen a lot of men die in those four years of war, and it made me determined not to follow suit. I wanted to cram as much of life's excitement as I could into every moment. After a few months of drifting, I joined some army friends up north and attended college for a few years, but I reckon my nature wasn't suited to studying all the time. I grew restless, bored. Before long I hit the trail again, heading west, intending to make a name for myself.''

"As a gunfighter?" she put in. She was seeing him in an altogether new light today, and she wanted more than anything else to believe that he was not the evil villain she had always pictured him.

"Yes, my innocent little tenderfoot, I intended to make a name for myself as a gunfighter," Jim Logan replied coolly. "I had always been quick with a gun, and the war helped me develop my skill. Afterward, I practiced diligently, and when I ventured back into the rugged territories of the west, I wanted to make men fear me, to watch them scatter like rabbits as I walked down the street, to show the world that I was a force to be reckoned with." He strode toward her, noting with bitter satisfaction her horror and dismay. "That shocks you, doesn't it?" he stated, a grim smile twisting his lips. "You hate the fact that I chose this profession, that I sought out the notoriety and fearsome reputation you obviously deplore. Well, little tenderfoot, that's what I did. I earned a name for myself as a tough, fast, hired gun, and I killed men who had to be killed, and lived the kind of life I wanted to live. I hired out my gun to men who needed protection, or who wanted help in a range war. I went from town to town, frequenting saloons and gambling houses, bedding every good-looking woman who took my fancy. I was a loner, allowing no one to come close to me, to know me or my past, but I did just as I damn well pleased and took no one's happiness into account but my own." He paused, and reaching down a strong hand, pulled her to her feet so quickly that the buckskin jacket slid away and she faced him naked, her long, slender body glowing with the luminosity of a pearl in the morning light as his narrowed gaze traveled over her, coming to rest at last upon her face.

"But there's one thing I didn't do despite all the rest," he said in a low, intense voice that held her attention. His hands tightened on her shoulders. "I never killed an innocent man. The people I shot were rustlers or bullies or murdering thieves. I was hired to fight them." His eyes pierced hers. "Sometimes, it's true, I was drawn into a gunfight with other men who sought to gain a reputation for themselves by killing the infamous Texas Jim Logan. As my reputation grew, these incidents increased, unfortunately for the two-bit cowpokes who wanted to kill me just to make a name for themselves." His lips compressed tightly. "I was forced to kill them in order to survive. But I never killed a decent, law-abiding man, or used my gun against one. The only men who have had cause to fear me are those who operate outside the law, or those who are stupid or loco enough to force me into a fight. Anything you've ever heard to the contrary is hogwash."

"If that's true," Bryony said softly, "then why did you kill my father?"

There was silence. He released her shoulders abruptly, and stood looking down at her, his eyes hardening.

"Ah, yes, your father," he grated harshly.

Bryony said nothing. She had listened to his tale with compassion, wanting desperately to understand what had driven him to a life of violence. She thought she understood his inner unhappiness, the bitter cynicism beneath the cold, indifferent facade, but she couldn't really reconcile herself to the life he had chosen, to a profession that violated every principle in which she believed. She had been raised to abhor violence; he practiced it almost daily. She believed in being an active part of the world around her. He was a loner, a man who sought no friends, who lived only for his own pleasure, commanding the fearful respect of those around him who were intimidated by his stunning skill with a gun and by his ruthless reputation. And there were other differences. She was innocent, having been raised to believe in a sacred love that she would one day find with a perfect man; he was a libertine who used women only to satisfy physical needs. She could sympathize with him, and regret the years of pain and guilt he had suffered, but she could not approve of him, nor excuse the life he had chosen for himself.

Their moment of closeness had vanished, and now the barrier that would forever divide them had been erected once again. She knew that she must forget the wondrous passion they had known together last night, and also the intimacy they'd shared in the cave this morning when they'd spoken from their hearts as lovers and friends. But first, first she would know the answer to her question. Why had he killed her father?

"Tell me something, Bryony," Logan remarked curtly. "How well did you know Wesley Hill?"

"What do you mean? He was my father!"

"I know that. But how well did you know him? What kind of a man was he? *What did you really know about him?*"

Under his questioning, she moved away from him and began to dress hurriedly, all too aware, suddenly, of her own nakedness. Logan watched her expressionlessly, his arms folded across his chest. When she had pulled on her dusty jeans and shirt, and had finished struggling with her boots, she stood up, tossing her black mane of hair and sending a fiery glance his way.

"If you must know, I've spent most of my time in boarding school since my mother died and so I didn't know my father very well. I was young when my mother died, and he was involved in his investments and things." Her tone was a shade too loud and too shrill, belying the calm composure she was trying so hard to convey. "One can scarcely expect him to have made time for a very young daughter, who must have been a burden to him. Can one?" She swallowed and went on defiantly. "But I do know that he built his ranch into one of the largest, most prosperous spreads in the territory, and that everybody for miles around respected and liked him. Now, I've answered your questions. Are you ready to answer mine?''

Surprisingly, her incensed tone didn't seem to anger him. His light blue eyes penetrated right through her, detecting much more than Bryony had meant to reveal. In those few, brief, angrily defensive words she'd flung at him, he saw for an instant the beautiful, lonely young girl shut away at boarding school, shut out of her ambitious father's busy life. He had a glimpse of the hurt and loneliness she'd always kept locked inside her, though she immediately glossed over her feelings, trying so hard to pretend they didn't exist at all. But there was no question in his mind that she had been deeply hurt by Wesley Hill's neglect, and not for the first time, he found himself cursing the man. Then he met Bryony's flashing green eyes as she awaited his reply, and he wished fervently that he didn't have to be the one to tell her, to hurt her more. Hell, she already hated him enough for what he'd done. Now he'd only be adding to that resentment. His lips twisted cynically. What difference did it make? She'd have to be told eventually; for her own safety, it was better if she knew the truth immediately. Maybe then she'd listen to reason and get the hell out of Arizona.

"Well, Bryony, I reckon you have a right to know why I killed your father," he stated grimly. "Daisy Winston was a friend of mine. A kid not much older than you, and all alone in the world." His lips were a thin, tight line. "Your father killed her."

His words were like a slap in the face. She nearly staggered backward as they hit her. "I don't believe you! You're lying!"

"No."

"Yes, you're making this up as an excuse for killing him!" Cold fury surged through her, making her tremble with the ferocity of her feelings; her eyes were wild with rage. "My father and Daisy Winston were lovers! Lovers! Why would he kill her? It's ridiculous! You're lying to me because you think I'm a stupid schoolgirl who will believe whatever you say, but you're wrong! I don't believe a word of it!''

His steel blue eyes grew even colder. "I'm telling you the truth. If you weren't such a damned stubborn little idiot, you'd shut up and listen to what I have to say." Impatiently, he pushed her roughly down onto the blanket near the fire and towered over her. When Bryony tried to scramble to her feet, he shoved her back, saying in a dangerous tone, "Stay right there! You're going to hear me out whether you like it or not! It's not a pretty story, but it's true, and you need to know it. I swear, Bryony, I'll hogtie you if I have to, but one way or another you're going to sit still and listen to me!''

His threatening words only intensified her rage, but she knew he could carry out his threat if he wanted. Fuming, she sat upon the blanket, regarding him with an expression of the utmost loathing, while her breast heaved with indignation. She brushed her rich ebony locks from her eyes and said between clenched teeth, "Go ahead and talk then, damn you! But I'll never believe a word of what you say!''

"That's up to you," he replied coldly. "Wesley Hill was a rustler, a thief, and a murderer," he began, ignoring her gasp of fury and continuing ruthlessly. "He and Matt Richards had been working together for years, rustling the smaller ranchers off the range, building up their own herds with stolen cattle at the expense of their neighbors. They'd stopped at nothing to line their own greedy, thieving pockets.''

"How dare you!" Bryony's voice was none too steady; she made an uncontrollable movement to rise and face him, but he swiftly knelt beside her and seized her roughly by the shoulders.

"It's true, damn it! Sam Blake hired me to put a stop to it before he's driven off the range. I've done a lot of checking, and one of my best sources of information was Daisy Winston—and believe me, she was in a position to know!''

Bryony pushed his hands away. "Don't touch me!" Her voice trembled. "Maybe you really believe what you're saying, but don't you see? That Daisy Winston fed you a pack of lies! What was she—a saloon girl? Do you really think what she said was reliable? Maybe she and my father had a fight, and she made up these things in anger! Maybe—''

"No, Bryony. Hear me out."

He sat down opposite her on the blanket. "Daisy had no reason to lie. She was a dirt-poor kid from the hills of Tennessee who lost whatever family she had during the war, and drifted west simply because there was nowhere else to go. Meg Donahue, the owner of the Silver Spur, took her in a few years back and gave her a job. Your father met her in the saloon and she became his mistress—his mistress! Though she was little more than an ignorant, scared kid barely older than his own daughter!''

"How do you know so much about her?"

"After Sam Blake hired me, I spent a lot of time in the Silver Spur, picking up range gossip and the kind of rumors cowboys thrive on. Daisy and I became friends.''

"Oh?" Her voice dripped contempt. "I can well imagine just how friendly.''

His eyes narrowed. "You're wrong, Bryony, if you think that Daisy and I slept together. I respected her too much to seduce her.''

This insult seemed calculated to inflame her. It succeeded.

"Why, you . . .!" Tears of indignation blinded her as she dove toward him, nails outstretched, but he grasped her wrists easily and rolled her onto the ground, pinning her there.

"I haven't finished what I have to say to you yet," he remarked coolly, as she struggled in vain to free herself.

It didn't take long before she realized the hopelessness of fighting him, and she ceased her writhing, staring up at him with fiery eyes.

"Go on, damn you," she spat.

He released her, and stood up. He began to pace restlessly about the cave, ignoring her stormy countenance. "It soon became clear to me that Daisy was frightened—frightened of your father, and of Matt Richards. It took some doing, but I won her confidence, and one night she told me . . . well, enough to make me realize what kind of a man Wesley Hill really was. She confirmed Sam Blake's suspicions, and even informed me that there was a third party involved, though she had no idea who this might be. That's something I still don't know. It could be anyone."

His voice grew bitter, and a haunted look settled over his features. "I reckon I could have shot down your father and Richards pronto to end the whole matter, but that wouldn't have helped me locate the unknown partner. Besides, Blake wanted proof he could show to a sheriff or judge in order to get some of his cattle returned. So I waited, doing my best to come up with some real evidence. And that turned out badly for Daisy."

He turned and frowned at Bryony. "She'd wanted to break off with your father after she learned what was going on, but he wouldn't let her. He and Richards both threatened to kill her if she spoke one word of what she knew to anyone. Daisy had guts, though. She told me what was happening, and I promised to help her. Then she mentioned that your father and Richards had quarreled after the Blake boy was murdered. Apparently, killing the boy shook up your father, and he told Richards he didn't want any more needless killing. Richards replied that he and the third partner had agreed the boy's death was necessary. Things got pretty ugly, I guess, and threats were made on both sides. Later, your father told Daisy that he was going to write a confession, implicating Richards, the third partner, and himself, which he would hide in a secure place, as protection in case Richards decided to try to get rid of him. He told Richards about it, explaining that the whole setup would be blown sky-high because the paper would fall into the appropriate hands if he should die. It was a shrewd move. He used that hidden confession to protect his life.''

"I never heard such a ridiculous story in my life!" Bryony burst out. "Do you realize the wild, unsupported accusations you're making against my father, a man who is dead and unable to defend himself, and against Matt Richards, the most respected man in Winchester? I think you're crazy! You and Daisy Winston!" An idea occurred to her and she added triumphantly, "If what that saloon girl said was true, and my father had drafted such a document, don't you think it would have come to light by now? He's been dead several months, and no such letter was found among his legal papers."

Logan gave her a long look. "You're quick, aren't you? The truth is, Bryony, I don't know why the document hasn't turned up. I don't know where in hell it is."

"It doesn't exist!" she cried staunchly. "It never did! And none of this absurd story is true!"

"It's true, all right. Now let me finish. Two days before she died, Daisy told me she was going to find out from Hill where he planned to hide the confession. She promised to tell me, and in return, I promised her my protection until the whole dirty business was finished. The next day I was in the saloon when I heard a prospector passing through town mention a name that was familiar to me. A man who had served with me in the Union Army was in trouble down in Mexico. I set out for Nogales, just below the border, to see if I could help him out." His eyes gleamed at her. "Sometimes, my reputation with a gun comes in handy. There are times when my name alone scares off trouble, and I never even need to fire a shot. Unfortunately," he went on with a frown, "this wasn't one of those times. It was an ugly business, but I managed to get him out of a bad situation. By the time I returned to Winchester, two days had passed. I went straightaway to see Daisy in the saloon, but she didn't have time to talk. Your father was coming to get her to bring her out to the ranch with him for the night. Meg Donahue came up just as Daisy was starting to tell me what she'd learned, and we had to break off our conversation. I figured I'd see her the next day and find out where Hill had hidden the damned paper."

He paused, but Bryony made no comment, merely glaring at him angrily, enraged by what he was telling her. From Jim Logan's calm, assured attitude, it was obvious that he believed what he was saying, but Bryony was convinced there was a dreadful mistake. Her heart told her that her father had been a good, decent, honorable man. He had been ambitious, that she acknowledged. But there was a big difference between ambition and lustful greed, between working hard to become successful, and stealing and killing to obtain one's goals. Her father had not been capable of viciousness or dishonesty. There had to be another explanation, she thought, as a fierce loyalty surged up within her. So she listened grimly to the tall gunfighter's story, while her keen mind tried to untangle the bits and pieces of information she was hearing. It was up to her to prove that Jim Logan was wrong. Her father was dead, and unable to defend himself and his good name. She must prove his innocence for him.

When she remained silent, Logan came to stand before her, his expression dark and impenetrable. There was no trace of satisfaction in his voice as he spoke, only a heaviness that indicated that what he was saying caused him considerable grief. "I never had the chance to talk to Daisy again, Bryony. Riding back to town from Blake's ranch the next morning, I saw vultures gathering in the sky above Cougars' Bluff. I rode over to investigate. I found Daisy.''

Involuntarily, Bryony gave a cry of dismay. Then she pressed her lips together, and clasped her hands tightly in her lap.

''She was lying under some scrub brush, her clothes torn and bloody, her hair matted with bl. . . .'' He broke off, slamming his fist against the wall of the cave. When he spoke again, his voice was steely. ''She had been beaten and strangled. It was one of the most brutal acts I've ever seen, and believe me, I've seen my share. And to top it off, that bastard had left her there to die in the desert sun.''

''Do you mean she was still *alive?*'' Bryony asked with mounting horror.

He nodded. ''Barely. She died within seconds of my reaching her—there was nothing I could do. But she did manage to whisper one word—your father's name. That's how I knew that Wesley Hill had killed her.'' The savage note in his voice frightened her. Murderous hatred shone in his eyes. ''There were fresh carriage tracks on the trail near her body and I followed them into town. He'd arrived just before me and he was on his way into the saloon. The saloon! Damn him—he had just killed a girl and he was aiming to sit down and enjoy a round of drinks! I called him out on the spot.'' A mirthless laugh escaped his tense lips. ''Oh, he didn't want to fight me. He knew he would be standing in hell before the sun had fully risen that day. But I challenged him, and by the code of the west he was obliged to face me.''

''What you did was like murder,'' she whispered.

''No, Bryony,'' he returned coldly. ''He had an even chance. He was armed and able to defend himself. Unlike Daisy, who didn't have a prayer in hell.''

The silence that fell between them then was long and painful. He seemed enraged all over again after reliving the memories of that awful day, and Bryony felt numbed by what he had told her. At last she spoke, forcing herself to meet his hard stare.

"There must be a mistake. My father wouldn't . . . he couldn't . . ."

"He could, and he did."

"No!" She buried her face in her hands, wanting to block his words from her mind. But she couldn't. She had to think, had to come up with the true explanation for the things he'd told her.

"There's still the matter of that document," she cried, grabbing at this thought. "If all this were true, then the document should have come to light by now, and since it hasn't, it probably doesn't exist, which means that Daisy Winston lied about—"

"The document exists. Apparently, it's so well hidden that it escaped everyone's notice. But it's bound to be discovered soon. I'm not the only one looking for it."

"What do you mean?"

"Matt Richards must find that confession—before you or I do. If you find it first, his game is up. Don't you see that? Don't you realize the threat you pose to him?"

She gasped. She was remembering that the Circle H had been ransacked after her father's death, and the study safe dynamited. She thought of her kidnapping off the stagecoach, and the attempt to murder her yesterday. All of the events that had puzzled and frightened her since she arrived in Arizona took on new meaning with his words. The chilling fear that had assaulted her as she listened to Zeke Murdock and Rusty Jessup from her hidden crevice in the mountaintop came back to her now. For the first time, the possibility that Jim Logan might be correct seriously occurred to her—and it was a devastating thought.

Logan seemed to be reading her mind. He studied her closely and then spoke urgently. "I found Shorty Buchanan's body when I rode out searching for you yesterday. I'd learned that Richards had asked you to marry him, and that you'd refused—for the moment. Tell me. Did he want you to move in immediately to the Twin Bars?'' The expression in her eyes gave him the answer he expected and he nodded, scowling. ''Don't you see, Bryony, he'll go to any lengths to get you off the Circle H so that he can have a clear field to find that damaging confession. As soon as I'd heard that you had thwarted his latest plan by turning him down, I knew he'd resort to violence again. And he won't stop until you're out of the way. That's why it's absolutely necessary that you leave Arizona until I get this settled—until Richards is dead or behind bars. As long as you're in the territory, you're a target for him and the coyotes who do his dirty work.'' He sighed. ''What actually happened yesterday before I found you, Bryony? How did you escape getting shot along with your foreman?''

In a dull, listless voice she related the events of the previous afternoon. When she had finished, Jim Logan pulled her gently to her feet.

''I reckon that confirms what I've been telling you,'' he remarked gravely. ''Rusty Jessup used to be your father's foreman. He was one of the small group of range hands who knew what was really going on. He and Zeke Murdock must both work for Richards now. They were hired by him to get you out of the way.''

Bryony felt too stunned and confused by all she had heard to argue. She merely shook her head and murmured in a dazed way, ''I know it can't be true. It can't. There must be another explanation for all this. My father—Matt—they're not evil men.''

Jim Logan drew her into his arms. He wanted nothing more than to hold and comfort her. She looked as white as parchment, and he could feel her slender body trembling within the circle of his arms. But even as he held her tenderly, his lips lightly brushing her hair, she pulled away in agitation.

''No, don't touch me! What we did last night was

wrong . . . it must never happen again."

"Why not, Bryony? You seemed to enjoy yourself at the time."

Tears stung her eyes and spilled onto her cheeks. "Have you no feelings? You know perfectly well that we shouldn't have . . . that there's no hope of any kind of friendship between us!"

"It wasn't friendship I had in mind." At her anguished cry, he scowled and the hard, glittering look returned to his eyes. "So, you still hate me for killing your father? Even after everything I've told you."

"What you've told me is a . . . a mistaken theory," she cried. "You killed my father for something he never did! And I can never, never forgive or forget that! Even if I wanted to, I could not. It will always stand between us!"

Logan made her a mocking bow. "Anything you say, ma'am." There was nothing but cold disdain in his tone, all traces of kindness and compassion gone. Before he could say any more, however, they were both startled by the shrill neigh of a horse from the mountainside, startlingly close. In two quick strides, he reached the mouth of the cave, pausing beyond Pecos, whose ears had pricked at the sound.

"What . . . who is it?" Bryony whispered, aware that her heart was hammering with awesome fear.

Logan returned swiftly to her side. "It's that loud-mouthed wrangler I knocked down yesterday, Buck Monroe. I reckon he's searching for you, little tenderfoot. It appears that our nice little hideout is about to be discovered."

Chapter Nineteen

Bryony flew to the jagged mouth of the cave and peered down the mountain trail, shielding her eyes against the sun. Outside the cave, the daylight was now quite strong, and there was every sign that it would be a beautiful morning. All traces of last night's storm clouds had disappeared from the sky and in their stead, a sapphire blue dome crowned the awakening landscape. The violets and paloverdes seemed more vivid than ever after the rainstorm, and the plain below stretched like a golden carpet until it merged with the rolling green foothills in the distance.

Some miles beyond, she knew, lay the Circle H in its own sprawling green valley, and by now, everyone would know that she and Shorty were missing. Her range hands were searching for her on the plain below; she could make out a number of figures on horseback fanned out amidst the cacti and scrub brush. Buck was one of them, only he was much closer, combing the trail of the mountainside, his flat-brimmed sombrero set squarely on his head. When he suddenly called her name, the sound came clearly to her ears across the quiet mountainside, just as his palomino's whinny had done. But Buck was still some distance away, well below the entrance to the cave. She would have time to gather up her things and go down to him. For more than one reason, she didn't want him or anyone else to discover

that she had spent the night in this secluded cave with
her father's murderer—the man who only yesterday had
knocked down Buck himself! Hastily, she turned back
to the cavern's dim interior, where Jim Logan was
regarding her carelessly.

"I have to go down to him," she said stiffly, stooping
to gather up her neckerchief, and checking automatically for the derringer in her holster. When she rose, she
paused for a moment, meeting the gunfighter's hard,
glittering stare with an expression of uncertainty in her
wide, brilliant green eyes. Without quite knowing why,
she felt a strange reluctance to leave now that the time
was actually here. She wanted to prolong this moment
alone with him for just a little longer. She knew it would
probably be their last.

If the situation was different, she might almost have
imagined that she was in love with him—but the
situation was not different. There was no hope that love
could flourish between two such different people. If the
first seeds of love had indeed been planted in her heart,
then she must do her best to destroy them; it was the
only way. Yet for one more moment, she lingered,
gazing into his eyes, aware of a curious ache within her.
Oh, if only things could have been different between
them!

"I reckon you're planning to leave Arizona?" he
remarked at last, breaking the electrifying silence that
filled the cave.

Bryony shook her head.

"Are you loco? Bryony, I told you, you're as good as
dead if you stay here now. Don't you realize that, you
stubborn little fool?"

She flinched under the fierceness of his voice, but
then retorted with a defiant toss of her head. "I realize
nothing of the sort. I don't believe a single word of your
extremely farfetched theory."

"Then how do you explain the attempt on your life
yesterday? How do you explain your abduction from
the stagecoach?"

"I don't know!" Desperation had crept into her voice. Why did he persist in badgering her about this? Why wouldn't he leave her alone.

"I won't leave Arizona—it's my home now. And no one is going to drive me away."

Logan's face tautened. He seized her shoulders and shook her furiously. "Why, you damn stupid little bitch! You deserve to get yourself killed! And I'll be damned if I'll lift a finger to save your stubborn hide one more time!"

Bryony wrenched away, carrying with her the image of his lean face livid with anger as she plunged out of the cave and into the sunshine. Choking back a sob, she hurried blindly down the rock-strewn trail, oblivious of the strain on her ankle, and trying to blot her final vision of him from her mind.

Buck was overjoyed to see her. He greeted her with a crushing bear hug and asked her repeatedly if she was all right. If he noticed that her cheeks were pale and her eyes wet with tears, he ascribed it to the ordeal she had been through, and listened closely as Bryony explained that she had spent the night in a cave after losing her horse and twisting her ankle. She didn't mention anything about Jim Logan, and Buck seemed to accept her story readily enough.

"We found Shorty's body this morning. He'd been shot," Buck said when she had finished.

"Oh, Buck, it was horrible. He never even saw it coming. They ambushed us. They shot at me too, and followed me up the mountain, but they didn't find me."

"Did you get a look at the men who shot at you? Could you recognize them if you saw them again?"

She hesitated. Then she shook her head. "No," she lied, not meeting his intent gaze. "It all happened so fast. . ."

Buck helped her to mount his palomino, then swung himself up in the saddle behind her. "Don't worry about a thing, Bryony. The boys and I will track down those hombres. It's the least we can do for Shorty." His voice was unusually grim and purposeful, without any trace of his customary good humor.

Later, Bryony was to wonder how she ever managed to get through the remainder of the morning. All those questions! Between Buck and the wranglers, Rosita, and Judge Hamilton, she was forced to repeat her story half a dozen times, each time refraining from mentioning that she knew the identity of her attackers, and also that she had been rescued on the mountainside by Jim Logan. She didn't stop to analyze why she kept these facts to herself; she only knew that an inner voice prompted her to do so. By the time she had collapsed in the study armchair with a cup of steaming coffee and a plate of buttered corn muffins supplied by Rosita, she wished only to be left alone. But it was not to be. Matt Richards came striding into the room, staring from her to Judge Hamilton and back again, and demanding in an imperative tone to be told what happened.

Judge Hamilton recited the story, sparing her the necessity of explaining again. While he did so, Bryony studied Matt. Could this dark, handsome, well-dressed man really be the calculating murderer Jim Logan claimed he was? Could he really be wishing her dead at this moment? It seemed incredible. Too incredible. There was concern in every feature of Matt's face as he heard what had befallen her. When he knelt by her side and took her hand in his, she searched his black, hooded eyes for some hint of insincerity, of malice. There was none. She found herself smiling at him, forgetting Jim Logan's ridiculous story. Matt was no more a killer than she was. And neither was her father.

Matt seemed to have forgotten the previous strain between them caused by her rejection of his proposal. His only thought appeared to be gratitude that she was safe. Bryony appreciated his solicitude, as well as the attentions of Judge Hamilton, but she found herself wishing for the peace and quiet of her own room where she could attempt to compose herself and to sort out the jumbled thoughts in her aching head. At last, they allowed her to excuse herself, promising that they would call again the next morning to see if there was anything they could do for her. Drained in both body and spirit, she fell into a restless slumber, stretched upon the blue silk bed quilt in her soiled clothes, seeking escape from her troubles in the murky depths of sleep.

During the next few days, Bryony wrestled with the questions confronting her. She turned over and over in her mind the information Jim Logan had given her, trying desperately to find a flaw in his reasoning, to discover an alternative explanation for Daisy Winston's death and for the attempts made on her own life, but there was too little information for her to go on. She did decide to search the ranch house, though. She told herself that she was merely exploring to amuse herself, but deep down, she knew that she had to prove to herself that the confession Jim had talked of did not exist. After an exhaustive search of the upstairs and downstairs rooms, she drew a breath of relief. So much for Jim Logan's suspicions! she told herself with a triumphant smile. There was no hidden document in this house, of that she was certain. This knowledge reinforced her belief that the whole ugly matter was a horrible, horrible mistake.

As much to keep her mind off her worries as for any other reason, Bryony decided to go ahead with her plans for a fiesta in June. She invited Matt, who accepted with his warm smile, assuring her that he wouldn't miss it for anything. Ever since the shooting incident, Matt had treated her with the utmost kindness and concern. He never once pressed her about marriage as he had done at the picnic, but seemed content to keep an eye on her, letting her know that he was there if she needed him for anything. She was grateful, and ashamed that she had ever, even for one instant, suspected him of being a murderer.

Her life settled down to its normal routine once again, and the terror of that late May afternoon on the mountain subsided into little more than a ghastly memory. The only event that disturbed the tranquility of the lazy summer days was the news early in June that Cochise, the brilliant Apache chieftain, had died on his reservation. The settlers in the area waited in trepidation to see the reaction of his people, for though the Apache leader had signed a peace treaty several years earlier with General Howard, it was known that some raiding bands still made forays from the reservation into neighboring areas, and now that the old chief was gone, the U.S. government was considering moving the Apaches to the San Carlos reservation on the Gila River, a place always unpopular with the Chiracahua Apache. So the white settlers in the territory waited uneasily for the Apache reaction to the new circumstances, and wondered bleakly if the old days of warfare would return. However, as time passed, and no new attacks occurred to warrant their fears, once again they settled into their routines.

Bryony, pondering the situation, couldn't help wondering how many raids were really instigated by the Apache, and how many were blamed on them unjustly. She remembered how Zeke Murdock and Rusty Jessup had disguised themselves as Apaches when they had attacked her and Shorty. This thought triggered something else in her brain. Buck had once told her that most of the people in the area believed that Indians were responsible for Johnny Blake's death, though Sam and Annie believed that her father and Matt Richards were behind it. She pressed her palms to her head, wanting to drive out all such thoughts. It couldn't possibly be true—it just couldn't! No doubt in the Blake boy's case it really *had* been renegade Indians who had killed him. She'd better accept that explanation and forget her own tormenting doubts or she would very likely go mad. Just because her own attackers had impersonated Apache warriors didn't mean that every death attributed to the Indians was the work of white men. How ridiculous she was!

This train of thought reminded her that she had neglected to invite the Blakes to her party. Bryony resolved to invite them that very day, determined to convince them that despite their suspicions, she was fully prepared to be their friend.

Dressed in a yellow shirt and a blue denim riding skirt, her hair twisted into a single ebony braid down her back, Bryony tightened the strings of her new Stetson as she stepped off the porch and walked toward the corral. Buck and Thomas had recaptured Shadow for her after a week of hunting for him in the wilderness, and then they'd found it necessary to break him in all over again. Though he had fought fiercely against recapture, the wild mustang had seemed glad to see Bryony again when she ran out to the corral to welcome him home. As she approached him now in the fenced corral, he greeted her with a high-pitched whinny and a prancing step.

"Mornin', Miss Hill," the red-shirted wrangler who was repairing a broken board in the corral fence nodded to her respectfully. "Ridin' out today?"

"Yes, Frank. Is Shadow's saddle in the stable?"

"Shore is. Want me to saddle 'im for you, ma'am?"

"No, thanks, I'll get it." She entered the long, rambling stable with its rows of stalls and feed bins, and its strong aroma of horses and leather. Buck Monroe was inside stitching up a saddle. He raised his head from his task and smiled at her.

"I just rode in from the north pasture," he remarked. "Rounded up a few strays and brought 'em back for slaughtering. That Army supply captain ordered a half dozen sides of beef—wants it by late afternoon."

"Fine, Buck." She answered him absently. Lately she had come to depend heavily on Buck to handle details of the cattle ranch. He'd been appointed foreman in Shorty's place, and she couldn't help thinking from time to time that if she had awarded him that position when she first came to the ranch, Buck might be the one now dead. She hoped fervently that he would not meet danger on her account, and for the first time wondered if she should indeed leave Arizona, at least until this perilous situation was resolved. Though she didn't believe for a moment that Matt Richards was involved, she couldn't deny that *somebody* had hired Murdock and Jessup to get rid of her, and this unpleasant thought made her shiver despite the intense heat of the sun. When she glanced up after lifting Shadow's heavy leather saddle from its peg, she found Buck watching her worriedly.

"Here, let me take that, Bryony." He tossed the saddle over his shoulder and walked with her to the stable door and out into the yard. "Mind if I ask where you're goin' ma'am?"

His good-natured grin didn't save him from her gesture of exasperation. "Yes, I do mind," she snapped, and then stopped in her tracks and sighed. "I'm sorry, Buck. I just don't like to feel crowded. Everyone has been so worried about me lately that I feel as if I can't even breathe without someone rushing up to ask me if I need fresh air, or a cup of tea, or a chair to sit upon. I'm well able to care for myself, and I'm not afraid to ride out alone! There, does that satisfy you?"

"Nope. Not after what happened last month," Buck replied undaunted. "Let me ride with you. I promise to let you handle any emergencies single-handed. Why, if a grizzly bear was to lumber on down and try to hug you to death, I reckon I'd just stand by and watch! Honest, ma'am, I would!"

She couldn't help laughing at that, and with a rueful shake of her head, told him he could ride with her.

"I'm going out to the Blakes, to invite Annie and Sam Blake to the fiesta," she said.

"Annie Blake—at your fiesta? Don't count on it, Bryony. That girl never went to no party in her life. She doesn't think of nothing but working her fingers to the bone on that ranch of her pa's. I'll wager she don't even know how to dance!'' With these careless words, Buck left to fetch his horse, while Bryony waited astride Shadow, a slight smile playing about her lips.

Oh, Annie Blake thinks of something besides her work, all right, she thought shrewdly, patting the mustang's long neck as she absently kept him under control. She thinks of you, Buck, and she thinks of you often unless I miss my guess. I'm going to do my best to help her rope you in like one of those poor, helpless calves you're always riding down. And as for knowing how to dance—well, we'll just see about that.

It was a perfect summer day, hot and dry, with the air refreshingly cool as it drifted down from the mountains, offsetting the burning golden glare of the desert sun. They rode in silence for the most part, Buck sensing Bryony's desire to be undisturbed. If he could have had his way, he would have snatched her from her horse and crushed her to his chest, showering kisses on that sweet, troubled face that kept him so bewitched. His infatuation with her was as strong as ever, though it was tempered now with deep respect, and with the knowledge that she was his employer, and thought of him merely as a friend—a reliable friend, yes—but nothing more. He didn't want to add to her problems by making a damned pest of himself like some moonstruck calf, but he was determined to keep an eye on her and see that she stayed out of trouble.

As they rode, he kept stealing quick glances at her profile, noting how she had changed since she'd come to the Circle H, and especially since she and Shorty had been ambushed last month. At first she'd seemed a little unsure of herself, and as fragile as a flower. She had been as much a product of the city as that fancy English riding habit she had brought with her. But now, she had shouldered the responsibilities of her position, and it showed in her face and bearing. Oh, she was still so damned beautiful that every wrangler on the ranch was loco in love with her, but she possessed an air of authority and competence that was obvious to see, and that had earned her the respect of her range hands. But something else was different, too. The enthusiasm and high spirits that had at first seemed such a strong part of her personality had waned with the passing weeks, and now, especially since the ordeal a month ago, she seemed quieter and somehow troubled. She no longer laughed as easily as she once had, and her eyes, those glorious green pools that had enchanted him from the first, now seemed clouded with worry, disturbed by thoughts she would share with no one. Buck wished she would confide in him and allow him to help her, but he knew her too well by now to try to force her to talk about it. Bryony was fiercely independent and she hated when anyone, even Judge Hamilton and Matt Richards, her closest friends, tried to pry into her private reflections.

While Buck was preoccupied with the workings of Bryony's mind during their ride to the Blake ranch, she was lost in somber reflection, dwelling reluctantly on a memory that she would like all too well to forget. Forget? How she wished she might! But the memory of one man and one night dominated her thoughts with cruel persistence, and it was not the danger in which she felt herself to be that accounted for her low spirits, but the haunting vision of a handsome young man talking to her before a firelight, a lean, tanned gunfighter who had opened his heart to her. She had been unable to forget the pain in Jim Logan's light blue eyes, or the way his voice had altered from its usual mocking drawl when he spoke about his father and the magnificent ranch in Texas. She had been unable to forget the unexpected gentleness with which he had made love to her that stormy night on the mountain, the way his hands and lips and eyes had caressed her with infinite tenderness. Despite her knowledge that he had bedded many women before her, she was aware that something special and powerful had happened between them that night. For her, it had been an initiation into a world of passion that before she had only guessed at; for him, she instinctively

sensed that something even more revolutionary had occurred. He had allowed himself to feel deeply, to react
not as a callous man casually taking a woman to bed,
but as a human being reaching out to another human
being for love and warmth and compassion.

How did she feel about this? That was what had been
worrying her ever since that night. She had come to
realize that she had matched his own need for love and
warmth with her own, seeking in him what she had
never had from anyone else. Love. Real love. The kind
of love she had read about and dreamed about, but
never experienced. She knew deep in her heart that now
she had found it. But it could never, never be realized.
So she tried to forget him—oh, how she tried. But the
memory of his touch, his voice, his eyes, tortured her,
making her soul ache with a pain that knew no bounds.
And as Buck Monroe trotted beside her across the
wilderness in all its dazzling summer glory, she wished
desperately a forbidden wish—that her companion were
instead the strong, sun-bronzed gunfighter who had
kindled in her the torturous flame of love.

It was with a startled gasp that she observed Jim
Logan as she drew up before the Blake's modest ranch
house. He was emerging through the doorway accompanied by Annie Blake. They were deeply involved in conversation and the chestnut-haired girl was standing quite
close to him, regarding him with fixed interest. Bryony
couldn't control a sudden stab of jealousy at seeing
them together, though she quickly realized she was being foolish. Nevertheless, she was aware that she was
flushing, and that her heart was pounding uncomfortably in her breast.

Jim Logan glanced up at the same instant Annie did,
but unlike the girl, who scowled in a most unwelcoming
manner, his expression underwent no change what-
soever, regarding the visitors indifferently, as though
they were complete strangers whom he had no interest in
meeting. Bryony stiffened under his cold glance, feeling

unexpectedly crushed. Buck Monroe, though, reacted more forcefully than any of the other three. He leapt down from his horse and stalked furiously toward the gunfighter.

"I reckon I've a score to settle with you, Mister Jim Logan!" he growled, his fists clenching.

"Buck, stop it!" Annie pleaded, desperately clinging to the cowboy's shirt. "What are you doing? He'll kill you if you try to fight him! And why you have a grudge against *him*, I wish I knew!"

"*He* knows damn well why I have a grudge against him! No man knocks me down and walks away without a bruise afterward!"

"I reckon that's not true, cowboy. I shore did it!" Logan remarked in his most infuriating drawl, a mocking smile curling his thin lips.

Buck began to struggle anew, but Annie clung firmly to him with mulish tenacity, and by that time Bryony had dismounted.

"Buck, stop being such a hare-brained idiot!" she ordered. "Forget what happened! You know perfectly well that Jim Logan could kill you instantly if he wanted, and I need you too badly as my foreman for you to get yourself killed over something foolish. Now simmer down and tie up our horses."

These words recalled the wrangler to his sense of duty, and he stopped struggling, though his face was still red and angry, in marked contrast to Logan's careless countenance.

"I wouldn't get myself killed Bryony," he muttered defensively. "Not if we'd used fists 'stead of guns. I can fight as well as any man—and I don't need no women-folk to protect me!"

"Of course not," the black-haired girl soothed, "but I came here to see Mr. Blake and Annie, not to witness a fight. So please oblige me by controlling your temper or I'll be sorry I agreed to let you come along."

Buck still looked as if he would like to fight, but

Bryony's words had calmed him, and he merely scowled darkly at the gunfighter, making no effort to approach him again.

Annie looked obviously relieved, while Bryony turned her eyes to Jim Logan's tall form. To her surprise, there was still no trace of emotion in the returning glance he sent her. Without speaking a work to her, but with that same maddening, mocking smile on his lips, he strode swiftly away, swinging himself easily onto his horse before calling a calm farewell to Annie. Devastated, Bryony stared after him. How could he be so indifferent to her? Could she have imagined the strength and nature of his feelings? She couldn't believe she had so misread the depth of his feelings. She was ashamed of the intense emotions that had instantly mounted in her own breast when she had first caught sight of him. She took a deep breath, fighting a very strong urge to burst into tears.

"What did you come for?" Annie Blake was asking curtly, her unfriendly voice recalling Bryony to her surroundings. Buck had obediently tethered their horses to the hitching post, and he, too, was watching Bryony curiously.

"I'd like to speak to you and your father, Annie. May I come in?"

"Suit yourself." The other girl shrugged. "Pa's out on the range, but you can speak your piece to me." She started to lead the way into the ranch house, but stopped midway up the steps and with heightened color glanced diffidently at Buck. "Want to come inside, Buck? I'll fetch you a glass of lemonade," she offered with an eagerness that was painfully obvious to Bryony, but completely lost on the sandy-haired cowpoke.

"Nope, Annie, I'm goin' to track down that no-good rangehand of yours, Bill Jenks. That varmint owes me twenty dollars from a poker game last week, and it's about time he paid up. Bryony, just give a holler when you're ready to ride for home."

Buck sauntered, whistling, towards the corrals, leaving Annie staring after him in disappointment. This time it was Bryony who recalled the chestnut-haired girl back to the present.

"Let's go in and talk," she suggested, a sympathetic smile touching her lips. "I think you'll be interested in what I have to say."

Inside the ranch house, Bryony couldn't help noticing how modestly the Blakes lived. In fact, the house was as plain as Annie herself. Only a single woven rug adorned the dark wooden floor of the adobe building, and the rooms were tiny compared to those at the Circle H. But everything was clean and in its place, and she followed Annie quietly into the sitting room, where a shabby chintz sofa and a trio of straight-backed chairs ringed a rough-hewn pine coffee table. There was a strong odor of tobacco everywhere, and Bryony noticed an assortment of pipes in a rack on the wall. She also noted the shotgun propped against the fireplace in the corner.

"Now, what do you want?" Annie demanded in her blunt way, eyeing her guest in anything but a friendly manner. "I've got chores to do and supper to fix, and I don't have time to dawdle around all day, so you'd best tell me what's on your mind."

By this time, Bryony had somewhat recovered from the shock of seeing Jim, and she was thinking more clearly. It was obvious to her that Annie's dislike hadn't lessened over the past few months, and she was determined to put an end to it. Suddenly, it became very important for Annie and Sam Blake to attend the fiesta. Bryony sat down calmly on the creaking sofa, folded her hands in her lap, and looked up at Annie with steady green eyes.

"I've come to invite you and your father to the fiesta at the Circle H on the twentieth of this month," she replied evenly. "Have you heard about it? I do hope you'll both come."

"Heard about it?" Annie laughed derisively. "Everyone in the whole territory has heard about it! That's all anyone ever talks about—the fancy fiesta Miss Bryony Hill is throwing up at her ranch! Well, you might have a nice big crowd for that there party, Miss Hill, but you won't see me or my pa there. We'd sooner drop dead then set foot inside your house.''

"I take it you still hold my father responsible for the troubles that have beset your family? And that you believe I'm equally to blame?"

"I reckon we don't hold *you* to blame for nothin'," Annie conceded reluctantly. "Jim Logan explained as how you had no idea what was goin' on, and never took no part in it.''

"He did, did he?" Bryony kept her voice level with an effort. She wondered what else Jim Logan had told Annie about her, but she didn't have time to reflect on this, for Annie had given her the opening she needed.

"That's fine, then," Bryony remarked. "Then may I ask why you don't care to come to the fiesta?''

Annie's lips tightened. "I don't hold with parties much, Miss Hill, and I don't aim to be obliged to your hospitality. I've got better things to think about than fritterin' away my time at some idiotic party, with a lot of drinkin' and dancin' and just plain foolishness goin' on. I don't want to come, and I won't.''

"You don't want to, Annie, or you're afraid to?"

"What did you say?" The girl took a threatening step forward, her eyes flashing. "I'm not afraid of nothing! And anyone who says different is a low-down liar!''

"I say different—and I'm not a liar!" Bryony retorted, meeting Annie's furious glare coolly. "You're afraid, all right! You're afraid to put a dress on and act like a lady! You're afraid to show that you're a woman, with a woman's feelings and cares and fears. You're afraid to go out and face Buck Monroe, to fight for him like a woman fights for a man. You're afraid you won't be pretty enough, or smart enough, or sweet enough to attract him, and so you just plain don't even try! Do you understand what I mean, Annie Blake? You're afraid, all right. Right down to the tips of your boots!''

White with fury, Annie charged forward. Bryony leaped to her feet, neatly side-stepping Annie's onrush, and pushed her unceremoniously down onto the sofa, staring down at her with sparkling emerald eyes.

"It's true, Annie, isn't it?" she said gently. "Look into your heart and you'll see that it's true."

Annie's mouth worked convulsively as she stared up at Bryony. Suddenly, her hazel eyes filled with tears, and she buried her tousled head in her hands, sobbing with all the force of her long pent-up unhappiness. "Yes, it's true!" she gasped brokenly, as Bryony sat down beside her and put an arm about her shoulders. "It's all true. I want Buck so much—I love him! But I know he'd never look at me twice. It's you he loves—I can see it plain as day!"

"Nonsense." Bryony's hands tightened on her racking shoulders. "Buck has an infatuation with me, a foolish infatuation that I assure you means nothing. I know, because I've had more than my fair share of infatuations with men, but none of them meant I was in love. Really, I didn't know the first thing about being in love until. . ." She broke off abruptly, as Annie raised glistening eyes to her face.

"Until what?"

"Never mind. It's not important. What is important is that I believe Buck *could* fall in love with you—if given half a chance. Look, I imagine he's known you for years, hasn't he? Well, for heaven's sake, that's part of the problem. He thinks of you the way he does his old saddle—not as a woman, a woman he could love. And Annie, I must admit that the clothes you wear, and the way you fix your hair, doesn't do very much to counteract that impression. The first thing you must learn is to have faith in yourself as a woman, and then dress and behave like one. Tell me, don't you have any other clothes besides these dreadful old baggy jeans and woolen shirts you're forever wearing?"

The girl sniffled and glanced at her shapeless clothes in some surprise. "I never needed none besides these. They're good, reliable work clothes, and that's about all I do is work."

"Would you like to do something different now and then? Would you like to go on picnics, or to fiestas occasionally?"

Annie wiped her eyes with the back of her hand. Her hair was falling stringily about her face. "I reckon," she shrugged, half resentfully. "But I guess what you said was right—I wouldn't know what to wear or how to act. Folks would just laugh at me."

"No one is going to laugh at you, Annie. I promise you that. If you let me help you, I'll see to it that half the cowpokes in the territory are swarming over your doorstep in two weeks! You'll see—attracting men is easy." Bryony's voice was earnest. "The important thing is to like yourself, and have faith in yourself. And show it! The rest will follow naturally."

"How do you know so much about these things?" Annie looked at her in wonder. "And why are you bothering to tell me? I reckon you could have any man you wanted. You're so pretty and all."

Bryony dismissed this with a laugh and a wave of her hand. "The only reason I seem to know so much is that I went to a silly girl's school all my life where learning how to attract and hold on to a man was one of the main topics of my education! That's all my friends ever talked about, and every accomplishment we ever mastered, be it painting or embroidery or music, was geared toward that purpose." She sighed. "We were expected to marry very attractive and wealthy husbands and spend all our time giving orders to servants and attending operas and balls! We were taught to be ornaments, pretty and accomplished in the things a woman is supposed to be accomplished in, so as to make a good impression on our husbands' friends, but never to be taken seriously. What a lot of nonsense! You have no idea how glad I am to be away from all that. Here in Arizona I am my own mistress, and I take care of myself. I work hard, and I've won the respect of my associates. That is more important to me than all the society teas in St. Louis!"

Annie was forced into a burst of laughter. It transformed her face, giving her clear hazel eyes a lively glow, and softening all the harshness of her features. "Seems you and me had opposite lives," she remarked ruefully. "Yours has been filled with—"

"Frivolity," Bryony supplied immediately, and Annie grinned. "Yes, frivolity, and mine has been filled with work. After all these years, I don't know if I could still learn all those things you want to teach me."

"Don't be silly, there's nothing difficult to learn! All we're going to do is get you some decent clothes, and teach you how to dress your hair more becomingly. And oh, yes, I'm going to teach you to dance."

"Dance!" Annie exclaimed, watching in amazement as Bryony leaped up in her excitement and began to pace rapidly about the room.

"Yes, you must learn to dance if you're going to attend my fiesta. Every man present will be begging for you to give them the honor!"

"There's only one man I'd want to dance with," Annie answered soberly, but there was a gleam of hope in her eyes. "You really think I could learn?" she wondered. "And do you think Buck might ask me to stand up with him?"

Bryony had been looking the other girl over appraisingly, and now she smiled confidently at her. "Annie, if he doesn't pester you the whole night like a fly buzzing around a honey pot, then I'll pack my bags and move back to St. Louis the very next morning. And let me tell you, that is something I have no intention of doing!"

This speech was greeted by a wide smile, but almost immediately Annie's face clouded with suspicion. "Say, why would you do all this?" she demanded in a low tone. "Why should Wesley Hill's daughter want to help me?"

Bryony returned to sit beside her on the sofa, her lovely green eyes meeting the other girl's intent gaze with great earnestness. "Annie, I don't believe that my father ever did you or anyone else a bit of harm. No, wait, let me finish," she hurried on as the girl tried to interrupt, holding up her hand for silence. "I know that you and your father feel differently, and I'm sorry for it. I only hope that one day the truth will come out and you'll see the error in your thinking. However, I don't see the point in our discussing that. The only thing that matters is that I want to be your friend—and your father's friend. You must trust me."

Slowly, Annie nodded. "I do trust you," she replied almost dazedly. "I never had a mother or a sister, or even a woman-friend. I'd like to have one, though. I get powerful lonely sometimes with only Pa to talk to."

"Then we'll talk to each other." Bryony smiled. "We'll have plenty of time for chatter once we start your dancing lessons, and sewing up your party dress. Tell me, what fabric shall it be? Do you have a preference?"

"Well, I've got a bolt of gingham upstairs that Pa brought me once from town," Annie began doubtfully, but Bryony interrupted her firmly.

"No ma'am! No gingham dresses for you! This gown is going to be made of satin or silk. And we'll drive all the way to Tucson to buy the fabric if we have to. And the color? Rose, I think. With your hair and coloring, it will be absolutely gorgeous! Oh, Annie, wait and see! After you've worn this gown, you'll be hard put to ever take it off! The night of the fiesta is going to change your entire life!"

And with all these words, the two girls put their heads together and began to plan in earnest. Bryony's enthusiasm was contagious, and she soon swept Annie Blake up with her in a fever of anticipation. Samuel Blake, arriving home some time later, discovered them laughing helplessly on the sofa after Annie's less than graceful attempt to follow Bryony's dancing instructions, and he completed the day's triumph by consenting to attend the fiesta with his daughter.

Bryony was both exhilarated and encouraged when she rode home beside Buck late that afternoon. She gave away no details to Buck about her visit with Annie, other than to say that both had agreed to attend the party. He seemed surprised, but didn't question her, evidently concluding that Bryony's charms had worked on the Blakes as effectively as on everyone else she met. Bryony herself secretly pondered his reaction when he saw Annie Blake decked out in the rose silk gown she would be wearing the night of the party, her hair arranged in fashionable curls. How happy Annie would be when Buck noticed her. And notice her he would.

As they neared the Circle H, some of her elation wore off, for the sight of her own impressive ranch house brought back the memory of her problems. She sighed to herself, as the horses instinctively quickened their pace toward home. Well, at least Annie and Buck had a chance for happiness. She must somehow learn to live without the man she wanted to spend her life with; she must learn to forget him. It was a gloomy prospect. She couldn't help thinking, despite her spirited words to Annie Blake earlier that afternoon, that she might have been better off if she had never left St. Louis, if she had never come west at all. Then she never would have met Jim Logan. She never would have known the torture of this forbidden love.

Chapter Twenty

It was the morning of June the eighteenth. Jim Logan stood before the tall oval mirror in the hotel bedroom, practicing his deadly ritual with the Colt as he did every morning. Today, though, his mind was not on his task. He handled the gun almost absently, as if he wasn't even aware of the incredible speed with which he drew it from the low-slung holster at his hip. He reacted automatically, without the intense concentration that normally characterized his pistol practice.

Logan had had a bad night. He had dreamed again, that same damn dream that had been haunting him ever since that stormy evening on the mountain with Bryony Hill. And to make matters worse, he had received another letter from Danny yesterday, another letter just like all the others. Hell! Why did the kid keep begging him to come home? Didn't he understand how impossible that was? Didn't he know what his older brother had become, that it was too late now to ever go back and pick up the ties from a life he had cast aside so many years ago? For an instant, his father's face swam into his mind's eye, a harsh, strong face, tough and leathery as cowhide. That face was a grim reminder of the main reason why he could never return to his father's cattle ranch—to Danny's ranch, he corrected

himself. He didn't have the right to return and he never
would.

And yet—that dream. That damn dream! It was as
clear to him now as the cheap painting on the wall
beside the mirror. In the dream he was home again, in
the huge, oaken mansion on the plains of Texas, where
he had been born. Spread before his gaze was the
bustling cattle ranch, vast and thriving, teeming with
wranglers and corrals and storehouses and cattle. He
could see the handsome interior of the ranch house, the
thick carpeting and fine furniture his mother had loved,
the parlors and sitting room, his father's study, the immense dining room and great, immaculate kitchen. And
upstairs, down the long, oak-floored hall, the enormous
bedroom suite that had belonged to his mother and
father. On the magnificent four-poster bed lay Bryony
Hill, in a sheer white silk negligee, her soft cloud of dark
hair falling temptingly over her milky shoulders, and
she was smiling at him, beckoning him closer, leaning
closer, beckoning, beckoning. . . .

He always awoke at that point, with sweat on his
face, and a twisting of desire in his heart. He dared not
admit, even to himself, how much he wished the dream
could be a reality. For to admit it would be too painful.
He stared at his reflection in the mirror. He had
changed. Bryony had done something to him that he
had not thought possible. She had made him love her,
made him care for her. After all these years of building
up his defenses, of remaining cool and uninvolved, and
independent of the whole damn world, he had fallen in
love with a girl whom he could never hope to win.

However much she had been drawn to him on that
unforgettable night when they had made such passionate love in the firelit cave, she would never allow her
feelings to continue. She would never contemplate a life
with the man who had killed her father. That had been
made clear to him from the expression in those deep,

gloriously green eyes. There was no hope of holding her
in his arms ever again, of caressing her soft, sweet
breasts, of kissing those exquisite lips, of knowing the
blinding joy that came from their union. And there was
no hope of any kind of future together, in Texas, or
anywhere else. The dream would never come true, so his
only course was to forget her, and to forget the terrible
feelings she'd awakened in him.

Logan was resigned to this, yet he could not shut her
from his mind. He knew that there was something he
could and must do for her before he packed up and rode
out of her life forever. He must get to the bottom of this
situation that threatened Bryony's life. He knew full
well the extent of her danger. It was only a matter of
time and opportunity before Richards and his filthy
partner got rid of her for good.

He had to find that damned letter! It was the only
way to prove Sam Blake's suspicions and provide him
with a reason to round up Richards and his men. Only
then would Bryony be safe. Replacing the Colt in his
holster, Logan found himself cursing aloud. If only he
weren't obliged to *prove* that Wesley Hill and Matt
Richards and their unknown partner were rustling Sam
off the range! Then he could merely challenge Richards
and the coyotes who did his dirty work for him to a gunfight and rid Winchester of them for good. He had no
doubt of the outcome of such a fight, for even distracted as he was by haunting thoughts of Bryony, he
still could outdraw any man in the territory. But he
couldn't settle things that way, not this time. Blake had
hired him to find proof that would help him to legally
recover some of his lost cattle. He was obligated to
stand by the deal. All right, he thought determinedly,
I'll get the proof and then I'll send those bastards to
their graves. I only hope Bryony watches her step until
then. Because if anything happens to her. . . .

He couldn't finish the thought. But there was a

dangerous glint in his eyes as he left his room and strode
downstairs to the hotel lobby.

Logan had moved out of Ginger's room in the Silver
Spur several weeks ago, no longer able to endure her
fawning attentions and her temper tantrums when he
responded to her with undisguised boredom. He didn't
have the smallest desire to be with any woman save one.
Maybe when he finished here and he rode on to another
town, he would regain his old interest in casual sex, but
not yet. Not yet by a long shot. It was too soon to think
of any woman but Bryony, for she filled his head,
crowding out every memory of every other woman he
had ever know.

"Mornin', Mister Logan," Edna Billings's lips
twitched uneasily into a smile as he entered the hotel
lobby, where she was sweeping the pine floor. Her nervous reaction to him was typical of what he encountered
from most people: they treated him with a kind of wary
respect and then breathed easier when he left the room.
He'd grown accustomed to it over the years. Only two
people had treated him differently. The first was Daisy
Winston. She had been his friend. The second was
Bryony.

"Mornin', ma'am," he gave Edna a nonchalant nod
and walked toward the door with his usual unhurried
grace.

Logan pulled the brim of his sombrero lower over his
eyes. At midmorning, it was already a scorching day,
with no breeze to relieve the oppressiveness of the sun's
beating rays that mercilessly baked the dry dust of the
street. The turquoise sky hung over the dirty little town
almost menacingly, and against its vivid backdrop, the
rugged mountains of red, purple, and lilac lifted their
craggy heads with regality, seeming to watch over the
landscape sprawled below. Logan, squinting at those
distant peaks, wished they could tell him the where-

abouts of Zeke Murdock or Rusty Jessup. Nothing had been seen of them since the attack on Bryony in May, though he'd checked everywhere. Well, he reflected purposefully, he'd find them, sooner or later. They couldn't hide out forever.

As he walked along the wooden boardwalk, he scanned the faces of the passersby around him. The town was in a bustle of activity; everyone was eagerly awaiting the fiesta at the Circle H ranch on the twentieth, only two days away. For the past week it had been the sole topic of discussion in the shops and in the street, and even in the saloon, where range hands had been busy bragging about the fancy duds they planned to wear for the occasion. Logan was fed up with hearing about it. Damn it, how could he forget Bryony Hill when her name was buzzed about all through the damn town?

He had just stepped around an old dog sleeping in the shade when he caught sight of her, accompanied by one of her range hands. Bryony was driving up in her freshly painted wagon, drawn by a pair of sorrel horses. As Logan paused to watch, oblivious of the people scuttling around him, the range hand helped her to dismount, then after a moment of conversation sauntered into the blacksmith's, while Bryony, attired in a red cotton dress and sandals, her raven-black hair loose and flowing over her shoulders, stepped quickly along the boardwalk toward the hotel.

Logan observed her through narrowed eyes as she came toward him, greeting acquaintances and smiling. He was shocked by her drawn appearance. There were hollows in her cheeks, enhancing the exotic, sculptured look of her delicate bone structure, but indicating to his sharp gaze that she was under considerable strain. Her lovely eyes were shadowed, with none of their usual vibrancy. Even when she smiled at those who spoke to her on the street, he could detect the effort behind it, for he saw immediately that she had changed dramatically since their encounter on the mountain. When he had run into her that time at Annie Blake's he had thought she looked somewhat subdued, but now, seeing her for the first time since then, when it had taken all of his willpower to refrain from running to her and crushing her in his arms, he saw that she was a ghostly vision of her former self.

Bryony hurried along the boardwalk, intent on reaching the hotel. Roger Davenport's stagecoach was due in this morning, and she was anxious to find out from Edna if there had been any word regarding what time it would arrive. She planned to bring him out to the ranch for supper so that they would have an opportunity to visit together. She was looking forward to his visit with mixed feelings. Remembering his condescending attitude the last time they met, she wanted the satisfaction of showing him how well she had adapted to her new life, but she also looked forward to the company of someone from her past, someone connected with St. Louis and the life she'd known there.

She hoped that talking with Roger would give her a brief respite from the depression that had settled so heavily on her, and that had been growing more burdensome every day. Peace of mind eluded her. She was still troubled about the allegations against her father, and she couldn't stop thinking about Texas Jim Logan. Her heart was a dead weight in her chest, paining her with every breath she took.

Suddenly, as she reached the corner of the feed store, she felt herself strongly grasped and jerked off the boardwalk. She gasped in fright, resisting automatically, and then found herself staring up at the man who for weeks had ruthlessly dominated her mind. She paled, and struggled in confusion against his iron hold.

"What—what are you doing?" she demanded breathlessly, her eyes widening. "Let me go at once!"

Instead of obeying this command, Logan dragged her into the further recesses of the alley, out of the sight and hearing of passersby on the boardwalk. His grip on her arms was firm enough to hold her helpless but did not hurt her. He stared down into her upturned face.

"What's wrong, Bryony?" he demanded. "What's happened to make you look so haggard?"

The blood rushed into her face. "Well, thank you so much for your kind compliment! I hadn't realized you were so concerned about my welfare!" Pride made her eyes flash as she recalled the indifferent way he had treated her at the Blake ranch. She was still smarting from that cold encounter. "I'll thank you to tend to your own affairs, and not concern yourself with me!" she told him icily.

"Shut up." He gave her a shake. "I'm not interested in your fancy talk, Bryony. I want to know what's wrong—and I want to know now!"

"It's nothing! I'm perfectly well!" She glared at him. What could she say? That she yearned to be with him again, for him to make love to her? That she was heartbroken and miserable because she loved him so hopelessly? No, never. She spoke, her voice a shade too shrill. "I'm a little tired from planning my fiesta, that's all. You have heard about my fiesta, haven't you? It's going to be a splendid party—the whole town is coming."

"So I hear." His lips were a thin, hard line. "I hope you enjoy yourself—dancing with Matthew Richards, the man who's been trying to get you killed. It's just the kind of stupid behavior I would expect from you."

"How dare you!" Her voice shook. "Matt Richards is a fine, upstanding man, and so was my father. You have no right to keep accusing them and I won't stand for it!"

"You don't have anything to do with it," he returned coolly. "But brace yourself, little tenderfoot. You're going to be in for a rude shock when the truth finally comes out."

"If you'll excuse me, I don't have time to listen to any more of this," she replied, her eyes sparkling like green ice. "I'm on my way to meet a *gentleman* arriving on the stagecoach. I wouldn't wish to be late. So if you'll kindly let me go . . ."

"Oh, yes, I heard about this easterner who's coming to your party. A former boyfriend, I reckon?"

Logan's hands tightened as she tried to twist angrily away from him, and he jerked her closer to him, his expression harsh.

"Listen, Bryony, I've heard about this dandy. Folks say he's on his way to San Francisco, that he's only going to be in town a few days. If you follow my advice, you'll go with him when he boards that stage for California. You'll get out of Arizona for good—go with this city boy and marry him, or do whatever the hell you want. Just leave Winchester before Richards tries another attempt on your life. It's the only thing to do. For once in your life, girl, be sensible!"

Her thudding heart pounded still faster as fury rushed through her. "Take your hands off me this instant!" she cried. "You have no right telling me what to do! I've already told you that I'm not going to leave Arizona and no one is going to drive me away! Yes, I know that *someone* wants to be rid of me—I'd be a fool not to see that, but I don't believe Matthew Richards is the culprit, and I intend to stay here until I find out who is behind it and why. But you needn't worry," she flung at him bitterly, "I take adequate precautions for my protection. I'm always armed, and usually accompanied by one of my range hands wherever I go. Does that satisfy you?" She took a trembling breath and tried again, in frustration, to break free of him. "Let me *go*, damn you!" She was half-sobbing, her black hair tumbling wildly about her pale face. "I don't see why my welfare is any of your concern anyway—I was under the distinct impression that you couldn't care less what fate might befall me! You told me so in almost those very words!"

"Did I?" There was a huskiness in his voice as he stared down at her from his towering height. "Then I lied, Bryony. I lied."

Abruptly, he pulled her closer, crushing her breasts against his chest as his lips found hers. He kissed her fiercely, bruisingly, hurting her mouth. Her senses reeled with the taste and smell and feel of him, and a faintness came over her. When he lifted his head, she dizzily perceived the agony in his eyes. "I love you, Bryony," he whispered. "Damn it, I love you. I can't stand the thought of seeing you hurt—and that's what's going to happen if you stay here in Winchester. You're not safe until I find that missing paper and expose Richards and your father and their filthy partner. You must leave."

Dazed, she swallowed once and tried to speak. No words came. She tried again.

"If . . . you loved me . . . you wouldn't do this," she said weakly. "You wouldn't accuse my father in this way. Don't you realize how it hurts me?"

"I'm sorry. It can't be helped."

"Yes, it can. *You* could leave town—now, immediately." She was shaking uncontrollably. "Forget these suspicions. Go away and let *me* forget them—let me forget *you!*"

"Is that what you really want?" He stared at her intensely, his light blue eyes searching her face.

"Yes . . . yes. I want to forget you—I must forget you. There's no hope for us together. What you are and what you've done will always stand in our way."

"I know that. I understand." There was a grim acceptance in his voice, and his eyes hardened. "But that doesn't change my intentions, Bryony. I'm going to stay in Winchester until I prove that your father and Richards and their friends have been rustling Sam Blake and others off the range. Nothing you can say will change my mind."

"Then you don't love me!" she cried tearfully, struggling away from his grasp. This time he let her go. "You don't care how much you hurt me!"

"I do care," he replied grimly. "But I'm going to do what I have to do. That's all."

"Very well." Bryony raised glittering eyes to his determined face, heedless of the tears streaming down her cheeks. "And I'm going to do what I have to do. I'm going to stay in Arizona. And I'm going to forget you! I only pray that we never meet alone like this again!"

He nodded, and the lean, handsome face was a mask of coldness. "I reckon that would be best for both of us."

She turned then and ran away from him, fleeing back to the main street of the town.

Chapter Twenty-One

Bryony wiped frantically at her tears, trying to regain some semblance of composure. She had little time to do this, though, for almost immediately after stepping onto the boardwalk, she saw the stage drawing up at the hotel, the horses steaming and tired after their long run. For a moment she leaned against the wood-frame wall of the feed store to steady herself. She watched as the driver jumped off his high seat and let down the steps for the passengers. Roger Davenport, looking stiff and uncomfortable, climbed gingerly down from the stage-coach, blinking in the bright southwestern sun.

"Roger!" Bryony ran to him and threw herself into his arms. "Oh, how happy I am to see you!" she cried, half hysterically.

Roger, elegantly dressed in a dark suit that was considerably wrinkled from the journey, held her off at arm's length, rather shocked by her enthusiastic greeting. He regarded Bryony with curiosity in his brown eyes.

"Bryony? My darling, you've been crying!" he exclaimed. "What is the matter?"

"Don't be silly, Roger!" her laughter was shrill. "I'm just so overjoyed to see you. You . . . you can't know how I've been looking forward to this!"

"I'm gratified, of course." Roger took her small

hands in his, smiling down at her in the old, indulgent way. "Well, you certainly look wonderful. As beautiful as ever. Though I'm not sure Arizona quite agrees with you, my darling. You're thinner than I remember, and pale." He flashed his quick, white-toothed smile. "Have you been missing me? Or have you been experiencing difficulty adjusting to his barbarous frontier? I warned you, you know. Come, Bryony, tell me the truth."

"Oh, no! Everything has been just wonderful! Perfect!" She couldn't meet his inquiring eyes. Instead, she hooked her arm through his. "Let's bring your baggage to the wagon, then I'll drive you out to the Circle H. You'll be amazed at what a competent cattle rancher I've become."

"Just a moment, Bryony. I have no intention of staying at the Circle H with you. I'm going to stay at the hotel."

"The hotel?" She stared at him. "But why? There's plenty of room at my ranch, and I assure you, you'll be most comfortable."

"No doubt." Roger gazed at her with the chiding look he might have used with a child. "However, it would not seem proper for us to stay together in the same house—unchaperoned. We must not set tongues wagging, you know, Bryony."

Amusement filled her. She couldn't keep the tart words from her lips. "How strange, Roger. You didn't seem overly concerned about wagging tongues that evening at Miss Marsh's School when you sneaked into the courtyard to visit me! That too, was highly improper," she reminded him with sparkling eyes.

Roger nodded at her, as if she'd proven his point. "Precisely, my dear. It was a foolish, careless act, and one I shall not repeat. Your reputation, and mine too, must remain unsullied, and I have no intention of damaging either by becoming your house guest. Besides," he added, "I intend to conduct a series of business meetings with the Tucson banker who will be driving to Winchester to see me, and it will be more convenient to conduct our discussions in my hotel suite.''

Bryony shrugged. "Very well, Roger, if that is what you prefer. But you must at least drive out to the ranch for dinner this evening. I expected you, and Rosita, my housekeeper, is preparing a banquet in your honor.''

He smiled down at her. "Sweet Bryony. Of course, I shall be delighted to dine with you. And I intend to spend every possible moment at your side.''

When you are not conducting business meetings, Bryony thought in silent amusement. But all she said was,"Very well. Let's dispose of your baggage in the hotel, and then we'll head out to the ranch. I'd like to show you around a bit before dinnertime.''

While Frank Billings took Roger upstairs to the hotel's only suite of rooms, Edna leaned confidentially over the wooden counter to speak to Bryony.

"That young dandy is mighty handsome, girl,'' she asserted herself in her blunt way, winking knowingly at Bryony. "And from the way he looks at you, I'd guess you could wear his brand any time you said the word.'' She laughed uproariously. "I reckon that fiesta of yours is goin' to be some wild party. Between this young feller and Matt Richards, and all those other crazy young cowpokes, you're not goin' to have time to breathe with all the dancin' you'll be doin', girl.''

Bryony made no reply, thinking that the only partner she wanted to dance with she could not have.

When Roger returned they left the hotel and walked to her wagon outside the blacksmith's. The wrangler who had driven into town with her was waiting for the horse he'd brought in yesterday to be shod, and would ride back to the ranch later, so Bryony and Roger drove back alone, she handling the reins with skill while he gazed about in grudging admiration of the glorious countryside.

"Tell me about St. Louis." Bryony tried to inject a note of enthusiasm into her voice. The almost hysterical fervor that had overtaken her after the scene with Jim Logan had dissipated, leaving her as brokenhearted and empty inside as ever before. Drained from the encounter, she now tried gallantly to listen to Roger's smug chatter, but she couldn't concentrate. The heaviness had returned to her spirit, and she only prayed that Roger wouldn't notice it and question her. She needn't have worried, though. He was no longer studying her; he was engrossed in his own witty recital of gossip involving the acquaintances they had once shared in St. Louis, and in an explanation of the importance of his business trip to San Francisco.

"And if I am successful in negotiating this matter, my father will be quite pleased with me. It will be a large feather in my cap, Bryony, I assure you."

"How nice." She tried hard to sound interested, but her thoughts were elsewhere. All she could think about was the expression in Jim's eyes when he kissed her, and those magical words he had uttered. *I love you.* She dragged her attention back to Roger Davenport with an effort. "I've planned a wonderful fiesta in your honor," she told him with forced cheerfulness. "Everyone in town is coming. I think you'll be surprised at how grand life can be in Arizona."

"Perhaps. But, Bryony, you must know that however grand it might be, it cannot hope to compare to the splendor of San Francisco. I've heard fabulous accounts of the gaiety and sophistication of that city. And I must tell you," he added confidentially, "if all goes well with these negotiations, I may very well be settling there, heading up a very important banking deal. How does that sound? Does the idea of living in San Francisco appeal to you?" He turned his head to study her delicate profile as she drove. He touched her fingers with one soft, manicured hand.

"You know, don't you, Bryony, my real reason for stopping in Winchester? I want to persuade you to accept that proposal that you so foolishly cast aside the last time we met." He hushed her as she began to speak and gave a little laugh. "Now, now, I know that we had a dreadful quarrel, and I may have said some unkind things to you. I apologize. I trust you've forgiven me by now, and that you, too, regret your loss of temper." His smooth hand closed on hers. "I've been able to think of no one but you, Bryony," he assured her ardently. "Tell me, has it been so with you? It must be the case. Say that it is!"

Before she had an opportunity to reply, they were both startled by a sudden hiss directed at them from the side of the trail. A mountain lion, its tawny fur stretched over a lithe, powerful body, was crouched to spring, snarling at them from the crest of a boulder. In panic, the horses reared up, screaming their terror. At the same instant, Bryony thrust the reins into Roger's hands and whipped her derringer from the pocket of her dress, firing unhesitatingly at the animal that was already bounding forward. The mountain lion dropped with a heavy thud to the earth, blood oozing from its lifeless form. But the horses, panicked out of control by the incident, bolted headlong up the road, dragging the careening wagon behind them.

"Oh! Help!" Panicked, Roger almost dropped the tautened reins, but Bryony acted swiftly, grabbing them from him and pulling with all her might.

"Whoa, there!" she called authoritatively to the plunging sorrels. "Whoa, boys—easy. There's nothing to be afraid of."

The animals gradually slowed, snorting and dancing nervously on the trail. Bryony halted them at last and jumped out of the wagon. She went to their heads, soothing them. When they were calm once more, she returned to her seat, glancing ruefully at Roger's sweating, white face.

"Are you all right?"

"D—damnation! How can you be so calm?" he croaked, wiping his face with a handkerchief held in trembling hands. "We were almost killed!"

"Oh, no such thing," she replied scornfully, replacing the derringer, which she had dropped onto the seat, back into her pocket, and gathering up the reins. With a click and a shake of the reins she sent the horses into a brisk trot. "There are lots of mountain lions in these parts. I learned long ago how to handle them."

"Where did you learn to shoot like that?" Roger stared as if he'd never seen her before. This unshaken, competent woman was vastly different from the flirtatious, vulnerable schoolgirl he'd courted in St. Louis. He couldn't believe the calmness with which she had acted, taking the entire situation in stride. "You fired so quickly—you might have missed."

"At that range? Impossible." Bryony couldn't help a burst of laughter as she saw Roger's incredulous expression. She remembered how important it had been to her to show him that she'd adapted to her new life, that she could take care of herself. Well, she'd done that. But she felt no satisfaction. It no longer seemed important. She sighed. How wonderful it would be to return to those carefree days, before love and danger had taken their toll on her. But she knew it wasn't possible to go back.

"We're almost home," she told Roger quietly. He had settled uneasily back in his seat, and was watching the surrounding countryside with darting eyes, as if expecting another ferocious creature to pounce upon him. At least the moment's danger had distracted him from his proposal, Bryony thought. She knew, though, that eventually she would have to give him an answer. This time she would have no difficulty deciding what to do. She didn't love Roger—she never had. She had met only one man with whom she would like to spend the rest of her life, and he was hopelessly ineligible. And then they drew near the ranch. She halted the horses, pausing to stare ahead at the Circle H ranchhouse and grounds set in the midst of the vast, sprawling valley. Beside her, Roger gave a low whistle of admiration.

"So. This is your father's ranch, is it? Quite impressive, I must say."

"Yes," Bryony returned in a low, strained voice. "This is my father's ranch."

Texas Jim Logan burst into the Silver Spur saloon like a man pursued, and stalked quickly over to the bar where Luke, the lumbering, bearded bartender, was wiping glasses with a worn cloth. Logan ordered a bourbon and downed it in one gulp. He was glad the place was nearly empty, except for a few old-timers playing cards near the wall. He wasn't in the mood for Ginger's attentions, or even for Meg's friendly conversation. He was in the mood for a drink—a strong one. Curtly, he ordered a second.

Logan didn't usually drink this early in the morning, but after the encounter with Bryony he needed a drink badly. Glaring at the liquid in his glass, he cursed to himself. Damn it! He hadn't meant to tell her that he loved her. But there was something so intoxicating about her presence that he hadn't been able to stop himself. Oh, hell, he thought philosophically, taking a gulp of the bourbon. He didn't suppose it made any difference, one way or another. Nothing would change the way things stood between them. The only thing that had been accomplished, he reflected, was to make him more determined than ever to find proof of Hill's and Richards's illegal activities, to protect Bryony from further harm. If only he could lay his hands on that missing document, it would solve the whole damn problem. He had covered every angle, talked to every person who might have the slightest knowledge of its whereabouts. And he had come up with nothing.

Suddenly, as he stared at the liquor in his glass, a

thought flashed into his mind. He remembered someone he had spoken to once, without success, who might now be more cooperative than in the past. Someone who might know more than anyone else in Winchester about Hill's criminal activities. Logan set down his glass, his eyes glinting. He'd have to find the right time for the interview. Later. Maybe tomorrow, or even the next day. They'd have to be quite alone. He smiled to himself with satisfaction, feeling more hopeful than he had in weeks. Soon he would know more. Perhaps there was still a way to save the life of the woman he loved.

Chapter Twenty-Two

The midafternoon sun slid into the western sky as Bryony rode for home on the day of the fiesta. Glancing up at the fiery golden ball that was relentlessly broiling the parched desert valley, she reflected that it was going to be a long, sultry desert night, ideal for romance and festivity. She couldn't help smiling bitterly to herself. Well, at least Annie would have the right atmosphere in which to bedazzle the unsuspecting Buck.

Having just come from the Blake ranch after making last-minute adjustments in Annie's toilette, Bryony was more than ever convinced that the girl would create a sensation when she arrived at the Circle H tonight. Clad in her new silk gown, with her chestnut hair sleek and shining, she would cause Buck, as well as a number of other men, to sit up and take notice. She would look a very different girl from the plain, tomboyish figure the young men of Winchester were accustomed to seeing.

Even nature was contributing to the aura of romance planned for the evening. Tonight, according to Rosita, would be the evening when the night-blooming cereus opened to reveal their beauty to the world. Every year in June on one night and one night only the fragile white blossoms of the unusual plant opened magically for a few hours, carpeting the desert with their lovely flowers before shutting themselves away again at dawn to sleep another year until their next fleeting burst of glory. And

Rosita had predicted that tonight would be the night of their blooming. Bryony looked forward to this event even more than she did to the fiesta. Somehow, the prospect of the dancing and gaiety in store held little appeal for her.

Her thoughts turned disconsolately to her father. If only he had not died—if only Jim Logan had not killed him! Things might have been so different for them. Perhaps she might have found love with both men, instead of being forced to do without the love of either.

She was galloping homeward, immersed in her loneliness, when she had the sudden urge to stop at her father's grave. As she neared the graveyard, she caught sight of a totally unexpected figure kneeling by one of the sites. Rosita! Her housekeeper was on her knees, head bent, her hands covering her face. What in the world is she doing here at this hour, with so many last-minute details needing attention at the ranch, Bryony wondered in amazement. She trotted forward, her brow wrinkled in puzzlement. At the sound of hoofbeats, the Mexican woman glanced up quickly, an expression of fear in her eyes. Seeing Bryony, she stumbled to her feet, giving a small, half-anguished cry.

"Rosita!" Bryony dismounted lightly and deftly tethered Shadow to a nearby ironwood tree. She hurried forward in concern as she saw the tears streaming down Rosita's face. "What is it, Rosita? Heavens, you look awful. What is the matter?"

Loud, racking sobs shook the brown-skinned woman, but she made no reply, instead turning her grief-stricken face away in embarrassment.

Bryony glanced down at the headstone before which Rosita had been kneeling. The name on the stone was that of Johnny Blake. Without knowing why, a chill came over her.

The woman finally turned to her. "Señorita, I am sorry!" she gasped in her heavy voice, her dark braids flying as she shook her head wildly back and forth. "I cannot bear this burden any longer. *Es malvado!* I told

him the truth . . . that cold-eyed hombre with the gun
. . . and I do not care if I die now because of it!"

"What are you talking about?" Bryony stared at her
in sudden, sick apprehension. "What hombre?"

Rosita wiped away her tears with the hem of her
flowered apron. Her thick voice shook with emotion as
she replied. "Señor Logan." She closed her black eyes
momentarily and a shudder passed through her.
"*Finalmente*, I have spoken out the truth."

"The truth! What do you mean?" Nervously, Bryony
met the other woman's bleak gaze. Her heart beat
rapidly in anticipation of the housekeeper's next words.

"The truth about this boy—this *pobre muchacho*,"
said Rosita, pointing with unconscious melodrama at
Johnny Blake's headstone. Staring at it, she sank down
again to her knees and fresh sobs shook her. "I know of
his murderers!" she gasped. "I have known *por mucho
tiempo*! He was killed by Señor Richards and others
. . . and I have kept silent about it for many, many
months!"

Bryony couldn't move, couldn't tear her eyes from
Rosita's guilt-ridden face. The woman glanced at her,
and something in Bryony's stricken expression must
have penetrated her own anguish, for she got heavily to
her feet and put a work-roughened hand on the girl's
rigid arm.

"*Por favor*, Señorita, forgive me!" she pleaded. "I
have shocked you, but it could not be helped. When you
found me here, you told me to tell you why I weep over
this poor grave, and I have done so. It is because of my
own wickedness in keeping silent. But you must understand, as *he* did, that cold-eyed one. You must understand that I kept silent because I was afraid. You see,
many was the time he had threatened to kill me—Señor
Richards. And your padre, too, Señorita, he also spoke
of my death if I did not remain silent about all that I
knew—all that I heard in that wicked house. And so until this day I have kept silent, never speaking of what I
know to any living soul. But today I spoke, and Señor

Logan has promised to protect me. He has promised to
see justice done to those . . . those *animales* who murdered *este pobre muchacho*. And so I told him the
truth.''

"Rosita." Bryony grasped the woman's hands in her
own trembling ones. Her voice was unsteady and her
green eyes bright with shock, but she managed to speak
coherently, her simple words carefully controlled, as if
at any moment her voice would crack and shatter like
fragile glass. "I want you to tell me everything that you
know. Everything."

And so it came out. Slowly, agonizingly, punctuated
by the housekeeper's own guilty condemnation of her
cowardice in keeping quiet. The long story of her
father's involvement with Matthew Richards in a
devious rustling scheme came tumbling out. Rosita had
tried to quit her position at the Circle H, to accept Edna
Billings's repeated offers of employment at the hotel,
but fearing that she might let something slip if allowed
to leave, Bryony's father had refused to let her go.

Bryony listened to the tale in numb silence. At one
point she broke in, asking in a tremulous voice, "But,
Rosita, why did you stay on after my father's death?
Why didn't you leave then and go to work for Edna
before I arrived here?" She remembered then the stolid
unfriendliness of the housekeeper when she had first
arrived. Now she understood the reason behind it.

Rosita shrugged in answer to her question. Her black
eyes were pools of distress. "I was frightened, Señorita," she replied with an air of finality. "Señor
Richards came to see me, and he told me that he would
be watching me closely, that if he thought I was talking
to anyone about what I knew. . . ." She made a gesture
with her hand across her neck. "*Un animal*, that one! A
beast for all his fine smiles!"

Bryony pressed her hands to her pale cheeks. "Oh,
what a fool I have been! But then, he seems so kind, so
decent! And he was a friend of my father!"

She made a small choking noise at this, and Rosita

nodded at her solemnly, pity showing itself in her face. "Si, Señorita, they were friends. *Compañeros.* I am sorry that you must learn this truth from me in this way."

Bryony gazed miserably at the tombstone before which they were both kneeling. "Tell me what you know about Johnny Blake's death. I need to know the truth, Rosita."

When Rosita had finished, Bryony had a fairly good picture of the type of life her father had led in Arizona, and it wasn't a pleasant one. She realized, as the housekeeper talked, that he must have become obsessed with greed, that obtaining land and wealth had become his ruling passion, blotting out whatever decency he had once possessed. Everything Jim Logan had said about him, she thought with repulsion, had been the truth. He had conspired with Matthew Richards, he had rustled cattle from Samuel Blake and others, and he had known of Johnny Blake's deliberate murder. According to Rosita, he had not learned of the boy's death until afterwards, and had quarreled about it with Matt. Bryony remembered that this coincided with what Daisy Winston had told Jim. She felt a stab of pain as she realized also that her father had probably killed Daisy, just as Jim Logan had maintained. Her father had been the one who had beaten and strangled her and left her to die in the wilderness. He and Matt Richards were guilty of every horrible crime Jim Logan had accused them of that morning in the mountain cave.

She passed a trembling hand across her eyes, and lifted her head to stare at the now silent housekeeper. "Rosita." She moistened her dry lips with her tongue. "Did my father hide a paper anywhere in the Circle H—a secret paper? One that might contain some proof about all these things you saw and heard?"

"No, Señorita," she replied wearily. "Señor Richards, he asked me about a missing paper many times after your padre died, and that night when those hombres entered the house and blew open the safe and turned everything upside down, I thought then that it was this paper they looked for. But I never saw any such thing. Today, Señor Logan, too, asked if I knew of it, and now, you. But no. I know nothing of such a paper. I am sorry."

Bryony sighed. "It must be there somewhere." She cast about in her mind for a hiding place they all might have overlooked. "Daisy Winston told Jim Logan that my father had written an incriminating letter that would fall into the right hands if anything were to happen to him. Daisy died before she could tell Jim where my father hid it."

"Daisy Winston!" Rosita gave her an odd look. "That one, si. I remember that she often came to la hacienda. *Una muy bonita niña.* I can remember the last time I saw her, all dressed up in a pink dress and a hat with flowers. She . . ." Rosita broke off abruptly and fixed bright, excited eyes on Bryony's face. "Señorita, I think I know where that paper is hidden. I remember it now!"

"Go on, Rosita! Tell me!"

"It was two, maybe three days before your padre was killed. That *niña*, she was at the house. I was scrubbing the floor in the parlor when they came down the stairs in the morning to leave—to drive to town. And your padre, he asked her, 'Do you have it?' "

Rosita nodded to herself. "Si, and then I remember that she took off her hat, not the one with all the flowers, but another one, one with feathers, so many feathers, and she showed your padre something that was inside the lining. Something tucked inside the band of that silly hat. Señorita, I think it was a paper, folded to fit inside. I never thought about it again, for I saw many strange things in that house, and I tried to forget them. But when you mentioned the name of Daisy Winston—si, I remember it now."

"Daisy Winston had the paper all the time, and that was why it was never found on Circle H property!" Bryony exclaimed. "That's why it never came to light

after my father's death. He killed Daisy, perhaps
because he suspected she had betrayed him, but then
Jim shot him before he could recover the document. In
fact,'' she recalled suddenly, ''Jim told me that my
father was entering the saloon when he caught up with
him. Jim thought he planned to buy himself a drink, but
actually, he must have intended to retrieve the letter. He
never had the opportunity, though.'' She stared at
Rosita. ''Do you remember what this hat looked like?
It's possible the paper is still there, hidden all this time
in the lining!''

''It was *rosado*—pink, you would say. With black
feathers.''

Something clicked inside Bryony's head at this
description. She remembered such a hat. The copper-
haired saloon girl had been wearing such a hat on the
day she accosted Bryony in the street. Could it be
Daisy's hat? Had her friends in the saloon divided up
her possessions after her death? Excitedly, Bryony wondered if the document were truly still hidden inside the
headband. Her lips tightened. She had to see that letter
for herself, read it with her own eyes.

''Señorita, what are we to do?'' Rosita asked ten-
tatively. ''It is growing late—have you forgotten the
fiesta? What is going to happen?''

The fiesta! Bryony noticed for the first time that the
sun was dipping low in the western sky. It would set
soon. Her guests would arrive, including Matt Richards.
Her heart jumped with fear at the thought. Yes, Matt
had indeed been trying to kill her. And tonight he would
be a guest in her home, eating her food, drinking her
wine, leading her onto the dance floor. She tried to
gather her wits. She needed time to think, for she had no
idea what she should do or how to proceed. She only
knew that she had to get her hands on that elusive
paper!

''Come, Rosita, let's ride back to the ranch. We
mustn't stay out here alone another moment—it isn't

safe." For the first time, Bryony fully realized the extent of her danger. In Matt's eyes, she represented a terrible threat. If she came across the incriminating letter before he did, she would have the power to expose him, to ruin him and see him hanged. Judging by his past ruthlessness, he would go to any lengths to prevent this. Anxiously, she peered about her. The countryside was deserted. A stillness had settled over the plains, as if the desert were listening, waiting. In the distance, the purple-misted mountains seemed to be brooding. She felt that they watched her, spying upon her thoughts.

"Let's go," she said nervously and hurried over to where Shadow restlessly pawed the dust, while Rosita clambered onto her aging mare that was tethered in the shade of a mesquite shrub. They galloped homeward, and both were relieved when they turned their mounts into the Circle H gates.

"Listen to me, Rosita," Bryony said quickly, as she dismounted in front of the stable. "Forget everything we talked of this afternoon. Act as if nothing has happened. Tonight, Señor Richards will be at the house. Whatever you do, don't let on that you have told me or anyone else what you know. Please, act normally. Will you do that? It's terribly important that he not suspect the truth!"

Rosita's black eyes flashed. "Si, Señorita, I will be careful. He will learn nothing from me."

"Gracias." Bryony squeezed her arm and watched the woman move swiftly toward the ranch house. One of the wranglers came over to Bryony and took the horses, whistling cheerfully, and making a remark about the festivities ahead. She scarcely heard him. Filled with anguish, she walked to the house and sank down onto the broad white steps.

One thing was firm in her mind. She had to get help. Despite her belief in her own capabilities, she realized that this was not something to be handled alone. There was too much at stake, and besides, several men had

already died at the hands of her adversaries. She had no
desire to join their ranks. She needed an ally to confide
in and consult. But who?

Her first instinct was to send for Judge Hamilton, for
surely he would know how to handle this situation. But
what if Judge Hamilton was the third partner? What if
he, too, was involved in this plot? She found this almost
impossible to believe, and yet . . . she had not believed
her father or Matt guilty either. She had trusted in them
as firmly as she trusted in the Judge. And that trust had
proved utterly baseless. If she was wrong about the
Judge, if she gave him the benefit of the doubt and was
betrayed, all would be lost.

In despair, Bryony ran her fingers through her heavy
black hair, casting about in her mind for someone on
whom she could rely. It didn't take her long to reach the
answer, the obvious, only answer. Perhaps she had
known all along that it was Jim Logan she must contact,
that he was the one she must call upon in this situation.
She was aware, suddenly, as she sat on the porch steps
with her head in her hands, while the wind whistled
sharply down from the mountains and a pair of cactus
wrens chattered inconsequently overhead, that she was
consumed by a sudden, overpowering desire to see him
again, to be held in his arms and comforted. If only he
was here with her now, to hold her close in his strong
arms, to make her forget all her pain and disillusion-
ment with the fire of his kisses. . . .

She moaned to herself, pushing away this line of
thought. She could not deal with it now. The most important thing at the moment was to get her hands on
that letter.

She got up and ran to the corrals in search of Buck,
but he was nowhere to be found. Her sense of urgency
grew. It was growing late, and the fiesta would begin
soon. After leaving word with Pedro to send Buck to
her the instant he returned, she hurried back to the
ranch house and entered her father's study. It was there
that Buck found her when he arrived a short time later,

standing in the doorway with his dusty Stetson in his hand.

"You looking for me, Bryony?" he asked, stepping into the room as she glanced up from the desk, pen in hand. "I been out at the south waterhole all afternoon, and—"

"Buck, I need you to ride to town on an errand for me. It's urgent." She rose from her chair behind the desk to approach him, holding the letter before her.

"Aw, Bryony," the young foreman protested, "I gotta get myself spruced up for the fiesta tonight. It's near sundown already, and those other varmints will be linin' up for their Saturday night baths! I'll have to fight my way to that old tub as it is! Tell you what," he offered suddenly, "I'll ride to town first thing in the mornin', rain or shine. I swear to it!"

"No!" Bryony spoke more sharply than she had intended, but the strain of the day was beginning to wear on her. She sighed at Buck's startled look, and tried to speak more evenly.

"You must ride to town now. Immediately. And you mustn't say a word to anyone about this—not to anyone at all. Do you understand?"

Buck's earnest brown eyes searched her face intently, his attention arrested by the desperation he sensed in her. "Shore, Bryony, whatever you say," he responded instantly. "I reckon I didn't know it was that important." He cleared his throat. "Uh, do you want to talk about it?"

"No." She returned to the desk and with her back to the wrangler, swiftly scanned the letter she had written to Jim Logan. It read:

Dear Jim,
You must meet me tomorrow in the alley behind the Silver Spur Saloon at eight o'clock in the morning. I cannot explain now, except to tell you that I know where to find what you have been seeking. Meet me—please. I place all my dependence upon you.

Then she had signed her name. After reading over the message hurriedly, she folded it and handed it to Buck with trembling fingers. "Take this to the hotel and hand it personally to Jim Logan."

"What! That low-down, no-good—"

"Please, Buck!" Bryony's voice rose shrilly. "Can't you forget your quarrel for my sake? It's vital that Jim Logan receive this letter as soon as possible. If he isn't there, see if you can find him at the Silver Spur. If not . . ." Bryony hesitated. She remembered that Jim spent much of his time at the Silver Spur and that he had mentioned Meg Donahue's name to her. From what he had said about the woman, she had sounded kind enough, despite the fact that she was the proprietor of a saloon. She hoped Jim would be there when Buck reached town, but if not, it seemed that Meg Donahue might be the best way to contact him. "If not, give this letter to Meg Donahue and tell her to get it to him as soon as possible. And don't mention this to anyone," she repeated, pushing him out of the front door. "Please, Buck, I'm counting on you."

He gave her a long, studying look and then nodded. "Don't you worry none, Bryony. I don't understand, but I'll do it. And I won't breathe a word."

"Thank you. Now hurry, please!" She watched him take the ranch house steps in one leap and run toward the corral for his horse. Then, her heart still pounding, she raced upstairs to her own room. As she burst into it, her reflection in the mirror over the dressing table startled her. Her cheeks were flushed and hot, her eyes bright with frenzy. Her hair cascaded wildly over her shoulders in an unruly tangle. She walked over to the mirror and stared at herself in shock. Then she pressed her shaking fingers to her hot cheeks. She must regain control over herself, she thought frantically. She must still this terrible pounding in her heart, still the fear and sickness permeating her body. It seemed an impossible task. The knowledge that she would soon be facing Matthew Richards in the parlor did nothing to soothe her, but she knew that if she was to stay alive long enough to see the proof with her own eyes, and to see Matt Richards hanged for his villainy, she must regain some semblance of poise. She must behave tonight as if nothing had happened, and above all, keep Matt from becoming suspicious. She had to get through this evening. Somehow. Anyhow.

When Buck shouldered his way through the swinging double doors a short time later, he saw that the Silver Spur Saloon was uncommonly empty for that time of day. Most of the cowpokes in town were getting themselves gussied up for the big fiesta at the Circle H, and only a scattered handful of gamblers and drifters remained.

Meg Donahue was enjoying a beer with a tall, slender, slate-eyed gambler in black when Buck arrived, and after glancing about for Jim Logan, he strode directly over to the red-haired woman, gazing down at her as she drained her beer mug and then grinned coquettishly at her companion.

"Meg, I got to talk to you."

She glanced up in surprise at Buck's tall, lanky form.

"Well, talk, cowboy," she returned good-naturedly, patting her flaming hair with one bejeweled hand. She winked broadly at the gambler, whose soft white hands rested unmoving upon the table.

"Alone, Meg." Buck's tone was firm. He nodded at the man in black and just barely tipped his Stetson. "If you'll excuse the lady, partner, I'd be obliged." Without waiting for an answer, Buck hauled Meg out of her chair and propelled her to the bar, which was empty of customers at the moment. Instead of being angry at this rough-shod treatment, though, Meg threw back her head and laughed. "All right, Buck, honey, all right," she declared. "Now why don't you tell me what's so all-fired important that you had to pull me away from my friend over there? I'm a 'listenin'."

With his back to the occupants of the saloon so that

they couldn't see what he was doing, he handed her the letter Bryony had given him. "This here is for Texas Jim Logan," he said in a low voice. "It's from my boss, Miss Bryony Hill."

Meg's eyes widened, and a wicked smile curved her painted lips. "You don't say, cowboy!" she exclaimed. "Could it be a love note from that pretty boss-lady of yours to the feller who shot up her pa? And here I reckoned she'd hate the sight of him! Now, won't this make Ginger madder'n a skunk? I do declare!"

"Listen, Meg." Buck gripped her arm. "I don't know what's in this letter, but whatever it is, it's secret and important, so don't blab to anyone about it. Just keep quiet and give it to Logan when he shows up. You expectin' him tonight?"

"Yep. He usually comes in for a few drinks, though he don't hang around here the way he used to. I think Ginger gets on his nerves." She laughed again, and nimbly folded the letter into a small square, then she placed it in the bosom of her dress, winking mischievously at Buck. "Don't worry, cowboy, I'll keep it safe till Texas comes. When he shows up, I'll deliver it pronto."

"Thanks, Meg—and remember, not a word to anyone."

"Whatever you say, honey." As he started to hurry off, she called out, "Hey, aren't you goin' to that fancy fiesta tonight? You'd best hurry home, honey, and get yourself a bath!"

Buck grinned. Now that his errand was discharged, he felt light-hearted, and he was looking forward more than ever to this evening, when he would dance with Bryony and actually hold her within his arms. "Yes, ma'am," he retorted, "I'm gonna have to throw those other coyotes out of that old tub, but I reckon it'll be worth the scuffle when every lady in the room comes abeggin' me to dance with her!" And with these brash words and a gleam in his eyes, Buck left. Meg ordered the bartender to serve another drink to the gambler in black. She waved to him with a friendly smile.

"Hey, mister, don't go away. I'll be back quicker than you can shuffle a pack of aces!" she called. The gambler leaned lazily back in his chair to wait. Meg strolled leisurely up the stairs to her private rooms above. She was gone some little while, during which time the piano player arrived and began to play loudly, as if to fill up the empty space with noise, and when she returned, the gambler had apparently grown bored with waiting, and had become involved in a poker game with some prospectors who were passing through the town. A few of the girls had come downstairs and were pouting at the lack of business. Meg quickly spotted Texas Jim Logan exchanging a few words with Lila, a half-filled whisky glass on the table before him. Smiling, she made her way to his side and Lila moved reluctantly away.

"Evenin', Texas." Meg sat down opposite him at the little table.

"Howdy, Meg. Business is pretty slow tonight, isn't it?"

"Yep. Most everyone in town is headin' out to the Circle H for that grand fiesta." She chuckled shrewdly, her bright blue eyes fixed upon his impassive countenance. "I take it you're not invited, honey."

"You take it right, ma'am," he said with his cool, careless drawl, but there was a tautness to his features not lost to Meg's sharp eyes. She did not comment upon it, though; instead she leaned forward on her elbows to speak confidentially in a lowered tone.

"Texas, I've got something to tell you," she said seriously. The sapphires at her throat winked brightly as she moved her chair closer to his. "Do you remember askin' me to keep a lookout for that Rusty Jessup hombre, who used to be foreman at the Hill ranch? And a fella named Zeke Murdock? Well, I don't know for sure, but a man passin' through town today mentioned something that made me sit up and take notice and I got a feelin' those two hombres are in Tucson right now."

Logan's eyes bored into her face, his attention riveted keenly on her. "Go on, Meg."

"He mentioned Jessup by name," she told him, "though I'm not too sure about that other fella, Murdock. But the description he gave me sounded like the man you told me about—big, brawny blond hombre with eyes that don't miss nothin'. He said they'd ridden into town a few days ago and were all set for a big poker game tonight—with pretty high stakes, 'cording to this cowboy. Flashin' money all over town, he said, until a gambler from New Orleans invited them to try to lose it at the card table. The fella who was in here couldn't stop talkin' about it, since it seems everyone was going to gather around and watch this high-powered game tonight. He was hurrying to New Mexico on business that wouldn't wait, otherwise he said he'd have stayed to see the show himself." She paused, regarding the man beside her speculatively. "What do you think, honey? I heard him mention Jessup's handle clear as a church bell, and it sure sounds like the other man was that Murdock fella. What are you goin' to do?"

Logan's eyes glinted. "What do you think?" He shoved back his chair and stood up. "I reckon I'll be back in a day or so. It shouldn't take long to track down those hombres and finish my business with them." There was a grim set to his lips that made several men who happened to glance in his direction at that moment feel a deathly chill creep down their spines. They were glad that Texas Jim Logan was not looking at them with that hard, steely expression in his eyes. Staring nervously, they watched him turn on his heel and cross the saloon with his long, powerful stride, his dark sombrero shadowing his frowning brow. They felt inexplicable relief when he shouldered his way past the saloon doors and out into the newly fallen dusk. With audibly exhaled breath, they turned back to their bourbon and their cards, feeling as if the devil himself had passed them by, going in search of other prey.

Meg watched him leave, a slow smile curving her lips.

For the second time that evening, she mounted the steps to the landing above. At the end of the hall was her suite of rooms, where she often did private entertaining. Jim Logan himself had spent some pleasurable moments there in the first few weeks after he'd come to town. Her rooms were large and comfortable, furnished with surprising, if somewhat gaudy, elegance. At this moment they were occupied by a guest, and as Meg quietly opened the entry door and stepped inside, she glanced with swift amusement at the face of the man who stared at her like a bear cub awaiting his mother's return, half-frightened, half-dangerous. She threw back her head and gave a great burst of laughter.

"He's gone," she announced, after she had regained control of herself. "And he'll meet up with Murdock and Jessup all right, but a mite sooner than he expects." The man in the room grinned in relief, while Meg sauntered forward and lifted the much-read sheet of writing paper from the gilt-edged marble table near the red velvet settee. She waved the letter gaily in the air.

"In a few short hours, honey, we'll have Miss Bryony Hill right where we want her," she declared, sinking heavily onto the velvet settee and stretching her legs in their gold satin gown and silk stockings out before her with leisurely delight. "And if we can't settle this little problem once and for all before the sun sets tomorrow eve, then I'll be damned if I don't run off and join a convent somewheres!" she chuckled, her great bosom heaving with laughter.

Matt Richards's black hooded eyes gleamed with satisfaction. Excitement began to pound in his veins. Meg was right. Tomorrow would mark the end of all their problems. Once and for all they would deal with the troublesome Miss Bryony Hill. And this time, there would be no rescue for that charming little black-haired beauty. This time they would have her all to themselves.

Chapter Twenty-Three

It was quiet in Bryony's room. She had dimmed her light in preparation to leave the small, private sanctuary of her own quarters and join the festivities already underway downstairs. Standing alone in the soft starlight that beamed in through the opened window, she could hear as if from a great distance the laughter and gaiety below, the muted voices of those guests who had already arrived for a night of merriment. The strolling musicians strummed their guitars as they wandered through the lantern-lit courtyard, serenading the ladies, and filling the air with their sweet, melancholy strains. Every now and again, above the dreamy music and the laughter, she could hear a man raise his voice to announce a toast, joined by a chorus of genial voices. She could imagine the extra servants she'd engaged bustling about under Rosita's brisk orders, and she could picture the bright, festive appearance of the ranch house, with everything cleaned and polished to a high gloss. Bryony still didn't know how she and Rosita had managed to ready everything in time, but somehow they had, and Bryony knew that it was time now for her to go downstairs, to smile and mingle and behave as if all was right with her world. It would be the hardest thing she had ever done.

At least, she reflected as she smoothed her gown, she looked well enough. Her emerald green satin dress, worn off the shoulders, shimmered enticingly in the starlight touching the room, emphasizing her creamy shoulders and full, firm breasts, accenting the tiny perfection of her slender waist as the heavy satin fell in soft, billowing folds to the floor. Emeralds that had belonged to her mother gleamed at her throat and upon her ears, and her luxuriant black hair was dressed in a fetching cluster of soft ringlets that framed her face, bringing out the dark, mysterious depths of her brilliant emerald eyes and setting off the sculptured perfection of her features.

At the head of the staircase she paused, gazing down at the scene below. Matthew Richards had just entered the ranch house; he was handing his hat to Rosita, who returned his cordial greeting with a stony nod. From Bryony's position on the landing above, she could observe the splendid elegance of his fine dark suit, the ruffles on his shirt, the neat arrangement of his black string tie. His black hair was carefully brushed, and the luster on his leather boots was impressive. He looked every bit the handsome, well-to-do cattleman, the gentleman most admired in this rough, frontier town. Suddenly, he glanced along the hallway and saw her poised at the head of the staircase, and a wide smile spread across his rugged face. He came to stand at the foot of the stairs, leaning one arm against the railing.

"Bryony! You look magnificent." The words were spoken with deep admiration, but even from that distance, Bryony could see the gleam in those dark, hooded eyes. Those murderer's eyes. For a moment, staring into them, fear threatened to consume her. She wanted to turn and flee to her room. But it passed quickly as she noted, with some surprise, the smugness about Matt Richards's smiling mouth, the hidden smirk behind his eyes. And at that moment, she had a mental picture of Johnny Blake's grave and its cold, lonely headstone. Something tightened inside her. Hatred entered her heart and it gave her unexpected strength. She found herself smiling at him, going down the stairs as if toward the man of her dreams.

"Matt, how good to see you," she said warmly, and raised glowing eyes to his face. "Isn't it awful of me to be late for my own party? I do hope my guests will forgive me."

"How could they not forgive you?" He took her arm to escort her into the parlor that was already becoming crowded with guests. "It would be impossible for anyone to be angry with a woman who looks as enchanting as you do tonight. I mean that, Bryony."

Oh, do you? she thought savagely to herself, though she merely smiled up at him and spoke with great sweetness. "Thank you, Matt. You always know just the right thing to say." She was grateful that Roger Davenport came up to them at that moment and took her arm possessively.

"Bryony, you look lovely. But I'm not surprised in the least. You're always beautiful, my darling."

"Roger, have you met my dear friend, Matt Richards? Matt, I'd like to present Roger Davenport of St. Louis."

Roger glowered at Matt as though he were his rival, but Matt appeared most genial to the easterner. "It's a pleasure, Mr. Davenport. Is this your first trip west?"

The men began to talk, and Bryony had time to think. She was formulating a small plan for her own protection. Roger was leaving on the stagecoach in the morning, and she had already explained to him, as gently as possible, that she would not marry him under any circumstances. As usual, he had refused to take her at her word, and had been persistently coaxing her to change her mind throughout his brief visit. Well, for tonight, maybe she would pretend that there *was* a possibility of her joining him in San Francisco. She hated to mislead Roger, but Matt would be less likely to try something desperate if he believed she might leave Arizona in the near future. Let Matt think her feelings for Roger were deeper than they actually were; let him be lulled into a false sense of security and hope. All she wanted was to make very sure that he made no desperate moves against her before she had an opportunity to meet with Jim in the morning.

With this plan in mind, Bryony began to flirt unashamedly with Roger, noticing with deft glances from beneath her eyelashes that Matt was watching most interestedly. After a short time, he excused himself from her side, and she and Roger were surrounded by other guests. Bryony behaved with all the gaiety and vivacity she could muster, for all appearances looking as if she didn't have a care in the world other than to see that her guests enjoyed themselves. Inwardly her nerves were taut, and the strain built as the evening progressed.

It was shortly before the supper was to be served that Annie Blake and her father arrived. Their timing was perfect. Buck Monroe had just emerged from the courtyard to pass through the candlelit dining hall and into the crowded parlor. Clad in a bright plaid shirt and new trousers, with his fancily stitched boots gleaming almost as brightly as his slicked-down blond hair, Buck looked even more handsome than usual. But as Annie Blake stood on the parlor's threshold, her arm entwined with her father's, the self-assured smile faded from his face, and he, like everyone else in the room, stared in incredulity at the girl in the hallway.

Bryony, watching breathlessly, felt the first real pleasure she had experienced that night. Annie was beautiful, far more beautiful than even she would have expected. The rose silk gown gracefully displayed the full, rounded curves of her tall figure that had always before been disguised by drab, baggy work clothes. Now, the woman beneath had been revealed. The rich color of the gown made her large hazel eyes glow with warmth. Her smooth chestnut hair, dressed simply in soft, silken curls that fell prettily from a smooth topknot on her head, shone in the candlelight. The plain tomboy was gone. Here was a lovely young woman, soft and pretty, with huge, sparkling eyes and a trembling smile that was at once both shy and newly proud.

The moment of startled silence was broken as Bryony

swept forward to draw Annie and Sam into the room. Annie's arm trembled slightly under her touch. "You're gorgeous!" Bryony whispered reassuringly, a hint of laughter in her voice. "Buck looks like he's going to faint! Mr. Blake, your daughter shall be the belle tonight. Don't you agree?"

Sam's gaunt, weather-beaten old face crinkled into a grin. His gray mustache twitched. "I shore do, ma'am. I never saw Annie look so purty before—reminds me real powerful of her ma, when I first laid eyes on her some twenty years ago."

They were interrupted by Captain Wayne Reynolds, a pleasant-looking young cavalry officer who had reacted more quickly than Winchester's cowboys to the sight of the charming new arrival. He bowed over her hand and spoke in a soft, eager voice.

"Miss Blake, what a pleasure it is to see you tonight. You look positively dazzling."

Annie seemed startled. She'd noticed the young captain in town on occasion, but he'd never even glanced in her direction. "Th—thank you, Captain," she stammered, a most becoming blush tinting her cheeks. "It's . . . real nice to see you, too."

"May I bring you a glass of punch, ma'am, or some other refreshment?" Oh, yes, the young captain's smile was most attractive. "Please, tell me how I may serve you."

"For one thing, you can let go of her hand!" a deep voice growled from behind the little group. Startled, Captain Reynolds turned around to find Buck Monroe's belligerent face. "Stop making a damned fool out of yourself, Reynolds," the cowpoke advised. "I'm shore Annie don't care nothin' about hearing a lot of flowery talk from you or anyone else. Isn't that right, Annie?"

Bryony held her breath as the cavalry officer frowned contemptuously at Buck, and Annie turned large, astonished eyes on him. Sam Blake, his gray eyes flashing angrily, seemed about to make a stinging retort, but to everyone's surprise, Annie spoke first.

"No, Buck," she replied, meeting his incredulous gaze with a defiantly uplifted chin. "Every girl likes to hear pretty compliments from a man. I sure do. And I thank Captain Reynolds very much for his . . . his courtesy!"

"Wal, I'll be a dog-eared Gila monster!" Buck exclaimed, running his big fingers through his thick blond hair in a gesture that destroyed the smooth, slicked-down appearance he had taken great pains to achieve. "*You,* of all women, putting on fancy airs! I never thought I'd see the day!" There was disgust and anger in his voice, but Annie was unflustered.

"You know something? Neither did I." Then, she turned sweetly to Captain Reynolds who stood, grinning, beside her.

"I reckon I *would* like a glass of punch, Captain Reynolds."

"Wayne, please." He took her arm and without a backward glance, they strolled across the parlor to the linen-draped table where refreshments had been laid out. As they passed through the room, a buzz of people surrounded Annie, complimenting her on her dress, her hair, fussing over the change in her. Captain Reynolds had a difficult time, since many of those competing for her attention were his fellow cavalry officers or the even more aggressive local cowhands, who showered Annie with the kind of attention guaranteed to make any girl blush. Annie was amazed at the stir she was creating. For the first time in her life, she felt young and happy and alive, and with every woman's instinct she possessed, she knew without having to look that Buck Monroe was watching every move she made.

He was indeed. After she walked off with Captain Reynolds, Buck glared after her in shock, while Bryony smiled delightedly. Good for Annie, she thought. She'd handled the situation as though she'd been collecting suitors for years, and she'd certainly given Buck a setdown. If tonight didn't teach him not to take her for granted, nothing would. Bravo, Annie.

Her lips curving mischievously, Bryony turned her attention to Annie's father, ignoring Buck. She tucked her arm in Sam Blake's and led him into the room. "Mr. Blake, I believe Judge Hamilton has been wanting to speak with you. He was in the courtyard with Frank and Edna Billings the last time I spotted him, so why don't we look for him there?"

"Shore, Miss Hill. I reckon I could use some fresh air. This here parlor is a mite crowded for my tastes," he remarked pointedly, with a fiery look at Buck, and then he and Bryony sauntered off together.

Buck stood alone in the hubbub of guests, glowering at Annie Blake. With clenched fists he studied her laughing hazel eyes, and the soft, glossiness of her hair, and ran his angry eyes over the ripe curves of her bosom and hips, stunned that he'd never before noticed their existence. But tonight, well, with that damned dress hugging every inch of her. . . . He cursed beneath his breath, and with a scowl, stomped out of the room, disgusted by the frivolous spectacle in the parlor.

Soon supper was served, and Buck had ample opportunity to take his mind off his troubles by indulging in the veritable feast that had been prepared. There were corn tortillas with chile sauce, oyster patties, tamale pies stuffed with chicken and tomatoes and garlic, a saddle of venison served with currant jelly, roasted wild turkey and plum stuffing, and a huge platter of thick, juicy beef, along with bowlfuls of delicious fried black beans. Dessert was a tempting assortment of fresh fruit, *sopaipillas*, and berry tarts, served with strong coffee and a half-dozen bottles of Wesley Hill's finest brandy. Strangely enough, however, Buck Monroe displayed little appetite. He picked at the food heaped on his plate, his eyes returning persistently though unwillingly to the girl in the rose silk gown, and Bryony, seated between Roger Davenport and Matthew Richards in the immense, elegant dining room overlooking the courtyard, took time out from her own concerns to notice Annie's triumph with delight.

She had little time to speculate about Buck and Annie, once the meal was completed and the dancing
began. She found herself on the festively decorated, lantern-lit courtyard, deluged with partners and barely able
to breathe between dances. She was even grateful when
Roger slipped his arm around her waist and suggested
they walk out among the orange groves. Matt stood
nearby and Bryony knew he would notice the rendezvous, so she acquiesced with a seductive smile and a
quick, "Oh, yes, Roger, I'd love it!"

The moon gleamed palely down on them as they made
their way toward the darkness of the trees. It was a
sultry night, hot and windless, with a sprinkling of stars
in the blue-black Arizona sky. Roger's arm squeezed her
waist. When they reached the seclusion of the fragrant
orange groves, he pulled her close to him and kissed her
fervently, his hands groping for her breasts. Bryony
jerked away, both angry and guilt-ridden. She *had* led
Roger on, but she wasn't about to make love to him out
here just to please Matthew Richards.

"No, Roger, let me go."

"Please, Bryony, why not? You do love me, I know
you do. I was beginning to wonder if things would ever
work out for us, until tonight. Now I see that your
feelings are getting the better of you." He flashed his
even, white-toothed smile, obviously pleased with the
situation. "Oh, darling, I'm so happy. When shall we
be married? You know, I have a splendid idea. Why
don't you come to San Francisco with me tomorrow?
You can pack after the last guests leave tonight."

Bryony stared at him in astonishment. "Roger, are
you mad? Don't you realize that I own a ranch
here—property, livestock? I couldn't just pack up and
go, even if I wanted to!"

He laughed light-heartedly, then grabbed her, kissing
her exuberantly. "Oh, Bryony, you're adorable. Don't
you realize that once I'm your husband, I'll take care of
all those financial details for you? We can dispose of the
ranch and cattle later. I'll handle everything. You see,

darling, after you become my wife, you won't have to worry your beautiful little head over such matters ever again.''

She could scarcely control her exasperation at his condescending attitude, but after all, she told herself, she couldn't really blame him for his optimism. The way she'd been acting tonight, half the territory must suspect that an engagement was imminent. She only hoped Matthew Richards was part of that group. But as for Roger, well, the sooner she set him straight, the better.

She sighed. "Roger, I'm sorry. I guess all the wine I've drunk tonight has made me behave very badly. I apologize if I gave you reason to hope . . . to think . . . Roger, the plain truth is, I'm not going to marry you and I never will. I don't love you.'' Her voice was firm. "I hope we can still remain friends, for I'm fond of you, but not in the way that a wife should be fond of her husband. Marriage is out of the question.''

He stared at her, stricken. "But tonight . . . the way you looked at me, spoke to me. Bryony, you must love me.''

She shook her head. "I'm sorry, Roger.''

His brown eyes lit with fury. "I see. You think I'm a fool, is that it, Bryony? You've just been using me tonight, haven't you? Trying to make some other man jealous! That's the reason you've been flirting with me so outrageously, like a . . . a common harlot. Tell me, who is the poor fellow? Mr. Matthew Richards? One of your hired hands?'' Contempt shone on his smooth-shaven, handsome face. "I see your game now, Bryony, and I have the greatest sympathy for the victim of this charade. I should have known what to expect from you after our last meeting in St. Louis. You showed yourself to be a foolish, silly girl then, and you've proved it now—however, I must add scheming to the description. I'm devoutly grateful to have escaped your clutches, believe me I am!''

Bryony's lovely green eyes pricked with tears. In a way, she deserved Roger's condemnation, and she regretted the pain she'd caused him. She touched his arm with a trembling hand, tears glistening in her eyes.

"Oh, Roger . . . please forgive me. I swear to you, I am not in love with anyone at the party tonight! I haven't been playing a coy, schoolgirl's game with you, I . . . I . . ." She found herself unable to continue, but to her amazement, her earnest tone and the tears on her eyelashes actually had an effect on him. His face softened, and somewhat mollified, he patted her arm rather awkwardly.

"For heaven's sake, don't cry, Bryony." He was dismayed by her obvious distress. "I apologize if I spoke rather harshly. I don't understand your behavior in the least, and I certainly have been hurt by it, but I suppose, since I'm leaving in the morning, we may as well part as friends." He cleared his throat uncomfortably. "After all, we probably won't meet again, and I'm certain you're as relieved about that as I."

She bit her lip. "I would like to remain your friend, Roger."

"Very well." His voice was stiff. "Then I won't trouble you any longer about my feelings. Shall we rejoin the party?"

What else was there to say between them? Dejected, but recognizing that she couldn't explain further without endangering both of them, Bryony merely nodded and they turned back toward the gaiety in the courtyard, silence heavy between them. As they neared the lights and the music and the happily twirling figures in the courtyard, Roger spoke formally.

"I think it would be best if I took my leave now, Bryony. I'm really in no mood for frivolity, and I have many preparations still to attend to before my journey tomorrow. You will excuse me, under the circumstances?"

"Of course," she replied quietly. Together they went in search of Frank and Edna, with whom Roger had driven to the party. Fortunately, they were ready to leave as well; the three were soon bidding farewell to

Bryony on the front porch of the ranch. Frank and Edna, with several nudges and grins and winks, went on to the buggy, leaving Roger and Bryony momentarily alone. Bryony touched his arm.

"I am sorry, Roger," she said gently. "Truly."

His smile was slightly wooden, but at least he made the attempt. "Let us not speak of it any more. I shall do my best to forget, and so, I trust, shall you."

She stood on tiptoe and kissed him lightly on the cheek. "Good-bye and have a safe journey. I hope you will find San Francisco to your liking."

"Thank you. I am certain it will prove a delightful and charming city. Good-bye, Bryony."

"Good-bye."

"Alone at last, Bryony." Matt Richards's eyes gleamed at her as she whirled about.

"M—Matt, you startled me!" she cried, with an attempt at a laugh.

"Sorry. You look so lonely out here. Aren't you enjoying your own fiesta, or are you merely sad now that Mr. Davenport has gone?"

So, he *had* noticed her performance this evening. That was a relief. She attempted what she hoped was a rather sad smile and replied in a low voice, "I'm afraid I shall miss Roger greatly. I'd forgotten how charming he could be. It was lovely seeing him again."

Matt nodded, his expression unreadable. "That was obvious. I finally realized why you turned down my marriage proposal that day when we had our picnic." A gentle expression came over his handsome face. "You were already in love with someone else, weren't you, Bryony? I guess my case was hopeless all along, isn't that right?"

She started to speak, but he interrupted her, taking her hand warmly in his. "It's all right, Bryony. Don't feel bad. All I really want is your happiness. Tell me, are you planning to see him again soon? When he returns from his business in San Francisco?"

Bryony's heart pounded with relief. Matt had taken

the bait. What an accomplished liar he was, she thought
venomously. But the important thing was that she had
accomplished her objective for tonight, and now it was
only a matter of hours before she met with Jim. She felt
safe. Her smile was dazzling as she tilted her head enchantingly up at him.

"Perhaps," she replied saucily. "But you must wait
and see! I am not at liberty to speak of our plans just
yet!"

There, that ought to satisfy him! She took his arm
with a tiny laugh and led him back to the crowd of
guests, chatting with great light-heartedness. Her relief
was so intense that at first she didn't notice Buck dancing with Annie Blake, or the way they were gazing as if
mesmerized into each other's eyes. Circulating among
her guests, she quickly heard the gossip of the evening:
Buck Monroe—according to everyone at the party—had
fallen head over heels in love with a girl he'd known
practically from the cradle. And the townsfolk were taking bets on how soon the wedding would take place.

Bryony smiled. She was delighted for Annie and
Buck. She only prayed that her own problems would be
settled as quickly, simply, and satisfactorily.

At last the fiesta was over. Bryony lay in her bed,
exhausted but unable to sleep. She was too tense, too
eager for it to be morning and time to see Jim.

It was after three when she finally drifted off to sleep.
She had taken the precaution of hiding her derringer under her pillow, but she didn't really expect any trouble.
Matt had believed that she was in love with Roger, that
she'd soon leave Arizona to marry him. He wouldn't try
anything tonight. . . .

Her sleep was deep, dreamless, heavy as sandbags.
She didn't hear the creak of the floorboards in her
room, the shuffle of a booted foot. She didn't hear
anything until Rusty Jessup spoke to her out of the
darkness, and by then, it was too late.

Chapter Twenty-Four

"Wal, now, if it ain't the little boss lady, and don't she look purty in her night clothes," came the hissed whisper out of the thick darkness. Bryony's eyes flew open in terror, but before she could scream, Jessup pounced on her, his sweaty hand clamping brutally over her mouth, his body pinning her helplessly beneath him. She fought like a demon; he swore as she bit his hand, and drawing his gun from his holster, he jammed it against her throat. Bryony's scream froze on her lips.

"One sound, boss lady, just one sound, and I'll kill you. And I'll kill that Mex housekeeper and anyone else who comes runnin' in here, too. But you'll be first. Thet's a promise, honey, you'll be first. Got it?"

She couldn't answer. Cruelly, he shoved the gun harder against her throat and his voice was vicious. *"Got it?"*

Bryony's entire body trembled convulsively and she could barely breathe, but she managed to nod. As Jessup removed the gun, still pointing it at her as he straddled her on the bed, tears squeezed from her eyes. "What . . . what do you want. . . ?" Her voice was a cracked, hoarse whisper, and Jessup grinned.

"Now, that's better. You're not so high and mighty tonight, are you, boss lady? Not like that day you fired me in front of all the hands. I told you then you'd be sorry, but I reckon you didn't take me serious. Now you do, though, don't you? Now you know for a fact that Rusty Jessup always keeps his promises!''

"What are you going to do?" she managed fearfully, dread engulfing her in an overwhelming tide. Why, why, tonight? She didn't understand what had gone wrong. . . .

Jessup's eyes ran over her exquisite body, tantalizingly revealed through her sheer negligee. Suddenly, he leaned down and fastened his lips on hers with lusty violence, sucking roughly at her mouth. She moaned and tried to squirm away from him, but he held her relentlessly beneath him and pressed the gun against her head as a terrifying reminder of what would happen if she screamed. He chuckled deep in his throat as she stiffened in alarm, and then his free hand found her breast and attacked her nipple, gleefully rubbing first one breast and then the other as he pressed his drooling lips against her mouth and throat with rising urgency. She felt him hardening, and a greater revulsion than any she'd ever experienced seized possession of her. Gun or no gun, she began to struggle wildly.

"Let me go . . . let me *go*!" she begged, shoving against him with all her strength, but he merely sat up and struck her a stunning blow across the face. Her head reeled back against the pillow, and a strangled sob escaped her throat. "No, no, please . . ."

Jessup grabbed her face in his hands, squeezing it between his strong, cruel fingers. Vicious satisfaction shone from his eyes. "It wasn't in the original plan, boss lady, but I reckon I'm goin' to have you here and now. I'm tired of waiting, tired of following orders. And there ain't much time . . ."

He ripped her nightgown aside and began loosening his trousers. Desperately, Bryony brought her knee up with all her strength and hit him ferociously in the groin. As he fell away from her with a cry of agony, she rolled off the bed, reaching as she did so for the der-

ringer beneath the pillow. Before she could grasp it, a
voice from the doorway brought her to a paralyzing
halt.

"Freeze, Bryony. Don't move, don't scream, or I'll
blow your pretty head off."

Matt Richards, gun in hand, stood by the door.

Bryony didn't move a muscle. She couldn't have. She
wanted to scream, to weep, to die, but she stood like a
statue as every vestige of hope drained from her half-
nude form.

"What the hell is going on here, Jessup?" Matt demanded in a whisper that was no less violent for the fact
that it was hushed. "You damned idiot, are you trying
to blow the whole plan this near to the finish? I ought to
shoot your damned eyes out!"

Jessup flushed, and fastened his trousers, climbing
off the bed with noticeable pain. "I couldn't help it.
Damnation, look at her. She'd tempt a saint, and you
know it. You'd have done the same as me, I reckon."

"There's plenty of time for that later. Meanwhile,
you were supposed to see that she got herself dressed
and packed. You've wasted time, and made an ass out
of yourself, by the looks of it. Now get downstairs and
wait with the horses. I don't want to hear a whinny out
of them."

With a dark scowl at Bryony, Jessup retrieved his gun
and his black felt hat and stalked from the room, the
door clicking shut behind him. Matt stood alone with
Bryony, his gun pointed at her.

"Get dressed, Bryony."

"Matt, what are you doing? I don't understand!"

"Don't try that innocent act, honey. It won't work.
You know exactly what's going on. Now get dressed and
start packing your suitcase. A small one. Just take the
things you might take for a short trip—say, to San Francisco?"

She gazed at him in shock. What was he talking
about? Her head ached from Jessup's blow, and she felt

dazed and frightened. Somehow, things had gone wrong and her danger was acute. She smelled death in the room with her, and knew from the cold, calculating expression in Matt's eyes that he would not hesitate to kill her if and when it suited his needs. She shivered uncontrollably.

"Of course, you're not really going to 'Frisco. But everyone around will think you did, especially after that nice little performance you put on tonight with that eastern dude. You played into my plans perfectly, Bryony, and I'm real grateful to you. We all saw you sneak into the woods with him. It won't take much to convince folks that you ran off with him. And by the time anyone learns different, it will be too late." Matt smiled maliciously at her. "Now, get dressed. We've got some riding to do, and I'm in a hurry."

"Matt . . . please . . . can't we talk?"

"There's only one thing I want to talk to you about. That letter your father wrote before he died. Now, I know that you've got it, or know where to find it. And I want you to share that information with me, pronto."

Chilled to the bone despite the fact that it was stiflingly hot in the room, Bryony reached for a dressing robe and wrapped it quickly about her semi-nakedness. She was trying to stall for time, to think this out. Matt knew that she had discovered the whereabouts of the paper, or so he said. But how? *How*? She pressed her hands to her temples, wishing she could block out the roaring in her head. It hurt her so, but she had to think!

"I don't have any idea what you're talking about . . ." she began, trying to put indignation in her voice. "I thought you were my friend, and here you are in my room, with that horrible Rusty Jessup, threatening me and making absolutely no sense. What letter are you talking about?"

Slowly, deliberately, he put his gun in his holster and walked toward her. Bryony, though she wanted to back away, held her ground. Matt grabbed her by the throat, his fingers tightening over the tender flesh. "Don't lie to me, Bryony. You're a clever girl, and I admire you for it, but the game is over. You know where that damned paper is and you're going to tell me." His voice was calm, firm, deadly. He released her as if with reluctance.

Bryony rubbed her throat. She was more frightened than ever, but she'd be damned if she'd let Matt see her beg or cry. At this moment she hated him with murderous intensity. She looked him straight in the eye and spoke softly, her eyes bright with loathing.

"The hell I will."

He smiled unpleasantly. "Oh, I reckon you will. Maybe not here or now, but when we get to the place I'm taking you, we'll have a chance to persuade you. And I promise you, Bryony, we *will* persuade you. Now, get dressed. And remember, I'll kill you, paper or no paper, if you make a sound."

To her dismay, Matt stayed and watched as she fumbled into jeans, a plaid shirt, and her boots. She thought yearningly of the gun under her pillow, but there was no way to reach it. As Matt once again drew his gun and ordered her to pack a small suitcase, she complied silently. When she had finished, he took the case and pushed her ahead of him out of the room. All hopes of reaching the derringer were gone.

Jessup was waiting for them at the gates leading into the Circle H grounds. He had three horses with him. Matt hoisted Bryony into the saddle of a gray gelding, and promptly tied her hands to the saddle horn. Then he and Rusty mounted their horses and led her gelding southward at a fast trot. Holding tightly to the saddle horn and trying to maintain her balance, Bryony's mind raced as she tried to imagine what had gone wrong, and what was going to happen to her now. She knew one thing: she wasn't going to tell Matt Richards anything. She set her lips together with determination and glanced nervously about to try to figure out where they were headed.

After some miles, she realized that they were on Twin Bars property. They had by-passed the ranch house, though, and were riding further east. The land was hilly and bright with the night-blooming cereus, but she could hardly appreciate the flowers now. Her heart was filled with dread, and she was reminded of the day she'd been kidnapped off the stagecoach. Then she'd been panic-stricken, too, but she hadn't had any idea what was happening to her or why. Now she knew the reason for her capture, and she knew just how ruthless those responsible for it could be. Her body grew clammy with sweat as she glanced at the hard faces of the two men.

Soon they began to climb a mesa on the eastern edge of Twin Bars property. Clouds now shrouded the moon and stars, leaving the countryside dark and eerily quiet. Bryony didn't even notice the little cabin stuck into the rocky plateau until Matt and Jessup slowed the horses. Then she saw the small, rough-hewn cabin set amidst rock and scrub brush and cacti. She bit her lip as she heard sounds of horses tethered behind the place, but she didn't say a word as Jessup deftly untied her hands and yanked her roughly down from the horse.

Oh, Jim, I'll probably never see you again, she thought as Jessup pushed her toward the cabin, and Matt grabbed her arm. All such thoughts died instantly as Richards led her into the dirty little cabin. As she came through the heavy wooden door, the first and only thing she saw was Texas Jim Logan's battered, unmoving form crumpled on the floor in a sticky pool of blood.

Chapter Twenty-Five

A terrible anguish rushed through her, worse than anything she'd ever known. She couldn't think of anything except that Jim was dead, and she had never told him that she loved him. Numb, stricken, she wished in that instant that she was dead too.

Bryony pulled away from her captors, running across the barren room to Jim, kneeling over his inert body. Tears streamed down her cheeks as she touched his face, his hair, murmuring his name over and over, heedless of the blood on her hands and clothes. And then she saw what she had not dared to hope for: he was breathing. Barely. He was alive! With a gasp of thankfulness, she grasped his hand and pressed it to her heart.

"Jim?" She smoothed his hair back from his brow. "Are you all right? Please . . . wake up. Jim?"

He didn't respond, and she saw that his breathing was very shallow. His lean, sun-browned face was bruised and there was blood running from his mouth. Most of the blood, though, was flowing from his left shoulder. Tearing away his shirt, she grew sickened at the sight of the raw, ugly gunshot wound. With anguished eyes, she turned to the people in the cabin, intending to insist that they help him, but before she could speak, she noticed for the first time Zeke Murdock's burly presence, and that of a woman.

"Bryony, meet Meg Donahue—my partner," Matt Richards announced as Bryony gaped in shock at the flame-haired saloon-keeper. Zeke Murdock and Rusty Jessup were grinning from ear to ear. Matt went on conversationally, "Meg's always been a big help to me, Bryony, honey, in my business affairs, and she was to your pa, too, when he was alive. We had a mighty lucrative partnership, you know, but now, it's just the two of us running the show—with a little help from a few of the boys, of course."

Meg Donahue—the third partner? So, Bryony thought numbly, *that* was what had gone wrong. Her mind leaped to yesterday, when she'd given Buck the note for Jim, the note he later reported to have delivered to Meg Donahue. And Meg, Bryony realized now in horror, had doubtlessly given it directly to Matt. With a chill, she realized that she had never deceived Matt Richards for a minute during that ridiculous charade with Roger. He had known all along she didn't love him, that she planned to meet Jim in the morning, and tell him where to find the missing letter. And Jim? He probably hadn't even received her note; instead, they had done *this* to him.

Suddenly, she took off her bandana and began to wrap it tightly about Jim's wounded shoulder.

"What's she doin'?" Zeke Murdock demanded. "We don't have time for her to play nurse. Let's find out where that paper is, pronto."

"I reckon he's right, Matt, we've waited a long time for this," Meg put in, sauntering toward Bryony. She grasped the girl's arm and jerked her to her feet. "Forget about him, honey, he's as good as dead. And so are you, if you don't tell us what we want to know."

Bryony shook herself free and, swept up in a terrible rage, she slapped Meg sharply across the face. "As good as dead?" she cried, her eyes glittering like fiery emeralds. "How can you say that, you horrible old bitch? *You were his friend*. He liked you. He trusted

you! You must be some kind of a monster—and so are
the rest of you. I hope you all rot in hell, and if I can
speed up that day by so much as one hour, or one
minute, you can be damned sure I will!''

With the blow, and Bryony's words, the smug smile
disappeared from Meg's lips. Her bright blue eyes were
like chips of ice in her heavily rouged face. "Honey, you
just made a big mistake,'' she pronounced slowly, eyeing Bryony the way a puma does a rabbit. "No one lifts
a hand against me and gets away with it. No one. And as
for your speeding up our appointment on Judgment
Day, well, honey, all I can say is, I hope *you're* real
prepared to meet your Maker, cause you sure don't have
long to go on this earth.''

Bryony's heart pounded. What were they going to
do? And what should *she* do? Should she tell them
where the paper was hidden? Then they would no longer
have a reason to keep her alive. The same held true for
Jim. She *must* not reveal the whereabouts of the letter—it was their only chance.

Warily studying Meg Donahue, she noticed for the
first time the woman's array of jewelry, which added
unnecessary decoration to her blazing blue taffeta gown
with its black sequined trim and feathers. Bright
diamond and ruby rings sparkled on her fingers, her
earrings were long, brilliant sapphires, and at her throat
. . . Bryony's mouth went dry. At Meg's throat was the
antique cameo brooch that had been stolen from her
months ago. Her mother's brooch. It was an island of
quiet good taste in an ocean of gaudiness.

Meg noticed Bryony's shocked expression, and she
fingered the brooch coyly. "Oh, you recognize this,
don't you, honey? Zeke told me he stole it from you
that day when you first came to town.'' She chuckled.
"I can't tell you how long I've been dying to wear this
pretty little thing, but I was always afraid to wear it in
town, in case I ran into you somewheres. Now it doesn't
matter, does it? And soon I'll be able to wear all my

pretty things, and folks will know they're real and not fake like they think in town." She touched her earrings with pride. "See these? They're worth a real handsome sum, and I've worn 'em dozens of times in the Silver Spur, but no one would guess that they're real. Where would good old Meg get genuine gems, after all? Well, honey, they're real, all of 'em. And soon, I'm goin' to move away from this hayseed town, maybe to San Francisco, or New York, or Paris, France—someplace fancy—and start all over. Folks will know they're dealing with a lady as rich and fancy as anyone who ever went to a private *boarding school*."

She spat out the word in disgust.

"Is that what you want?" Bryony shook her head scornfully. "To prove you're a lady? I'm afraid you're doomed to failure before you even begin, Meg. You've taken on an impossible task."

Meg laughed, totally unoffended by the insult. "All I want, honey, is to wear my pretty clothes and jewels, to find myself a string of good-looking men to keep me company, and to live a life of leisure. I sure don't want to spend the rest of my life playing trail boss to a bunch of lazy whores, fetching whisky for drunks, and cleaning up that damned saloon! I've had six years of doin' that on my own, and nine before that working with my husband. I put in my time at hard labor, and now I'm going somewhere where I can put my feet up and enjoy my hard-earned money."

"Hard-earned? By stealing, you mean?"

Meg placed her hands on her broad hips and regarded Bryony mockingly. "Well, I couldn't save up enough from the saloon to live the way I've a mind to, so I decided years ago I'd better start planning for the future. Everything fell into place when Matt and your pa moved into the territory, and we hit it off right away. We saw how we could help each other out, and working in the saloon, I sure picked up a lot of useful information for 'em. But, honey, even with the rustling deal, it's

taken me years to get to a point where I can think about
retiring and moving away. I reckon I deserve a nice, soft
life by now.''

Bryony thought of the Blake's modest ranch house,
the way Annie and her father worked their fingers to the
bone trying to make a meager living off their ranch, just
like dozens of other small, industrious ranchers in the
valley. And here was Meg Donahue bragging about
stealing from them so that she could set herself up like a
queen. Bryony's eyes blazed. ''I think you're disgusting,'' she told Meg coldly. ''Thole whole filthy lot of
you.'' Her gaze flicked to Matt, who had sat down on
one of the few rickety chairs in the dirty, sparsely furnished cabin. He was observing her dispassionately,
though she sensed that he was growing impatient
because he kept tapping his booted foot against the
floor. ''And as for you, Mr. Matthew Richards, the
most deceitful, reprehensible man in Winchester, I'm
very grateful I didn't accept your marriage proposal
that day. I'd rather be dead than be married to a man
like you—or should I say, a no-good, stinking *skunk*
like you?''

Matt raised his eyebrows at her as an unpleasant
gleam entered his black eyes. ''Be careful, Bryony.
You're in enough trouble already.''

She laughed contemptuously. ''Then what difference
does it make what I say? You're going to kill me
anyway, aren't you? *Aren't you*? Well, Matt, if you
ever decide to get out of the rustling and murdering
business, you can always enter the acting profession.
You play a fine, upstanding gentleman most con-
vincingly, I assure you.''

He got to his feet and approached her. He touched
her cheek with mock gentleness, grinning as she recoiled. ''Look at the trouble you're in now because you
refused me. I'm forced to take actions I would rather
have avoided.'' His lips tightened. ''Nevertheless, I will
take them, Bryony, honey. I have a business to protect,

to say nothing of my own life. Oh, yes, I'll settle this matter at any cost."

She stared at him with outward calm, though inwardly she trembled at the ruthlessness in his hooded eyes. "Don't be so sure," she spoke coolly. "You still need to find that paper, and I have no intention of telling any of you where it is."

Matt's eyes narrowed and he gestured angrily toward Jim. "No, but you'd tell *him*, wouldn't you? The man who killed your father! A dirty, bloodthirsty gunslinger—"

"Stop it!" Bryony hissed. He's a finer man then you'll ever pretend to be! He's honest, and kind and decent, and you're . . . you're nothing but a lying, cheating, murdering *rattlesnake*!"

Matt seized her then and pulled her up against him, his usually handsome face ugly in its viciousness. "There's one thing about rattlesnakes, honey. They're deadly."

He abruptly twisted her arm behind her back and dragged her with him toward the cabin door. "Let's go, boys. It's time we found out what we need to know. When we're done, this little lady is all yours."

Rusty Jessup shoved his hat on his head and walked toward the door with relish. Zeke Murdock grinned as he followed Matt and Bryony outside. Meg started to join them, but Matt stopped and glanced back at Texas Jim Logan's unmoving form.

"Stay here with Logan, Meg," he ordered curtly. "His gun's in that pile on the table; take it and keep an eye on him. A sharp eye. If he comes to and tries anything, you know what to do."

"You bet I do, Matt, but I sure hate to miss all the fun," Meg replied, her eyes shining maliciously as Bryony struggled uselessly to free herself from Richards's bearlike hold. The door shut behind the little group and Meg, taking up the black-handled Colt, hurried eagerly to the window to watch.

Dawn was breaking as Matt hustled Bryony out onto the mesa. She gasped raggedly as Matt cruelly jerked her arm, forcing her along with him. Murdock was on one side of her and Rusty Jessup, gleeful as a fox in a rabbit hole, marched on the other. *What did they plan to do*? she wondered with a sickened, churning stomach. She now saw that they were dragging her along toward the edge of the plateau. She stiffened, every muscle screaming with terror as she had her first inkling of what was in store. "No!" she shrieked as Matt drew her brutally forward. "No, you can't, you can't!"

"We shore can," Jessup hooted, enjoying the expression on her face. This would teach the stuck-up bitch a little lesson. She'd not only tell them what they wanted to know, she'd beg them to let her live by the time they finished this little game. And afterwards. . . . He grinned in anticipation of the pleasures awaiting him.

Matt brought her up short at the very brink of the plateau and forced her to stare down. It was a sheer dizzying drop that Bryony saw as she trembled in Matt's powerful grasp. Nothing but rock and cacti and slithering lizards. Sweat drenched her as she gazed through widened eyes down, down, down to the jagged rocks far below. She felt herself growing faint, swaying. Desperately, she closed her eyes. Matt's voice rasped in her ear.

"You've given us a lot of trouble, Bryony, honey. Too much trouble. The boys and me wouldn't mind seeing you lying down there on those rocks, dead—or maybe just bent and broken. The thing is, even if the fall didn't kill you, I reckon you'd be dead before long." His tone was matter-of-fact, almost pleasant. "You see, if a rattler didn't kill you, or starvation, well, the heat would—or the buzzards. One way or another, it wouldn't be too pretty or too pleasant, that's for sure. Now, honey, are you going to tell me where that paper is or do I send you flying down onto those nice, sharp rocks?"

Bryony couldn't speak. She swayed helplessly in his arms.

"Talk, Bryony!" Matt growled. He shoved her closer to the cliff.

"No! I won't tell you," she sobbed.

Matt spun her about and backhanded her across the mouth. She staggered to her knees at the cliff's edge, her head exploding with searing pain. The next thing she knew, Zeke Murdock had seized her, tossing her like a puppet to Jessup, who held her by the hair and warned, "Talk, boss lady, or you'll be damned sorry!"

She struck out at him blindly, but he delivered another stunning blow, and this time Murdock caught her before she fell. Snatching her up in his brawny arms, he jerked her to the brink of the cliff once more, only his huge hands preventing her from hurtling down onto the sharp rocks far below. Bryony screamed, a high, piercing wail echoing across the bleak landscape.

"Well, honey?" Matt's voice was cold. "Ready to talk or does Zeke let you go, here and now? I don't have time for any more games. This is your last chance!"

She gasped for breath, dizzy from the blows and the awesome height of the ledge she was so precariously balanced upon. Her thoughts flashed longingly to the cabin where Jim lay shot, beaten, and unconscious on the dirt floor.

"Where's that paper, dammit?" Matt shouted. "Answer me!"

She slumped brokenly against him, tears streaming down her face . . . tears of fear and rage and frustration. She didn't have the strength to fight anymore. She just didn't have the strength. . . .

Jim waited tensely until the men had left the cabin with Bryony. Cautiously, he opened his eyelids slightly, enough to see Meg Donahue settling herself by the window, his gun held loosely in her hand. He closed his eyes again for an instant, bracing himself.

He had regained consciousness shortly before Bryony's arrival at the cabin. His head ached and his shoulder vibrated with a pain so intense it made lights dance in front of his closed eyes. But he had fought the agony with every ounce of will power he possessed, and he'd pretended unconsciousness though every nerve in his body screamed for action. He knew that if he was to overcome the odds against him, he had to wait for the right moment to make his move.

As he lay there, his mind was keenly filling and sorting information, making sense at last of the puzzle that had mystified him all this time. Meg Donahue! Her involvement, he recognized now with bitter anger, was the key element in the whole damn mess! It was Meg who had walked in on his conversation with Daisy when the girl had been about to tell him where Hill's confession was hidden. And after that, Daisy had been killed. Hell, Jim reflected furiously, Meg must have gotten the news to Hill that Daisy was betraying him. Damn her! She had obviously set him up last night by sending him out on a wild-goose chase, giving Murdock and Jessup the chance to ambush him at Beaver Pass. And like a greenhorn, he'd fallen for it. . . .

This was it. Meg was alone in the cabin, engrossed in the happenings outside the window. He tensed his muscles, took a deep breath, and with agonizing effort hurled himself to his feet and across the cabin toward her. Even with the shoulder wound and the effects of the beating, he was quick enough to take her by surprise. He pulled her against him, one hand jammed over her mouth, while the other struggled for possession of the gun. She fought vigorously, but he overpowered her and gained the weapon. He sucked in his breath as his shoulder throbbed unmercifully, but his iron hold on Meg Donahue never slackened.

"Sorry, Meg," he muttered through his teeth, "but I reckon you've got this coming," and he raised the butt of the gun and hit her on the back of the head with a carefully measured blow. She sagged against him like a leaded sack. Lowering her roughly to the floor, he stepped to the door. Fresh blood from his wound poured down his arm and across his chest, but he held the Colt steadily as he edged out the door to swiftly survey the scene by the brink of the cliff.

When Jim saw Bryony at the cliff's edge, surrounded by the three men, red-hot fury coursed through him. His eyes glinted like polished steel as he moved with the stealth of an Indian toward the group at the ledge. Ten feet from them he halted and leveled the gun.

"Let her go, Richards." Logan's voice rang loudly in the clear air. As he spoke, the other four all whirled to face him, shock registering on their faces. Then, everything happened at once. Roaring, Murdock raised his gun, but Jim's shot exploded first, killing Zeke instantly. At the same moment, Rusty Jessup hurtled forward in a diving tackle aimed at Jim's legs, while Matt threw Bryony to the ground and joined the fray.

Bryony pushed herself to her knees, her heart pounding as she saw Jim wrestling with the other two in the dust. Without his injuries, he would have been more than a match for either of them, but now, wounded and hurt, she saw in horror that he was in terrible trouble. Matt landed a thumping blow to his stomach, while Jessup hit him in the head, sending him slumping to the ground. Somehow he found the strength to get to his feet, kicking Jessup and stunning Richards with a powerful blow from his good right arm at the same time. Instantly the two men closed in on him again. The gun had been thrown aside in the fight and Bryony saw it glint from under a rock. She was on her feet, running toward it, her heart in her throat, even as she saw Richards pull his gun, trying to get a clear line on Jim. She screamed to Jim, but he was busy with Jessup, aiming right-handed blows at the ex-foreman's swollen face, driving him, with an unexpected surge of strength, into unconsciousness. Just as Jessup collapsed in a heap, Matt took aim, rapidly releasing the safety.

Suddenly, a gunshot thundered. Logan spun about as Matt toppled into the dust, blood splattering everywhere. Stunned, Jim just stared at him. Then he turned. Bryony stood a few yards away from him, her face white as parchment, shock written all over her beautiful features. The Colt was in her trembling hands. As he watched, she dropped it and stared in horror at Matt Richards's corpse. Her shot had been straight and true—right through the heart. She opened her mouth to speak, but no sound emerged. Then she dropped the gun, and began to weep.

Logan limped toward her. "Bryony. My Bryony." He spoke with great weariness as he gently took her in his arms.

She clung to him, crying, shuddering. "I know, Bryony, I know it's rough—killing a man, especially a man you knew and cared for at one time—"

"No!" she cried suddenly, breaking away to stare at him with a tormented, tear-streaked face. "It's not that! I'd kill him again—all of them, if I could. I had to help you—save *you*!" Her green eyes glistened with tears. "Oh, Jim, I love you so! If anything had happened to you, I wouldn't have been able to bear it! I would have wanted to die, too!"

He stared at her. For the first time, his own heart began to thump with an unbelieving hope. He searched her eyes keenly.

"Bryony," he spoke huskily. "I love you—there could never be another woman in the world for me . . . never!"

He kissed her then, with the fierceness that came from almost having lost her. She closed her eyes, answering his kiss with a tumultuous passion more savage and sweet than any she had ever imagined, a surging, overwhelming force rushing through her, washing aside any shreds of hesitancy or doubt in its path. Love flowed through her, cleansing her soul, buoying her heart, drowning her in a rapturous, raging passion that knew no beginnings and no ends.

At last their mouths parted and he gripped her even more tightly, bruising her flesh as he searched her face intently. "Doesn't it matter anymore—my shooting your father?" he demanded tautly.

Did it? Her heart told her the answer. Wesley Hill had been a criminal, an unscrupulous, greedy, conniving rustler—a man who had stolen from his neighbors, murdered his mistress. Had he ever been a real father to her? Had there been anything good and decent and honorable about him? She doubted it. She gazed at Jim, who for all his cool, cynical exterior, was capable of great love and understanding. A man—despite his tough, arrogant manner—of compassion and true decency. Her eyes reflected the depth of her feelings as she spoke to him in a voice that was soft with love.

"No. It doesn't matter." Tenderly, she touched his battered face with her fingers. "It couldn't . . . not now. I'd be a fool to throw away your love. My father wasn't worth that sacrifice. I know that now."

In spite of his pain and exhaustion, Jim smiled. Here they were in the midst of death, surrounded by corpses and blood on this forsaken mesa, yet he felt reborn, as if he'd been given a second chance at life, at happiness. He stroked the thick ebony hair of the woman in his arms, knowing that she was responsible for this. His sweet, spirited Bryony with the emerald eyes and honeyed lips. He kissed the top of her head.

"In that case, little tenderfoot," he drawled in his deep, lazy voice, "I reckon there's only one thing to do. We're just going to have to get married."

A smile to match his lit her eyes as she lifted her lips for his kiss. "Yes, Mister Logan, I reckon you're right."

Chapter Twenty-Six

Bryony soaked lazily in the big porcelain tub in her bedroom at the ranch. It would be her last bath in this tub, her last night in this room. Tomorrow morning she was to marry Texas Jim Logan.

She sighed happily, leaning back languorously in the perfumed bath water. Ten days had passed since that awful dawn on the mesa, and a great deal had happened. Her father's hidden confession had indeed been found inside the lining of Daisy Winston's black-feathered pink hat, and on the basis of the information it provided, as well as their blatant crimes against Bryony and Jim, Meg Donahue and Rusty Jessup were in jail in Tucson, along with several other rustlers implicated as accomplices in their activities.

Bryony had sold the ranch piecemeal to several neighboring ranchers—Sam Blake among them. At the price Bryony asked, it was a bargain, for she was eager to be rid of it and everything it represented. She was starting a new life tomorrow, making a new beginning, and in order to do this, she felt she had to free herself of all reminders of her father's illegal past. After the ceremony tomorrow, she and Jim would depart on the afternoon stage for their honeymoon in San Francisco, leaving the bulk of her possessions to be shipped later. To where, she didn't know. They hadn't planned beyond their honeymoon, but whatever plans they eventually made, she knew she would be happy. Jim's presence assured her of that.

Her lips were curved dreamily in a happy smile when suddenly, without warning, the door to her bedroom burst open. She shrieked, her heart hammering in cold apprehension as she bobbed up in the tub, staring with parted lips and widened eyes. What she saw astonished her. Jim Logan, dressed all in black with a red bandana at his neck, stood in the doorway. He lounged there, tall and muscular, with a cool glint in his vivid blue eyes and a sardonic smile on his lips. Bryony gasped.

"J—Jim! What are you doing here? Never mind! Get out, and I'll come downstairs and talk to you after I've dressed. I can't imagine why—"

To her amazement, his smile merely deepened, and he strolled casually into the room, shutting the door behind him and coming to stand a few feet away from her, leaning his tall frame against the fruitwood dresser. His shoulder wound was healing cleanly, and he looked stronger and more intimidating than ever. But Bryony was not intimidated. She glared at him, her breasts beginning to heave with indignation.

"What do you think you're doing? Please leave, and wait for me downstairs!"

"Sorry, little tenderfoot," he drawled, amused by the expression on her exquisite face. "I reckon I'm staying right here."

"But why?" she cried in bewilderment. "What's wrong?" For a moment, she wondered wildly if he had changed his mind about getting married, if he had decided at the last moment that he preferred his freedom. Was he leaving her? A sick feeling rushed through her, but this faded to anger as he continued coolly.

"I've reached a decision about our future after the honeymoon, and I wanted to tell you about it. I've got a few other ideas, too."

From the way his eyes gleamed as he studied her in the tub, Bryony hadn't much difficulty guessing what was on his mind. Furiously, she dipped lower in the tub, crossing her arms defiantly over her chest. "Jim Logan, you . . . you . . . beast! We're not married yet, you know, and if you think you can just burst in here and expect me to . . . to give myself to you the very night before our wedding—"

He grinned. "It wouldn't be the first time, little tenderfoot. And I reckon I don't feel like waiting."

She glared at him, eyes blazing. His arrogance was unbelievable! But she would teach him that he couldn't always have his own way! Stubborn, arrogant man!

"I'll see you tomorrow at the courthouse," she told him angrily. "Now please leave this house immediately."

He picked up the thick towel she had left on the little table beside the tub and held it teasingly. "Come on, Bryony, you can't stay in that tub forever, you know. I'll help you get warm and dry."

"Jim!" A not unbecoming flush entered her cheeks. "It's getting quite cold in this tub, and I really do wish to get out now, so if you'll *kindly* hand me that towel and get out of my room, I'll be *most* obliged." Her voice dripped icicles, but he just chuckled, his eyes glinting with amusement.

"If you want this towel, little tenderfoot, I reckon you'll have to come and get it," he drawled politely.

"Ohh!" Bryony's eyes flashed fire. It *was* growing cold in the tub, damn it. Her teeth clenched tightly together as she quickly stood up, and with as much dignity as she could muster, she stepped out of the tub, reaching swiftly for the towel in his hands. But he grasped her wrist and pulled her close to him, wrapping the towel about her slender, shivering form, and to her fury, he began to rub her dripping body with it.

She struggled to escape him. "Jim! You're despicable! If you think you can come in any time you please, and expect me to . . ." But her angry words trailed off as warmth and pleasure seeped through her. His hands on her body always had this effect, numbing the anger in her mind and bringing every inch of her flesh tinglingly alive. He held her nude form crushingly against him, letting the towel slip unnoticed to the floor while his hands slid to her breasts. Fire flared in her as her mouth searched his hungrily and her arms entwined themselves about his neck. Effortlessly, he swept her up and carried her to the bed, lowering her gently onto it, their lips still locked together. She helped him shed his clothes swiftly, and then he moved atop her. Bryony ran her fingers ecstatically over the hard muscles of his back as together they rediscovered each other, their mutual passion mounting to a towering peak. When he plunged inside her she cried out in pure pleasure as the gnawing ache inside her found fulfillment, and together they were consumed in a torrid world of fierce, intoxicating sensuality. It was a long time later that they lay peacefully in each other's arms, their nude bodies shiny with sweat and entwined as though they were one person. Bryony's lips moved tenderly against Jim's hard shoulder.

"I love you."

"And I, you, my darling little tenderfoot."

She snuggled closer, her lovely eyes half opening as she remembered something he had said earlier. "Jim?" It was the merest whisper on the night breeze.

"Yes?"

She touched his broad, muscular chest, her fingers tracing a pattern on the dark hair there. "What was that you said about a decision you reached? About our plans after San Francisco?"

"So you remembered." Gently, he moved her head on the pillow as he pushed himself up on one elbow to gaze down at her. "How would you like to live in Texas, my love?"

She stared up at him, her black hair flowing over her

creamy shoulders, her green eyes brilliant in the moonlight that spilled softly into the quiet bedroom. "Texas? Do you mean your home? Your family's ranch?"

She could scarcely believe it when he nodded. A joyous smile lit her face as she threw her arms about his neck. "You know that I'll be happy anywhere as long as we're together," she whispered, "but I'm so *glad* you decided to return home. Does this mean . . ." she searched for the right words, "that you've come to terms with your father . . ."

"Yes." Jim stroked her hair as he spoke quietly. "I reckon I've been doing a lot of thinking lately. I took a good, long look at myself. Remember what I said to you that day in the cave about not being able to forgive myself? Well, I think maybe I can do that now. I've seen the way you handled this whole ruckus with your father, and that you came to terms with it. You've broken your ties with him, and with the past. That took a lot of courage and a lot of guts." His deep voice went on thoughtfully as Bryony leaned against him. "I reckon it's my turn to come to terms with my family, my past—to face it, and stop running.

"My father wanted to make peace before he died; that's why he left the ranch to me as well as Danny. I couldn't accept that before—didn't think I deserved it, but now . . . now I reckon I can. Damn it, Bryony, I've got to. I owe it to him and to myself to forget the feud that separated us and go home. That's the one way, the only way, to heal the old wounds, to make peace in the family once and for all." He grinned at her, though she sensed the painful introspection that had gone into this decision, and that lay behind his words. "And besides, Danny's been begging me to give him a hand running the place for so long, I'm beginning to wonder if the grand old homestead can survive much longer without me. That kid—"

"You miss him, don't you?" she interrupted, laughing.

His vivid blue eyes gleamed with warmth. "Damn right I do!" He chuckled. "And now that I'm going to have a wife, and someday a family to look after, well, it's time to go home." He kissed her gently, and smiled. "Think you'll like being mistress of a seventy-five thousand acre spread?" he drawled. And then his expression grew serious.

"You know, Bryony, we've always had plenty of household help and all, but I thought you might want to ask Rosita if she'd like to move to Texas with us and stay on to give a helping hand. Would you like that?"

She kissed him exuberantly, bouncing up in the bed. "Jim, that's a wonderful idea!" she exclaimed. "It would be lovely to have Rosita with us—I'll ask her first thing in the morning!"

"Morning's coming soon enough," he replied, glancing out the window where the midnight blue sky was just beginning to fade. "Just make sure she understands that she'll be traveling to Texas alone, *not* coming along to San Francisco on our honeymoon with us! I want you all to myself on that little excursion, lady."

Bryony tossed her head and her jade green eyes danced. "Oh, you do, do you, Mister Logan? Well, I have some news for you. I received a letter from Roger Davenport just yesterday, and he told me about this *marvelous* young lady he met at the theater his very first night in San Francisco!" She could barely conceal the mischievous sparkle in her eyes. "He said he only wished I could meet this paragon of every possible feminine virtue, and so I thought—"

"No, Bryony," he growled, pulling her fiercely against him, his hands beginning to stroke her again, but she squirmed away, laughing, and went on.

"Listen," she insisted, but he cut her off.

"I don't want anything to do with that dandy and his lady-friend," Jim told her firmly, but she put her fingers to his lips, silencing him with a burst of laughter.

"Do you know who she is?" Bryony asked, laughing.

"Diana Oliver—a girl I traveled with on the stagecoach! A horrid, odious, stuffy girl! Roger sounds as if he's *in love* with her!" She collapsed against Jim in a fit of laughter. "Oh, I believe they will suit each other admirably—most admirably! Almost as well as Annie and Buck, for that matter!" She stroked his chest soothingly. "And no, my love, I do *not* wish to visit them in San Francisco, though I would like to get in touch with Dr. Brady and the Scotts, you know, since they were so kind to me when we traveled together."

"Bryony!" Jim pulled her to face him, staring with dangerously glinting eyes into her face. "I'm not going to spend my whole damn honeymoon socializing with a crowd of people."

"No, my darling." She kissed him sweetly on the lips, the glow of passion kindling once more in her eyes. "Not the entire honeymoon. Most of it will be spent exactly like this."

And she leaned close against him, her lips warm and sweet on his, her body pressed invitingly against his as they fell back upon the rumpled sheets. Their bodies thrilled with desire, and their voices whispered of love as outside the amber dawn rose softly over the black mountains. Together, Bryony and Jim celebrated the new day.